My First Murder

My First Murder

Dolores Stewart Riccio

ISBN: 1516975944
ISBN 13: 9781516975945

For the remarkable women—
courageous, intuitive, resilient, practical, clever,
and sometimes eccentric—
who have graced our family, past and present.

Warmest thanks to the dear readers who have proofread these pages:
    my husband, Rick, Anna G. Morin, and Joan Bingham;
    to first readers Leslie Godfrey and Lois Karfunkel,
    to Jennifer Caven for her careful editing,
    and to Nancy Erikson who remembered and smiled.

Chapter 1

In which I pocket a love letter and
learn the true meaning of guilt.

In March of 1943, when the ice finally broke up on Silver Sand Pond, I knew I was in the worst trouble of my life so far.

The bloated body of Winston Snow had floated to shore several hundred yards south of the ice house. Gordon Fisher, the jovial town moderator, who'd been delivering orders from Fisher's General Store that morning, saw the old man's swollen arm hanging over a sand bar. As Gordon tried to lift the body out of the water, a wriggling mass of eels spewed out of Snow's intestines and fled back to the darkest depths of the pond.

Gordon's younger brother Tristan brought me the grisly details, smiling and licking his lips. "Hey, Mellie! You shoulda seen them squirming away inside the old guy's gut. Them eels sure made a meal out of him. Wouldn't want to go eel fishing in that pond any time soon, nosiree, not me."

I was thirteen, and this was the first time I'd ever felt the wrenching guilt that burns inside you until you want to throw up. I hadn't needed any Medusa picture squirming around in my head to make me even sicker.

If I were going to play the "glad game," like in the book *Pollyanna* (the girl who could find joy in a barrel of crutches!) I suppose I could have felt pleased that Mr. Snow's family would be able to give him a decent burial at last—casket closed, of course.

Dr. Tyrell, who doubled as our coroner, verified that the cause of death had been accidental. Late one afternoon in January, Mr. Snow had gone out to check his "tilts"—ice-fishing flags. Dusk had come on faster than expected with a driving rain from the east. As Mr. Snow headed for shore, he must have stepped onto the thin new surface where blocks of ice had been cut out near the ice house. A dreadful mistake, so everyone agreed.

But I knew differently. Mr. Snow had died because of me and the letter. I might as well have gone out there and held the old man under the ice myself.

By the time Mr. Snow's body surfaced, I'd figured out most of the real story, but no way was I ever going to tell it. I thought about those warnings I saw everywhere these days of the dangers of careless words. *Someone talked*, exclaimed the poster of the drowning sailor on the post office wall. *Loose Lips Sink Ships*. I knew the accusing finger in the poster was pointing directly at me—if my lips ever got loose, our whole family would be sunk. Not that anyone would have believed me. Being afflicted with a vivid imagination, I was often accused of its next of kin—outright lying. Yet part of me longed for the truth to come out, as it always did in stories.

Sure, I might have shed a few tears over some baby bird falling featherless from its nest, but I had mixed feelings about the passing of that crotchety old man. To tell the truth, for our family, Mr. Snow's death was more of a win than a loss, because of the inheritance. And that meant I had to protect Aunt Bette. Not to mention, hide my own part in what everyone was calling "a needless tragedy." If I hadn't meddled in his affairs, Mr. Snow would still be alive and well.

I should have put that letter back the moment I found it, or if I couldn't do that, at least ripped it up into a hundred little pieces. I knew in my gut that it could only mean trouble. But I was so flabbergasted that someone had written a real love letter to a wizened old curmudgeon like Mr. Snow that I kept rereading the spidery handwriting. The ink had faded to purple. *Purple passion*, I thought. And each time I read those passionate words again, our boring small town took on an exciting new glow. If someone had once swooned over the

Winston Snow I knew, such hot romances might be going on secretly all the time in Whitford. Hidden desires might be lurking in any breast, even among the ample bosoms of the DAR.

Of course, I didn't know then who the woman who signed herself "Pan" was, but I did know "Win." I invented countless stories to explain why the letter had been written, and I hid it in my trustiest hiding place—the space behind the built-in drawers under the eaves in my room. It was the only place my mother never thought to clean.

Housecleaning—the more vigorous, the better—seemed to give my mother some deep satisfaction, second only to her pride in cooking. She'd got a reputation for being the best cook in Whitford. And people in town sometimes paid Mother to cook for them—baked beans, fried chicken, breads and pies for wakes, or simple tiered cakes for emergency weddings. We had a lot of those during the war. And sometimes she'd hire out to clean for Whitford's well-to-do families, as she did for Mr. Snow each spring and fall.

Mother's cooking and cleaning, our boarders, and some money put aside from selling Dad's lumber yard to Nathan Whitcomb was pretty much all the income we had. Keeping a Victory Garden was not a great new challenge for us Byrds, as it had been for some of our neighbors. Mother's garden had gone a long way toward putting food on our table ever since my father had died of pneumonia in the winter of '39. Every morsel of summer that could be preserved was put up in mason jars and bushel baskets stored in the cold room of our cellar.

Mother probably wished she lived nearer to one of the defense plants where a woman could bring home almost the same wages as a man. Aunt Bette, who wasn't tied to a house and a child, had taken a room in Southport and worked at the yard where Liberty Ships were being hastily welded together. That daring move lasted for only a few weeks. As usual, steady employment proved to be too much for her. She soon became weak and sickly again and had to move back with us "to build up." She brought me a *Soldiers Without Guns* poster—three women dressed for rough factory work, eyes shining with noble purpose.

Scrubbing and polishing someone else's house definitely lacked that sense of glorious sacrifice. *A waste of a perfectly good Saturday*, I thought, when Mother—looking like a Viking queen with her blonde-gray braids wound tightly around her head and her mouth set in a determined line—bustled Aunt Bette and me along to Snows' for the fall cleaning on that day in September when I found the letter. I wouldn't have minded the dismal prospect so much if I had been allowed to dust in the library, but that most fascinating room was forbidden to me. I couldn't imagine why I was shut out of this treasure, unless the room held some murderous secret, like Bluebeard's castle. Which it almost did, as I was to find out later.

"That dirty old fool!" Mother had exclaimed to Aunt Bette when she had a look around in there herself.

"Don't be such a prude, Catherine. Say, here's a weird one," Aunt Bette had whispered, shutting the door so that I was left out in the hall. I pressed my ear against the dark panel. I could barely hear as my mother continued to exclaim with horror while Aunt Bette drew her attention to...*what?* I burned with curiosity. Anyone would think Mr. Snow had a row of severed heads on those shelves.

The Snow house was located in Frietchie Circle, facing the Friendship Unitarian Church across the town green. "Shamefully neglected until Win bought it," is how Aunt Bette described the handsome house. The last owner, Mrs. Whitcomb (*nee* Frietchie) of the funeral-parlor Whitcombs, had sold the place to Winston and Frances Snow in 1932. Due to his foresight in pulling out of the stock market while it was still riding high, Winston Snow had been able to retire to a country estate while other financiers, so we heard, were leaping out of Wall Street windows in that black year of 1929. After moving to Whitford with his fortune intact, Snow had devoted himself to buying antiques and Oriental treasures at bargain prices.

"And a delightful Georgian brick was restored to our town!" my aunt declared, as if she shared the glory of it somehow. The "delightful" shutters had been painted a rich blue to complement the dark red brick. Because of its distinctive, graceful style, the house was greatly admired from cupola to portico by everyone in town. The library was located in the back of the house, with a bay window overlooking Mrs. Snow's rose garden. Mrs. Snow had been dead for over three years, but her roses kept right on blooming abundantly every June and were still producing a few brave blossoms in September—which inspired my mother to warble "Twas the Last Rose of Summer" while stringing up a clothesline in the backyard.

My plan to get into the library was the only bright spot in a day that promised to bore me to tears. After a morning spent outdoors smacking Persian rugs with a rattan rug beater and imagining myself as a galley slave in ancient Rome, I was only allowed inside when Mother spread our lunch out on Snow's kitchen table.

My petite, dark-haired aunt often cooked dinner for Mr. Snow in that bountiful kitchen with its pantry full of S.S. Pierce tins. She'd started to help out in Mrs. Snow's last illness and continued after her death—except for those few weeks in Southport. But when Aunt Bette had come home, humming patriotic songs in a weak little voice—eager, she said, to get back to her welding torch— Mr. Snow had raised her wages to twelve dollars a week.

Cooking for Mr. Snow was "duck soup," Mother said. He lived nearby, and that easy job made it possible for Aunt Bette to buy the attractive clothes and pretty little shoes (size three!) that meant so much to her, as well as to be nourished by some healthful red meat. I'd taken on my mother's concern for Aunt Bette's anemia, so I was thankful that Mr. Snow always seemed able to have a supply of beef, coffee, and sugar on hand, in spite of shortages and rationing. But I was dumbfounded that anyone would employ my aunt to cook. She could make a nice onion sandwich on buttered toast, but that was about it. And Mr. Snow didn't seem like the onion-sandwich type to me.

As I listened to the talk at lunch that day, I think I got my first clue that there might be something more than cooking a hot meal going on between my aunt and old man Snow. Although I tried to look utterly absorbed in the copy of *American Girl* in my lap, my presence wasn't forgotten, as my mother's use of vague or dangling phrases indicated.

"He's very well educated," my aunt asserted. "Some school in Switzerland, then Harvard, you know. And he likes to teach me about property and investments. He says I have a natural aptitude for business."

"Some school in Germany, you mean. And you know what all that big talk amounts to..." Mother let that trail off. "Remember your natural aptitude for real estate."

"You don't have to remind me of that, Catherine. That's dead and buried, and nobody blames me. I was practically a child, and he took advantage. So you just let it alone. Win's been very generous."

"Silk stockings and cigarettes? You call that generous?" My mother used a piece of waxed paper to pinch to death a foolish fly buzzing our egg salad.

"Well, I just don't know what you expect." Aunt Bette pushed aside her crusts and lit a Parliament.

"Much, much better things for you. You'll be thirty-six in March. I'd just like to see you settled and secure."

"This just might be my best chance. He's been talking about doing something substantial for me."

"How do you mean, 'something substantial'?"

"You know…so I'll be taken care of."

"What about the brother?"

"Oh, they don't even speak, for heaven's sake. It's a sort of religious war. Hamilton's an Episcopal bishop, and Win…well, you know how he is." Aunt Bette dropped her voice to a whisper. "I mean, you've seen the books…"

I kept my nose in *American Girl* as if my only interest in this world was How to Be a Heroine of the Home Front.

"Well, then there's Eunice. She's a niece and very close to him, so I understand."

"I might be a little closer." Aunt Bette had a mischievous smile, but Mother gave her that not-in-front-of-Amelia look.

My aunt turned to me, still smiling. "She has an old head," she said to Mother. It sounded like a compliment. Inspired by her confidence, I took a chance and looked up with what I thought was a mature and trustworthy expression.

She frowned with delicate distaste. "Must you fill your mouth so full?" I could see where the two faint lines between my aunt's eyebrows were getting not-so-faint.

"I hope you won't be taken in by false promises." Mother polished our oily fingerprints off the enamel tabletop with a paper napkin that disintegrated under the punishing pressure. "How will you know, really, unless you see it on paper with your own eyes?"

"He's already called Mr. Fenner. It's in the works, Catherine. I know it."

"You do, do you? Well, maybe. What's his age now, anyway?"

"Sixty-five. Sixty-six next April."

"That old goat! I hope you know what you're doing."

But then they changed the subject to *Science and Health* by Mary Baker Eddy, a book they were both reading and which they agreed was the most inspiring book ever written—the same as when they were both reading *Don Quixote,* it was the greatest novel. They used to read parts of *Don Quixote* aloud, laughing and crying, and it put them in quite a good humor. I loved those *Don Quixote* evenings. Even if Aunt Bette did call me "Dulcinea" for weeks afterward, it was a lot more fun than Christian Science.

After lunch, I was presented with a pail of hand-scalding water, a torn piece of toweling, and a cake of gritty Bon Ami to wash the painted woodwork in the hall.

"Now use plenty of elbow grease and get into all the crevices. But no dripping water on the floor, for God's sake. And don't you dare sit on any of the furniture!" My mother's voice descended into the low warning range, a lioness defending the den. "Practically all those chairs are antiques, and if you put your big foot on even one rung there'll be the devil to pay. He's got them all written up in a list with notes on every dent and wormhole. And *stay clear away* from the china vases."

"Chinese porcelains," Aunt Bette corrected her.

"Listen, Bette—'vases' she understands. And you know how things have a way of just jumping off the shelves when Amelia is around."

"It's her karma," my aunt said calmly. Then she turned to me, seeming somehow taller although I already had two inches over her. "If any one of Mr. Snow's precious belongings breaks in any remote corner while you are in this house, I will kill you. Do you have that straight?" Her dark blue eyes were chilling.

"I don't think anything will break today, honest," I assured her, although never sure myself. "And who wants to sit in those hard wooden chairs, anyway! Our own furniture is much nicer than those ugly things."

I could hear them laughing with some merry private knowledge—possibly because, among other rare pieces, one of those "old things" was a genuine Governor Carver chair that Aunt Bette called "a museum piece."

Washing away at the paint, I worked my way toward the library while Mother and Aunt Bette wiped down walls and polished furniture in the parlor. I could smell pungent paste wax and hear the rise and fall of their continuing argument. With newfound energy, I'd soon rounded the door frame into the mysterious library with its perfume of leather, rich old wood, and dust from crowded book shelves.

Drying my hands on my shirt tail, I chose an extra large, dusky orange book titled *Indika Illustrated*. I was fascinated by drawings of snake charmers, turbaned royalty riding elephants, cringing "untouchables," sacred cows, and an alarming custom of widow-burning called "suttee." This last foreign tidbit was scarily like my worst nightmares, always about being trapped in a house on fire.

There were more books about India and other Eastern lands, but most of the books on nearby shelves were about religion—or rather, against it. I was drawn to a picture book featuring caricatures and ribald interpretations of Joseph and the Pharaoh's wife, Lot and his daughters, and other familiar Bible stories.

On the other side of the room there was shelf after shelf of what seemed to be medical books about sex. Some of the titles were in Latin. I didn't recognize any of the words, except little ones like *et*, *per*, and *que*. Naturally I planned to get over there, but my eye was caught by the mythology shelf right below religion. I'd developed a fondness for mythology ever since I'd got too old for fairy tales. It was in a thin, dark green book on Greek gods that I found the folded letter written in ink which had aged to a faint purple. Just as I unfolded it, I heard my aunt's light step coming down the hall from the parlor. Quickly I stuffed the letter in my shirt pocket, pushed the book back in place, and went back to washing woodwork before she looked into the room.

"Amelia, are you going to get it!" she said in a conspiratorial whisper. "First, you're not supposed to be in this room bothering the books. Second, this kind of woodwork should be waxed not washed. Get yourself out of here and finish in the hall. Now I'm going to keep my eye on you, and if I see you in here again, I'm going to call your mother."

Later I tried to tell myself that it wasn't my fault that the letter went home in my pocket, since I never did get the chance to return it to *The Gods on*

Olympus—a simple mischance that led to Mr. Snow's death, and almost got me murdered, too.

⌒⟶

Warfare was alien to Whitford, as foreign as Tobruk or Stalingrad. Although we listened to the news each night, clustered around our domed radio, the reality of killing and being killed eluded us in the early years of the war. Even when telegrams from the War Office began to arrive and gold stars appeared in windows, these tragedies in other families seemed unbelievable. How could a young man we used to see playing basketball or pumping gas be dead and buried in a foreign land where no one had ever been? At least my dad had a resting place right here in the cemetery beside Friendship Unitarian.

The brutal violence of war had no place in a small town of modest church spires, unlocked back doors, tumbled-down stone fences, and the rich green fields that only a yearly dressing of manure can yield. All that distinguished our town from others just as pleasant and unremarkable was its many small lakes. We called them "ponds," although the largest was more than a mile long.

Living near the ponds, we swam in their fresh warm water every day in summer. Clusters of brown or green cottages, with names like "Pleasant View" and "Lazy Daze" printed on board signs tacked above leaning porches surrounded the ponds. On the ribbon shorelines, there were simple wharves with rowboats tied to them and an occasional bright canoe overturned on a narrow beach. Whitford's larger homes, distanced from the ponds, fronted on main roads at the center of town, with ample space between them for wide lawns and great, old shade trees—elm and chestnut.

Our house, once part of a farm, was in a stratum between, not hemmed in by cottages, but having several acres of land that led right down to the shore of Silver Sand Pond; not on a main road, but at least on a paved one. Like the ducks and turtles, we too were part of the pond's world.

Almost once a year, sometimes skipping a year, one of the ponds took a life. A few were lost in summer. Youngsters swam from an early age in Whitford, and parents didn't always watch closely. But most of the drownings happened in winter, when a sheet of ice over one pond or another created irresistible short-cuts across town.

People said it was foolish of the old man to go out there at dusk and careless to cross the ice-cutting section. In his panic, in the freezing black water, he'd likely trapped himself under the true ice that bordered the deceptive skim. Of course, we'd all been warned not to trust that end of Silver Sand Pond. And Winston Snow had been an intelligent, prudent man. Yet no one questioned the accident.

The alarm had been given by our boarder, Alex Carver. Beryl and Nathan Whitcomb, neighbors who were block wardens making their rounds nearby that evening, immediately called for help. Volunteer firemen rushed into action, in a scenario they'd played many times before. But they didn't find him, though they broke through the ice and dragged for the body with hooks all that night. They couldn't use searchlights, of course, because of the blackout. We were only a few miles from the Plymouth coast.

When I woke in the morning, some of the searchers were still there, and others continued to drag through the raw, windy day. Some unknown spring beneath the surface, they concluded, must have pushed the body into a nest of rocks.

That was in January, four months after I found the letter. Although it was no longer in my possession then, it never left my mind. I remembered every word.

My Darling Win,

I have read your brief words a hundred times, and each time the anguish is greater. You say that your love is unfair to me, that we must not see each other again.

What you have not said, I know, knowing you so well. You have worlds to conquer of which I can never be a part.

You know how much I love you——and so you also know that I cannot resist whatever you want, even if what you want is never to return to our summer palaces and pleasures.

How easily I could follow the way of the Lily Maid and send my body floating down the river to you on a barge——but for your sake, and the sake of others, I shall live.

And I shall live to remember——as you will remember, whether you wish it or not. When I wander alone in dreams we shared, perhaps I will glimpse your shadow sometimes drifting in those same love stories we made our own. The great love stories never have happy endings——had you realized that?

This is my first letter to you, and I shall never write another or intrude upon you in any way. I have always understood we could not make a life together, for your future was already written when we met.

Summer is over. Winter is forever now. Be happy, my love.

   Always
    Your...
    Pan

         January 15, 1910

Chapter 2

In which my so-called friends dish
the dirt about Aunt Bette.

When I'd finished my last allotted chore that Saturday and gone home to change into clean shorts and a Camp Pocahontas shirt, I noticed the letter in my pocket and read it. How romantic it was! How much trouble I'd be in if it was found in my room! After hiding it carefully, I went straight to Daisy and Jay's house to tell them about the strange collection of books I'd found in the Snow library—and maybe about the letter. As I walked the familiar mile through the woods, the fatigue of housecleaning slipped off my shoulders with every step. It was only quarter to three when I arrived. Plenty of afternoon left.

My friends, the Eliots, were twins, but they looked more like a regular brother and sister. Jay was taller and leaner. Daisy was paler and her straight brown hair was a shade lighter than Jay's. For the twin part, they both had dark eyes with straight brows like brush strokes, and they ran the same way, as if they were moving in slow motion, but gracefully, like some kind of African deer. They were standoffish, with a wicked sense of humor—especially Jay, who drew mocking cartoons of other kids and even teachers.

Daisy told me they had been named for characters in one of her mother's favorite novels, which they hadn't read yet. *The Great Gatsby* was in the "racy books" cabinet that the librarian, Miss Pratt, guarded with fierce looks and threats to tell our folks. May Beth Eliot, their mother, was "away working for the government" in Washington, D.C., Jay said, and wasn't expected up north "for the Duration."

I'd heard Aunt Bette tell Mother a different story about May Beth. One day when her children got off the school bus, instead of cookies and milk, they'd found two notes on the kitchen table, one for them and one for their father. Their mother had run off with a trombone player in the Army Air Force Band stationed in New Jersey. So they had been sent to live here in Whitford with their grandmother, Mrs. Alma Eliot, who pressed her lips together into a thin line if we got into a fit of laughing or played records too loud or ran down the stairs.

Hiding out in Daisy's bedroom to avoid the silent disapproval of Mrs. Eliot, I livened up their afternoon with tales of *suttee*. When they tired of young brides being burned to death on funeral biers, I said I knew a real love story I could tell but they would have to swear eternal secrecy or I would get killed. They crossed their hearts and hoped to turn into toads, so I told them about the letter. I even remembered the date.

"My God," said Daisy. "That was over thirty years ago."

"Thirty-three," Jay said. He was sitting on the window sill with the window open, his feet dangling over the porch roof. I peeked over his shoulder at the sketchbook in his lap. The woods across the street and nearby houses began to appear under fast strokes of his charcoal pencil. Jay had a stack of similar sketchbooks in his closet, but only one drawing hung on his bedroom wall, a framed sketch of May Beth Eliot wearing a straw hat and laughing. She was as pretty as a movie star, so probably it wasn't her fault that she got herself into trouble with a guy in uniform.

"Well, Mr. Snow is really ancient—way over sixty. He would have been just middle-aged, in his thirties, when the letter was written," I explained. "She called him 'My Darling Win.'"

"Your Aunt Bette wouldn't like that at all," Daisy snickered. "You'd better not make her jealous with that lovey-dovey letter to her sugar daddy. Grandma says your aunt and Mr. Snow…"

"Shut up, you moron," interrupted Jay, swinging back into the room—but I'd already caught the drift.

Embarrassed and angry, I said, "Tell your stupid grandma that my Aunt Bette is taking a business course from Mr. Snow that's going to make her very wealthy. And when she's rich, we're all going to move out of Whitford *forever*." As if to put this boast into immediate action, I stormed downstairs and outside, back to the woodland path that linked the twins' house on School Street to ours on Pond Street.

It was a rutted dirt road between forsaken cranberry bogs. The woods that day were bronzed with autumn, deserted except for a sprinkling of industrious little creatures putting by their winter stores. The only sounds were of birds calling, some soft scurrying in the bushes, and the occasional breeze in the tops of pines. Even my footsteps were muffled; the ground was padded with pine needles and rotted oak leaves. Trees grew together overhead, blotting out the sunlight, always making the path darker than it should be for any given hour of the day. I loved the cool, ripe, spicy smell and the curious pale growths that pushed up between brown leaves—Indian Pipes and puffballs. To me, this was an enchanted place, and it worked its spell on me that day. Halfway home, I forgot to be angry.

In a deep stand of pine, a hollow in the earth under low sweeping branches, was my secret hiding place. I was about to check that the old metal cash box I'd buried there was still suitably camouflaged with pine needles when I heard Jay and Daisy, loping up behind me, humming ghostly music.

"Listen, Amelia—Daisy didn't mean anything," Jay said by way of apology. "You know how the church ladies gossip when they get together to sew for Old Home Day." Fluttering his elbows, he cackled and pecked like a flock of chickens.

I tried to scowl at their two concerned faces, but it was no good. Jay could always make me laugh.

Seeing a crack in my armor, Daisy said, "So...got anything to eat at your house?" The pencil-thin twins always seemed to be hungry, as if nothing their Grandma cooked would ever fill them up.

"How about if I beat you two at Monopoly again?" Jay offered, gazing into the woods as if he couldn't care less about my answer.

"Yeah, okay, but no cheating this time. I could make cocoa. There's not much sugar in my jar, but I'll filch some out of Aunt Bette's. And there's cheese for sandwiches."

I didn't mention that old man Snow had given Aunt Bette a five-pound wheel of cheddar. Food was getting to be a sore subject around town as shortages began to clear out shelves and meat cases at Fisher's General Store. When shipments of scarce items did arrive, Guy Fisher would tip off special customers in advance. My family knew this because Winston Snow was on Guy Fisher's select list, and we suspected that Dr. Tyrell was, too. Since Aunt Bette often benefited from Mr. Snow's well-stocked larder, we refrained from complaining to outsiders, although my mother had a few sharp words to say about Fisher's favorites when she couldn't fill her own shopping list.

Chapter 3

In which I receive an inspiring gift—
and a promising invitation.

*P*erhaps *Pan's real name was Elaine.*

    I was reading the sad tale of Lancelot and Elaine, the Lily Maid of Astolat. It was Sunday, an unusually warm day for October. I'd fled the probability of being called for chores and settled outdoors under the pines in the backyard, with a few Macintosh apples to munch. The cool odor of pine sap mixed with the tart juice of apple in my mouth. I'd almost forgotten the letter until the Tennyson story brought it to mind.

    But somehow I couldn't fit the Mr. Winston Snow I knew into the Camelot legend. He was not my idea of a romantic hero, with his lipless mouth that turned down at the corners, frosty blue eyes, and that gray grizzle on his chin, the bow-legged old man I sometimes saw flapping around in backless leather slippers and a faded green coat sweater with leather elbow patches, his Boston terrier panting after him. The little fellow was named Ollie, short for Oliver Wendell Holmes who had been a Harvard man like Mr. Snow.

    I was seeing Mr. Snow more often now because of being drafted by Aunt Bette to deliver groceries from Fisher's to Snow's place, pulling them along in a squeaky old red wagon. She was doing most of Mr. Snow's marketing as well as his cooking and spent time there in evenings, too. I guessed she was still being educated about business.

The kitchen was about as far as I ever got when I carried in boxes for Aunt Bette. Mr. Snow always looked at me as if I had mud on my shoes, even after I'd scraped them clean on the welcome mat. He probably didn't like children since he didn't have any. He liked dogs, though, because Ollie was allowed to run all over the house and do worse than muddy the floors, according to Aunt Bette.

Whenever I was at Snow's, Ollie used to follow me like my shadow, not just because I'd slip him a biscuit, but also because I was the only one in his little circle of people who liked to run as much as he did. Ollie and I had some good sprints out back of Snow's.

When no one else was listening, I talked to him like a person. He'd settle down with a sigh, his pug snout fitting snugly between white paws. His pointed black ears would quiver with the intensity of his listening, and his eyes looked troubled as if he were struggling to understand.

Remembering the letter had given me a horrid pain in my stomach. What if Mr. Snow began looking for it, and the letter wasn't where he'd left it? What if he told Aunt Bette, and she guessed that I'd taken it? What if Aunt Bette complained to my mother? I tried to tell myself that Mr. Snow must have forgotten all about that old letter, or why would he leave it where Mrs. Snow (when she was alive) or anyone else could find it? Still, I'd have to find a way to put the letter back so that Aunt Bette and Mother would never know I'd taken it.

From where I was reading that Sunday, I could see Sarge Curry come out of his cottage and wave me over. Although Sarge was well past fifty, I considered him to be one of my good friends. He always asked me what I was reading, and we'd talk about that and his favorite books, too. Sometimes he gave me books he didn't want anymore or had two of. Although I'd never told him, he seemed to know I'd been forbidden to go inside his cottage and didn't invite me. So our talks happened when the weather was fine and we could sit out on his little porch.

Sarge's cottage was right behind our other neighbors' house, Beryl and Nathan Whitcomb. Mrs. Whitcomb and Sarge had once been married, and after they were divorced, Sarge moved into the small beach cottage in back that they used to rent out in the summer. All he'd had to do was to put in a heater and build some bookcases, which he said were better than insulation. He also added a sort of lean-to shed which was his shop out back of the cottage. Sarge was a kind of genius at repair, and he was kept busy fixing everything from toasters to tractors now that all machines were irreplaceable for the Duration—which is what people called wartime, not knowing when it would end but believing that it somehow must.

When Beryl married Nathan Whitcomb, he'd moved into the big house where Sarge used to live and bought my father's lumber yard. Sometimes when Beryl made a roast chicken or a boiled ham dinner, she'd call me over and hand me a pie basket with a plate of food, swathed in a blue checkered dish towel, to bring out back to Sarge.

"It's almost your birthday," Sarge said that day, "and that calls for a gift." With his sleeve, he dusted off the book he was carrying and handed it to me, his sad spaniel eyes looking merry for once. He moved aside a fishing rod, leaning it carefully against the window frame, and we sat on the two oak rockers on his porch. The aroma of fish chowder with fried salt pork drifted out through his window.

"*The Adventures of Sherlock Holmes,*" I read the title aloud. Then I thanked him and looked through the pages a bit. The print was very small, but there were some interesting illustrations of a tall thin man in a plaid cap.

"Was Holmes a real person?"

"Well, no—not a *real* person," Sarge said. "But definitely alive in people's minds. He was a highly logical, observant, and scientific detective, the first of his kind. He believed that all puzzles could be solved by rational deduction. Holmes said, 'Eliminate all other factors, and the one which remains must be the truth.' "

Wondering if the puzzle of the letter could be solved by "rational deduction," whatever that was, I said, "I'm reading *Tales from Tennyson* now. I'm at

'Lancelot and Elaine.' It's about King Arthur and his knights going on quests, and courtly love."

"Let me see what you have there." He took the Tennyson book out of my hand, looked it over carefully, and read a few pages, while I read the first page of the first Sherlock Holmes adventure. We were quiet and comfortable—until the fishing rod fell over, which knocked the bait can off the porch into a washing machine standing beside the cottage.

I started up guiltily. "I didn't touch it!"

"I know." Sarge laughed as he went around to clean up the mess. "Things just happen, don't they? I should get the washing machine into the shop and out of Beryl's sight, anyway, before she has a conniption fit." He picked worms out of the tub.

I helped him walk the washing machine around to the shop. Since it wouldn't fit in the door, we covered it with canvas. Like my mother, Beryl kept her yard very neat with the grass cut short, but Sarge never cut his part of the lawn. He said he wanted to simplify his life. This made Beryl quite cross with him all through the summer months. I think if she'd asked him nicely, he would have fixed up his half of their yard (her backyard, his front yard) but she never spoke to Sarge after the divorce. Instead, she'd come over to our house and yell at Mother about how embarrassed she was by that field of weeds, and how reading Thoreau had ruined Sarge's mind. Or she'd ask me to carry a note to him, with words scrawled so angrily that they ripped through the paper. And she wouldn't send him any baskets of home-cooked food for a while.

I always wondered if Beryl realized that Sarge was a pretty good cook for a man. Probably he never did mess around in the kitchen while he was married to Beryl. But sometimes we'd have root beer and gingerbread on his porch, and I knew that he'd made them both himself.

Last February, some of Sarge's root beer exploded about ten in the evening while Nate Whitcomb was out learning how to be an air-raid warden in a class organized by the American Legion. Hearing repeated blasts from Sarge's cottage, Mother and Aunt Bette imagined that Sarge had lost his wits and was shooting at Beryl's house, so they called the police. Beryl thought so, too, because she came screaming into our kitchen in her old pink chenille bathrobe.

She'd been brushing her teeth. Mother took one look at her neighbor with white foam oozing out of her mouth and tried to wrestle Beryl to the sofa, so she wouldn't topple onto the floor. It was past midnight before Police Chief Ferro got everything sorted out.

After that, everyone in town knew about Sarge's homemade root beer but not about his baking. He brought out a plate of gingerbread that October afternoon while we rocked and read. It was dense and heavy with extra molasses. I hoped that Sarge would never simplify his sweet tooth.

Sarge suggested I ask Miss Pratt, the librarian, for *Idylls of the King.* "The same stories of King Arthur and all, only told in poetry. You like poetry, don't you?"

"Yes, but Miss Pratt doesn't always allow me to take out the books I want, if she thinks I'm not old enough."

"She'll let you have that one, Amelia—it's a classic. I don't exactly agree with Miss Pratt, but I do think you should realize that reading junk can make you as sick as eating too many hot dogs. But the classics, now, will nourish you forever. And another thing—you only have time to read so many books. So you may as well choose the feasts and not the garbage."

Sarge's own words seemed to make him sad. His shoulders and his brown mustache drooped a little more than usual. I didn't know how to make him feel better, and besides, I was having a hard time thinking cheerful thoughts myself. That part about what you read staying with you forever applied to letters, too.

I wished that Sarge were the librarian instead of Miss Pratt, and I told him so. He said he liked being nothing best, but at least he smiled.

"But you're not nothing," I protested. "You used to own Fisher's garage, and now you have your own repair shop. And I've heard some people say you'd be a better town moderator than Gordon Fisher, if you wanted the job."

"I deny it," he replied, still smiling. "I've no taste for politics. The garage was Beryl's, and that isn't a shop back there, it's a tinkering room. Do you see any business signs out front?"

"Nope." I could have said that people paid him to tinker with their broken machines, but there wasn't much point in arguing with grown-ups. They got fixed into their grooves, like toy hockey players in a penny arcade game.

After Sarge and I finished my last two apples, I saw by the shadows that it was getting late. Thanking Sarge again for the birthday book, I went home to help with supper before my mother had to holler for me, which always made her so cross. I wondered if Sarge was making biscuits to go with the chowder. I liked swishing through Sarge's tall grass better than our plain short lawn, anyway.

Korhonen's rusty blue truck was parked in our driveway. He'd be making a delivery of eggs, cream, and maybe a chicken—and no doubt having a cup of coffee with Mother, exchanging town gossip. His daughter Minna had come with him, so I escaped to the barn to show her my animals. She was a freshman, like the twins, but they didn't hang around with her much. Or anyone else for that matter. They knew kids were whispering about their mother, except for me. What with the gossip about Aunt Bette and Mr. Snow, I was in no position to get all shocked over May Beth Eliot.

Minna was friendly and lively, a solid kind of girl, but not fat. She had a square jaw, milky skin stretched over high cheekbones, and hair as yellow as late corn, the same color as the cardigan she was wearing. She was easy to be with and I liked that, although she was inclined to think that animals were something you fattened up to eat. So I explained about my little animal refuge in the garage—that Romeo the rabbit was not going to be our dinner, as we didn't eat rabbits, not even when meat was scarce. Prince the frog I had found in the street, and I was planning to bring him back to Silver Sand Pond so he could settle in there for the winter.

Minna petted Romeo, who was cowering in the corner of his cage. She peered at Prince and at Merlin the turtle through the glass of the old fish tank. "You have so many pets," she said. "I have to keep my cat Louhi in the barn, too."

Moving Merlin to a cracked enamel washbasin, I invited Minna to help me carry the fish tank over the field path to the pond.

It was colder down at the pond's edge, shaded by birches and maples. The wind coming across from the Town Beach brought a faint odor of yellowing reeds and crushed green clams. Once the swimmers stopped tramping in the shallows, fresh-water clams took over the sand. I could see them through the water, lined up in soldierly formation. In the spring, we'd have to rake them up to take back our little beach.

Prince sat frozen in one corner of his glass house, pop eyes staring ahead. We turned the tank sideways near the reeds, then sat on the wharf, which had been pulled in and stacked away from shore for the winter.

"You must come and visit us, sleep over," Minna said. "We have lots of animals. We can ride the horse. And take a sauna in our bath house."

Such a neat idea, I felt sure it would get shot down at home "I'll have to ask Mother," I said. "I've never ridden a horse. Is a sauna like a steam bath? We won't get cooked, will we?" Maybe I wouldn't tell Daisy and Jay, who would surely be scornful of a farm adventure. Minna was such a sunny person, I felt warmed just sitting beside her.

She wasn't the kind of friend you wanted to horrify with *suttee*, so I asked her who she liked, and she said there was a boy named Juhani in Kates Hill who was seventeen. Their families were friends, both owners of cranberry bogs (only Juhani's family had an orchard and bees instead of a farm like the Korhonens) and both members of the same Lutheran Church and Temperance Camp.

"In school, of course, he's called Johnny," Minna added. "Miss Cronin, your boarder, comes from Kates Hill. My brother Will is engaged to her sister Emily."

"Do the sisters look alike?"

"Yes, very much. The whole family looks like each other, nice people, so talented with their music.

Minna seemed to be missing the point.

"Is Emily any prettier?"

"They look almost the same. Emily's hair is lighter. Both good cooks and hard workers, too. My brother will be lucky to have the Cronins for in-laws."

It was another way of looking at it. When I talked to Miss Cronin, who was my science teacher as well as our boarder, I didn't think about how homely she was because she was so interested in others and so enthusiastic about everything from plant pollination to star constellations. Maybe it was like that with Emily and Minna's brother.

I'd always hoped that someday I'd turn out to be beautiful, as were all my favorite heroines, but I seemed to be growing up ordinary and tall. My face was too thin, my color too pale, my freckles too noticeable, and my hair, a dull sandy color, wouldn't curl no matter how much Aunt Bette singed it with the curling iron. My eyes weren't too bad, I thought. If only I'd got Mother's ocean-blue eyes instead of eyes that were greenish like pond water. It would be a sensible idea to learn to be as pleasant as Miss Cronin in case my looks didn't improve.

"You should see their hope chests, filled with such beautiful work, embroidered linen towels and crocheted scarves. So clever, those two!"

Would the hopes in Bernice Cronin's hope chest be fulfilled in Whitford? Or would she be disappointed like Elaine, the lily maid? For a wild moment, I imagined her floating dead on a raft on Silver Sand Pond, orange maple leaves trailing across her board-flat bosom.

Then Minna's father began yelling for her across the field. When we looked, Prince had finally found the courage to escape, and we hadn't even seen his departure. I picked up the empty tank, and we went up to the house.

Before Korhonen's old truck had sputtered its way out of the driveway, my mother was already busy crushing ice wrapped in a towel. She used a hammer to whack at it with as much vigor as if she were attacking the Enemy. I stayed out of the way until she put the deep bowl of thick cream into the larger bowl filled with slivers of ice and took out the eggbeater.

Thinking I might as well practice being pleasant right away, I offered to help whip the cream into butter, which Mother was going to tell me to do anyway. It took forever, with the bowl of cream sloshing around in the melting ice, but at last the whole mess sort of curdled into globs of yellow fat floating in thin whey. Mother skimmed out the butter and pressed it together, squishing and kneading out every last drop of liquid.

"There," she said with great satisfaction, forming the butter into a loaf with greasy hands. "Fisher may not have any for sale, so he says, but we've got two pounds or more. Maybe I'll make some muffins. They really don't taste right without real butter. Very good, Amelia!"

Once in a while some small thing made Mother happy, and a weight I carried in my chest suddenly lifted.

It seemed like the right moment to ask for something, so I asked if I could spend a weekend at Minna's, and I got a half-promise just as Aunt Bette came in the door with a paper bag held at arm's length and screamed, "Butter! Is that butter, Catherine? How grand!"

"And what's there, Bette? Fish again?"

"Oh, you know how the old fool loves to fish! And he's too damned good at it, always comes home with a huge catch, looking pleased as punch. Don't worry, I made him clean and fillet them properly this time. Bass. And they couldn't be fresher, just a few hours out of the pond."

"Well ... mustn't look a gift bass in the mouth." Still in a good humor, Mother whipped the bag out of my aunt's hand and into the Frigidaire. "I'll fry them for supper. Guess I'll make some tartar sauce, too."

"What's that book you're taking upstairs, honey?" Aunt Bette lifted *Sherlock Holmes* out of my hands. "Not a library book. Where'd you get it?"

"Sarge gave it to me. For my birthday."

"You didn't go into the cottage, did you?" My mother took her head out of the Frigidaire and wheeled around to fix me with her fierce "tell the truth" look.

"No, of course not. We sat on the porch."

"Amazing that you could get over there without a machete," Aunt Bette said, handing me back my book with two fingers.

"A young lady doesn't go into a man's room alone." Mother brought out one of her favorite axioms as if imparting this wisdom for the first time.

"He's such a tragic figure." My aunt went to the kitchen sink and began to wash all vestiges of fish off her smooth white hands. "I wonder if he's becoming a little odd from being so solitary. I mean, really, *that yard*! When I left here this morning, I believe there was a washing machine leaning beside the porch. Yesterday it was a broken tiller. The place is beginning to look like the town dump. I wonder that Beryl, with her high-strung temperament, doesn't do something drastic."

"There's nothing wrong with Sarge," I protested, hastily setting the kitchen table for three. "He's not crazy or anything like that."

"What do you know about it?" my aunt exclaimed tartly, shaking the moisture off her hands into my eyes. "All that *marching to a different drummer* is probably going to lead him right off the deep end."

No point in debating. Aunt Bette wasn't big on seeing another person's point of view. I slipped away upstairs and got started on my algebra assignment, which I had ignored all weekend. I liked algebra, so pure and logical, but I couldn't see what good it would do me because it was nothing like life.

Chapter 4

In which my best-laid plans go
awry...but I am undeterred.

Inspired by Sherlock Holmes's smoke bomb ruse in "A Scandal in Bohemia", I'd enlisted the help of Daisy and Jay in my first try to get the letter put back. Their collecting for the scrap drive from Aunt Bette would provide a diversion, while I pretended to feel sick and headed for Snow's bathroom, but really to sneak into the library. My aunt had not been fooled for one moment and had tossed us all out with harsh words. Aunt Bette certainly proved to be stronger than she looked and probably didn't need to be built up anymore.

Not only was I now in great disgrace with the Eliot twins, but by the time I arrived home, Aunt Bette had called my mother to tell her that I'd almost thrown up and was probably coming down with the grippe. Being fanatical about such things since my father's slight cold had turned into pneumonia, my mother made me get right into bed and brought my supper upstairs, a plate of milk toast, which I despised. There was nothing more disgusting than warm milk with oily butter floating on top and soggy bread underneath! After a while, I sneaked into the bathroom and flushed it down the toilet.

The aroma of Mother's crusty fried chicken and cornbread wafted up the back stairs, but when I checked the Frigidaire later, there wasn't a wing or a crumb left.

"Are you all right, Amelia?" Mother called anxiously from her bedroom.

"I couldn't sleep, so I'm getting an apple. I'm fine now."

"The apples are in the pantry, so what are you doing in the icebox?" We'd had the Frigidaire for two years, but Mother still called it the icebox.

"Just looking."

"Well, get to sleep so that you can go to school tomorrow if you're well enough. You can have a Uneeda biscuit. It'll help settle your stomach."

"I'm fine, Mother. Don't worry." I went back upstairs with two apples and a handful of Ritz crackers. It was only nine o'clock. Turning out the light, I raised the window shade. A full moon had risen over the lake. I felt wide awake, as if some magic thing was supposed to happen that I wouldn't want to miss. I sat perfectly still at the window for a while, but nothing changed. It seemed to me that the world was a dreary and boring place compared to stories. There was a lot of milk toast in real life. So I listened to Mystery Theater on the radio and smoked one of Aunt Bette's Parliaments, using my musical powder box as an ashtray. It played "Dream, when you're feeling blue..."

My bed, which my father had made years ago, had fox, squirrel, and raccoon heads carved into the posters. In the daylight, their faces looked like those of real animals, but at night, when the moonlight touched the carving, with their half-closed eyes, they seemed as mysterious as the beasts in fables. I was just letting my thoughts drift into their world, as I did almost every night, when I was inspired with a second plan to return the letter.

I'd have to break into the Snow house when no one was there. Only it wouldn't really be breaking in, because I would unlock the pantry window beforehand, while I was putting away groceries for Aunt Bette the following Saturday morning.

My plan seemed to be working out perfectly. Mother and Aunt Bette were going to the movies Sunday night, and Mr. Snow was going to visit his niece Eunice in Worcester. Probably no one would notice the unlocked pantry window. It was a funny, high window, the kind that doesn't get used often enough to be checked out by the few Whitford residents who went in for nightly lock-ups, like Mr. Snow.

"Where does he get the stamps to waste gas on these trips to Worcester?" my mother wondered aloud.

"How would I know?" Aunt Bette snapped back. "Do you want me to ask him?"

"Well, it's very strange. People can't even buy enough gas to get to work."

"He doesn't go to work. He's retired."

"I see that he keeps you well supplied with cigarettes. And all those steaks. Where does he find them? Not at Fisher's! Guy Fisher hasn't had a porterhouse in the meat case since the day after Pearl Harbor. You'd think the Japs had bombed the Chicago stock yards."

"Amelia, are you going with us, or what?" Aunt Bette called upstairs. I went back to my room to answer so that they wouldn't know I'd been listening from the stair landing.

"No, thanks. I have to finish my book report."

"It's Charles Boyer and Rita Hayworth in 'Tales of Manhattan.' "

"The book report is due Tuesday, and I haven't finished reading the book."

"I think she's still feeling sick. Maybe I should call Dr. Tyrell," my mother said. "She never misses a movie."

"What for? Dr. Tyrell doesn't believe in medicine. You can hardly squeeze a prescription out of him unless you're dying." Aunt Bette, who was often sickly, liked to have something to take for it, or better yet, several medicines in a variety of colors to be taken exactly on time at different hours. Even an evil-looking, brownish extract of liver that tasted so bad, she had to lie down after taking it.

Mother came upstairs and felt my forehead. She told me to get to bed as soon as possible because I felt flushed to her.

As soon as they left, still arguing about Dr. Tyrell, I stuffed the letter into my shirt pocket and ran all the way to Snow's. Every window shade was drawn for the blackout. I thought I detected a faint light in the hall, probably left on so that Mr. Snow wouldn't have to come home to a totally dark house.

I should have looked in the garage.

I dragged the milk box from the back step to the wall outside the kitchen. Standing on the box, I could reach the pantry window. I slid it up an inch or two. It squeaked, but I moved it as carefully and quietly as I could, a little at a time, until it was high enough. The sash rope was broken, so I had to hold it open. With my other hand, I pulled the shade down a bit in order to raise it, so that I could climb in the window. The shade slipped from my hands and went up with a loud *TWANG* followed by a *FLAP-FLAP-FLAP* as it spun around the rod. My other hand just froze right there, holding the window up. Then I heard Ollie racing down the stairs at full tilt, barking like a crazed dog.

I began to let the window down again very gently. Ollie was snuffling, scratching, and growling at the pantry door, which was almost shut. Then the worst happened! Mr. Snow's slippered step shuffled into the kitchen. I felt like a statue of ice with a great hot thumping heart in the center of it.

He flung open the pantry door, and there was my hand holding up the window.

"Jesus Christ!" he yelled and ran toward the library.

As I jumped down from the box and ran, I heard him coming out the back door with Ollie. By then, I had reached the trees. I glanced back over my shoulder long enough to see him standing in the light from the doorway—holding a rifle! I hadn't even known that he owned one. He must keep it in one of those locked cases in the library. Cold shivers rippled from the backs of my arms to my scalp.

Ollie was standing beside him now, not barking at all, quietly wagging his rear end. "Go get him, Ollie!" Mr. Snow ordered. I heard the dog run after me, no doubt feeling he was part of some merry game. But in my panic, I easily outdistanced the little fellow scrabbling and panting after me.

After that, I just kept running and never looked back. By the time I reached home I could hardly breathe. At least Ollie, in his doggie wisdom, had known I wasn't a robber. Actually I had been trying to put something back, not steal it, I reassured myself.

When she returned home from the scene of the crime late on Monday afternoon, Aunt Bette related her dramatic version of the incident to Mother. Her voice was shrill with anger. I was at the dining room table, finishing my book report on *The Count of Monte Cristo.*

"It's a miracle that he came back early from Eunice's. They could have had the house completely cleaned out if he'd stayed the evening in Worcester. The sterling, the Nippon chests, the Chinese porcelains, the Governor Carver chair, Mrs. Snow's collections ..." Her voice rose higher with each valuable item she named. She seemed to be keeping some kind of list in her head.

"Eunice tried to keep him, of course, but he became very restless, he said, with her and Rollo bringing the conversation around to wills. You know how he hates Eunice's father, Hamilton. They haven't spoken in years. But Eunice is a favorite of his, and well she knows it. Winston said he thinks there were three of them, and they had a truck parked down in back of the church. Lucky for them, he said, that Ollie didn't catch them. He'd have never let go. A great hairy hand holding up the window! If the moon had been out, Winston would have got a shot at them, but it was pitch black."

My mother murmured something about Eunice already having inherited some of Mrs. Snow's best jewelry and how it's pretty hard to run through the night carrying antique chairs, but Aunt Bette was starting the story all over again, beginning with the infamous hand at the window. My mother poured two glasses of the port wine she keeps to build up Aunt Bette. I could see them through the open dining room door. When the Ritz crackers and Kraft pimento cheese spread came out, I went into the kitchen for a pre-dinner snack.

"Amelia, you're awfully uninterested in all this excitement," my mother said in a questioning tone. Her sharp eyes looked especially tired that night, and her gray-blonde hair, usually neatly braided and coiled, was straggling over her cheeks and neck. Her hand around the glass looked knotted. I remembered that it was washing day and the wringer was broken.

But my aunt sparkled with enthusiasm, looking fresh and bright as a doll in her blue dress embroidered with tiny pink flowers. The big white collar reflected light onto her face. She looked at me with narrowed eyes.

"What's the big deal?" I said, casually spreading a Ritz cracker with cheese. "I guess nothing really happened to Mr. Snow's house, though. I mean everything is just the way it was before, isn't it?"

"What do you mean!" my aunt exclaimed crossly. "It was a dastardly crime, breaking and entering with the intention to steal."

I wanted to say that nothing had been broken or even entered, but I knew she'd just get madder and scream at me.

My mother got up and refilled both their glasses, then stashed the bottle in the cupboard and firmly shut the door. She put the crackers back in the pantry, snapped the cover shut on the glass jar, and wiped the crumbs off the table. Aunt Bette lit a Parliament and tried to blow a smoke ring. Sometimes she could do it.

"Catherine, I have an idea," she said. "Why don't you read the cards to see if they'll reveal something about the criminals."

"Wouldn't the Ouija board be better?" my mother suggested.

"Perhaps you're right. Wouldn't it be wonderful if we could get their names! Mellie, please go upstairs to my room and get out the Ouija. It's in the bottom drawer of my bureau—you know, where I keep my carton of cigarettes."

Taking note of the dig, I headed upstairs without argument, but my feet were as heavy as if I were going to the guillotine. *Like Marie Antoinette*, I thought, and I held my head proudly. *Peasants screaming for my death were stupid and wrong to think me guilty of any real crime.*

After a few hollers from my aunt, I trudged back down to my doom with the Ouija.

They warmed up the pointer by circling it around the board, slowly at first, and then faster and faster. Ordinarily, I loved the spookiness of the moment when the Ouija came to a life of its own. This time I leaned my back to the sink and watched them fearfully.

"Can you tell us, O Ouija," my mother said in a low dramatic tone, "who tried to break into Winston Snow's house?"

The pointer flew to "Yes" as if it were greased, though they held their hands lightly above it, with fingertips hardly touching the polished wood.

"How many men were involved in the crime?" my aunt asked.

The pointer hesitated this time, shuffling back and forth for a minute. Then, in the blink of an eye, it thrust itself over to the number 1, and skidded straight off the board.

"There, I thought so," said my mother. "Probably some kid."

Sometimes she scared me. She seemed to see right inside people's heads, especially mine. Of course, it could have been a lucky guess.

"Nonsense!" my aunt exclaimed crisply. "Let's see if we can get a name. O Ouija, will you tell us the name of the robber?"

Again the pointer hesitated, longer this time than it had before. Then it began to move, ever so slowly, scuttling like a crab back and forth. But I could see where it was headed. I knew it was going for the A. *The blade was about to fall!*

Just as that guillotine scene flashed through my mind, a funny thing happened. The china bread board that hung in the center of the double window over the kitchen sink fell off its nail into the dishpan.

My mother, who was facing in that direction, screamed blue murder. The onion-patterned bread board was used only for decoration. She jumped from her chair, knocking the Ouija askew, and ran to the sink, pushing me aside and looking as if she expected to find a heap of china splinters. It turned out that only one little corner of the server was chipped off. But it might as well have been dashed to smithereens. "It's ruined," she moaned. "It's just ruined. Can't I ever have anything nice?"

She turned and looked at me accusingly.

"I didn't touch it," I protested. "I was just standing here. You could see that yourself, Mother."

"Black Tuesday," said Aunt Bette, lighting another Parliament from the one that was still burning in the ashtray. That's what she called me sometimes, because my birth date was on the same day as the great stock market crash.

"What about when you washed the dishes after supper last night. Did you touch it then?" My mother wasn't going to give up so easily on blaming me.

"No, I did not." I put a little sob into my voice.

"Do you really think, Catherine, that the child looked for extra work to do after the dishes and took down the china server to give it a wash? Here, you're tired. You sit down, and I'll make you a nice cup of tea to settle your nerves." Aunt Bette got up and took hold of the kettle daintily.

"Now, you let me do that. You need *fresh* water." My mother whisked the kettle out of my aunt's hands, rinsed it out twice, then filled it with cold water before setting it on the stove.

My aunt gracefully resumed her seat and puffed her cigarette. "With all this worry about the burglary, I almost forgot to tell you," she said. "Winston has asked Mr. Do-Right to help catalog his library. Ugh." *Mr. Do-Right* is what my aunt called Mr. Carver, my English teacher, another of our boarders. My mother always said you couldn't go wrong with teachers because they were clean and didn't expect much.

"I think he's a very sweet person, Bette." My mother took out blue willow mugs and two teabags. "I only hope that cheapskate Winston is planning to pay him decently."

"Oh, there's nothing to cataloging a library. I could have done it for him, just writing titles and authors on little cards. I don't even see why he wants it done, all those dreadful books ought to be burned, not cataloged. There's something odd about all this. I mean, why Win asked him in the first place. Remember one night at the end of September when you sent Mr. Do-Right over to Win's place to bring me a coat in case there was a frost?"

"You ought to take better care of yourself, Bette. You know how susceptible you are to colds."

"Well, naturally he wormed his way right in so that I'd have to introduce him to Win who was holding a gold and leather volume of something or other that Alex recognized and commented on, so they began to chat about books. Win was just being polite, of course. Alex raved on and on about how he's been interested in great books ever since he crawled out of his cradle because of his mother who was the librarian. You remember that sad story he tells about her coughing her guts out with TB, and his eyes always fill with those crocodile tears."

"Honestly, Bette—be fair! It's not a sign of depravity in a man that he re-members his mother's death with sadness. Amelia, do you want a cup of tea?"

"No thanks, Mother." She always made it half milk for me. "Cambric Tea" she called it, as if it was something special and not hot watery milk. After pour-ing boiling water into the mugs, Mother took hers to the sink to sip while she cut up leftover chicken for the casserole she was making for dinner. With a few vegetables, a lot of noodles, and her rich golden gravy, Mother could really stretch a chicken.

"The next thing I knew, they were in the Sacred Room. Win was showing off some of the rare volumes, and Alex was rambling out his life story, boring as it is. Honestly, that man is so self-centered!" Aunt Bette crushed her cigarette out in the full ashtray.

"You know, I believe you're jealous, Bette."

"Jealous? Of that pompous little sneak?"

I hate it when they fight, and I could see it coming, so I went on up to my room. I thought about Sherlock Holmes and Dr. Watson, how well they got along, always so polite and logical.

And then I had my brainstorm! Would Mr. Carver put back the letter for me? Why not! He'd be in Snow's library lots of times alone if he was going to catalog those books. But would he tell? I might be able to convince him that it would break my mother's heart if she knew I'd taken something that didn't belong to me. I could cry and say how sorry I was for doing wrong.

This, I felt sure, was my best idea yet. Positively foolproof.

Chapter 5

In which I enlist the help of Mother's
boarder and breathe a big sigh of relief.

A few days later, about four in the afternoon, Skipper Davies had stopped by our barn where I was trying to nurse back to health a baby squirrel I'd found half-dead on Pond Street.

"Have your own zoo now, Byrdie? Don't you know that you can get a nasty bite that way? Squirrels don't let go." He'd dropped his bike outside the door and poked his head into the barn. "Ah, I see. You're doing your bit for the Red Cross, is it?."

Of all the dumb things, I was still in my Camp Fire Girls uniform. That stupid red scarf! After school, Miss Cronin had force-marched us on a field trip to collect geological specimens and earn Nature Lore honor beads. Her skinny bow legs climbed steep hills as easily as a mountain goat's, while we girls all struggled to keep up. We were loaded down with canteens, homemade sit-upons (oilskin over layers of newspaper) and canvas bags in which to stow our finds. My arms got scratched, I was still sweaty, and my white blouse was smeared with leaf rot.

While Skip and I were growing up, we were the only two kids living within a mile of each other on Pond Street. Being three years younger and a girl, I only got to be the outlaw lassoed by the Lone Ranger, the evildoer stalked by the

Shadow, the gangster run down by the Green Hornet. Once he'd left me tied to a tree in the woods across the street and gone home for lunch, later pretending it was only a joke and I shouldn't get mad.

Then Skip got a job at Fisher's, bought an old bike, and raced off to hang out with the guys. I hardly ever saw him after that, except at school, where I wasn't supposed to say "hi" or even let on we knew each other.

"I know how to handle squirrels. You don't have to worry about me," I said. "This guy's probably not going to live much longer anyway. At least he didn't get run over like he would have if I'd left him in the road."

I pushed a stick through the wire mesh to move the squirrel's water dish closer to his nose. He just lay there on his side, staring blankly. If a furry animal could be pale, he was. I'd named him Geraint, which I didn't tell Skip for fear he would laugh. I stroked Gerry's tail where it hung out of the cage.

"Squirrels have fleas and nasty parasites, you know. Better keep your hands off him." Skip was poking a straw at Merlin the turtle, who was trying his best to look like a rock in the cracked enamel dishpan that was his new home.

"Any news about your dad?" When Skip came over to see me these days, he generally wanted to talk about his father, Frank Davies, who was a chief petty officer in the Navy.

"I think the old man was at Midway. He couldn't tell us anything, of course. Anyway, we haven't had a letter from him since June. I know Ma is worried but I'm not. I'm sure the old man is okay. You know what a tough guy he is. His letters are just held up because of the fighting."

I didn't know very much about Midway, so Skip took a stick and drew a map in the dirt outside the barn door. The Japs had come from all sides, ships and planes, like a pincer. Despite their three-pronged attack, we had defended Midway and won, but we'd lost many ships and hundreds of men. Skip must be plenty worried about his father, not having had a letter for several months. I remembered how miserable I felt when Daddy got sick.

"Your mother would have heard from the war office if anything happened, like if your Dad got wounded. You'll probably get a dozen letters all at once. Mrs. Gilbert says that's how letters came from overseas. 'Feast or famine,' she calls it. Ask Glenn—he'll tell you."

Glenn was the postmistress' son. He and Skip and Tristan Fisher all hung around together. They called themselves "The Troops." Glenn was the best-looking but he wasn't much of a talker. Skip was better company and usually had a funny story to tell. Tristan only mumbled about drinking and cars. I bet Skip didn't confide in them about not hearing from his father.

"Yeah," he said, pushing the stick into the ground right in the middle of the battle. "A whole bunch at once. That'll make Ma's sciatica feel better. Then she won't have to see Dr. Tyrell so often." Skip took a quarter out of his pocket and practiced making it disappear between his fingers. Even when I watched every move, his hands were too quick and clever for me.

"Could be any day now those letters will show up."

"Hey, let me borrow that red thing for a minute." He pulled the scarf from around my neck and began to fling it this way and that until suddenly it vanished, I thought behind his back. "Ma sure has been a crank ever since she threw her back out. I tell her not to go to work when it hurts, but she won't listen. Every afternoon I hear her swearing, trying to get dressed for Whitford Inn. Then I hear her come in at one in the morning and go through the same thing again, trying to get her waitress's shoes untied." He reached over my shoulder and pulled the red scarf up and out as it if had been in back of me all along. My skin felt warm and tickled where his fingers grazed my neck.

"Is your Ma working today? Would you like to have supper with us? We're having meatloaf." The meatloaf was only ground pork. Lively Ames, who ran the Poor Farm, had slaughtered a pig and sold us part of it, a nice change from chicken.

"Hey, thanks, but no thanks. I'm on my way over to see Daisy Eliot. Promised I'd show her some magic tricks. Gonna meet the Troops there."

Jay wouldn't like that much—he called Skip & Company "The Stupes," but Skip didn't seem to care, just mooned around Daisy with that wet look in his eyes. Maybe it was a mistake to have a best girlfriend who was as graceful as a doe, with long sweeping eyelashes and a smile that could make anyone feel important. And she wasn't too tall, like me—really lucky that way.

"Just thought I'd stop by to see how you're doing with the zoo. Keep up the good work, Nursie!"

He jumped on his bike and rode it around in a fast circle twice, finishing off the map, then down the driveway with his hands in his pockets, whistling "Daisy, Daisy, give me your answer, do…" His light hair stood up around his thin face, making him look devilish. The gravel driveway was too bumpy for a bike. Serve him right if he fell on his head. Serve him right if Daisy told him what Mrs. Eliot said about his Ma and Dr. Tyrell.

When I went back into the barn, Geraint was dead. I could tell because he looked smaller, the way creatures do when the life goes out of them. I covered him up with a piece of flannel, thinking I would bury him tomorrow. I already felt bad enough without organizing a funeral, too.

I fed some cabbage leaves and carrot tops to Romeo, who fell to munching them right away, with one eye fixed sideways on me, just as a large shadow loomed over my shoulder. The bunny dropped his carrot top and skittered into the covered corner of his cage. At first I thought Skip had come back, but it was only Mr. Carver.

"Hi there, 'Melia," he said. "Would you tell your mother that I'm going over to Snow's tonight to talk to him about his books. I won't be back for supper, but I would like to have a sandwich when I get home, if it's not too much trouble." He looked into Geraint's cage.

"The squirrel died today," I explained. "I guess he was just too small to live without his mother."

"So I see. But don't you feel bad. He'd probably fallen from a tree and was badly hurt. There wasn't anything you could have done to save him."

I didn't reply, since I was too close to tears at that moment. At the same time, I was getting the feeling that Mr. Carver was in a sympathetic mood.

"Are you going to be working with Mr. Snow's books—I mean, like writing up the book titles and stuff?" I asked.

Mr. Carver looked a little uncomfortable. Probably because there were so many weird sex and anti-Christian books in that library, but he didn't know I knew that, and I didn't intend to tell him.

"Yes, he's asked me to catalog his library. Do you know what a catalog is, Amelia?"

What kind of a dummy did he think I was? "You mean a card file like Miss Pratt has at Whitford Library?"

"Exactly. And when that's finished, I'll type a list of the books from the cards. It may be that Snow is planning to sell some of his or Mrs. Snow's collections. Her volumes of poetry are very beautiful. At any rate, I enjoy working with books, and I have the spare time right now. I'll make a little extra money, too." He laughed and clapped me on the shoulder. "Do you think your Aunt Bette recommended me? I don't know how else it would have occurred to Snow to hire me."

Not a chance! Aunt Bette was the one person in all of Whitford who thought Mr. Carver was a real jerk.

"Mother might have mentioned that you're an English teacher and all. She works over there sometimes."

"Yes, that might have been it. Or Bette." He smiled at me brilliantly. He had a pencil mustache, like Ronald Colman's, and a mouthful of bright even teeth—his Ipana smile, Aunt Bette called it. And he smiled often, dazzling my mother. "It was certainly nice of your mother or your aunt to recommend me." He got up from where we had been watching Romeo watching us.

"Mr. Carver," I said quickly, "if you take something that's not yours by mistake and then put it back, it's not stealing, is it?"

He squatted back down and looked at me in an earnest, teacherly way. "Now, what exactly do you mean by that, Amelia?"

So I told him about the letter, how it had practically fallen into my hand while I was dusting, and I'd put it into my pocket thinking it was waste paper. Then later, I'd read it, realized it was personal, and didn't think I should throw it away.

"Then why didn't you tell your mother about it?" He tried to entice Romeo by wiggling a cabbage leaf. Romeo was playing Frozen Statues, never moving a muscle except for the trembling.

"Because I was in that room by mistake. I'd forgotten that I wasn't supposed to be dusting in there." He'd understand that all right, considering what most of the books were like.

"Hmmmm. You're asking me for a pretty big favor here, don't you think? What's the letter about?" He stood up again and brushed off his trousers.

I felt my face getting hot. "I'm not sure. Maybe it's a love letter."

"A love letter! Well, what do you know..." He smiled another dazzler.

"A very old love letter. From before Mr. Snow was married."

"And what book did you say it was in?"

"Something about Greek gods. *The Gods on Olympus.* A small green book on the shelf right near the religious books."

"I tell you what, Amelia. You leave that letter on the desk in my room, and I'll see what I can do. Maybe when I'm working on the books later on I'll put it back for you." He turned and headed out the barn door. *Didn't he realize that when my mother cleaned his room, she read everything on his desk?*

"Mr. Carver, wait!" I chased him out the door. "I'll put it in the middle drawer, okay? Under something."

We crunched down the driveway together. I looked up and saw he was still smiling, only now it was sort of a knowing grin—a good sign.

"Okay, 'Melia. If that will make you feel better. I hope I won't forget it's in there."

I didn't think he would. I thought maybe he was a little curious. So I said good night and ran back to close up the barn. It was getting pretty chilly, so I piled up extra hay in Romeo's cage for a warm place to burrow, laid newspapers over Merlin's pan, leaving just a little air space, and wedged out of the barn door that didn't close right.

Hurrying into the house before my mother came home to put the meatloaf in the oven, I took the letter out of its hiding place behind my built-in drawers.

Mr. Carver's room was very tidy and smelled just the way he did, citrusy and sweet, like an overripe orange. Moving very quietly, although I knew I was the only one home, I crossed to his desk. A letter opener, scissors, and ruler were laid out next to a neat pile of English compositions. There were six very sharp pencils in a jar, four regular and two red. A bottle of black ink and a fountain pen still in its blue velvet box. A photograph of his mother, I guessed, in a silver frame. She was wearing a filmy scarf around her neck and looking up in profile. The light on her thick curls was like a halo. The hair was tinted red, the eyes violet. I opened the middle drawer. On one side there was a stack of business letters. On the other side, a photo album. I put Mr. Snow's letter under that and shut the drawer.

Good-bye, trouble!

Chapter 6

In which my idyllic visit to Korhonen's farm ends with a suspicious fire.

"Don't call my brother 'Wilho,' even though my parents do," Minna whispered that Friday after school when I arrived to spend the weekend at the Korhonen's farm. "Call him 'Will.' That's the name he goes by *outside*. He's my step-brother, really. My father's first wife died many years ago."

"Oh, doesn't he like 'Wilho'? It sounds ever so much more interesting than 'Will,' " I whispered back. I didn't think I should say 'foreign'—or 'dashing,' which was the new word I was trying out that week. And Wilho himself was not what I'd have called a dashing figure.

We were sitting at the big wooden table, worn smooth and light-colored with scrubbing. Looking out the kitchen window, we could see Minna's brother against the cheerless November sky, smiling kindly at nothing in particular as he limped from the barn to the house with two bright pails filled with milk sloshing a bit on his overalls. He was a tall man in his early thirties with sandy-colored hair and plastic-rimmed glasses.

Minna's mother, who was round as an Eskimo doll and wore her hair covered with a flowered kerchief, was standing at the sink with her back to us, having just sterilized a milk can with boiling water. Will stamped in the back door, letting in a chill whip of wind and the faint odor of barn animals. After he poured the milk into the waiting can, Mrs. Korhonen clapped on the lid and directed him to do something right away. The language was Finnish but I understood the tone of voice. He picked up the milk can and went down cellar to store it, I supposed, in the cold room. Then Mrs. Korhonen turned to us.

"Would you girls like a cup of coffee? I make it now for Wilho," she said, almost shyly.

"Oh yes, Mama!" Minna answered for both of us. "And some of the *pulla,* please." She gestured toward the two shiny braided loaves partly covered with a towel on the cupboard shelf.

Mrs. Korhonen poured boiled coffee from a blue enamel coffeepot and laced it with rich cream. The sugar bowl on the table was full, and I followed Minna's example in helping myself to a heaping teaspoon. At home I was only allowed to drink Postum because coffee might stunt my growth (which I wished devoutly would get stunted. I already towered over most of the boys in my class.) The bread—tender, fragrant with cardamom, golden from egg yolks and butter— ah, it was prewar heaven!

Will came and sat with us, downing a huge mug of coffee and several slices of *pulla* thickly slathered with butter. I was struck dumb watching him, thinking of how careful we'd learned to be with butter at home.

"Well, girls," he said when he had finished, "I'll get a good fire going later, and you can have the sauna all to yourselves after dinner tonight."

Minna giggled. "You have to try our steam bath, Amelia, because Will is making the fire especially for us."

"Sounds like fun," I said weakly.

Will smiled and studied us quietly. "It's good for Minna to have a friend like you," he decided. "Your mother is a hard worker, with your father gone. You must be a great help to her, a strong girl like you. But she let you off your chores this time, eh? Very nice of her."

"We keep a garden, too—a Victory garden." I sat up straighter, trying to look steadfast and noble. "And I do most of the weeding. But no chickens anymore." Because my mother had discovered that she wasn't, after all, a dab hand at neck wringing. No more collecting eggs smeared with chicken shit for me, thank God.

Sitting at the table with brother and sister, all smiles, I felt warm and happy, not worried about a mess of things like at home. "That was wonderful *pulla,* Mrs. Korhonen," I said.

Minna's mother turned from the potatoes she was lustily mashing for fish cakes. "You like it? You want more?"

"Oh, no thanks. I just think it's awfully good." I stacked our dishes and brought them to the sink.

Mrs. Korhonen laughed behind her hand and said something to Minna in Finnish.

"Mama says you have very good manners, but you're too thin," Minna translated.

At supper a few hours later, Mrs. Korhonen did her best to fatten me up, heaping my plate with fish cakes and home-canned vegetables—pickled beets, corn swimming in melted butter, shell beans, and scalloped tomatoes. Instead of bread, they passed rye crackers called "hardtack"—and a great round dish of butter. The family ate earnestly, without conversation. Minna's father, a thinner, older version of Wilho with yellow-stained fingers and horn-rimmed glasses, sat at the head of the table, bent over his plate.

After the creamy rice pudding with a crusty cinnamon top, I could barely move, but less than a half hour later, Minna grabbed my arm. "Come on," she said. "Let's get into our robes for the sauna!"

Out in the sauna hut, which smelled pungently of pine splits, we sat on worn wooden bleachers, thick white towels wrapped around us like Dottie Lamour's sarongs, Minna threw buckets of cold water on the heated stones until I was gasping with the effort to breathe the hot, moist, pine-scented air. Nevertheless, I managed to ask questions.

"I suppose your brother won't have to go in the army because of his leg?"

"Yes, there's some good in such a terrible thing. At least he won't get killed. He fell down under the tiller, and it ran over his leg."

"What are these for?" I pointed to the peeled white branches that stood in the corner. Salty sweat ran down my forehead, stinging my eyes.

"They're to hit and scrape yourself all over." She laughed and held out a branch to me, relenting only when, finally, I reached out reluctantly to take it.

I was relieved to see her stack the branch back with the others. "Only my father does that now. The rest of us think the steam is enough to clean our skins."

Curiouser and curiouser, I thought. But the best was yet to come.

"Had enough?" she asked at last. "Let's put on our robes and boots, and run around outside."

"Are you crazy, Minna! There's snow on the ground." A dusting of snow had fallen during supper, giving the farm buildings and the cranberry bogs out back a storybook glow, as I imagined Heidi's home in the mountains should look—whitened roofs, fragrant smoke rising from the chimney, snug windows glowing with lamplight, and the low sounds of animals getting ready for the night.

"Cold air is good for closing the pores. You'll see," she insisted, pushing me out the door. I pulled my robe around me tightly, and gingerly tested the outdoor temperature. Our warm breaths misted the frigid air.

But we didn't feel the cold—we felt marvelous! No longer heavy from supper and chilled by November, we whooped and hollered, dashing around through the trees like two little madwomen.

"Keep moving! Keep moving!" Minna slapped my arms and shoulders as well as her own.

The oil lamp we'd used in the sauna hut, dancing madly where it hung on Minna's wrist, apparently attracted Will's eye, for he leaned out the back door and called to us.

"Enough, Minna! Bring your guest in now. She must be hungry."

Hungry!!

Well, yes, I admit I found room for a dish of "blueberry soup" Minna took out of the refrigerator with a glass of fresh milk on the side. I did forego the heavy cream, however, that Minna and her brother spooned onto their berry desserts.

"Miss Cronin boards with you," Will stated as he carefully scraped up the last of the thickened juices with his spoon.

"Yes, and she's such an interesting person outside of school. I like talking with her about plants and animals. Do you know we have seven kinds of poisonous plants growing right in our own yard? Let's see...there's yew and lily of the valley and rhubarb..."

"Rhubarb?" Minna interrupted with a look of disbelief.

"Just the leaves, not the red stalks we eat."

"It's a wonderful thing to be a teacher," Will said in an admiring tone.

"Will is engaged to Miss Cronin's sister, Emily," Minna announced solemnly, as if she hadn't already told me.

"How nice!" I replied politely, turning toward Will. "I hope you will be very happy." He nodded and smiled at his empty dish.

"The wedding will be next May, and I will be a bridesmaid in pink. With Emily's help, we're making our own dresses," Minna added.

"And your other boarder, Alexander Carver," Will continued. "We were in school together. Every grade, but we were not buddies. He was so smart, the pet of all the teachers. Class president, too. It's good that your mother has such fine boarders, both clever, both teachers, eh?"

"My mother's very fussy about her boarders," I agreed.

"Will was there when Mr. Carver's father fell down the stairs," Minna said. "Mr. Carver was in an awful state, wasn't he, Will? Just a year after his mother passed away—so tragic!"

"Yes, very sad for a boy to lose his mother, I know. I drove up to the house, delivering eggs, right after the father's accident happened. Broke his neck on the stone floor. Had a workshop down there for covering books with leather."

"Bookbinding," I said.

"Yes, beautiful work. I looked around while I was waiting for the hearse. I had to give Alexander a whiskey and put him to bed. Then I stayed in the cellar with the body. Old Waldo Whitcomb himself came, with Junior. All they could think about was who would embalm the embalmer. They had no one else to do that work except Jeremiah Carver, and there he lay, all broken."

"Like a prince in an Egyptian house of the dead," I murmured, thoroughly enjoying the morbid turn of our conversation.

"I will never forget the crooked neck, his head was turned backwards." Will, for once, was not smiling. Then he went on to a subject he found pleasanter. "I went to school with Lively Ames, too, same year. We all graduated together, 1928. Such plans we had—who could have known what was coming? After the crash, Lively and me had to buckle down and help our folks.

Alexander worked on our farm that summer. Such a smart guy, he learned from me and my father to speak Finnish almost perfect. Then he got away to a fancy college, even in those bad times. The father was dead set against it. But a year after the father died, Alexander sold the house and land." He stood up, stretched, and yawned. "Can you imagine selling that fine piece of land? I never would."

Minna picked up the dishes and put them in the dishpan. "I might have," she said. "Who wants to live on a farm all her life!"

"Those were the days! Lively and me were in track together. He was the sprinter, I was long distance. What a time we had." He chuckled, remembering. "Well, young ladies, I'll say good night. I guess you're going to stay up and gossip till dawn."

He limped off up the stairs, still smiling to himself.

Talking all night was exactly our intention, but the state of sheer physical satiety we had reached put us out like two candles in the November wind whistling around the snow-painted roof of the farmhouse. I slept in Minna's bed, and she slept in the cot that had been set up for my visit. We knew nothing more until Louhi, whom Minna had sneaked into our room, walked across our chests in the morning, tickling our faces with her black and white tail.

Minna jumped up and put on overalls, an old shirt of Will's, and saddle shoes. "Up with the chickens" was not just an expression at the Korhonens'. Savory aromas of salt pork frying and coffee boiling wafted up the stairs, dispelling any low impulse I might have had to pretend I was still asleep. With a mighty yawn, I pulled on slacks and a sweater. I wished I had a male relative whose shirts I could borrow. Minna and I grabbed our almost identical lumber jackets (hers was blue and mine green), and hurried down to breakfast.

After two cups of sweet creamy coffee, a big plate of eggs fried with salt pork, toast with wild strawberry preserves, and baked apples, we were off to the henhouse to feed hot mash to the cackling hordes. I felt so full I was practically waddling like one of the ducks the Korhonens kept in a separate housing near their chickens.

"Oh, it's such fun to have you here," said Minna, giving my arm a friendly pinch.

"Do you realize it's only about six-thirty," I complained, but actually I was feeling quite brightened by the unaccustomed coffee.

"Want to ride Edvard when we finish our chores?" Minna asked, luring me into a better humor.

But when she pulled the old farm horse into the field later that morning, I thought something important was missing. "Did you forget the saddle?" It was surprising how tall the sway-backed animal looked when we were standing beside it, breathing in the sweaty smell of its great shiny flanks.

"I'll help you up and get on after you." Minna clenched her hands into a stirrup. Once she'd heaved me up to where the saddle should have been, nearly casting me over onto the frosty grass, she hopped up in front, using the split-rail fence for a ladder. Edvard was the soul of patience as we plodded around the field under the grave gaze of her father. I clung to Minna's waist for dear life during the first few turns, but at last I was able to sit up straight and merely hang on to her shirt.

Suddenly she turned the horse and sped him toward the barn at the fastest rate he would go, which could only be called a brisk walk.

"What's the matter?" I asked breathlessly.

"Don't you hear the alarm? There's a fire somewhere! If we hurry, we can ride in the truck and see it. My brother will be running out in a minute—he's one of the volunteers." Minna whipped off the bridle and shut the horse in his stall, tossing a blanket over him in place of a rubdown. The two of us rushed to the old blue pickup truck parked just outside the barn and threw ourselves over the rusty tailboard. At the same time, Will was racing in his uneven gait from the house, fastening his jacket on the way. By the time we fell onto the old car seat that was perched under the rear window of the cab, Will had started the motor and was letting out the clutch.

"Hang on, girls!" he hollered through the open window. "Here we go!"

Mrs. Korhonen had run out, apron flapping, to open the big double gate as the truck rumbled across the clumps and ruts of the rough paddock at full speed, with Minna and me bouncing in back. As we whizzed out the gate, honking and waving, two brown and white cows at the far side were startled into lifting their heads from the hay they were munching. Mr. Korhonen held up his pitchfork in a solemn salute, then disappeared into the darkness of the long hen house.

We ducked under an old gray horse blanket for warmth. Will continued to honk as we rumbled down Temperance Street. We could hear the harsh blasts of horns from other volunteer firemen's vehicles all getting louder as they converged, following the signal the alarm whistle gave—two blasts and then three, repeated over and over.

"Where is it? Where are we headed?" yelled Minna, who didn't know the code. Riding backwards, we twisted around to see where the ragtag parade was going.

"I think I can see the smoke," I hollered back. "Over there toward Silver Sand. Oh, Minna, you don't think it's my house, do you?"

"No, Amelia, no! It can't be yours!"

We grabbed each other's hands in delicious terror, but logic prevailed over drama, and Minna added, "It's one of the cottages, for sure. There've already been two this month—summer places, nobody home."

"Things happen in threes," I shouted, echoing a pronouncement my mother liked to make, as we screeched off Pond Street onto a dirt road that led to the shore, following the fire truck followers. There were so many cars there already, pulled hastily to the side of the dirt road, that we had to park a long way back from where the fire was blazing and billowing in the Simmons' "Pine Bower" cottage.

"You girls stay out of the way now," Will cautioned. He hurried to join the crew pumping pond water, since there was no hydrant on that back road. As soon as Minna's brother was out of sight, we climbed on Gordon Fisher's Chevy, parked right behind the fire truck, for a better view. Gill Ott, the fire chief, was running back and forth, shouting to his men. The firefighters crashed about in the underbrush trying to aim their hoses as he directed. It was apparent, even to us, that the fire was raging out of control. The most they could hope for was to keep it from spreading to the cottages on either side by dousing them liberally with water.

A pine tree between the cottages went up like a giant candle flame. The crowd of onlookers, many of them on cars like ourselves, exclaimed in unison, a sound half between horror and excitement, like you hear when a trapeze artist slips and nearly falls. The roof of the cottage on that side, "Wee-Like-It," that belonged to the MacLennans, soon caught. It was quite burned through before the blaze was finally reduced to a sour, steaming pile of blackened timbers.

By then it was two in the afternoon. Will was still busy with the crew who were hosing what remained of the cottages. Since we were "starved," we walked over to my house, where we made a stack of peanut butter sandwiches to take back to the truck.

Will ate two of them in very few bites as we drove back to Korhonens' again, the three of us squashed in the cab this time.

"How did the fire start?" Minna asked.

"Ah, the chief thinks it was set. What a damned thing!" Will sighed.

The cab reeked of smoke and sweat, so I was riding with my head half out the open window, but I pulled back in to hear more. "Does Chief Ott know who did it?"

"Let's say he has his suspicions." And that's all we could get out of Will, although we peppered him with questions all the way back to the farm.

Chapter 7

In which a suspect is named, Mother reads the cards, and we Camp Fire Girls visit the Poor House with gum-drop trees.

Gil Ott's quiet conclusions about an arsonist in our midst had been broadcast throughout Whitford as if by loudspeaker. Coming home on Sunday night, I walked into a heated discussion in the kitchen. Supper had been cleared away. It was only vegetable soup, and I was still stuffed anyway from the Korhonen's Sunday dinner, baked ham and scalloped potatoes swimming in cream and butter.

"They're saying it's Jason Fisher, you know!" Aunt Bette's exclamations often had a slightly hysterical edge. She looked up from the blue wool skirt she was hemming with quick, nervous stitches.

"Just because he's not quite right. You should know how people like to gossip, Bette." Mother was making a shopping list on the back of an envelope with a pencil stub, the braids around her head shining more blonde than gray under the overhead light. She studied our ration books and sighed.

"It's not only because he's slow, Catherine. Jason has been right on the spot at every fire, so I'm told, with his mouth hanging open and a wild, glazed look in his eyes. Obviously gleeful over his handiwork."

"So were half the town enjoying themselves. Fire appeals to a man's baser instincts."

Aunt Bette laughed and took another precise invisible stitch. "It's true. Everyone loves a good roaring fire, preferably out of control."

"At someone else's cottage," Mother added, stashing the list in her old leather pocketbook that always hung on the doorknob behind the kitchen door. "I don't know what I'm going to do for sugar the rest of this month."

"Oh, for goodness sake, can't you bake with honey ... or molasses?" suggested my aunt who'd never baked a cake in her life. "Save the real sugar for our tea. Would you believe that Win has ten-pound sacks of the stuff in his cellar? Maybe I can sweet-talk him into supplying us with some. And I certainly hope you're collecting all of Mr. Do-Right's coupons! He may be seeing a lot of Penny Fisher but he's living here. If you ask me, there's a weird streak running through the whole Fisher family. Remember Gramps Fisher?" My aunt put down the sewing and reached for her box of Parliaments.

Mother was in the pantry getting the ginger brandy she keeps to aid Aunt Bette's digestion. "Oh, the General," she reminisced, her mood instantly brightening. "Toward the end, he used to shoot at anything that moved outside his bedroom window. Now you have a thimbleful of this, Bette, and it will set you right." She poured the amber liquid into two double-shot glasses. "And I'll have a drop myself. Remember his campaign table with all the lead soldiers?"

"How about Gert Fisher, who saved all the newspapers that were ever delivered, floor to ceiling in every room. Good thing, with all those cats." Aunt Bette reached for her glass and sipped daintily but steadily. "Well, now there's this younger generation. There's Gordon, he's fine—runs the town meetings like a professional. But Penny—when she was little, she was a sleepwalker, and she couldn't eat anything except bananas or she'd come out all over in a prickly rash. Mercifully, she outgrew all that when she became a young woman. Then there's Tristan—he's a drunk, and so young, too. And Jason, our probable arsonist."

"One red, one white, and two pink flowers," I said.

"What's that, dear?" Mother asked.

"Mendel's law of genetics," I answered.

"If he weren't a *Fisher*," Aunt Bette continued, "Jason wouldn't have got away with this for so long. You know the whole family protects him, especially Gordon."

"Oh, Bette, you talk as if he started his career with the Chicago fire. I feel in my bones that it's not Jason at all."

"Well, who do your bones feel it *is*, Catherine?"

"Someone...someone we'd never suspect. Someone with a dark side we rarely see." Mother stared dreamily at the light reflected in the kitchen window. Suddenly she screamed and jumped up. "Oh, my God, we've forgotten the blackout! Amelia!" After we'd raced around pulling all the shades downstairs, Mother sat down heavily in one of the kitchen chairs and stared into space.

"Listen, Catherine...why don't you read the cards? I mean about the fire. I think you're having the Sight," Aunt Bette suggested.

Mother smiled in a mysterious fashion. She got up and took the dog-eared deck of blue Bicycle cards out of the hall desk and began to shuffle them thoughtfully. After a while, she cut them into three packs and picked them up with her left hand, so that the packs were in a different order. Then she slowly dealt out three rows of five cards each, while we hovered over her.

"Here he is, light and dark together." She pointed to the Jack of Hearts and the Jack of Spades side by side in the first row. Lowering her voice, she looked over her shoulder to make sure Miss Cronin wasn't on the stairs. The boarders weren't supposed to know that Mother read the cards. "A young man with two sides to his character. See, next to him, the Five of Hearts? That's his changeable nature. Seven of Diamonds and Nine of Spades—a loss of property and money. But this...this is funny, here in the bottom row. The Ace of Hearts, that's our home, and the Eight of Spades, like a warning." She and Aunt Bette looked at each other. Then Mother studied the rest of the cards without saying anything more.

"It's time for *The Shadow*," I reminded them. I'd been watching the kitchen clock, just waiting for this moment. "Want me to turn it on?"

"Why don't you listen to the radio in your room tonight, honey," said Aunt Bette. "I have rather a headache, and I think your mother is tired, too."

Damn! I was going to miss what Mother really saw in those last few cards. Or I was going to miss *What evil lurks in the hearts of men, the Shadow knows.*

So I went upstairs and knocked on Miss Cronin's door, which was half open, and asked her if she wanted to join me and my little radio. "My mother doesn't want to listen," I told her. "They're reading cards in the kitchen."

"Are they really!" Miss Cronin only believed in science and found our family's interest in the supernatural rather eccentric. "Well, why don't you come in here, dear, and we'll listen on my radio. I don't usually, but it will be fun, for once."

That was what I hoped she'd say. The sound was clearer on her radio than on the old static-y one that Dad used to keep in his workshop, and which was now mine.

Miss Cronin had a little box of maple sugar candies shaped like turkeys, a present from one of her classes, and we ate those. After *The Shadow,* I told her about my horseback ride, and she told me how the horse was first introduced to this continent by the Spaniards, and that the horse used to be a much smaller animal before it evolved to its present size, and about Charles Darwin's voyage on the *Beagle.* Her face was shiny with enthusiasm. It seemed as if nothing was as important to her at that moment as sharing the entire development of the horse with me. Miss Cronin was that way about everything, from dissecting a preserved frog with unbounded delight and excitement (unaware that some of her eighth graders were horrified) to illustrating the proper method for starting a fire without matches for the edification of the Camp Fire Girls who only wanted to toast their marshmallows without delay.

After listening to the horse lecture and *The Shadow,* I went off to bed, first stopping at my aunt's room to see if there was an open box of Parliaments. No luck there. It was almost Thanksgiving, anyway, and getting awfully cold for smoking out the window.

We had roast chicken for the big feast, just like a regular old Sunday and not Thanksgiving. But Mother invited Sarge, whose stories of local Civil Defense misadventures kept Aunt Bette in good spirits. And he earned Mother's approval by fixing the broken washing machine wringer.

At Christmas, however, Mr. Snow gave us such a large rib roast of beef that Mother was afraid of what other people would think, so we three dined in lonely splendor. Mother made a little plum pudding and served it blazing with ginger brandy.

I thought of Ebenezer Scrooge and the Cratchits. The week before Christmas, when Miss Cronin had taken us Camp Fire Girls to sing carols in Frietchie Circle, Mr. Snow had opened his door to wave us away before we were half through our repertoire and then let Ollie out to bark hysterically during Miss C's recorder solo of *What Child Is This?*

After the caroling, we'd all gone over to the Poor Farm to give our hand-made gum drop trees to the indigent folk who lived there and thus earn a Community Service honor bead. Our presents were made of small tree branches stuck with gum drops at the ends of every twig to look sort of like Christmas trees. It did seem that roomful of lost souls brightened a little with our singing. Lively Ames and his sister, Merry, the two hulking redheads who ran the Farm, had thanked us properly with cocoa and graham crackers.

"Do you think Mr. Snow gave us this roast because he was visited by the Ghost of Christmas Yet to Come?" I picked on the golden, crusty fat of the huge standing ribs.

"Amelia, don't be a smart alec." Aunt Bette pushed my hand away from the meat.

I smiled at her in a saintly way. "God bless us, every one," I said—and ducked when she swung at me.

Chapter 8

In which Mr. Carver moves on and leaves me in suspense.

"I'll miss Alex, and I'll certainly miss the board money." Mother banged a wooden spoon on the rim of the soup pot, frowning at the thick brown liquid that bubbled up with carrot chunks from time to time. The last of the Christmas ribs, although picked quite clean, still managed to give a rich, savory aroma to our steamy kitchen.

"Good riddance to bad rubbish, I say," my aunt murmured to me in the conspiratorial tone I loved so much. Sometimes she acted as if we were sisters, when I wasn't getting on her nerves.

"What did you say, Bette? He always paid right on the dot, and he kept his room spic and span, with everything arranged so neatly in his bureau drawers. Bette, will you see that this soup doesn't stick? I put a lot of barley in it." Mother donned my father's floppy old hat, barn coat, and black rubber boots. She grabbed the wood basket. "I'm going out for a few more logs." The wild January wind, screaming for any entry, blasted its way into the kitchen as my mother thumped out the back door.

"Let him mooch off the Fishers. Who cares?" Aunt Bette spoke up crisply to the closed door, then turned her dark-lashed blue eyes toward me and winked.

"Come on, Amelia. Pick up that stuff and come into the living room. Your mother's going to make a nice cozy fire."

"What about the soup?"

"I'll check it out in a minute. It'll be just fine."

I gave the pot a quick stir myself, picked up the tray of Camp Fire Girl honor beads I was stringing on a leather thong, and followed my aunt out of the room. "I think I'm over two inches taller than you are," I said.

"Maybe you would be," she admitted, not turning, "if you'd hold your shoulders back and straighten your spine." She settled herself on the softly cushioned sofa with the otter arms that my father had carved and lit a Parliament, taking a deep long drag of the smoke and gazing off into space thoughtfully.

I put my tray on the floor and sat beside it, cross-legged, eye to eye with one of the otters, liking the winsome sweetness of its glance.

"So he's engaged to Penny! Poor girl," Aunt Bette sighed.

"Shouldn't he wait until they're married to move in?" I asked.

She chuckled. "Free rent, honey. How that All-American Boy loves money! The Lord only knows how much Win is wasting on him for that so-called cataloging job. He won't tell me what he's paying. And there's nothing to it! I could have written out those little cards for Win myself."

I was hoping she wouldn't work herself into a temper just when it looked as if we were going to have a pleasant Saturday afternoon, and it was too cold to walk over to the Eliots'.

"Maybe he doesn't want you to look too closely at his library," my mother suggested as she came into the living room with an overflowing basket of wood and set it down by the fireplace. "What kind of a mind collects such trash?"

"There's nothing wrong with Win's mind. He's like most men, that's all. Godless and grabby." My aunt crushed out her cigarette crossly.

As I sat there stringing the bright beads, trying out different patterns of blue, red, orange, and green, I started to worry about Mr. Carver's departure. Had he really returned the letter to Mr. Snow's book? Or was it still in his desk? Would he forget and leave it for my mother to read?

Suddenly I had to know.

"I'm going upstairs for another leather thong," I said.

"While you're up, stir the soup, honey," Aunt Bette said. "Bring down the book on my night table, too, please. And a box of cigarettes." She lit the last one in her pack and threw the empty box into the fireplace where my mother was laying out twisted newspaper and kindling.

I sped into the kitchen, swirled a big wooden spoon in the soup and banged down the pot lid, then ran upstairs to my aunt's room for *The Master Christian* and the Parliaments. With those in hand, I crept quietly into Mr. Carver's room. It was as tidy as always, despite the couple of cardboard boxes in the corner. Cautiously, I opened the middle desk drawer where I'd left the letter and paged through the bills, papers, and photo album. The letter wasn't there. It wasn't in the cartons, either. Or in any of his other drawers or his closet. That must mean he'd put it back in Mr. Snow's library, but still I didn't feel quite easy in my mind. I'd have checked everything again, but Aunt Bette had begun to call me impatiently.

I ducked into the bathroom and flushed the toilet. "I'll be right there," I shouted, splashing water in the sink and slamming the door. As I hurried downstairs, I realized that, much as I hated even to bring up the subject, I would have to ask Mr. Carver himself about the letter.

It wasn't until Sunday night, when he came to his old room to pack the rest of his things, that I got the chance.

"Want me to help you carry those boxes?" I offered, standing in the hall outside his open door, as I'd been taught to do. I held my jacket ready in one hand. Mr. Carver had borrowed Fisher's Chevy and was up and down the stairs, filling it with his belongings.

"Well, that's mighty nice of you, Amelia." Mr. Carver flashed one of those smiles that would have made Daisy Eliot swoon. He looked as handsome as always, with his little dark mustache and up-tilted nose, but his cheeks were strangely flushed and his eyes glittered. Perhaps he was coming down with the grippe, or maybe he was just feeling happy about his engagement, or he had been drinking with Mr. Fisher, or all three. "Why don't you carry these suits. They're not too heavy." He handed me the two suits he wore alternately to school, brown and dark blue.

I stood there for a moment, screwing up my courage. "Mr. Carver," I said at last, "about that letter I gave you ..."

"What letter was that?"

"Don't you remember a few weeks ago you said I could put the letter—the one I took by mistake—in your desk drawer and you would return it to Mr. Snow's library?"

He paused in his packing, looking out the window as if giving the matter some thought.

"Oh, yes. I remember now. Say, that was so long ago, I'd almost forgotten about it."

"Well, did you?"

"Did I what?"

"Did you put it back, Mr. Carver?" I heard that babyish whine creeping into my voice.

"Amelia, you had no business reading that letter." He was looking straight at me now. "You are a very nosy young lady. Nosy people get into a lot of trouble."

Tears were itching my eyes, but I persisted. "But did you put it back? Did you find the right book, the small green one, *The Gods on Olympus.*"

He looked back at the window. "Don't worry, Amelia. I've taken care of the letter. We need never speak of it again, and it would be much better for you if you'd let it go from your mind completely." He took the silver-framed picture of the lady with the red-tinted hair off the desk and packed it between folded shirts in the middle of a carton.

I stood there with my mouth hanging open like a dope, feeling muddle-headed as I always did when adults behaved queerly. After a long while, he said, "Do you understand? You're to forget all about the letter."

Way on the other side of the tiny sitting room that separated their quarters, Miss Cronin must have heard his cold commanding tone and wondered at it. She peeked her head around the corner of her door and said, "Is everything all right, Amelia?"

"Oh, yes, Miss Cronin. I'm just helping Mr. Carver with his moving." I hurried down the stairs with the suits he'd put over my arm, I threw them in a heap at the back of the Chevy, and I didn't go back upstairs again. Instead I went out to the barn to see if Romeo and Merlin were warm enough. I'd covered Romeo's cage with a tattered old quilt and wrapped Merlin's enamel pan in layers of newspaper. They seemed to be all right, just sluggish. After I saw Mr. Carver drive away in the Chevy, I sneaked up the back stairs with Merlin's enamel dishpan and put it under my bed.

Right then I was as glad as Aunt Bette that Mr. Carver was moving. I was thankful not to see him, except at school, where I wasn't even in any of his classes. As it happened, he wasn't in our house again until the night of the accident. January 25th.

Chapter 9

In which Mr. Snow suffers a tragic accident,
Mr. Carver goes off the deep end, and
Mother and Aunt Bette gird up for battle.

Shortly after the New Year, Mr. Snow went away for the weekend to a house party given by his niece Eunice for her theater friends. Aunt Bette said that Eunice used to be a well-known singer and wanted to dazzle her rich uncle with some of her impressive contacts. So my aunt and I went over to Snow's to fetch Ollie and take him back to our house. Since Mr. Snow had already left, she took me inside with her, using her own key. While we were there, she went down cellar to check something on the heater so the pipes wouldn't freeze and left me holding Oliver on leash.

It didn't take me more than a moment to realize the chance I'd been waiting for had at long last arrived. I hooked Ollie's leash to the back of a kitchen chair and whipped around the corner to the library to look for the thin green book that held, I hoped, a secret love letter within its pages.

I rifled through the shelf with growing apprehension. What a shock! *The Gods on Olympus* wasn't even there. It looked as if piles of books had been rearranged. Shelves were empty that had been full, some books were packed in cartons, and others were lined up in a much neater way than they had been before.

On the long, heavy library table, I saw two wooden boxes full of little white cards—the catalog, I guessed. There was no time to check the cards for the book I sought, however, because just as I finished my lightning survey, a fearful crash brought me running back down the hall. I reached the kitchen a hair's breadth before my aunt shot out of the cellar.

Ollie had plastered himself against the back door, shaking with fright from the crash. The kitchen chair was lying on its side, fortunately not broken.

"Can't you even do a simple thing like watch the dog?" my aunt asked tartly, while I picked up the chair. "Here, let's take a few of these cans of fruit home to your mother. He'll never miss them."

"Oh, good—peaches," I said, holding open the cloth shopping bag she'd unfolded from her purse. "Don't you want to bring some dog food, too?" Only dehydrated dog food was legal now, but at Snow's there were cases of canned dog food stashed away in the cellar.

"Your mother's table scraps will be much better than canned horse meat, believe you me. Now you carry this bag, and I'll take Ollie." She put Ollie's little red sweater over his back and fastened it underneath. He frisked about delightedly at the prospect of going outdoors.

The bag was heavy, but I half-dragged, half-carried it along. "What happened to the books in Mr. Snow's library?" I couldn't help asking while we walked home.

My aunt's voice was muffled because she was holding her pink wool scarf in front of her face to shield it from the wind. "Ambitious Alex has talked Win into reorganizing the whole thing. Of course, the longer it takes, the more he makes. They're closeted in the library for hours, real chummy over the catalog. I can't even see why Win takes such an interest in him, must be a passion for dullness. Old men have strange tastes."

Aunt Bette gave me almost complete charge of Ollie for the weekend—that is, I got to walk him and feed him, but he slept in my aunt's room.

"I hate having that dirty animal in my house," my mother declared. "Remember, Bette, *When you lie down with dogs, you get up with fleas.*"

Ollie seemed clean enough to me, and I was envious of my aunt having a dog to cuddle with at night. I couldn't imagine how she got around my mother in the matter of bedding down a "dirty animal" in her room. Anyway, Ollie's company was a great treat, and I pretended I'd been permitted to have my own dog at last. That made it all the sadder when he was taken home on Sunday night.

Sometimes things we've longed for come to us in ways we never thought and wouldn't have wished. Only a few weeks later, Ollie lost his master and became my aunt's dog. From that time on, he was always in and out of our house.

It happened on a Monday night. We'd opened a can of Mr. Snow's peaches for dessert, because Miss Cronin was having her supper elsewhere and so couldn't be scandalized by this weekday largesse. We were just scraping the last of the peach juice out of our dishes when we were startled by a resounding knock. My mother, who'd been uneasy all evening, opened the door with one hand on her heart, as if to keep it from fluttering out of her chest.

Hulking on our back step was Gil Ott in a great black poncho with his arms around Mr. Carver, who was stumbling and weeping.

My mother gave a cry, took her ex-boarder in her arms, and led him gently to a chair, while the fire chief said, in his booming voice, "He's chilled to the bone, Catherine. Can you get him into some dry things and give him a shot of something? Got to get back! I'm afraid that Winston Snow has fallen through the ice. Alex here saw what happened. Tried to go in after him. Nate and Beryl were driving by the icehouse and spotted Alex thrashing in the ice. He called to them to get help, but it was too late. Guess Snow's a goner."

Aunt Bette screamed and ran for her coat. "Oh, my God! Oh, my God! I knew it!" She dashed out the door and ran down the dark path that led to the pond faster than Gil Ott could collect himself to return to the scene.

I wanted to follow them and reached for my jacket on a hook beside the door, but Mother grabbed my arm in her steely grip and sent me to find some of my father's clothes that were packed away in the attic. "Be sure to get a thick sweater! Wool trousers! And some underwear. Don't forget socks!" She hollered the last of these orders as I was racing up the stairs.

By the time I got back, Mother had Mr. Carver wrapped in an afghan, his clothes a sodden lump on the floor. He was sobbing and drinking a double shot of ginger brandy while she poured the water out of his shoes into the sink.

"Sweet, merciful Jesus," he cried. "I tried to reach him! His hand...I almost had him, but he slipped away. Oh, I'll never forget his face."

"Now Alex, you go into my room and get into these dry clothes before you catch your death. Amelia, is this the best sweater you could find?" She shook it out with disgust, showing me the hole in the sleeve. The odor of mothballs, more pungent than smelling salts, wafted under our noses.

"Can't I go down to the pond now, can't I, Mother? Don't you want me to look after Aunt Bette?"

"No! Absolutely not. You're only going to be in the way right now. Besides, when I'm ready to go down to the pond, I'll need your help."

Later, she called me down from where I was peering out my bedroom window, trying to see through the dark, wind-drifting shapes of the trees to the shore of Silver Sand. Mr. Carver was lying on the living room sofa, dressed in my father's clothes, rolled up at sleeve and ankle, moaning to himself, "Sweet Jesus! Sweet Jesus!"

Mother had taken down the big old camp coffee pot from the top shelf of the pantry and made a gallon of steaming brew, boiled and strong. "Here, you help me with this," she said, gesturing toward my jacket at last. When we were well wrapped up, she took the coffee and I carried a box of old white mugs as well as Aunt Bette's scarf, boots, and gloves, down the path and around the pond shore to the ice house.

The moon had come out from the blowing clouds like a blessing on that strange, grim scene. Some of the men were breaking through the thin ice and poling the frigid black water. It had barely frozen over places where great blocks of ice had been cut, then packed in sawdust in the ramshackle building. Other men had pushed the police motor boat as far as they could through the thin ice at the ice house and were chopping their way through the thicker layer beyond. Their quiet hopelessness hung heavy in the icy air. Mother caught hold of Aunt Bette—who was crying and pacing back and forth, wearing some fireman's slick coat over her own, the hem dragging—and made her put on her scarf, gloves, and boots. Then we poured steaming coffee for the wet, chilled rescuers. When it was gone, we went back to the house and made another pot...and another.

Mr. Carver had pulled himself together and come down to the ice house, Mother's bright afghan around his shoulders. He stood there talking earnestly with Chief Ott. I came up behind him and listened. "...insisted he could smell a storm coming, and he'd better check his traps and get some fishing gear or other off the ice. I got to worrying about him, put my coat on and followed. He'd already pulled up his pickerel and packed the gear. He set off ahead of me. Moon wasn't up yet, and I couldn't see which way he was headed at first. Then when I did, I shouted a warning. He seemed confused, staggering, maybe it was his heart. Next thing I knew, he'd gone through. Tried to get him, but I was too late. Sweet Jesus! Slipped right out of my hands." He mopped his tears with the edge of the afghan and caught sight of me, standing in the shadows. We stared at each other for a moment. He stopped crying. The chief patted him on the shoulder, and I ran back to where Mother was heading up to the house again.

It was after midnight before anyone thought to send me to bed, but I stayed up much later, hanging out my bedroom window. Finally, I smoked one of my aunt's Parliaments, closed the window and got under the covers. After a while, the chill in my shoulders began to wear off. As I fell into sleep, I could hear my aunt and my mother still talking in low tones in the kitchen.

When I got up in the morning, although it was only seven, the house was empty. A note on the kitchen table read: "Gone to Snow's. If Mrs. Eunice Durer calls, tell her to call back at lunchtime."

What were they doing over there? I made two peanut butter sandwiches and ate them on the way to Mr. Snow's house.

"I came to help with Ollie," I announced as soon as I opened the back door. They were upstairs, so I went up after them. Ollie, who was lying in the middle of Mr. Snow's bed, bounded off to greet me.

"What are you doing here?" my mother asked crossly. She looked exhausted. I repeated my excuse, crouching down to scratch Ollie's back.

"Did they find Mr. Snow?"

"No, dear." My mother sighed heavily, turning back to the open bureau drawer and lifting a pile of folded shirts. "They didn't find him. Chief Ott thinks now that they may not locate the body at all...that is, until the ice breaks up. It's often that way when someone goes under in winter."

Aunt Bette, red-eyed and bedraggled, did not look up from what she was doing, which was going through the papers in an old drop-front bedroom desk. I marveled at their cool efficiency after the panic of the night before.

"Since you're here to help, take Ollie and go along home," Mother said. "I'm expecting Mr. Snow's niece to call back, and I need to know what time she'll be here. You listen for the phone and get the message straight. I'll want to know every word she says, so you call us here right off. Now, go!"

"I'm sure it's here in his room somewhere," my aunt was saying in an abstracted fashion, starting on the desk's bottom drawer.

"Maybe there's a secret compartment," I suggested. I swooped up Ollie from the bed and placed him on the floor, then headed for the bedroom door. "What are you looking for, anyway?"

"An important paper," said my aunt. She began to rattle the various knobs and pigeonholes on the desk top.

"Get going!" my mother ordered in her top-sergeant voice, pitched low and strong. I went.

As I scampered down the stairs, allowing the dog to follow merrily, I could hear my mother say, "You know, Bette...I'll bet it's in Mrs. Snow's old room."

"Why would it be there?"

"I just have a feeling..."

I got Ollie into his red sweater, and we set off for home, without my learning whether Mother's intuition would turn up the important paper, as it often turned up other lost items.

Ollie and I were having a snack of pimento cheese and Ritz crackers when the phone rang just after ten. "This is Eunice Durer. May I please speak to Miss Cabot or Mrs. Byrd?" The woman's voice had a slight accent that sounded almost British, like Merle Oberon.

"They're not home right now." Some instinct for survival held me back from telling Mr. Snow's niece where they were and what they were doing. "May I take a message?"

"Yes. Please inform Miss Cabot that my father, my husband, and I will arrive about two this afternoon, and that we will require entry to the Snow residence." There was a slight hesitation, and then she asked, "Has anything been learned? I mean, Uncle Win…has Mr. Snow been located? Oh, I suppose you really wouldn't know anything about that."

"They're still looking for him down at Silver Sand, but they don't think they'll find him now. My mother said Chief Ott believes they may have to wait until spring."

There was a pause while Eunice relayed this information to someone else, then a man's voice on the phone. "Rollo Durer here. Young lady, do you have Chief Ott's number?"

"Yes, but he won't be there. He's still down at the pond. It's WHI-772."

"There must be someone at the fire house."

"It's more like a garage. Maybe Mrs. Ott will be there."

"What about the police station?"

"WHI-787. The Chief's still down there at Silver Sand. And Officer Bugbee—it's his boat. Maybe some part-timer is manning the station, though."

He said good-bye in a cool tone. As soon as I hung up the phone, I dialed Snow's and repeated all that had been said. I had to say everything twice more, with Mother asking if I were sure of each word.

"Stay there," she ordered. "We're coming home to change."

I sat watching for them by the kitchen window. Ollie was sleeping on a folded blanket beside the stove.

When they flung open the back door, they were smiling. Aunt Bette gave me a little hug.

"It's okay, honey. We've found what we were looking for, all right. Your mother's a wonder, do you know that? Let them come here now and try to order me around!"

Mother was looking extremely pleased with herself.

Their meeting with the Durers and Hamilton Snow, Mr. Snow's brother, was an appointment they dressed for with great care, Aunt Bette in black with a small cameo at the throat, and Mother in dark purple with a double strand of pearls that looked almost real. At one-thirty on the dot, they set off on foot toward Frietchie Circle, proceeding with a sober and dignified air.

But the recounting of the afternoon's events that I heard later bordered on hysteria, always a possibility when Aunt Bette got herself wound up. It was my first experience with the passion that blossoms like a rash at the prospect of money. I sat in the shadows at the top of the stairway and got the gist of the afternoon's encounter. It seemed to me that everyone had quite forgotten Winston Snow. I imagined a dark shape floating somewhere under the black ice, his drifting hands scratched skinless in trying to break down that unrelenting wall. What mattered now was his "estate," a concept that was new to me but one that I was to hear about constantly in the months ahead.

"I have a copy of the will right here," my aunt had informed Eunice Durer when she demanded that the house be sealed until the will was read. "Win gave it to me for safekeeping. As a co-executor, I believe I'm obligated to take charge of Winston's house and belongings until the estate is settled." Aunt Bette held out the will then, allowing the Durers to read the pages without actually letting go. "Mr. Fenner will have a copy for you."

The entire Whitford property—every last delicate porcelain, every moldy stick of Puritan furniture, every rose in the garden, every tempting book in that crowded library, along with every blue chip stock in Mr. Snow's portfolio—everything that any of us had admired and cared about—was bequeathed to my aunt, according to the will she waved just out of the Durers' reach. I was as surprised and thrilled as if it had happened to me. This was the ultimate happy ending, like *Rebecca of Sunnybrook Farm*.

Only Mr. Snow's Worcester property (of considerable value, actually) had been left by her beloved Uncle Win to Eunice. Eunice's father, Hamilton Snow, a distinguished Episcopalian bishop, was to receive only one bequest, the Snow family Bible, which was kept unsullied in Mrs. Snow's bedroom. The brothers had not spoken in a decade—except once, at Mrs. Snow's funeral.

"Uncle Win must have been out of his mind—senile!—when he drew up that will," Eunice had declared. "Just this year, wasn't it? His lawyer informs me that Uncle Win had already contacted him in reference to drawing up a *new and revised* will, or adding a codicil, or something. I'm certain Uncle Win meant to reconsider in favor of his own flesh and blood. I know he did. He told me so, didn't he, Rollo?"

"It seems very strange to me, and I think it will seem so to the probate judge," my aunt imitated Rollo Durer's drawl quite cleverly, "that my father-in-law, his closest relative, was hardly remembered at all in this document, whatever it is, that you've got there. That smacks of a mental deficiency in Uncle Win. And I think I can speak for all of us in saying that we've noticed how he's gone down-hill this year."

"He could hardly remember his own name," Mr. Snow's niece had screamed. My mother remarked to my aunt, in recalling this part of the encounter, that it was interesting to witness Eunice's well-bred composure cracking to pieces.

"And yet, Winston was able to handle his own business affairs just fine," my aunt had retorted. With each retelling in the kitchen through that long evening, her replies to Eunice became progressively more formal. "Just fine" became "very well," then "very competently" or "very competently indeed."

There was one question to which my family had no answer. "If Uncle Win was in his right mind," Eunice had insisted, "what was he doing walking on ice that he knew to be dangerously thin? I'll tell you what happened. He was dazed and mentally disabled, that's what happened. He'd forgotten about the danger near the icehouse, which according to Chief Ott, was something known by everyone in town."

And so the battle lines were drawn between the two factions before the rescuers had even put away their iron hooks and given up the search for my aunt's former employer, and (it seemed now) dear friend.

Later that night, I heard my aunt crying quietly in her room. I thought her tears were for the loss of that friendship, but I wondered, too, if she weren't angry and afraid of what the Durers would do to spoil her glorious prospects.

Chapter 10

In which Skip joins the Navy, a suitor
calls on Miss Cronin, and the unknown
arsonist strikes closer to home.

With a wink, as if pulling some magic trick, Skip whipped a birth certificate out of his sleeve and showed it to me.

"What's this fabrication?" I asked.

"Jeeze, Byrdie. Don't use those fifty-cent words on me." He ran his fingers through fine brown hair, which did little to make it neater.

How was I supposed to talk to him other than in the words that just popped into my mind? We were sitting on the windowseat in my living room, watching huge flakes of snow squish against the glass, then soften on the edges and run down the panes in droplets

"A fake, then," I said. "This makes you eighteen, and you're only sixteen."

"I'm getting out of Whitford. I'm going to join up. Navy, if they'll have me." He busied himself at pulling out the fringe on one of my mother's handmade cushions. I hesitated to say anything, because he was in such an ugly humor, practically giving off sparks.

As always, he'd turned up at our door unexpectedly. This time, he was on his way home from shoveling Rosemary Gibbs' driveway so that she could get to the night shift at the telephone office. Skip often did chores around her little house, since her husband Roger was with the Army somewhere in North Africa.

At first I'd been delighted, thinking Skip would brighten up this dreary February afternoon with jokes and teasing, but he'd only wanted to confide in someone he knew wouldn't squeal. His thin face, so often lit up with a mischievous grin, was solemn today. His hair looked greasy and kept falling into his eyes.

"Have you told Tristan and Glenn?" I asked

"Later. Can't let on to the Troops just yet. You know how Tristan is when he's had a few beers. '*Careless Talk—A Needless Sinking.*' "

"What's your ma going to say?"

"I don't give a damn what she says. It'll be too late by the time she finds out anyway. I've got it all figured, don't you worry." Some of the fringe had completely unraveled. When I took the pillow away from him and replaced it on the windowseat, he took out a quarter and began to play tricks with it.

"But she needs you at home. You owe it to your father to look after her."

"Ha, ha! The old lady's not exactly lonely, you know. She's keeping herself pretty busy. I guess everyone knows about it, huh? All about that little pipsqueak Dr. Tyrell and his *treatments?*"

I made my expression as blank as possible. He grinned knowingly and pulled the quarter out from behind my ear, but I turned away as if studying the glass case that housed my mother's collection of arrowheads, most of which she'd found on the pond's sandy shore.

Ollie, who wasn't allowed in the living room, could see us over the card table barrier we'd put in the doorway and was frantically leaping and yipping at me. Skip picked up the pillow again and punched it with his fist, adrift in his thoughts. A small smile hung about his lips as if some pleasing notion were attempting to take hold.

I tried a different tack. "I bet they'll be able to tell that the date's been changed. They'll probably bounce you right out of the enlistment office. It's liable to be pretty embarrassing in front of all those other guys."

"Nah, they won't even guess. I look eighteen, don't you think? Rosemary says I do."

"Well…" I didn't want to insult him. "Seventeen maybe. You could pass for seventeen all right." Actually, I thought he might make it.

"That's all I need to enlist without permission. I added an extra year so it wouldn't look too phony. Pretty good job, if I do say so myself."

"Did you tell Rosemary what you're up to?"

"Hell no. Might as well broadcast it from the town hall steps as to let her know anything. I've had an earful from her though, I can tell you. There ain't nothing those telephone operators don't know."

"I always thought she was different."

"Younger. A lot prettier. But not different, Byrdie. They're all the same under the skin."

"Kipling said that. I read it in *Bartlett's*."

"What d'you mean, 'Kipling'? I said it. I'm right here talking to you, Birdbrain. Who's this Kipling?"

"Just a writer. Never mind."

Skip leaned on my shoulder to examine the case. "See that?" He tapped on the glass, pointing to the star of our collection, the time-blackened vertebra with an arrowhead half buried in it. The sound sent Ollie into paroxysms of whining and barking. "Some guy probably never knew what hit him. Just keeled over on his face in Silver Sand. Wonder if he drowned or bled to death."

"Drowned, if he was on his face," I said. "Takes less time than bleeding to death." I thought of Mr. Snow. They hadn't found him yet, and Aunt Bette was half-crazy from waiting for it to happen. The suspense, she said, was killing her. Maybe they never would find him, or when they did, it would be a scattering of anonymous black bones, so far into the future that no one would know or care who he had been.

"If I was going to drown, I'd rather be in the ocean than a dumpy little pond like Silver Sand." Skip was tapping on the glass again, this time using his quarter, making the arrowheads dance inside. Something else for me to worry about.

Ollie began to scratch the floor, trying to burrow under the barricade at the doorway. I gave up and moved the folded table. He hurtled into the parlor and landed at my feet.

"Hey, Skip! Want to play a few hands of poker? I have some pennies." Skip, who had taught me the game, usually enjoyed taking my money. With his clever fingers, he could pull Aces out of thin air.

He stopped jarring the glass. "Nah. I've got to go. Things to do, you know. Just thought I'd drop by and say 'so long'."

"If you send me your address, I'll write to you," I said, brightening at the idea. Most of the girls in school were writing to servicemen. Daisy Eliot was writing to three different guys, and I didn't even have one.

"Okay, Byrdie. But no fifty-cent words, you hear? Say! I'll even let you know where they send me after training, if you promise to keep it a secret from every-one—and I do mean everyone. Can't be too careful with information like that."

"Isn't that against the rules?"

"Yeah, but my old man always lets the old lady know anyway."

"How come the censors didn't black out that part? Did your dad use a code?"

"Sure. Now you're sworn to secrecy, right? Cross your heart. Okay, then. My dad carries his *Goode's Atlas* with him wherever he goes. Took the cover off, you know, to save weight. And I'm doing the same."

"I can get that at the library. What's the code?" I asked.

"Well, I don't exactly know what their code is, but I have this idea of how it could work. I'll send you a page number, see, and when you look at that page, you'll see where I am."

"Isn't that kind of obvious?"

"It would be, but here's how I'm going to do it. Just add up all the number of words in my letter, and the sum will be the page number. Then I'll add a P.S. that will tell you the name of the town or whatever. Just take the first letter of each word—get it?"

"Of course I get it. You may end up with a weird sentence, though. What would you write in the P.S. if the town was Whitford?"

"Let's see ... 'Wow, have I got a thirst for...a thirst for...old-fashioned root beer drinks.' I guess there's a few extra letters. Is root beer one word or two?"

"It'll be the way you write it. I could figure it out all right. Super idea." Skip had such a quick mind, I wondered why he never did well in school. "Those page numbers—we'll have to have the same edition, like printed in the same year."

"You bet. But mum's the word, right?"

"You can count on me, Skip."

"Figured you were the one who'd keep it all under your hat. Well, see you later, Alligator."

He punched me in the shoulder, not hard. Then he gave me a quick kiss on the cheek and left. From the bay window, Ollie and I watched him trudging through the snow until his blue jacket faded in swirls of flakes and he disappeared into the falling gray sky.

I went back to *Pollyanna,* which I'd been reading for the third time, since the library wouldn't be open until it stopped snowing. Unlike the Glad Girl, my mood was as bleak as the landscape. At least Skip had entrusted me with his secret plan and had promised to write to me. I could be a little glad about that.

All week I wondered if Skip would get away with it. We said "Hi" if we passed on the school grounds, but he was always with the Troops. I knew better than to embarrass him in front of his friends by starting a conversation. The following week he was gone, having taken advantage of his mother's busy weekend work schedule at Whitford Inn.

"He's joined the Navy, Catherine! And he's so young, so young. Oh, what will Frank say? He'll blame me, I know it!" Cora Davies sat stiffly at our kitchen table the following Saturday, letting the tears slide down her face. Some of them dripped into the cup of tea my mother had made for her. I sat cross-legged on the floor with Ollie, sharing his blanket, hoping not to be noticed...or questioned.

My mother and Skip's mother were on-again, off-again friends from way back, sometimes seeing each other almost daily and sometimes going for months without a visit, although the Davies' house was just down the street a half mile. This was the first time she'd been over since Mr. Snow's accident, but we'd probably see a lot of her while she was upset. Cora was a pretty woman, except for the two scowling lines between her eyes. Her thin, angular features were like Skip's but her red-gold curls were of a particularly vivid shade that her son claimed had come out of a bottle.

Although Cora protested that she couldn't force down a bite, Mother was making her a cheese omelet "to keep up her strength." She whipped the eggs with a fork so vigorously that the pale yellow liquid almost leaped out of the bowl.

"Well, Cora, since he's only sixteen, surely you can pursue the matter. Why don't you notify someone in the recruitment office? The identification Skip used must have been fiddled with."

"It's no use. He won't come home, even if they bounce him out of the Navy." The steady flow of Cora's tears must be making her tea salty.

"Why ever not?" my mother asked sternly, pouring the well-beaten eggs into a bubbling tablespoon of butter in the hot iron skillet.

"We had words last week, before he left."

"Words about what? My goodness, he's just a child, Cora. You should *insist* that he come back home. Why, he hasn't even finished high school."

"Oh, he said some dreadful things to me, Catherine. I don't know. I don't know what to do."

"You should wallop him, that's what you should do." Mother banged the stove with her spatula "There's no need for you to take a lot of lip, working as hard as you do to keep a home together with Frank gone God knows where." Mother chopped the cheese into submission and sprinkled it over the sizzling eggs. The aroma made my mouth water, and Ollie was drooling, but I supposed we wouldn't get any, since we'd already had our breakfast—oatmeal again.

"Someone filled his head with a lot of stories about me. I don't know for sure *who*, but I can guess. That *hussy* shouldn't be the one to talk, either." Cora rubbed the small of her back with one hand and finished the tea with the other.

"Stories…" my mother said thoughtfully, flipping that whole three-egg omelet oozing with cheese onto a plate for Cora. "Now, how about a nice slice of toast to go with this?"

"Oh, I don't think I can eat a bite," Cora said, picking up her fork. Mother stood two slices of wheat bread in our ancient toaster whose sides opened like a book.

"Well, you want the truth, don't you, Cora?" My mother said this firmly, as if she'd already decided upon the appropriate reply.

Cora looked up from the omelet pathetically. The tears welled up again "Truth? I...what do you mean?"

"Those busybodies up at the telephone office have it all over town, my dear. Hasn't it occurred to you that someone standing at the window there can see right into your driveway? And they listen to every blessed word you say on the phone. Skip was bound to hear something sooner or later." Mother rushed the toast over to Cora along with our last jar of strawberry jam. "Here, you have this with your eggs. It will put heart into you."

Ollie came out of his lethargy and barked at the fast disappearing omelet. Ordinarily, he could count on a nibble if Aunt Bette or I were at the table.

"Amelia," my mother said, suddenly regarding the two of us, "why don't you go upstairs and strip the beds. Bring the sheets and the laundry from the hampers down cellar." Cora's visit had delayed Mother's energetic washday, and she seized this means of catching up and getting me out of earshot at the same time.

"Thanks a lot, Ollie," I whispered in his ear, and then went leaden-footed to my chores. The terrier shook his head and sank back on his blanket with a frustrated sigh. The omelet was gone. As I left, Cora was piling jam in juicy red heaps on her toast.

Later, while I was trudging down to the washing machine with several pillowcases full of laundry over my shoulder, I heard Cora say good-bye. The Inn was short-handed, and she was wanted earlier than usual. Standing at the door, she added, "I'm not the only one, Catherine. It's him should be blamed, taking advantage of his patients that way."

This didn't make a lot of sense to me then. But I remembered that conversation the following summer when Dr. Tyrell's wife, the sallow, sour Inez, who devoted most of her energy to her perennials, discovered her husband in a compromising position with one of his patients. Mrs. Tyrell had been out in the yard on a ladder, clipping the withered blooms off her massive rhododendrons, when she happened to glance in the uncurtained top half of the examining room window. The Tyrells separated as a result. Inez kept the large white house with the beautiful garden on Frietchie Circle. Her faultless floral borders adjoined the late Mrs. Snow's rose garden. They had been great friends once, conspiring over afternoon tea to improve on nature—although unlike Inez, Mrs. Snow had employed a gardener. That fall, after their bust-up, Dr. Tyrell moved to Cape Cod where doctors were even scarcer, and Inez carried on in tight-lipped martyrdom, vigorously combating beetles and yellow leaf blight.

Meanwhile, after her chat with Cora, Mother wouldn't allow Aunt Bette or me to visit Dr. Tyrell under any circumstances, although my aunt came up with some hysterical symptoms in the interim, and I had some equally alarming fantasies of perishing from a ruptured appendix. Mother gave us both double cod liver oil capsules and urged Aunt Bette to reread Mary Baker Eddy's *Science and Health with Keys to the Scriptures.*

"Really, Catherine," my aunt protested, clutching her side where the pain was pinching her, "a stiff wind would knock him over. I wonder what they all see in him, with that baby face and those little round wire glasses. Small all over, I bet."

"Big trouble can come in small packages," my mother shot back, rolling her eyes in my direction. "Poor Cora..."

After Skip left at the end of February, his mother didn't hear from him for months, nor did she try to find him and reveal his deception. I got a scrawled letter, in pencil on lined notebook paper, while he was still at the Great Lakes Naval Training Station. It was full of jokes, exclamations, and misspellings, but he signed it, "Love, Skip." There was a photograph, too, of Skip and his two new buddies leaning against an anti-aircraft gun on shipboard, white hats tipped at rakish angles, grinning and squinting at the sun. I put it in a frame on my vanity so that Daisy would notice.

I told my mother that Skip was getting along fine and hoped "everyone at home" was well, knowing she'd pass that along to Cora. Then I wrote Skip that his mother missed him and wanted to hear from him soon. I made it just a brief casual line, not wanting to rile him just when I had my own serviceman whose morale I could lift with amusing letters from home.

By then it was March, and the branches on our beach willows were getting thick and yellow with spring promises. American troops, almost as inexperienced as Skip, were fighting bitter battles in Tunisia. Mr. Snow's bloated body was floating to shore under the breaking ice. And I was getting ready for the Camp Fire Girl Ceremonial, beading a headband with significant symbols of my progress as a Trail Blazer. I had designed it myself, drawing the pattern out on graph paper with colored pencils, under Miss Cronin's supervision.

We were working on it one Sunday evening in her room, when a caller appeared at our back door. My mother called up the stairs, "Bunny! There's someone here to see you," and Miss Cronin started, upsetting the bead tray. Her face went red and white by turns, and her prominent eyes popped with anxiety.

"You can stay here and work out this part by yourself, dear," she said. "Oh, I'm sorry. I think I've mixed up the colors, but they're all on the bed. You'd better begin sorting them while I'm downstairs." She skittered away like a frightened rabbit.

After I got the beads straightened out, I went downstairs myself, passing by the living room where voices could be heard. It was Lively Ames from the Poor Farm. I'd never seen him in a suit with his rough orange hair all slicked down. Miss Cronin was telling him about the migratory routes of the Northeast Indians while he peered into our glassed-in collection of arrowheads. Having no good excuse to linger, I went into the kitchen, where my mother grabbed me by the arm and pulled me into the pantry.

"You stay out of there, Amelia," she whispered fiercely. "He's come to call on Miss Cronin. He even brought her a present." Her mouth quirked into a funny smile.

"Chocolates?" I asked hopefully.

"Better than that. A side of bacon. Just look at this, will you!" She slapped the greenish-gray slab of home-cured pig with pleased anticipation. "She's going to give us half. It'll help stretch our meat and fat stamps."

The bacon had sizzled out and my headband was complete by the middle of March when the Camp Fire Ceremonial was held. My beaded symbols were pine trees, arrows, stars, hearts, and a cross at the forehead center. I modeled the headband, wearing my ceremonial robe—the Camp Fire Council had decreed an Indian maiden motif—much to the delight of Aunt Bette. Our troop's identical robes had been designed and cut out of brown cloth by Miss Cronin, then stitched by us Camp Fire Girls on the school sewing machines. On most of us, the shapeless, fringed garments fell below mid-calf.

"Your own unique decoration will make your robe an individual creation," our Guardian, Miss Cronin, had assured us.

"Obviously a white captive," said my aunt, yanking my straw-colored hair, braided and bound with leather thongs for the occasion. "From the bleeding heart brigade."

"The red hearts stand for love."

"Some affair of the heart you haven't told us about?"

"Not that kind. The brotherly kind...or sisterly." I really knew there was no use explaining my symbols to Aunt Bette while she was enjoying her sarcastic misinterpretation.

"If brotherly love fails, there's always your bow and arrow?"

"The arrowheads symbolize truth. Aw, come on, Aunt Bette."

"And this is for target practice." She put her finger on the cross.

"Worship," I said.

"As in going to church?"

"Miss Cronin said to include goals and good intentions as well as our accomplishments."

"Well, I can't say we set you a very good example there. The last time your mother and I went to church was Thanksgiving. An event which you skipped, I might add. I remember that Reverend Pinch announced that the sermon was to be 'An Attitude of Gratitude,' and we barely escaped without disgracing ourselves."

"*You* nearly disgraced yourself, you mean," my mother chimed in as she grabbed my shoulders and positioned me for re-braiding my hair.

"You were laughing, too, Catherine. You said it had a kind of beat and snapped your fingers in rhythm."

"I smiled. You laughed. There's a difference in decorum."

"Ouch!" I complained. "That hurts, Mother!" A small clump of hair, not aligned with the rest, was being pulled right out of my scalp.

"*You have to suffer to be beautiful*." Another favorite adage. So far, all I'd got was the suffering part.

"Win used to say that religion is the great swindle." My aunt's pretty face assumed a Lillian Gish expression of wistfulness. "I'd better take Oliver Wendell

Terrier for company over there, don't you think?" She'd decided to move her things into Snow's house, the better to guard his treasures until the will could be probated and settled.

"I should think so! You know if you hadn't begged and pleaded, that dog would have had to sleep in the barn here. I don't hold with animal dirt in the house."

"He'd have frozen. We'd have found his poor little body stiff as a board, for God's sake. Do you think Gordon Fisher would carry my things over to Snow's in their car?" She rummaged around in the hall desk. "When this is all over, I think I'll make it a habit to attend church every Sunday. Amelia can go with me. I'll get her a decent outfit. After all, if I'm going to live on Frietchie Circle...I mean, it's a community thing, not just a matter of religion."

"Winston will be rolling over in his grave, if he ever gets one. What on earth are you hunting for?"

"Twine. I want to tie up some cartons."

"Look, it's right here in the fourth drawer." She slapped the ball of twine into my aunt's hand."Alex would be happy to borrow Fisher's Chevy and move your belongings."

"That unmitigated idiot. I'm never speaking to him again. How could he be so stupid as to let Win head off toward the icehouse?"

"It wasn't his fault. He was broken-hearted. You didn't see how he cried on my shoulder like a baby."

"I bet you loved that."

"If we're going to throw bricks, Bette, how could you play the part of a fine lady and plan to grace the church with your presence if bullheaded Win hadn't stomped into that thin ice?"

My braids were now so tightly woven that my scalp was sore. It seemed like a good time to get out of the line of fire. I bundled up in jacket, boots, and mittens—the night was raw and windy—and waited for Miss Cronin to come by and pick me up in her ancient Ford. It was a Sunday night, and she'd taken a circuitous route from a visit to her parents' house in Kates Hill, picking up Indian maidens for the Ceremonial every mile or so. Some of us were riding on the running boards by the time we arrived at the barely heated Grange Hall.

Miss Cronin had chosen the hall for this event because it had a huge old fireplace. Hitching up her fringed skirt over her skinny legs, she set about making a roaring fire.

Another strain on our friendship—Daisy Eliot looked like the poster girl for Camp Fire in her perfectly fitted costume. I suspected that some judicious tailoring by Mrs. Eliot had made that brown sack almost chic. Her golden-brown hair was pulled loosely into a single braid down her slim, straight back. Ringlets escaped around her face. My double braids suddenly felt unbearably tight, as if they were pulling my eyebrows toward my ears.

With an arch little smile, Daisy informed me that she'd had a post card from Skip and was adding him to her weekly letter list.

"I got a letter. Two pages," I decided not to ask how he'd signed *her* post card.

"Jay said that Rosemary got a letter, too," Daisy told me. "They were wondering why at the post office, he said. After all, Skip only worked around her house sometimes."

"Why didn't they just steam the letter open so they wouldn't have to wonder anymore?" I felt angry with my gossipy friends, but on the other hand, chumming around with the twins meant always being first to know all the good gossip. Other girls were looking enviously at Daisy and me whispering together.

"Opening other people's mail is against the law. I'm surprised at you, Mellie." Daisy frowned prettily. "Grandma said it's a disgrace that Cora let Skip join up so young. Grandma said she could guess why, though."

"Someone told Skip stories about his mother." I looked Daisy straight in the eye.

"Not Jay and me," Daisy said. "And not Grandma, either. Maybe Glenn, or Tristan. Or it could even have been Rosemary who squealed. Oh, I forgot to say, the Troops got post cards, too. Pictures of practically naked girls in sailor hats saying 'Great Lakes Loves the Navy.' Skip just printed in big letters, 'Plenty of action, lots of brew, great bunch! Join up and see the world, you guys.' "

"One good thing about post cards—you don't have to heat up the kettle to read them," I commented.

Miss Cronin was giving us a fishy stare. "Let's all hold hands and form our circle of sisterhood." Her teacher's voice reached into the darkest corners of the Grange Hall.

"He signed my post card 'love and kisses,'" Daisy offered, and giggled.

About twenty minutes after our Guardian's first melodious "Wo-He-Lo" call to the circle, we heard the fire whistle blasting out its signal. No one there knew the code, so we proceeded through the recitations and awards to the song fest, until Lively Ames burst in the door with the grim news.

"Excuse me, ladies," he apologized. "Bunny, that's over in your neck of the woods. You, too, Mellie. Right next door to your house. Sarge Curry's shack is burning. Just thought you'd like to know. Going over there myself right now." He blushed furiously and stamped out again, crashing the door shut after him.

Miss Cronin drew the ceremonial to a dignified if hasty close and dispersed the camp fire in the prescribed manner. There was a quick announcement that we would be giving a musicale for the Poor Farm at Easter, as part of our community service. Apparently, caroling there at Christmas had provided a real lift to the inmates of that dismal establishment. Then, with a final ringing Camp Fire Call, our Guardian rushed us all into her car and we raced away. When all the passengers had been hastily dropped off, except Daisy who insisted on going home with me so as not to miss the fire, we banged and rattled down the icy roads at a reckless thirty miles an hour, skidded down Pond Street, and came to rest in our driveway with a mortal screech of brakes.

It was the first time a house ablaze was more to me than a sort of glorified Fourth-of-July display. What a horrid sight! The whole back of Sarge's little house was on fire. He was sitting on the ground between his cottage and Beryl's house with several piles of books he must have rescued from the flames. Crowds of people were milling around, trampling our foundation plantings and Beryl's backyard. There was a terrible odor, like burning tires, drifting with the smoke from his repair shop. Great clouds of acrid steam rose where Chief Ott's men were dousing the fire with hoses attached to the hydrant on Pond Street.

Miss Cronin, Daisy, and I rushed over to Sarge. He looked up at us helplessly with soot on his face and a sagging mustache. "Here, let us help you with those before they get all wet in this mess," Miss Cronin said, picking up several volumes and motioning to us girls to do the same. "You come with us, too, Sarge There's nothing you can do here except catch the grippe. Oh, I'm so sorry about this, you poor dear man!"

"We can take the books into our house," I said, piling them up to my chin. Daisy picked up an armful, too.

"An excellent thought, Amelia," said Miss Cronin. She was carrying a big canvas Camp Fire Girl bag which she filled with books.

Where was my mother? Looking around, I saw Aunt Bette holding one of Beryl's arms while her husband Nate hung on to the other. It looked as if Sarge's ex-wife wanted to throw herself into the flames and only their efforts were keeping her from self-immolation. She was screaming periodically in short, sharp bursts. Some of the young men—I recognized Gordon Fisher and his slow brother, Jason, and Glenn, the post mistress's son—were gawking in the shadows behind Aunt Bette. She looked back at them with a murderous glance from time to time. I couldn't see my mother anywhere.

I found Mother in the kitchen, cutting sandwiches. The gallon pot of boiled coffee was being kept warm on the back of the stove. "We're bringing in Sarge's books for safekeeping," I said, "Is it okay if we put them in the hall?"

"No, no!" said Mother, taking charge at once. "As long as you've got them in your hands, take them right up to Mr. Carver's old room. Sarge has to spend the night somewhere."

"Your mother is quite an organizer," Daisy whispered to me as we trudged upstairs. "All those sandwiches! I'm a little hungry, too, aren't you?"

Sarge staggered in behind us with a huge armload. "I hate to be a bother like this," we heard him say.

"Oh, nonsense, Sarge," Mother replied crisply, wiping the bread knife on a towel. "Listen, you're going to stay right here tonight, and I won't take no for an answer. Now you don't have to carry those books any farther. Just put them right down on that chair. Amelia and Daisy will take care of them. You just go out and watch that no one tramples your things until we get them all into the house."

He went like a zombie to do as he was told.

After we'd lugged all the books Sarge had saved upstairs, and we'd helped Mother carry coffee and sandwiches out to the porch, I saw Minna leaning on Korhonen's truck wedged in the muddle of other trucks and cars belonging to volunteer firemen and the usual gawkers. She ran over to join us.

"Oh, Minna," I wailed, "most of Sarge's library and his repair shop! Do you know how this happened? What started it?"

She took my hand in both of hers. "No I don't, but I'll find out what I can from Will, and we'll talk at school."

"They say it's Jason who's been setting these fires," Daisy whispered. "Do you know anything about that, Minna?"

"Look!" Minna pointed toward the smoldering shambles. "I think they've got it under control, don't you? You can't see the flames anymore. Some things in the front room may be okay."

It was true. Billows of wet foul smoke were cascading out of Sarge's workshop, but no blaze. Somewhat cheered, I said, "There's coffee and sandwiches on the porch." We jumped the railing on the dark side and helped ourselves until my mother got hold of us. Then we were kept busy running with mugs of coffee to any of the firemen who were taking a breather. Although the men were grateful enough to gulp hot drinks between forays, how embarrassing it was for me to be pushing refreshments at every neighborhood disaster!

"Jay is going to be *so sorry* to have missed all this," Daisy said, sloshing along beside me with two steaming mugs. "It's definitely a shame about Sarge, but let's face it, that rundown cottage of his *was* rather an eyesore. I must say, though, I admire your mother! So nice of her, too, to offer Sarge a refuge. She's a real home-front heroine. If the fighting ever got as far as Whitford, I bet your mother would be taking in refugees and tending the wounded." Minna's sympathy might be a comfort, but Daisy had that cheerful way of putting a bit of sparkle into the gloomiest events so that they seemed more like an adventure.

Minna's brother Will swung up on the porch, tugged on my braids in a friendly way and picked up two cheese sandwiches in his huge, smoke-blackened hand, consuming them in a few mouthfuls. A moment later, he limped back to the silhouetted scene of running, shouting firemen.

Gordon Fisher and Lively Ames came by and took coffee from Miss Cronin. Daisy elbowed me in the ribs so that I wouldn't miss seeing Lively squeeze Miss Cronin's hand before the men hurried back to the now nearly quelled fire.

The smell was in the house for days. Mother put a kettle on to boil with some of our precious, dwindling supply of spices to sweeten the air. She swore the smoke had dirtied all our curtains, so we'd need to take those down and wash them. The ones in the dining room would have to be stretched to dry, hung on a rack by a thousand sharp pins that framed it and held the lace taut—always my job. I never finished a row without jabbing my fingers.

After the firemen departed, our yard and Whitcombs' looked like a war zone right out of *Life Magazine*. The very next morning, Mother was out there in my father's old boots directing the clean-up of debris, sometimes with Nate and sometimes with Sarge (Beryl's husbands generally stayed clear of one another). Beryl remained inside. Nate said she was too distraught over her damaged property to raise her head off the pillow and that as soon as she recovered, she meant to ask Police Chief Ferro to arrest Sarge for careless smoking and endangering the war effort by tying up essential personnel. My mother sent over a pot of baked beans and a freshly steamed brown bread so that Nate would have something to eat until Beryl's vapors dissipated.

Fortunately, that same week we had a little warm spell that freed the ground from frost, so the restoration effort went forward without delay. Sarge's little cottage was in ruin. Half the townspeople's broken appliances were lost, and couldn't be replaced for the Duration, but as Minna had predicted, he did save a few of his possessions from the front room of his cottage. Not the books though. Those had been damaged beyond recall by smoke and dampness.

Aunt Bette had sweet-talked Gordon Fisher at the fire, so a few days later he helped her move her things into Snow's house. I missed her and Ollie sorely. But like Pollyanna at her cheeriest, I found something to be thankful for in the midst of this disastrous March. My good friend Sarge was installed in our front bedroom—but for how long?

Chapter 11

In which Sarge fixes everything, I begin pursuing the real Pan, and Winston Snow's body surfaces at last.

he fire had forced Sarge out of business, without benefit of a fire sale. For a few days, he just sat in a rocker at the front bedroom window, reading a rescued copy of *Walden* and looking out mournfully at the wreck of his kingdom. When I was sent to fetch him at mealtimes, he joined us like a sleepwalker. Mother kept a sharp eye on his plate, making sure it was heaped with nourishing foods—*the best of medicines*, according to her. I don't know whether it was the quiet contemplation of Thoreau's philosophy or Mother's chicken noodle soup and baking powder biscuits that eventually brought him out of his slump, but one morning we woke to the sound of hammering outdoors. Hurriedly, I got dressed and ran outside, where I found Sarge on a ladder, repairing a tumble-down gutter.

"*To those who keep pace with the sun, the day is a perpetual morning*, Amelia," he recited cheerfully. "Give me that piece of wire right at your feet, will you?"

"It *is* morning, Sarge," I said, handing it up.

"*Only that day dawns to which we are awake*," he added.

"We're all awake now. Mother said to tell you she's fixing apple pancakes and she wants to know how long you'll be." We owed this and other special treats to Sarge's distressed status.

"For your mother's pancakes, I'll be finished and ready to attend breakfast in two shakes of a lamb's tail."

So Sarge began his interim career of fixing everything that had split, cracked, worn out or broken since my father died. It was his way of earning his board with us until he developed some other source of income. Whatever that might be, it would not involve working for an employer in the usual sense, which Sarge said he had given up for religious reasons.

He offered to move into a smaller room, perhaps Aunt Bette's since she was going to inherit Snow's house, but Mother said, "Time enough for that when I get another boarder." She meant *cash-paying.* "Besides, we don't know yet how Bette will manage all alone over there. She may be back sooner than she thinks. She's not strong, you know."

Mother had been addicted to solitaire, but now in the evenings, she and Sarge fell to playing ruthless games of gin rummy. Sarge was the better player but had such phenomenally bad luck that Mother often won, giving her great satisfaction and a number of worthless IOUs.

She never read the cards with Sarge around the house but took particular note if a card fell out of the deck by accident, and I knew she felt it held a message for her. When that had happened in the past, she would say something like, "Ah, the Ace of Diamonds—that's money coming into the house, possibly through the mails." Since I was used to living with omens and portents from the cards and other seemingly accidental events, such as three crows perched on our beech tree predicting a wedding, I missed the drama of consulting the cards or the Ouija. In all other ways, having Sarge boarding with us was an intense pleasure for me that I was fearful would come to an end at any moment. There was no predicting what grown-ups might do to stir up a change just when life was going along smoothly.

I hardly ventured to speak of my worries, but Sarge himself brought up his precarious position in our household. "If it weren't for your mother," he said, "I fear it would be the Poor Farm for me."

"I hear that Mr. Fisher is looking for help now that Gordon's been called up," I suggested. It wrung my heart to imagine Sarge becoming one of the Poor Farm's colorless flotsam—Sarge, whose sad brown eyes held so much understanding and warmth, and whose mind was like a library of great books.

He looked at me as if I'd suggested robbing the Kates Hill Savings and Trust. "Parcel out my life with a pound of nails and a yard of oilcloth?" He reflected on the prospect dismally. "Sell my soul for a few dollars in my pocket? Surely, Amelia, that would be a poor trade."

Maybe Miss Pratt would die, I thought fiercely. She was ancient anyway. Then Sarge would be offered the librarian's job. I didn't know how long my mother, who worked with gusto from dawn to dusk, would put up with someone whose heart was in the woods at Walden.

Sarge's rescued books were heavy reading. With his encouragement, I looked through them anyway, a few lines here and there. Generally, I sat cross-legged in the upstairs hall, only going into Sarge's room to exchange volumes, thus almost keeping to my mother's rule of staying outside the door of any man's room.

"There's an Oliver Wendell Holmes in one of your poetry books," I said to Sarge while he was up on the roof nailing down loose shingles. I'd followed him up the ladder. "Is that the same famous person from Harvard who Ollie was named for?"

"Winston Snow probably admired Holmes as a Harvard teacher, but he was better known for his verse." With his mouth full of nails, which gave him a peculiar mumble, Sarge recited:

'And if I should live to be
The last leaf on the tree
In the spring,
Let them smile, as I do now,
At the old forsaken bough
Where I cling.' "

"Doesn't seem to fit our Ollie much," I said. "Tiresome stuff about nature and old age."

"Try Elizabeth Barrett Browning," he suggested.

Her poetry wasn't any easier to understand, but the biographical note about her and Robert Browning carried me through, as Sarge must have imagined it would. Then I came to a Browning poem called "A Musical Instrument," that began with the words "What was he doing, the great god Pan, down in the reeds by the river." It brought back in one searing flash all the worry I'd endured because of that old love letter signed "Pan." Thinking of Elizabeth and Robert Browning, the story behind the letter began to intrigue me once again.

"I have always understood we could not make a life together," Pan had penned in her wavering script, "for your future was already written when we met." I knew from Aunt Bette that, after a long engagement, Winston Snow had married the heiress, Frances Coffin, of the chemical industry Coffins. Pan must have known that Winston intended to marry for money and position, not for love.

When this notion locked into place—like a red flower or an eye in a jigsaw puzzle—it was a key piece that made me eager to put together the whole picture. Most especially, who was Pan? Was that a private love name or a nickname that others might remember?

"I'd just like to find out who she was," I said to the Eliot twins. Daisy yawned and complained again about my fascination with dead love affairs, so I went back to tossing out review questions for their upcoming Latin quiz. We were holed up in Jay's room, killing the pain of verb declension by playing swing records very quietly. I would never have admitted it to my friends, but I was really looking forward to First Year Latin. Passion, betrayal, and tragedy might lurk in those stories of ancient times.

Then Daisy made a brilliant suggestion. "Find out where Snow used to live, where he worked, who he hung around with, when he was romancing the mystery lady. How old was he then, do you figure? Thirtyish? At least that will give you some idea of where she could have been located. Otherwise, you might as well just blindfold yourself and stick pins in the map, for all the chance you'll have of finding some old dame who used to be called Pan."

Jay picked up his sketch book and flipped to a blank page "I don't know what good all this digging up old scandals is going to do. You're as bad as Grandma." He began drawing some stout guy in a toga. After he sketched in the face, however, I could see it was their Latin teacher, Mrs. Bombard. "I mean, it's like having to learn Latin, isn't it? Who cares about some dead language anyway? *It killed the ancient Romans, and now it's killing me.*"

Whether he was truly indifferent to worldly possessions or was simply too depressed to care, after the first shock, Sarge appeared to be uninterested in the origin of the fire that had destroyed his livelihood. But I *was* interested. During the days that followed the fire, I had numerous conferences with Minna, who did her best to pump Will for information on that very subject. Suspicion still hovered over Jason Fisher, whose brother Gordon had given the alarm.

When Chief Ott had arrived at the scene, Minna said, he'd found Gordon, who had a reputation for protecting his slow brother, with Jason firmly in tow, trying to put out the runaway blaze with Beryl's garden hose. Jason was gaping and smiling at the licking flames. Gil Ott suspected that Jason had set the fire, and Gordon had come upon the scene soon afterwards. Discussions had taken place between Gil and Police Chief Ferro, and Ferro had had a serious talk with Jason's parents. Guy Fisher, a big blustery man, like his son Gordon, had threatened to punch Ferro. Lillian Fisher, the boys' mother, had cried hysterically.

"Is Chief Ferro going to arrest Jason?" I asked Minna eagerly. I'd never known anyone who was arrested.

"No, the Chief just gave Guy a warning to keep an eye on his son, that the Fishers might have to put Jason in a home. Will said Ferro always tries hard to give kids a break, especially someone like Jason who probably doesn't realize what he's doing."

"What about the people whose summer cottages have gone up in smoke? And poor Sarge who lost his business and most of his books? Are they supposed to give Jason a break, too?"

"The thing is, Mellie, there isn't any real evidence."

Chief Ferro might have required real evidence, but in our home and in most of Whitford, Jason Fisher had already been tried and convicted.

The March thaw, which had made it easier to clean up our yard in the aftermath of Sarge's fire, did something even more important for our family. It produced a body that could be declared dead. Only a few days later, Mr. Snow surfaced at the water's edge several hundred yards "down pond" from the ice house. When Gordon Fisher, who'd been delivering a grocery order to Rosemary Gibbs, spotted one arm overhanging a sandbar and rushed down to the shore to pull out the rest, the sudden black writhing of eels from Snow's torso sent Gordon scurrying back up the embankment in quite a panic for so hulking a man. For once, our town moderator had been at a loss for words. After driving hell-bent to the Whitford Police Station—a tidy two-room law enforcement domain next to the Whitford Firehouse—he'd jumped out of the truck and stood mouthing the news soundlessly at the open door.

Not an expert in lip reading, Police Chief Dom Ferro followed the silent discourse as best he could.

"Eels, you say?"

Gordon's mouth moved convulsively.

"Eels in the pond is no big news, Gordy. Whatever are you so worked up about?"

Gordon shook his head and gestured frantically.

"Oh, eels in a *body,* you say. What body? Where?"

Later, Dom Ferro reported this exchange to us with a macabre chuckle. He and Wayne Bugbee, the only regular police officer, and Gil Ott, the fire chief, had pulled the body out with a couple of rakes. Now Ferro was looking for someone to make an official identification of the corpse, which despite its ravaged condition, they knew was the body of Winston Snow.

I'd already heard the story from Tristan Fisher, who'd sped over on his bike to regale the Eliot twins and me with every possible twist of those wily scavengers in Snow's midsection. Immediately, Jay took out his sketch book and began drawing the scene Tristan described, only he put little bibs on the eels.

"*Boys!*" Daisy had commented with profound scorn. Nevertheless, we listened avidly to every sordid detail of Tristan's tale. And I realized that this was the news that everyone was waiting for at my house.

Immediately, I jumped up and raced home, arriving breathless to tell Mother. Afterwards, I threw up as quietly as possible in the bathroom so as not to risk being put to bed with a bowl of milk toast for supper.

So Mother and Aunt Bette were suitably composed, attired in their deep purple and black crepe respectively, and sipping restorative cups of tea with ginger brandy when Dom Ferro arrived that afternoon with his sad announcement. He was a roly-poly man who usually wore a beaming smile and had the light step of a good dancer, the sort of person you'd expect to be leading a choir rather than a posse.

"You'll want Hamilton Snow to identify the deceased," Aunt Bette told him. "He's next of kin, Win's brother. I've written out the phone number here. Do you want to call or shall I?" She held out a slip of paper which Dom did not take.

"Oh, please, Miss Cabot. If he's a friend of yours, I'd really appreciate it if you'd do the calling," the police chief begged. "I'm sure you'll break it to him nicer than me. I can't take no more hysterics today."

"Very well, I'll call then." Aunt Bette drained her tea to the last drop and took a deep breath.

"I'll ring the number for you, Bette," said Mother, taking the note out of her sister's hand. She grabbed the black wall phone and rang for the operator. When the long distance call had been put through, she said, "Bishop Snow, please. Miss Cabot calling," and gently put the receiver in Aunt Bette's hand.

Then Mother made Dom sit down at the kitchen table while she fixed him some warmed-up coffee and a ham sandwich which was made from a lovely big Virginia ham my aunt had found in Mr. Snow's cold room.

Aunt Bette, standing on tiptoes to reach the mouthpiece, steeled herself to cope with the bishop's long distance disdain. We listened eagerly to her end of the conversation.

"Yes, it's required…No, there won't be an inquest. Dr. Tyrell is the acting coroner, and I'm sure he'll find this a case of accidental drowning. He's the only doctor we have left in Whitford." Aunt Bette paused and listened for a minute. "You can call at the Whitcomb Funeral Parlor. It's just in back of the Friendship Unitarian Church. Take Whitcomb Street out of Frietchie Circle, pass the cemetery, and there you are. Oh…but I think the street sign is missing. Well, all right, if you wish. But I feel I should inform you that I've taken up residence there, to protect the property. What do you mean! I had every right to do so. I'm an executor. Of course, it's a proper will. Come now, Bishop Snow, I'm sure you checked all this out with Win's lawyer." Aunt Bette's dark blue eyes were flashing dangerously. Instinctively, I stepped out of their range.

"There is no hotel in Whitford. Oh, wait ... I think there are a few rooms at the Whitford Inn. You could stay there."

Mother laughed as she refilled Dom's cup. "Not exactly the place for a bishop, eh?" she commented to the chief, who smiled affably and reached for another oatmeal cookie from the plate she'd located conveniently near him. I reached for a couple myself, pushing one under the table to Ollie. He crunched it appreciatively.

"Amelia, how many times do I have to tell you not to feed that animal at the table?" Mother scowled at me.

Meanwhile, Aunt Bette had rung off. "You could hear the operator breathing heavily," she said with a wry chuckle. "Whoever it was, she didn't miss a word."

After Dom Ferro left, being assured that proper identification would be forthcoming that afternoon, Aunt Bette voiced her new worry. "The bishop's determined to stay at the house. Eunice and Rollo are coming, too. They're going to remain here through the funeral. Do you think I should clear out and leave the place to them?"

"Not on your life!" my mother replied instantly. "Don't you dare give in now. And don't so much as make them a cup of coffee. Remember, you're not an employee there any more. Just have the coffee things out where Eunice can't miss them if she looks down that long nose of hers for a minute."

"You're right. I wouldn't put it past her to pick up a few mementoes either. But I'm ahead of her there. I've been making an inventory." With a worried frown, Aunt Bette reached for two cookies and pushed one under the table to Ollie. "You know, Catherine, I'm just a little nervous about this visit. Do you think I could borrow Amelia for morale support?"

"If you're willing to tolerate the breakage." In our most recent accident, Mother's Blue Willow turkey platter had fallen from its customary high shelf while I happened to be standing there studying it in absent-minded fascination. Luckily, it didn't break, having landed in a basket of folded laundry. After she'd calmed down, Mother had threatened to make me wear dark glasses in the dining room from then on.

My aunt turned to me with an unexpected dazzling smile. "You'll come and protect me from the dragons, won't you? Just don't stare at any fragile treasure." So it was agreed that I'd stay with Aunt Bette at Snow's while his family was there for the funeral. "And you keep a sharp eye on them every minute." Aunt Bette gave me my assignment. "Especially that Eunice. Let her know you're watching."

"And don't give up Win's room," my mother continued her warnings. "Put the bishop in the guest room. It's small, but it fronts on the street. The Durers can take Mrs. Snow's old room, and Amelia can bunk with you."

Oh, what an adventure! What responsibility! What fun! I packed three times. The second time, I took out my books, because, after all, there was Mr. Snow's glorious library to browse through, and I really needed a little more room for underwear. Then Aunt Bette made me take everything out of my Camp Fire Girl duffel bag and put my belongings into a regular leather suitcase, in case Eunice Durer should look with scorn at my choice of luggage.

Leaving Sarge to whatever fate might befall him with my impatient mother was my only regret in embarking on this vacation from dreary routine. A note had been sent to the school office asking that I be excused from classes all week due to a family emergency. Although I was given assignments to complete at home, the days ahead promised to be gloriously exciting.

"That Ferro is a milksop," declared Aunt Bette, flipping a clean sheet over the bed we were changing at Snow's house, getting ready for the relatives to descend on the premises. "We could all be burned up in our beds, and he'd still be up at Fisher's holding Lillian's hand and patting Jason on the head."

"I don't think it's Jason, Bette. I think they're looking in the wrong direction," my mother insisted, while she polished the bureau top with vigorous swipes. "Remember when I laid out the cards on it? I have to tell you the truth, though, I was a little relieved that it was Sarge's cottage next. I was afraid it was going to be our house. *To you and your house,* the cards read. Now wasn't that foolish of me?"

"Yes, I know," said Aunt Bette. "Better him than us. Oh God! I think I've broken this nail."

"Don't even say that, dear. I feel so guilty."

"It was only a shack, an eyesore preying on Beryl's nerves every time she looked out her kitchen window."

"It was Sarge's *Home*, Bette." Mother always said that word with a capital H "Well, you don't have to feel responsible, you know. Is that why you have him lodged in your best bedroom? That's just crazy! It was only a stray thought you had. Everyone has thoughts like that."

"*Thoughts are things*," my mother said with conviction. "I'm just helping him get on his feet again. And besides, he's kept himself busy at the house. I didn't realize how many things needed fixing. I should have taken care of that roof myself long ago."

"Don't be ridiculous! That's a job for a man. A person could fall and get killed from that high dormer."

"You're right. Maybe I shouldn't let him go up there. Perhaps I'd better do it myself."

"Catherine...listen to me, will you?" Aunt Bette stopped making up the bed and fixed my mother with her steely gaze. "Let Sarge fix the roof, and you stay off it. That's what I meant."

Mother was gazing abstractedly into the mirror she had just finished cleaning, no longer listening to her sister. "It's a double image," she said.

"What is? What are you talking about?"

"The arsonist. It's not Jason but it's not clear. I'm seeing a double image." With that, Mother swept regally out of the room with the laundry. My aunt got no more out of her that I heard. Finally, I managed to escape the whirlwind of preparation for a quiet hour in the woods with Ollie.

Chapter 12

In which the Snow relatives descend on Whitford, I become resident snoop for Aunt Bette, and Winston Snow is buried.

Once my mother was satisfied that everything was in order, and she had left for home, staying with Aunt Bette was like a slumber party, with late-night fun and gossip and giggles—and at Snow's there was always exciting new territory for me to explore. Even in the attic I found turn-of-the-century *Punch* magazines with illustrations of women in leg-o'-mutton sleeves, and a trunk filled with large feathered hats and exotic wraps. But I felt bilious most of the time from eating strangely, sleeping too little, and reading too much.

Refusing to be relegated to housekeeping, Aunt Bette had referred the Snows to Whitford Inn for their meals. One afternoon when the coast was clear, Aunt Bette and I had snuck home for "a decent dinner," as my mother called it, a pot roast from Snow's freezer, smuggled by me past the Snow relatives that morning. Uncertain of the roast's legal status now that meat was rationed, Aunt Bette had concealed it under my poncho, where only Ollie had detected it, guarding me zealously all the way back to Pond Street.

"I'll bet they're dining on Spam Surprise at that gin-soaked inn," my aunt said gleefully.

The pot roast, now succulently browned and surrounded by glistening carrots and potatoes, ornamented our dining room table like a noble monument to our own resourcefulness in coping with the hardships of war. We dug in bravely, Aunt Bette and I not forgetting to share scraps with our loyal defender under the table.

"I hope you're not letting that animal get grease on the rug," my mother said.

When we walked back to Snow's later, my aunt seemed quite cheered up by the good meal, despite having a houseful of Mr. Snow's hostile relatives to face.

During the week of my employment as resident snoop at Snow's, one particular post became a favorite of mine. The sofa in the library faced the fireplace, and when I sat on the floor there, I was hidden from anyone glancing in the library door or even walking partway into the room. Thus I was able to spend many a stimulating hour poring over selections from the shelves of forbidden books. If I heard anyone approaching, I had only to push the book I was reading under the skirt of the sofa.

One rather fascinating textbook on abnormal sex lapsed into Latin in what must have been the raciest passages. As luck would have it, I'd also found a Latin dictionary and was able to translate quite a few of the difficult nouns and verbs. The Eliot twins were definitely mistaken about the study of Latin, I decided. It was not such a "dead language" after all.

Not to neglect my duties, every once in a while I would make a tour of the premises, checking to see if Eunice Durer was rummaging through the desks or had purloined any of the valuables. Despite my best efforts to be an invisible spy, there always seemed to be some bang, crash, or squeak to announce my arrival. Although once or twice I thought I heard, or sensed, the quick shutting of a drawer, Eunice was always at her needlework when I peeked in. I believe it was an embroidered vestment for her father. Often she arranged herself by the window, thus allowing sunlight to fall on her sleek ash-blonde hair. When I got to be old, like twenty or so, I would wear my hair coiled just that way. Mine was similar in color, although slightly darker and usually in need of a good brushing. I would wear clothes like Eunice's, too, I vowed, recognizing the quality if not the costliness of her faultlessly tailored wool suits and pastel silk blouses. I think that was the week I gave up orange as my color of choice and reconsidered blue.

I did count one major coup, a conversation between Mr. Snow's brother and niece. The day before the funeral, I heard them come into the library, and I hastily pushed my book under the sofa. It was only *Sears' Pictorial History of Russia*, which was harmless enough, but I never could be sure how grown-ups would react. It soon became obvious, however, that they didn't even know I was there.

"Look at these books of his," the Bishop exclaimed in a booming voice that must always have projected without difficulty from the pulpit. "Obscene. Sacrilegious. Abominations fit only for casting into the fire."

"Trash, indeed, Father. I feel as if I've observed a whole new side of Uncle Win since I came here. I feel..." and here Eunice paused delicately, "soiled. If Aunt Frances had lived, he never would have sunk this low."

I sank pretty low myself, trying to be as small and quiet as possible.

"Well, perhaps. Frances had her problems with Winston, poor brave invalid that she was. She complained to me, you know, about this very collection of filth and ... certain other activities of his." The bishop attempted to lower his voice, but it was quite audible still, like a stage whisper. "I felt it was my duty to have a talk with him. Well, as you know, that was our last talk in a decade."

"Aunt Frances would never have allowed her lovely things to go to a stranger, a common person like that Cabot," Eunice Durer said in a real whisper I had to strain to hear. "I mean to ask her for the Cheng Te hibiscus dish. Don't you remember that Uncle Win wanted me to have that? He mentioned it several times."

"My dear Eunice, I'm sure that he did, but you recall that Win stayed rather clear of me for these past years. Pure guilt. Couldn't look me in the eye. Perhaps it was Rollo who heard him promise you the Cheng Te. It's a pity that Frances didn't leave you more of her beautiful things directly rather than abandoning the whole disposition to Winston."

"Yes. A few nice pieces of jewelry, but—at least the Worcester property will be mine. That's something. Unfortunately, Uncle Win's bequest means I have no other claim. I had a little phone chat with Fenner yesterday, when *that woman* was out of the house. Fenner thinks this will is a travesty, of course. He didn't say that in so many words, but it was implicit in his manner."

Ethically, his hands are tied. I brought up our conclusion that Uncle Win was mentally disturbed. Fenner won't go along with that. He did suggest one avenue, though. He said, since *you,* his closest living relative, were so minimally named in the will, it might be considered an oversight. Poor Fenner could say no more, but I got the impression you might be able to lay a claim against the estate, Father, should you choose to do so. As soon as this pitiful funeral is over and the will is read formally, I think you should consult your own attorney."

At that moment, Rollo Durer, a ruddy, muscular man with thinning, sandy hair, leaned his head in the library door and reminded his wife and her father that it was time for afternoon visiting hours at the funeral home.

As they left the room and went down the hall, their voices faded, but I heard one last exchange.

"You mean, bring the matter to court?" The Bishop sounded shocked but not uninterested.

"Well, it might not need to come to that. We might try for a reasonable settlement with Cabot."

The rest was mumbles, and then the front door closed. Hearing a sound that signaled action, Ollie came trotting downstairs from my aunt's bedroom, no doubt fresh from a cozy nap on her bed. He found me in less than a minute, and I hugged him. It was good to breathe aloud again.

We ran to the parlor window, where I watched the departing relatives from behind the heavy, dark blue drapes, father and daughter, two slender, distinguished figures, so similar in aristocratic profile and bearing. Rollo loomed over them like a medieval knight guarding the royal party.

When I repeated their conversation to Aunt Bette, it nearly drove her into a frenzy. I was made to recount it word for word several times. She and my mother discussed it endlessly, while cigarette after cigarette smoldered in the ashtray. The ginger brandy was brought out and not immediately returned to the cabinet.

I didn't tell the part where Eunice Durer called my aunt "a common person." Surely my Aunt Bette, from her snapping blue eyes to her size three shoes, with her quick, nervous intelligence and valiant soul, was quite uncommon.

On the day of the funeral, Aunt Bette sat with close friends of Mr. Snow's in the row behind the Snow relatives, who were in the front pew. Eunice's black crepe dress showed off a triple strand of pearls that my aunt said had been Mrs. Snow's. My mother and I sat in the next row back. I wore a new coat, navy blue.

"It's ridiculous," my mother had said to Aunt Bette, "for this child to be draped in black, just so you two can look like the Bobbsey Twins. If you want to buy her a spring coat, choose some color that she can wear all season. After all, the old crank hardly ever spoke to her except to say 'wipe your feet.' "

We tied a black ribbon on Ollie's collar, but he was not allowed in the church. It seemed wrong to me that the one being who mourned Mr. Snow most wholeheartedly and didn't care a fig for the money should be shut out of the ceremony.

I'd worried that the church would be mostly empty except for the Snows and us, and Aunt Bette would be embarrassed. Winston Snow had been known around town as an old grouch who thought he was better than ordinary folks and a sharp dealer when it came to financial matters. I didn't know anyone who really liked him except Aunt Bette. So I took a deep breath and said a little prayer of gratitude when I looked around inside and saw practically everyone in town had shown up in their funeral best. It made me shudder to see the dark handsome casket that dominated the front of the church. I kept remembering Tristan's description of the body. I guessed the eels were gone, though, and there were plenty of fragrant flowers to mask whatever was in there.

The early morning rain had cleared away as if on cue to a sparkling if chilly March day by the time we reached the cemetery. It was a slow, stately, winding procession—the hearse, the one black limousine (which didn't have room for Aunt Bette, so she said) and the rest of us mourners on foot, since it was only a few hundred yards from the church. At the burial site, which was next to Mrs. Snow's monument *Beloved Wife*, my aunt collapsed upon me, weeping. As I regarded the entwined sleeves of our new coats, I saw that we would indeed have presented a more pathetic picture if we had both been dressed in black. I held Aunt Bette upright while Reverend Pinch spoke a few words at the gravesite.

Unitarians aren't big on the Saved going home to Jesus in Heaven, so there's not a lot they can say at funerals. Bishop Snow had been invited to officiate but had declined. He did, however, say rather a long prayer making some reference to God welcoming his brother like the Prodigal Son.

After the mourners had left the cemetery and the caretaker had shoveled the dirt over Mr. Snow, I walked Ollie over to the burial site and tried to explain matters to him while he sniffed around and pawed the fresh earth. He had a limited vocabulary, but he did understand "all gone," a phrase that generally meant "no more biscuits" or whatever treat he was begging for. So I said to him, "Ollie, Mr. Snow is all gone, all gone." I think he understood. I snapped off a white rose from the heap of flowers mounded over Mr. Snow and took it with me.

Then we visited my father's grave, which was in an older part of the cemetery, near a huge old maple tree that would soon be offering a deep leafy shade. I brushed off the dead leaves that had rotted near his stone through the winter and placed the rose where a few tender spikes of new grass were just pushing through. The ground was wet and muddy, so I sat on a nearby slab of granite and studied the monument. *Franklin Byrd 1900-1939, Beloved Husband and Father.* It didn't seem real that my big laughing father should be there under the sod. Instead I imagined him being welcomed by St. Francis to Heaven, if there were a heaven. And what about Mr. Snow? Would he be wearing that old leather-patched coat sweater and backless slippers into Paradise? Or would he be young and handsome again, and would Pan run to meet him?

I retied Ollie's ribbon, which had become somewhat bedraggled. He relieved himself on the maple, and we went back to Snow's together. The after-funeral gathering had shed some of its gloom and almost taken on the air of a party. We made our way to the refreshment table, where one of Mr. Snow's old cousins was recounting a story to a gray little man wearing rimless glasses. Later, I learned this was Guy Fenner, Mr. Snow's attorney.

"I didn't realize," said Fenner, "that Winston had ever lived in this part of the state—I mean, before he and Frances bought the house and settled in Whitford."

Still chuckling over his tale of Winston as an eager young businessman being taken in by a "swamp Yankee" with a bogus Brewster chair, the cousin wiped his eyes with a white linen handkerchief and said, "Ah, yes, he was running back and forth to Boston on weekends to squire Franny to tennis matches and concerts, and then home to his folks in Worcester, then back to Kates Hill through the week, partnering with a real estate attorney. It was a hectic time in his life, all right."

"I always wondered where he'd got the notion to buy here in Whitford," Mr. Fenner said. "Must have liked it here when he was a young man just starting out. Pretty country, you know, and fine for antiquing, but really, between you and me, it's the back end of nowhere."

Mr. Fenner and the Snow cousin wandered out to the bare, bloomless rose garden. It had turned really warm and pleasant outdoors. I made up a hearty plate of ham salad sandwiches and marble spice cake for Ollie and me, and we ate our funeral lunch on the back stairs outside the kitchen door. As I cleaned up Ollie's discarded lettuce leaves, I thought about what I'd just overheard. It seemed that Mr. Snow had lived in Kates Hill about the time that Pan had written the letter. That meant she might just be a local girl. What luck!

Mr. Snow had married the heiress Frances Coffin. I wondered what had happened to Pan then. If she hadn't died of a broken heart, she might very well still be alive somewhere, but she would be very, very old.

That afternoon, the Snow relatives left, much to our family's relief. The will was to be read the following week in Mr. Fenner's office in Boston. As Rollo Durer was putting their luggage into the Packard, Eunice turned to Aunt Bette and, in her sweetest voice, said, "Bette, do you think I could have that little yellow saucer with the hibiscus as a memento of Uncle Win? You know, he often spoke of wanting to give it to me."

Aunt Bette gave Eunice the full benefit of her killing look. "You mean the Cheng Te?" she asked, just as pleasantly. "Such an important piece. It's strange he didn't make you a bequest of it in his will, isn't it? Well, these things can all be talked over at the reading. I'm sure you're much too grieved to discuss the details this afternoon."

The way Eunice Durer glanced at my aunt right then was almost respectful.

Chapter 13

In which we celebrate the reading of
Snow's will, the Allies land in Sicily,
and I find the girl who was "Pan."

"Since you're immersing yourself in ancient Egypt," said Sarge, who was washing the outsides of the dining room windows while I sat at the carved pedestal table with *Herodotus for Boys and Girls*, "why don't you have a look at Shakespeare's *Antony and Cleopatra*? The story is straight out of Plutarch, best historical account we have."

"Who's Plutarch? Did you know that 'some Egyptians made pets of crocodiles?' " I read aloud from the chapter on Egyptian customs, 'They each of them train up a crocodile, which is taught to be quite tame; and put crystal and gold ear-rings into their ears, and bracelets on their fore paws.' Do you think Ollie would like a bracelet? When a dog died in Egypt, the dog's human family shaved their entire heads and bodies, but for a cat only the eyebrows. Isn't Shakespeare too hard? Although, next year when I'm a freshman, we'll read *Julius Caesar*."

"Plutarch was a biographer who compiled a kind of Who's Who in Ancient History. A shame they don't start you off with *Romeo and Juliet*, so much more sympathetic to your age." He shut the window and moved the ladder to the next in the row of three. "*Antony and Cleopatra* isn't too hard at all. Just skip the difficult passages as you usually do. And how about giving your mother a thrill by washing the insides of these windows? She must have clean windows for Easter, you know, but she hardly has time to do everything."

I groaned, but actually it wasn't too boring. We continued our talk about Egypt and Cleopatra while pointing out streaky corners to each other by tapping the glass. After we had finished and extravagantly admired our sparkling handiwork, I made an omelet for us both, a bit too brown on one edge. It was a rare pleasure for me to cook, which only happened when Mother was out of the house. This was the glorious day that she and Aunt Bette had driven to Boston in Snow's Oldsmobile for the reading of the will, although everyone involved already knew what was in it.

"Is it too early for white gloves, do you think?" my mother had asked. The day had begun unseasonably hot and sunny.

"No white until after Memorial Day," my aunt had declared firmly. "Your tan kid gloves will be very nice with that burgundy dress. Oh God, I wish I had a new pair of silk stockings! I could always count on Win for silk stockings. Do you think this run shows? I've caught it with nail polish. Will I be able to employ Fenner as my attorney, since Eunice and her gang already have their own lawyer?"

"Keep your skirt down and the run won't show. If you'd saved your silk for special occasions, you'd have a good pair to wear today. Did you check Mrs. Snow's bureaus? I wouldn't have anything to do with Fenner. Remember where they got the bright idea that Winston forgot a substantial bequest for his own brother when he wrote that will?"

"Well, we'll see," Aunt Bette had said. "Win thought a lot of Fenner, and you know how particular he was. I've been through all the bureaus. Apparently, Frances wore lisle, which bags around the ankles. I suppose when you're an invalid sitting with a rug over your legs day after day, you don't bother about silk stockings."

It was clear that my aunt was as impressed with Mr. Snow's attorney as she was with everything that had been Mr. Snow's. Even later, when there was ample evidence that engaging Fenner had been a mistake, she was liable to gloss over the notion that she might have chosen differently.

It was past five, and I was beginning to be concerned about our dinner, when the sisters came home. Sarge and I ran out on the front porch when we heard the Oldsmobile come to a steaming, bucking halt, as if it objected to strange hands on the wheel. To my horror, there was a sudden deafening noise. The car seemed to explode! A tremendous bang as the hood flew up. Hissing billows of steam rushed out of the engine. The sweet spring air was filled with the rank odor of overheated metal.

The two women screamed and jumped out of the car doors as if their clothes were on fire—laughing, exclaiming, dancing, and hugging. Their wild exuberance made no sense at all with the disaster taking place in our driveway.

It was official! Aunt Bette had inherited the Snow house, its contents, the bank accounts, the stock portfolio—everything except his property in Worcester. So who cared if a little radiator blew its top? They would have the car fixed—everything fixed or even new—forever! Meanwhile, the explosive phase being over, Sarge was approaching the radiator gingerly with a window-washing rag in his hand.

That evening was even jollier than a *Don Quixote* night, and I was only sorry that Sarge missed it because of being called to the Poor Farm to resurrect their hot water boiler. There was a bottle of red wine from Mr. Snow's cellar, even a little glass for me, plus all kinds of glorious S.S. Pierce tins from his pantry. To me, it was like an elegant picnic. Some of the tins were spread out on the table to be served cold, and some of the foods had been heated up in small saucepans and skillets. There was even a cracked blue willow saucer on the floor for Ollie, who liked the liver pâté and Vienna sausages quite well. He kept his paw on the dish, as if holding it in place, long after it was empty.

Besides the sausages and pâté, we had shrimp paste on melba toast, mock turtle soup, lobster newburg, tinned ham, baby gherkins, baby peas, and for dessert, two kinds of fruit, bing cherries and Dakota figs in heavy syrup—all unobtainable for the Duration. We used Mother's best china with the pink flowers (not the old blue willow), the Oneida silver that she had bought piece by piece through the mail, and linen napkins.

"A festive spread, appropriate to welcoming spring," Sarge called it when he returned. Mother insisted on fixing a plate of goodies and some strong tea for him, but he took them up to his room (as I was beginning to think of it) on a tray. Perhaps he was considerate enough to realize that the sisters had quite a lot more to digest than S.S. Pierce delicacies.

Aunt Bette—still wearing her best powder blue suit, white lace blouse with little pearl buttons, and blue high heels that I couldn't have fit half my toes into—talked about all the things she'd always dreamed of buying and doing if only she had a little money. Some of these were the things she wanted to give her sister, but "No, no, that's not necessary," Mother kept insisting. Except about college for me. On that subject, she simply said, "I've always wanted that for Amelia."

"Well, naturally she must be properly educated," Aunt Bette agreed. "My only niece, and with an I.Q. up there." Mother gave her The Look. I was not to be spoiled by praise for things over which I had no control, whether green eyes or a working brain. In her philosophy, only the development of a disciplined character was to be commended.

Then I was to have an entire new outfit for Easter—"from the skin," Aunt Bette said. And Mrs. Snow's old typewriter, if I'd liked. (I was ecstatic!) Aunt Bette would use Mr. Snow's portable for her business correspondence.

"You'll need it, Bette," my mother said thoughtfully, whisking the crumbs off the table into her napkin. "I think you'll have some corresponding to do. You haven't heard the last of the Bishop yet."

My aunt sliced a fat Dakota fig in two with her spoon but didn't eat it. "Oh, I'm not going to worry about that tonight, Catherine. Tonight is for celebrating, tomorrow for worrying."

"Shades of Scarlett O'Hara," my mother warned. Just what I was thinking but didn't dare say.

Mother had carefully checked that the blackout curtains were completely closed, lest the neighbors observe our feast and think we were in the black market. As it happened, Miss Cronin had been out that evening, having supper in Kates Hill where she was teaching an evening course for homemakers called Safety in Home Canning so they wouldn't all poison themselves with lethal green beans. Although she'd gone straight to her room when she returned, she came down to make herself a cup of tea just as we were cleaning up in the kitchen. There was a great bustle to rush the evidence into the refrigerator or out to the pantry. Except that Ollie burped and Aunt Bette giggled.

"Would you like a glass of wine, Bunny?" my mother invited in her most dignified manner, looking tired but royal. Even though she was wearing her old chef's apron over the good wool dress, her faded gold braids, catching the overhead light, shone like a crown. "We're just celebrating Bette's birthday with a family party."

That would be a few weeks early, I thought.

"Oh, no thank you, Mrs. Byrd. I love my cup of tea at this time of night. I wonder, though, if you have a little milk?"

She headed for the Frigidaire, but my mother got there first and had the milk bottle out in a flash. There was hardly time to see the leftover sausages and ham before the door was firmly shut again. I became aware that the odor of shrimp and pickles hovered about us.

Miss Cronin lingered. "Such a noise when the car radiator exploded this afternoon. It quite startled me. Was that poor Mr. Snow's Oldsmobile? I hope it wasn't too badly damaged. It's so difficult to get anything fixed these days. Not knowing what was going on, I rushed to the front window."

"The front window in Mr. Curry's room?" my mother asked.

Aunt Bette began explaining before Miss Cronin could reply. "Catherine accompanied me on business—for the estate, you know. I'm taking care of the house until everything is settled. And taking care of Ollie, too." She reached down and scratched the dog gently behind his ear. Ollie sighed and licked his chops, without ever opening his eyes. "So naturally we took the Olds," she continued. "I think a hose broke. It hasn't been driven since January."

"Mr. Curry was downstairs and the door to his room was open," explained Miss Cronin, squeezing the teabag against the cup with a teaspoon. She went to throw the teabag away.

"Here, I'll do that!" My mother whipped the teabag out of her boarder's hand and disposed of it, letting the lid bang shut.

Miss Cronin seemed to want to say something else but then thought better of it. She poured a little milk into her tea, sipped for a minute, wished my aunt a happy birthday, then said good night. I guessed that she'd seen the scratched word on the windowpane. I remembered the day we'd first seen it ourselves, when my English teacher Mr. Carver was renting that room.

"See, he's as crazy as a bed bug. I always knew it. I always told you so." Aunt Bette had exclaimed when Mother showed her the damaged window.

"He must have been nervous. A nervous habit," Mother had said. "You know how people pick at things when they're nervous."

"*Catherine*!" my diminutive aunt had screamed at her, jumping up and down with excitement. "It says 'MAD'! It's scratched right into the glass. And that's what *he* is. Not nervous. Mad as a hatter!"

"It doesn't say 'mad,' Bette, for goodness sake. Must you be so dramatic? It says 'MAB.,' probably a club he belongs to, some kind of Masons. I think I'll fix us a nice cup of cocoa."

"Well, are you going to speak to Mr. Perfect about this or what?" Aunt Bette had demanded.

"There's something so comforting about cocoa," my mother had said.

It wasn't like Mother to let any willful destruction go unpunished. If ever I'd scratched initials into a windowpane, I'd be running for my life. But strangely, she never said a word to Mr. Carver. Aunt Bette was right. Mother did have a blind spot where he was concerned. Then, of course, Mr. Carver moved to Fisher's, and that was the end of it. Now the big front bedroom was Sarge Curry's room.

While he was continuing his window washing campaign through the upstairs, Sarge asked my mother if she'd like him to replace that windowpane. "Nathaniel Hawthorne," Sarge told me while he was re-puttying later, "scratched his initials into the glass at his cousin's house, the very home he used as a model for *The House of Seven Gables*."

I was outside in the hall, sitting cross-legged in the doorway.

"Then maybe it isn't so freaky," I said.

"Nothing freaky about Hawthorne," Sarge declared.

For some curious reason, I kept the discarded glass, placing it slightly ajar over Merlin the turtle's washbasin home, moved to the barn now that spring had come. The letters were M-A-B, I definitely decided, and not M-A-D as my aunt had imagined, but the indent on the B was so slight as to cause the confusion.

On Easter, we all went to church in our new outfits. Besides a white lace collar on my navy blue coat, I had a pale blue linen dress with embroidered rosebuds on the bodice, a lace-trimmed slip, and most exciting of all, *a real bra*. Aunt Bette had bought me two of them. The smallest possible cup, but now I would be spared the embarrassment of being the only girl in eighth grade gym class who was still wearing snuggies and an undershirt.

"I wish I could have bought you shoes, too," my aunt said, "but your mother said the shoe stamps must be saved for fall. Is that the best you could polish those horrors?"

I looked down at my brown loafers. I myself thought I had done a rather incredible job of covering the scuffs.

All through the service, I worried that my family might be struck with another fit of the giggles, as they had at Thanksgiving, but the Reverend Pinch's sermon, "V for Victory Over the Forces of Death!" did not undo their resolve to be as reserved and regal as befitted the almost rich.

After dinner, which was only roast mutton (mutton not being rationed), Miss Cronin came by in her creaking Ford to whisk us Camp Fire Girls to the Poor Farm, where we gave our much-practiced Easter concert for the ghostly inhabitants and earned more Community Service honor beads for our Indian ceremonial outfits. We began with "Christ the Lord Is Risen Again."

There was a strange odor in the high-ceilinged, under-furnished rooms of the old house—a combination of Lysol, tracked-in manure, thrice-fried fat, and something else, perhaps old age. Lively and his sister Merry, with their ungainly height and flaming hair, appeared all the brighter in those colorless surroundings. They gave us tea and brought out some limp graham crackers, possibly left over from their Christmas party. It seemed as if they really tried and really failed to give the place a homelike atmosphere. Lively sat hunched over, cracking the knuckles of his huge hands in a disconsolate manner, and Merry banged the kettle around the stove while we politely sipped the odd tan liquid she'd brewed, sweetened with their own honey in lieu of sugar.

But Miss Cronin was wonderful. You would have thought she was having Earl Gray and petits fours at the Ritz as she sat perfectly straight in a peeling yellow kitchen chair, discoursing on the construction of natural cement cells by the solitary mason bee of Southern France. The cords in her thin neck stood out above her crisp, white Camp Fire Girl shirt, but in the vacant eyes of the old folks around her, there was a stirring of interest, whipped up by her unflagging enthusiasm. She had her audience.

Following tea, the Camp Fire troop executed a parting hymn, "For the Beauty of the Earth," and murdered a few phrases of Bach's "Passion According to St. Matthew" as we backed out of the kitchen yard past an unearthly assortment of underwear flapping in the spring breeze. Once on the main road, we girls fell into a more rollicking rendition of "Roll Me Over in the Clover" until Miss Cronin, although in a jovial mood herself, threatened to dump us all on the road and let us walk home.

Shortly after Easter, I received a second letter from Skip, this one from New Orleans where he was taking some special training in shallow landing boats at a boatbuilding plant on the Industrial Canal. Although he was allowed to tell me where he was and what he was doing that spring, in later letters, after he was sent to North Africa, he used our code to let me know his whereabouts. I was thrilled at how well it worked. A lengthy anecdote about poker winnings gave me page 138 in the Atlas, the bulging cranium of North Africa. He signed it, "Love, Skip," and added, "P.S. Been assigned to the galley all week, but that's okay. Always Love Getting Extra Rations." "ALGER" was on the map! Underneath, in parenthesis, it read, "Algiers."

I kept my pledge of silence without difficulty, since I was certain that one careless word would send Skip to the bottom of the Mediterranean. It was his hand I always saw reaching up through the waves in the "Loose Lips Sink Ships" poster. I didn't want to burn his letters, though, so I hid them in my usual safe place, behind the built-in drawers with my diaries.

In May, while Skip was still in New Orleans, Rosemary Gibbs had been taken ill with one of those mysterious disorders that were not discussed in detail in front of my friends and me. None of the regular operators wanted to handle the night shift at the telephone office. In the end, they had to split the shift between two new, hastily trained operators, one of whom was Mother. Often I spent those nights with my aunt at Snow's, where I was allowed to have Mrs. Snow's lovely yellow and white bedroom, with two bookcases full of her collection of plays and poetry. What with all this shuttling back and forth, no one really knew of my excursions to Kates Hill, seeking the elusive Pan.

Riding over after school on a bike borrowed from the Eliot twins, I spent many an hour at the library in Kates Hill paging through old yearbooks. Since Mr. Snow had managed an office there at the time the letter was written, I thought Pan might be a Kates Hill High School graduate. All I got for my pains were a few paper flea bites and the chance to learn my way around another library. Several afternoons that spring I searched, never guessing how close I already was to Pan's disquieting story. But when summer vacation began and swimming was the order of every sunny day, I let go of my obsession with dead lovers.

Mother's temporary job at the telephone office stretched into a semi-permanent position. Rosemary had almost died. Her parents came and took her away from her little cottage to the family farm in New Jersey for a long rest. Like the faint underground roar of an oncoming earthquake, the rumor rumbled around town, inevitably to the ears of the Eliot twins, that it was a mishandled abortion that had nearly killed the young telephone operator. I'd only recently learned what that was, and I found it hard to believe.

"Glen's mother says it was Dr. Tyrell did it before he moved to the Cape. Punctured something, and then let the hospital clean up after him," Daisy whispered. We were sitting in the Eliot backyard, among the bursting roses of early July. She and I were playing Chinese checkers while Jay flipped through his sketchbook. We sipped Coke from bottles that were now lukewarm from being held in our sweaty hands. Coke was quite a treat for me, since my mother didn't buy any sodas, which she said would ruin my skin. Daisy jumped a pink marble over three others into her home triangle.

"Grandma and Mrs. Frietchie say Dr. Tyrell would never do anything illegal," Jay disagreed.

"Your grandma! Did she talk about it?" I was aghast even to speak of pregnancy with Jay, but he whistled in an offhand way and kept his eyes on his drawings.

"Not to us, of course. The Old Home Day Committee met at our house to knit socks for soldiers. They can't use their meeting room in the library cellar anymore because the ceiling may fall in." Chuckling, Jay finished his Coke, then took up his charcoal pencil. "Gil Ott says they have to have supports installed. All those thousands of books above them." He began to draw ladies' legs sticking out of a heap of books.

"You can hear everything in the parlor through the old grate in Grandma's bedroom," Daisy explained. "We opened it just before the meeting. We knew there'd be gossip, but we didn't know how awful it would be."

"Jason Gibbs hasn't been home in a year." I thought that should conclusively prove that Rosemary couldn't possibly have been pregnant. We knew Rosemary. She was cheerful, pretty, and guileless. She wore a Peter Pan collar with a silver circle pin. Well, maybe she talked incessantly, but that was her only fault that I could see, making it all the more doubtful that she'd be harboring such an unthinkable secret.

"Exactly," Daisy said meaningfully. "What else could she do?"

"But it's against the law. Dr. Tyrell...we'd better not talk about this. He could go to jail, couldn't he?"

"Mrs. Frietchie says absolutely he didn't do it. She says Rosemary did it herself, with a knitting needle, and Dr. Tyrell probably saved her life." The slight figure of Dr. Tyrell, holding his black bag, appeared on Jay's sketchpad.

"How could she do that?" Not only was I horrified, I had reached the limits of my medical comprehension.

"We couldn't hear that part." Daisy frowned. "They went and whispered all the details so low they could hardly hear each other. At least, Miss Pratt couldn't. She kept saying, 'WHAT? What did you say she used?' "

"How did the committee find out? I'm sure Rosemary didn't tell them," I wondered. Although Rosemary was such a talker, you never knew what would spill out once she got started.

"We think it was Inez Tyrell," Jay said. "She and Mrs. Frietchie have been real chummy lately, having that red, white, and blue flower bed planted on the town green. They got Ed Lyons to weed it, and the committee donated money for his wages."

"They don't need Ed," I said. "They can dig the dirt pretty well themselves."

"The question is," said Jay, in an even lower tone. "If Rosemary was pregnant, who was the guy who knocked her up?"

"I won!" Daisy exclaimed. All the pink marbles were home.

Mrs. Eliot came out the back door with a basket on one arm and a pair of garden shears in the other hand, so the question remained as we had left it, unanswered. She smiled at me in a pleasant way, which was unusual in itself. Clearly, she was after something.

"How's your aunt getting along in that big old house, dear? That estate of Snow's seems to have bogged down a bit in Plymouth probate, hasn't it?"

"Aunt Bette's very comfortable, thank you, Mrs. Eliot. And everything is just fine, no problems at all," I lied. In truth, Bishop Snow had thrown a major monkey wrench into the settling of the Snow estate, and Mr. Fenner was urging my aunt to come to some kind of out-of-court settlement with the Snow family, plus a healthy percentage for him as negotiator. It looked very much as if Aunt Bette wouldn't be getting her hands on the money unless she were willing to give up a third of it, a dilemma that had generated many a screaming fit in our kitchen.

The Cokes were gone, and the game was lost. I decided to head for home before Mrs. Eliot nailed me with any more kindly questions.

"Good news, Amelia," Sarge told me when I came in the door. "The Allies are landing in Sicily." He'd been fixing our old domed radio, which had needed only a new tube. It was still on the kitchen table, along with a grimy screwdriver and greasy pair of pliers.

"We'd better clean this up before Mother sees it," I said, always conscious of Sarge's precarious situation in our household. I got the dishcloth and Bon Ami from the sink.

"Listen...*listen*," he exclaimed. "This is history, Amelia. They said the Italians are falling back easily. Did you hear that?"

In our household, Sarge was the person who got most excited about the war news. He scrounged maps from everywhere and kept them rolled up under his bed. He'd never wanted to travel, but he loved to see the world through a map. I knew he'd have Italy spread out on the floor of his room tonight. I would sit in the doorway while he showed me just where the troops were landing and where he thought they would make their push.

"Is Mother still asleep? Maybe we'd better turn that down a bit."

"Oh, of course. You're right. How thoughtless of me. She was on that late shift last night." He turned off the radio and brought it back to the living room.

"She's not working tonight, though. So I'll be at home. Did the Allies cross from North Africa?" I asked after Sarge returned to the kitchen.

"Right you are, they crossed from Algiers."

"Then they probably used shallow landing boats?"

"Sure. LCIs, LCTs. Troops, tanks, trucks, pontoons. Everything has to get to shore through shallow water. But if the landing area permits, they might use LSTs. They're bigger and hold more. Why do you ask?"

"Just wondered. Something I read about in *Life*. Did the news report say if there were many Allied casualties?" I asked.

"Didn't say. I expect there were. Awfully unprotected coming in on an enemy beach like that, you know."

It didn't seem real that Skip could be getting shot at, maybe wounded or killed, while I was playing Chinese checkers with Daisy. I said a prayer for him, although I didn't have much faith that anyone was listening. If only Mother had sent me to Sunday School when I was little, at least I'd know how to say a proper prayer.

Still, on a perfect July day, with a breeze from the west fluttering blue and white gingham curtains and with a bunch of daisies in a white pitcher dropping petals on the windowsill, who can believe that war is real? The uneasy feeling in the pit of my stomach began to define itself as hunger. I eyed the row of fat beefsteak tomatoes sitting on the sink's porcelain drainboard. I'd make my favorite summer sandwiches for Sarge and me. One thick tomato slice covered a whole piece of Wonder bread, with mayonnaise slathered on, and nothing else except a sprinkle of salt. They went down so easily, I soon had to make seconds.

"Aunt Bette says, if you want a job, the Olds is acting up again. She thinks maybe it's the carburetor, but she doesn't really know," I told Sarge while we ate our lunch. "She says she'd as soon have you fix it as to bring it to Fisher's garage, be a lot cheaper."

He chuckled amiably. "Better than that, I won't charge her anything."

"Oh, Sarge," I said, with the first cross feeling I'd ever had toward him. "Be practical. You have to charge something, or you won't be able to make a living. Aunt Bette can pay you all right. She has the executrix's account to draw on while the will is being probated."

"You know, Amelia, you sounded just like your mother right then. I do believe you're going to be a very practical young woman one day."

I wasn't really flattered. In my view, there weren't any two people in the world more different than Mother and I. "We don't look alike," I said.

"Not so much now, perhaps, but what about when she was your age? Have you seen her high school graduation picture?"

"Yup. It's in the album in the living room."

"Well?"

"I guess. A little. What about you, Sarge? Did you go to Whitford High, too? Do you have a picture?" I was sorry as soon as I'd said it. All those photographs must have been lost when his cottage was set afire.

He went right on talking without rancor. "As it happened, among the books I carried out the night of the fire were those old yearbooks, of all things. I really wasn't thinking straight. If I had been, I would have rescued my fifteen volumes of Dickens. Do you remember them? Leather bound? Gilt edges?"

I said I did. Sarge sighed, his mustache drooping as it did when he felt sad.

As we were clearing the table, I asked if I could see Sarge's high school pictures, and he went upstairs and brought down four yearbooks, one for each year he was in high school. We looked at the Class of 1910 together and admired his graduation portrait. "The Inventor," it said underneath his name, followed by a quotation: *I am an intellectual chap, And think of things that would astonish you.* Gilbert, *Iolanthe,* Act II.

Mother got up in a cranky mood and made herself a cup of Postum, since there wasn't any more coffee or blue stamps to buy some. Sarge borrowed my father's toolbox and set out for Snow's to fix the Olds. Mother told him to tell Aunt Bette for God's sake to send back some coffee, Snow must have a couple of dozen cans of it in the cellar. I took the yearbooks upstairs. Before putting them back in Sarge's room, I paged idly through the other three volumes.

It was in the Class of 1907 that I found her. Margaret Ann Burns. A lovely, dreamy face that looked somehow familiar. Underneath her name, in quotation marks, the single word "Pan" leaped out at me. The verse her classmates had chosen for her: *Not speaking much, pleased rather with the joy Of her own thoughts."* Wordsworth, *Margaret.*

That afternoon, I checked out *Poems of Wordsworth* at the library. Miss Pratt smiled at me for the first time in memory. "YOUR TASTE IS IMPROVING," she shouted at me in ringing tones. "Wordsworth...now that's poetry you can get your teeth into. Head and shoulders above that simpering Millay you're so fond of."

From the library, reading "Margaret" as I walked, I headed around Frietchie Circle to Snow's, where Sarge was still working on the Olds—*and no one came But he was welcome; no one went away But that it seemed she loved him.... She was a woman of steady mind, Tender and deep in her excess of love.* Wow! I was dying to learn everything Sarge knew about the mysterious Pan.

Chapter 14

In which Mr. Carver breaks his engagement, Aunt Bette runs a practice air raid drill, and I discover that a little knowledge really is a dangerous thing.

"Margaret Ann Burns…" Sarge repeated the name thoughtfully. "Do you know how to start a car, Amelia?"

"Nope. You must remember her. She would have been in high school when you were, just a couple of years ahead," I said "You might have called her Margie."

"Well, come on, I'll show you. I just want you to start up the motor while I watch how the carburetor behaves."

"I can't, Sarge. I don't know how. What if I wreck something?"

"I don't believe I'm hearing this from a girl who was named after Amelia Earhart. Go ahead, get in! Time you learned anyway. It's really very easy."

I felt like an impostor sitting behind the wheel, but it was quite exciting. Someday I would really know how to drive, and I'd have my own car, a groovy red coupe.

"Now, under your right foot, that's the gas pedal. The brake's on your left. In the middle is the clutch. And up here is the key. All you have to do…" he continued patiently with careful instructions until he was sure I understood. Then he went back to the carburetor. Raising his hand, he signaled me through the windshield.

"All right, start it." A moment later he was yelling at me, " Ease up on the gas, for God's sake!"

I took my foot off the gas pedal in a hurry, and the motor coughed and stalled.

"Okay, Amelia...let's try that again." So it went for twenty minutes or so, until Sarge was satisfied. By then I was getting rather proud of my new skill, thinking of how I'd brag to Skip in my next letter.

"Purring like a baby tiger. We'd better take it for little test drive, don't you think?"

"Sure." I moved reluctantly to the passenger's side as Sarge got in to drive. "Was I really? How do you know?"

"Were you what?"

"Named after Amelia Earhart."

"She made her first transatlantic flight just before you were born. It was your mother who told me that. Quite a heroine, much admired. To my mind, the two things go together." Sarge brought the Olds out of the garage, and we drove around Frietchie Circle in style. I waved at Miss Pratt, who was out watering the geraniums in the library windowbox. She scowled back, the glaring July afternoon turning her steel-rimmed glasses into two flashing signals.

"Do you think they'll ever find her? Miss Cronin said she could've been taken prisoner by the Japs, like if she saw some top secret military stuff, and she might be released after the war."

"Way back in 1937? Miss Cronin is a romantic. I hope she's right," Sarge said, turning the wheel to negotiate Frietchie circle with obvious pleasure.

I imagined myself in the cockpit of an airplane, wearing a leather helmet and goggles, white scarf blowing in the cool breeze. The sky was sparkling blue, the clouds were wisps of veil that blew aside to let me dive through. On an island, far below, a mysterious new Jap weapon was glinting in the sunlight, catching my attention, drawing me down for a closer look. But as

I came back to earth, the sharp dart of curiosity, my nemesis, struck me again.

"Margaret Ann Burns," I said firmly, above the sound of the motor that was purring and the scatter of gravel as we circled the town green with its lush grass and the patriotic red, white, and blue flower garden at the center. Why did that color scheme seem so unnatural? "Did you know Margie Burns, Sarge?"

"Sounds familiar. I'll have to look at the picture. Did she have blonde curly hair? No, that was Mary Margaret." He sighed, remembering.

"Darker than that, but not real dark hair. Beautiful eyes. Must have been the silent type, from the quotation."

"What was the quotation?"

I gave him the Wordsworth right from the book in my hand.

"Oh yes, of course. Margaret Ann."

"What about her?"

"Lovely girl, quiet. Auburn hair, violet eyes. *A face to launch a thousand ships.* What a surprise when she married the undertaker. Hey, I'm getting carried away here. Mustn't waste any more of your aunt's gas." He slowed up at Snow's and backed the Olds into the garage. "I'll drop off the key, and we'll walk home. Your aunt told me to throw it in the pantry window when I finished. Hope she finds it. She's off somewhere with Beryl. Gave me this pound of coffee first, though, so let's not forget to bring it home with us."

"They're taking Red Cross first aid training," I said. "Here, I'll show you where to leave the key."

We went around back to the unlocked pantry window. I stood up on the milk box and dropped the car key neatly on the table inside. There was a bowl of peaches, not quite ripe. I helped myself to two of them, cheap enough wages.

I handed one of the peaches to Sarge. "She married a Whitcomb?" I asked as we began our walk home, savoring the still-tart and crunchy peaches.

"No, no. She married Jerry. Jeremiah. The Whitcombs' embalmer. He absolutely worshipped her, used to follow her around slavishly in school. She was kind enough about it, in a regal sort of way, you know, as if he were her pet hound. Every once in a while, she threw him a smile. Certainly never thought she'd marry him. Ah, small towns do make for desperate marriages."

"Jeremiah?"

"Jeremiah Carver. Well, they're all dead now, all dead and gone. He only lasted a year after she died. Broke his neck in an accident. He fell down the cellar stairs, one of those stone floors."

"Carver? *Carver!*" A horrid realization stopped me in my tracks. I felt as if all the blood in my body rushed down to my shoes, making my head light and my feet heavy. The peach dropped from my nerveless fingers.

"Come on, Amelia. Let's pick up the pace a bit, shall we? *Left, right, left, right.* I promised your mother I'd pick the string beans before supper. Must be bushels of them. If victory depends on your mother's ability to produce vegetables, the Nazis are finished. And you know what? You can help me."

"I suppose that means we have to put them up tomorrow."

"Yup. Now tell me, what's your great interest in Margaret Carver?"

I was ready for this and had practiced an answer. "I thought I'd seen her face somewhere before, maybe she'd become famous, an actress or a murderess or something."

"Going to keep it your little secret, eh?" he chuckled. "Actually, she was the librarian in Whitford for many years, before your time though. Died right there in the library. Maybe she's haunting you—you spend enough time over there. Consumption they used to call it. Tuberculosis, you know. Damn shame. Might have lived longer if she'd gone to Plymouth Sanitarium, but it was against her religion to see a doctor."

"Why was she called Pan?"

"Fancied herself a pagan, you know, until she got into Christian Science later. A woodland creature. Girls used to take such dramatic notions when I was a young man. Anyway, there was a theatrical they got up one summer, and she played the god Pan in a green tunic and tights. Pointy ears, too, as I remember. Danced around through the trees, of which yours truly was one, a skinny oak with pimples. Ah, my sapling years!"

He smiled and walked with a lighter step back in time, as if he were no longer my short, round, gray-mustached, unemployed friend. I knew enough about grown-up reveries to keep quiet for a bit.

"So, I guess, after that, she doffed the costume but kept the moniker," Sarge said finally. "*A rose by any other name...* And to think she married Jeremiah! Well, she had the boy. I've heard she doted on him."

"Alex," I said.

"Yes, of course. Alexander Carver, your inimitable English professor."

"He's just a teacher, really."

"A manner of speaking, Amelia."

We walked the rest of the way in silence. It was hot, and my thoughts were tumbling around like burning leaves. Not until late that evening did they settle down to one smoldering conclusion. The letter I'd given to Mr. Carver to return to Snow's library had been written by his mother! Surely he knew she was called Pan as a young woman. And her handwriting, he must have recognized her handwriting, too. What would he have thought of his mother and old Mr. Snow? What would he have done?

I was sick for most of a week. "The summer grippe," my mother called it. Fortunately, the weather was too hot for milk toast, so I was given saltines and medicinal coke without the fizz to settle my stomach. Through the open windows, I could hear swimmers down in Silver Sand Pond, splashing and laughing. It sounded as if everyone in the world were carefree except me.

"What worries me," I overheard Mother say to Aunt Bette, "is that she doesn't even want to read. Except the Bible. She's lying there in a room where she has storybooks piled up to her eyebrows, and she's reading the Bible. Now what do you make of that?"

"Let me have a look at her," said my aunt.

I'd been listening at the top of the stairs after yet another trip to the bathroom, so I hurried back into bed and assumed what I hoped was an invalid's plaintive expression.

"What are you smirking about?" asked Aunt Bette by way of greeting. "You've got your mother half crazy. Here, let me feel your forehead, honey."

"It's at least a hundred," I said.

"You'll live. Give me that cloth on your head, and I'll just run it under the cold water."

"Oh, thank you, Aunt Bette," I said faintly when she'd hurried back with a freshly chilled washcloth for my forehead.

She sat lightly on the edge of the bed, wearing a yellow polka dot playsuit with a halter that tied in back of her neck. At first glance she looked about sixteen, but her dark blue eyes pinned me to the pillow like a butterfly mounted on corkboard. "Well now, honey," she said, "are you worried about something?"

I squirmed and looked out the window. "Oh no, what would I be worried about? I just have the grippe, that's all."

Without looking away from my face, she picked up the Bible that lay open at the foot of the bed, keeping the place with her finger. "So what's this, then? Preparing to meet your Maker?"

"I don't know what's wrong with the Bible," I whined. "I mean, it's supposed to be the Good Book, isn't it? Why is everyone getting so excited because I happen to be reading it? Maybe if you'd sent me to Sunday School..."

"Very commendable. Very understandable that you should choose to read the Bible rather than that stack of Flash Gordon comic books under your bed. We just wonder how it happened to gain your attention. It's not on your summer reading list."

"I finished that list in June."

"All right. Let's see how far past the *begats* you are." She opened to the page where I'd left my Camp Fire Girls bookmark. "Ah, Proverbs! 'He that guardeth his mouth keepeth his life; but he that openeth wide his lips shall have destruction.' Say, this is cheery stuff."

"I liked the story of Esther. And Ruth. And Moses."

"So then, it's all stories to you, is that it?"

"Well, I was wondering about the ten commandments. I mean, I wasn't sure if I knew what all of them were exactly. So I just began reading."

She closed the Bible and reached for my comb and brush. "Your hair looks like a bird's nest. Sit up here, and let me get at it. Now I want you to be a whole lot better by tomorrow morning because we've planned an air raid drill—'incident' they call it—for Saturday, and I need you for a victim. And ours is going to be a bigger and better incident than that pitiful spectacle the American Legion conducted last month. Beryl and I need a dozen victims for everyone to practice bandaging. All the volunteers will be taken to Kates Hill for ice cream sodas directly after the drill."

"Are the Eliot twins volunteering?" I glanced at the mirror on my bureau. Aunt Bette was rolling my hair back on the sides the way she wore hers, like a movie actress, maybe Ann Sheridan.

"No, they've been invited to a picnic and hayride somewhere, the selfish gadabouts. But Minna's going to be a victim, too. That'll be fun, won't it? So you get well by Saturday, you hear?" She took two hairpins out of her hair to skewer mine to my head, then tied the back with a ribbon she took off my old teddy bear.

"Who're they going with?" I felt revived suddenly and swung my feet over the side of the bed to the floor. "Where is it?"

"Ah, Lazarus returns from the dead. Some Sea Scouts from Plymouth, I believe. Jay has a buddy who invited them, but really I think the buddy has his eye on Daisy. She has a pretty cool way with the fellows, I notice. Now don't you get any ideas. Nice girls don't go out with guys in uniform. If you're out of bed by Saturday, you're on my list of volunteers." She gave me a quick kiss on the forehead and then wiped off the lipstick with a Kleenex. "Fatal Apple," she said, holding up her matching nails for my approval. "Pretty shade, isn't it?"

"The Sea Scouts aren't guys in uniform,'" I protested. "They're just Boy Scouts in sailor suits."

"With sailors' ideas, no doubt. Forget it. No niece of mine is going to become one of those Victory Girls."

I slumped back on my pillow, struck dumb by the unfairness of fate and family.

On her way out the door later, I heard Aunt Bette reassure Mother, "I don't think she's planning to become a nun, Catherine."

There must have been some magic in her visit, because I was indeed much better the next day. So on Saturday, Minna and I were carried on stretchers to the church lawn, where we were wound up in bandages like two Egyptian mummies, while the Eliot twins were at a clambake with the Plymouth Sea Scouts.

Ollie tugged at my bandages, valiantly trying to free me from my aunt's enthusiastic first aid. Although muffled by her broken jaw, Minna had a good laugh at me trying to fend off the determined terrier. But just then a shadow fell over us. We looked up into the round hazel eyes, trim mustache, and brilliant smile of Mr. Carver.

"Well, well, I do believe I'm recognizing Amelia and Minna under all those bandages. It's nice to see you giving some of your vacation time to an important civic purpose like this. Amelia, is your mom here today? I'd like to say hello to her if she is." He glanced round vaguely.

I looked down at the ground, hoping the blush I felt going clear up to my scalp would be hidden under my head-wound bandages. "Oh, hi, Mr. Carver. Nah, she's home sleeping," I mumbled.

"Sleeping! I can't believe that. Why, it's past noon."

"I guess she's just tired." Instantly, I was sorry I'd said anything, and I refrained from explaining further.

But Minna volunteered on my behalf. "Mellie's mother works nights now, Mr. Carver."

"I guess Penny did mention something about that. At the telephone office, right?" I could feel him looking down at the top of my head while I kept my eyes riveted on the blackened Indian pennies tucked into my loafers.

After an endless pause, him studying me, me looking down, Mr. Carver turned his attention to Minna, asking how she was progressing with the summer reading list he'd given the freshman class in June, which was different than the one for us eighth graders. She confessed to getting bogged down in *Pride and Prejudice*.

"Such a lot of silliness in that mother and those sisters over getting a husband," she complained.

"Don't you think that's what girls are like, even today?"

"Not that foolish about it," she declared, her square jaw looking firmer than ever.

I thought of Minna's muscular little mother, wearing her flowered kerchief, hefting those heavy cans of milk, and I could imagine how foreign the pretensions of Mrs. Bennett were to Minna. I supposed I should feel the same, but somehow I always stepped into the world of a novel and disappeared until the story was finished. Rafting on the Mississippi, searching for the Holy Grail, or sharing the social preoccupations of the Bennett family—I lived each one wholeheartedly.

Thinking of books steadied me somehow. I felt that my blush had faded. Mr. Carver didn't know that I'd learned about Pan, I reassured myself, and possibly had even put the letter out of his mind. I looked up bravely, as high as his knee anyway, still avoiding his eyes.

"And where is your Aunt Bette?" he asked, suddenly switching his interest back to me. Crouched down, so that he was at my eye level, he patted Ollie, who was now taking a nap under the stretcher. Ollie opened one eye, growled and moved away from the disturbing hand. "I suppose she's here somewhere, doing her bit?"

"Inside. She's very busy coordinating," I replied, motioning toward the church. I hoped he wouldn't go in and bother her, in case I should be blamed for it.

"It's good of Miss Cabot to devote her time to this. I understand she's rather involved in her own affairs these days. It's true, isn't it, that she's come into a rather substantial inheritance?"

"Um," I muttered. If there was one rule that had been impressed on me, it was that I was never to discuss family business with outsiders. In any case, my mouth had gone so dry I couldn't speak.

"That's all right, Amelia," he said. "I know the whole story already, so you're not giving anything away. Yes, she's a fortunate young woman, as we both are aware. In the right place at the right time and ready to take advantage of whatever came her way—that's what luck is all about." Admonishing us both to plug away at our reading lists, he turned and sauntered into the church. I didn't think he even heard me say that I'd finished mine already and was working on Minna's.

"Did you hear that the engagement is off?" Minna whispered.

"What engagement?"

"Penelope Fisher and Mr. Carver. It's off."

"Since when?"

"Who knows? Not too long ago, though. All I heard was that Penny gave him back his ring even though it was really him who broke it up. Isn't that awful?"

"Why? She's probably better off."

"*Why?* Mellie, are you crazy? Penny doesn't have all that many chances, and now he goes and breaks off the engagement."

"I suppose so." Then it hit me. "Oh my God! He must have moved out of Fisher's then! Where's he going to live?"

"I hear he's staying in one of those summer cottages that didn't get rented on Silver Sand Pond. But he's going to have to find something else before fall. No heat in those cottages, you know, and there's spaces between the boards where the wind can really whistle through. They're just shacks really."

I shivered. "I wonder if my mother knows that," I said, more to myself than to Minna.

"Well, why don't you tell her. She could use another boarder, I bet. But you have Sarge Curry, don't you? Does he pay anything?"

"Of course he pays board," I said indignantly, but I had the frightening thought that Sarge's room was now in jeopardy. And how willingly he would move out of it, into a smaller room or even the barn, rather than to cause my mother a moment's concern. Oh, he would end up at the Poor Farm for sure, if he didn't smarten up. Suddenly I felt quite angry with Sarge.

"It's funny, though, that Mr. Carver didn't tell Mother himself, Minna. It's almost as if he doesn't want to board with us. If he'd said even one word about being homeless, my mother would have welcomed him back with open arms. He was her favorite of all the boarders we've had."

"Maybe he's embarrassed. To move out and in again like that. Or maybe he just wants to be alone with his grief," Minna said dramatically.

"What grief? You just said it was he who jilted Penny, so what's he got to grieve over?"

Minna shrugged and smiled impishly. So we both laughed and forgot about the complications of Mr. Carver' love life for the time being.

Later on, Aunt Bette took us victims in the Olds to the Frietchie Farm ice cream stand, where there were cows but no cream. We had to have our ice cream sodas made with sherbet. Ollie was very disappointed and licked indifferently at his cup of orange sherbet. I reminded him that we all had to make sacrifices for the war effort, and Minna said I was a nut for reasoning with a dog.

"A strange thing," Aunt Bette said to me as we were driving home. "Alex Carver showed up at the church and helped us move all the first aid equipment back into the storage room. And you know what else, Amelia? He asked me, practically with hat in hand, if he could stop over this evening and have a talk with me about Mr. Snow's books. Some of them, he says, are valuable, and that Win had noted which ones while they were working on the catalog. I don't even know what I did with that damned catalog."

"It's in the cabinet under the bookcase to the right of the fireplace," I said. I'd been looking for her carton of Parliaments without success.

"My, you certainly do get around, don't you? Well, I suppose I'm going to have to hear what he has to say. When you get home, you be sure to tell your mother that Alex is coming over to call on me tonight. That'll tickle her."

It did. She was frying cornmeal-breaded bass that Sarge had caught in the lake. "Well, well, will wonders never cease! Amelia, mix up some tartar sauce, will you? Put a half cup of mayonnaise in that bowl, and I'll tell you what else to add." She flipped the fish to the second side, golden and crusty now on top. "Half cup piccalilli, heap it up. No man knows how to clean fish properly. I had to go all over these fish myself," she continued happily. "Yes, indeed, wonders will never cease. Alex invited himself, and she didn't put him off, is that it?"

"Yup. What else should I put in?"

"Grated quarter of an onion. Mind your fingers. I don't want any blood in it. Did it seem to her that he really wanted to talk about books?"

"Didn't say," I said through my tears. There always seemed to be some grating involved whenever I was lending a hand in the kitchen. It was a wonder that my knuckles had any skin on them at all. "She just laughed a lot," I added, feeling important. A gold mine of information.

"Don't go getting any wrong ideas," Mother said, wiping traces of breading off her hands on the old chef's apron she wore. "He's not engaged anymore. He's perfectly free to call on anyone he likes, your aunt included."

"Minna told me. But Aunt Bette hates him. She says terrible things about him."

"But today she just laughed. We'll see what we'll see," Mother said. "Go call Sarge for supper. He's out in the barn trying to fix the broken door. I told him he couldn't manage that alone."

Grabbing the turtle food off the hat shelf near the back door, I headed outside to our victory garden where I liberated a bunch of baby carrots and a handful of outside cabbage leaves. Then I filled the old galvanized bucket with water from the outside faucet.

Our barn had one oversized door, so warped on its hinges that it was stuck open. Now that Sarge had worked on it, however, it was stuck closed.

"I guess I'm going to need help with this," he said. "I'll see if a couple of the guys at the firehouse will give me a hand on Saturday."

"Supper's ready. And would you tell Mother I'll be right there. I'm going to get in around back," I said.

"You mean you're planning to go up that rickety ladder carrying all that stuff? Oh no, you don't."

"I have to feed Merlin and Romeo. And fill the water dish, too." There were still tears in my eyes from grating the onion.

"All right...all right. But I'll hold the ladder and hand up the water when you're safe in the loft."

I'd gone into the barn through the hinged window in the loft many times by myself without a second thought. I'd also escaped that way on numerous occasions when my mother had been looking for me to do some detested chore. It had never occurred to me that there was anything wrong with the ladder. Now I noticed that certain rungs had a bit too much spring when I stepped on them.

"Ollie's coming to visit next week, but Mother's going to make him sleep in the barn," I told Sarge when we'd finished and were on our way back to the house. "It's not like when my aunt was living here and Ollie could sleep in her room.

"Your aunt's going away?"

"Boston. She's going to see Snow's broker and his lawyer and some appraiser. And do a little shopping, she said. So I'm dog-sitting. She's going to pay me fifty cents a day."

"Not bad," said Sarge, who probably hadn't earned a dollar since he'd been burned out of his shop. "You're quite an animal person, Amelia. Ever thought of becoming a vet?"

"I used to, when Dad was alive. But now I think being a librarian would be heaven. You know that scratched pane of glass you replaced in your room?" I'd looked at it with new eyes while feeding Merlin. "M-A-B?"

"Yes?"

"Margaret A. Burns."

Sarge was silent for a moment. Then he said, "I'd thought of that. You don't miss much, do you, Holmes?"

I grinned. "Elementary, my dear Curry."

Right at that moment, I might have told Sarge about the letter, but Mother leaned out the back door on the verge of a scream. "Supper's getting ruined while you two are dawdling," she yelled in exactly the same tone she might have used to say, "Rome is burning, Nero, and you're just fiddling around."

Chapter 15

In which Aunt Bette shows off a treasure, and all that glitters turns out to be real gold.

Two days later, on Monday, my aunt rolled into our driveway in the Olds and hopped out carrying two handbags. Ollie jumped out after her and ran to greet me.

"Wait until you see what I have to show you," she said to my mother. "Let's go into your bedroom and shut the door."

I sidled in after them. My mother's room was on the ground floor, opposite the parlor, looking out on the front yard. Beryl was out in her garden, chasing something with a bamboo rake.

"Okay, big eyes," Aunt Bette said. "You can see, too. Pull the shades."

"Get that dog off my bed, Amelia," said my mother. I had to sit on the floor, holding Ollie down. He was getting used to many indulgences, living with my aunt.

Aunt Bette dug into the larger of the two bags and pulled out a knotted blue kerchief. "And I thought the jewelry had gone to Eunice. Pearls, a gold choker, an engagement ring, cameos. She got all Frances Snow's traditional pieces. But boy, that was just a drop in the bucket!" she exclaimed as she undid the knot with her Fatal Apple fingernails and spilled the contents of the kerchief onto Mother's bed.

What a dazzling cascade of jewels tumbled onto the pink chenille spread! It looked to me like a pirate's hoard—sparkling bracelets and rings, ropes of necklaces and lockets, a rainbow of brooches and jewel-encrusted watches. Then she dumped the contents of the second handbag beside the first glittering heap. Beaded evening bags with jeweled straps, a slim silver flask, gold cigarette cases, and even two miniature revolvers with inlaid mother of pearl, one gold handled and the other silver, or perhaps even platinum.

Sharp intakes of breath greeted this sudden splendor. Mother clutched my hand as if fearing I would reach out for some priceless bauble.

"Just look at what I found in Win's safe deposit box!" Aunt Bette exclaimed. "Well, not in his official safe deposit box in the Bank of Boston. I'll have a look at that in a few days when I go up to town on estate business. Yesterday morning I came across a second key in a little green envelope in Win's desk. Turns out he'd rented a second box in the Plymouth Shawmut, can you imagine that? You know, at first, I wondered if any of this stuff is *genuine!*" Aunt Bette's voice was rising to that hysterical note we worried about. "But I took two of the gold and diamond pieces to Reliable Jewelry and got a quick appraisal. And *they are!* The jeweler—Dick Flash, is his name—almost dropped his *loupe* when he took a gander at what I had in my hand."

My hand slid toward one of the revolvers. Quicker than a cat, my aunt slapped my fingers hard. "They're not loaded, but they are real," Aunt Bette said in a low tone.

Mother put her hand on her breast and sat back against the pillows. "I can't believe my eyes," she said faintly.

"Catherine, will you just look at this one!" My aunt fished out a diamond ring and held it up in triumph. Even in the dim light of the shade-cloistered bedroom, it shown with incredibly deep fire. "I wonder how many carats? Three? Four?"

Mother picked up the silver handled revolver. "It looks so much like a toy."

"I'm told they're not."

"And who else did you show all this to?"

"Alex. But *just the guns*, Catherine. I needed a man's opinion, you know."

"Since when, Bette?"

"Oh, look," I exclaimed, reaching out with my still smarting hand. "Isn't this darling!" It was a jewel-encrusted pin, a perfect little antique automobile with diamonds and sapphires and a tiny ruby on the head of the stick shift.

Delicately, my aunt took it out of my fingers and pinned it unerringly on the collar of her blouse. "I love this," she said, caressing it, holding her little chin high so that we could admire the beauty of the miniature. She lit a Parliament, and the smoke encircled her head like a tiara.

"You'd better wrap that all up again, Bette. Looks to me it's the real McCoy. What if someone were to see this cache?" My mother was coming to life. "Will these pieces be yours legally, do you think?"

"Everything is mine except the Worcester property. And the other jewelry that was left to Eunice in Frances Snow's will. The best pearls, that opera strand. But never mind, I've got *all this* now. Only, I don't know what I may have to sell, to settle with those vultures. Should I believe Fenner that I'd better not let Hamilton Snow bring me to court?"

"I wouldn't trust Fenner any farther than I could throw him." Mother looked fierce enough to toss the little gray lawyer a pretty good distance. "Eunice has him in her pocket." She lifted a diamond and emerald bracelet, gazing at it with awe. "This doesn't look like Mrs. Snow's style to me."

"I don't know where they came from, but I know they never belonged to Frances. All her pieces were appraised and insured. There's something very Twenties about these pieces, don't you think? Win had such varied business interests."

"Some illegal business, I wouldn't doubt," my mother said. "Look how easily he filled his cellar with all those canned goods that are scarce as hen's teeth—and that freezer full of meat. Black market contacts, certainly. Maybe even gangsters. You and I wouldn't even have had the faintest idea who to hit up for a rib roast at Christmas. Certainly not Fisher's butcher."

They began to laugh, falling back on the pillows...then quieting...sighing... and beginning again, infecting one another with their merriment. Perhaps they were picturing Fisher's meat case, which currently displayed only tripe, beef kidneys, and some mutton that looked as if the animal had died of old age. Or else they were imagining Mr. Snow conferring with some Edward G.

Robinson-types in the back room of a gambling house. Or maybe they were simply hysterical, like bobby-soxers at a Frankie Sinatra concert.

"It doesn't matter where this swag came from, it's in my hands now, and I intend to hang on to every last ill-gotten gem." Aunt Bette sat up finally, her voice getting that hard, determined edge I knew so well. I doubted that Fenner or anyone would get this fortune away from my aunt's dainty grasp.

One by one they picked up each piece and exclaimed over it, placing them all back in the kerchief, which my mother then tied up with a ferocious knot.

"Oh, Lord," she said. "With all this to beguile me, I haven't even asked you how it went with Alex last night. Come on, let's go have a glass of iced tea while you tell me about it." Mother stood up briskly and snapped up the shades, letting light back into the room.

My aunt shrugged prettily. "Oh, you know. Alex is Alex. Sort of boring. But he did go through the catalog and mark all the cards with the book values that Win mentioned to him, as best he could remember. I suppose I ought to be grateful for that," she said without conviction as we all went into the kitchen.

"You'd better put that jewelry back in the Plymouth safe deposit box tomorrow," my mother said, shaking her finger at my aunt. "And lock your door tonight."

"I always lock my door, unlike you, Catherine. I'm all alone there, in a strange house full of valuable things. First I'm taking all this to Boston next week, to be appraised by some jeweler a little farther from home. Then I'll stash it all back in the bank, don't you worry. You know what he said? He said I was the most beautiful woman in Whitford."

"Did he now! You see...he's not such a tedious fellow, is he?" My mother turned away with a small quirky smile. "What did you wear? I hope you offered him a cup of coffee, at least."

My aunt wrinkled her nose. "My pink silk blouse. You should see how it looks with that cute automobile pin. Yes, I gave him coffee—and cookies, too. Boy, were they dry out of that old tin. And about the worst pot of coffee I've ever made in my life. I don't know what went wrong. But he claimed it was delicious and accepted a second cup, what a liar he is! There's a disagreeable sweet smell about him, too, that I don't like very much. Like a bad orange. So don't get any ideas, Catherine. I know you. You think he's Mr. Right. But he isn't Mr. Right for me."

I breathed a secret sigh of relief and went into the pantry for three tall glasses, wondering why I was allowed to have all the iced tea I wanted whereas the caffeine in hot tea was supposed to stunt my growth. Which would have been a blessing, since I was now too tall to dance with any boy of my own age. I decided against pointing out to Mother the illogic of her thinking process.

"You could do worse," my mother said, thumping ice cubes out of the stubborn metal tray.

"Not much. Look at poor Penny."

"They weren't right for each other, obviously. Amelia, you can get the spice cake in the bread box. And napkins, please. And don't you repeat one word of anything to the Eliots or to Minna."

My aunt grabbed my wrist with her crimson fingernails so that I almost dropped the cake. Ollie looked up hopefully.

"And no one," she said, "*no one at all* is to know about the jewelry. On your honor, Amelia?"

"On my honor, Aunt Bette," I promised. "You want to know where I think you should hide the loot?"

"It's possible that you've been reading too many detective stories, young lady," my aunt said.

"Listen, Aunt Bette. You know in Mrs. Snow's room underneath the vanity, the loose heating grate? There's a little shelf inside. And you can't even see the grate with the vanity in place. The skirt covers it."

"Who do you think you are, the fire inspector? What were you doing fishing inside my grate anyway?" Aunt Bette's blue eyes grew dark and menacing.

I was sorry to have given away an excellent hiding place for nothing but grief. "Aw, Aunt Bette. My pencil rolled under. The mechanical one you gave me."

She shot me her killing look, then turned to her plate and dug into the spice cake hungrily while a Parliament still smoldered in the ashtray. "I didn't have any breakfast or lunch," she explained.

"Bette! You're going to get all run down again! Let me fix you a sandwich."

"No...no...it's too hot. This is lovely." A moment later, she stopped eating, pushed the rest of the cake away, and picked up the cigarette. "Oh, God!" she exclaimed.

"Amelia, you've had quite enough for now," my mother said quickly. "Why don't you take Ollie out to the barn and give him a good brushing. Fleas are probably bothering him in this heat, so put some pennyroyal on the brush. There's a big bush of it beside the chive. Has a minty smell...you know the plant I mean?"

My aunt was looking down at her cigarette, and I noticed a line from the side of her mouth that I'd never seen before.

After Ollie and I went out the back door, I stood by the open window over the sink wondering why I'd been rushed out after being allowed to view the treasure hoard.

"Jack was the only one for me," Aunt Bette said.

Jack? That name meant nothing to me. We didn't even know anyone named Jack. Was Jack the tall guy with his arm around my aunt in the photo she'd cut to fit in her wallet? Both squinting in the sun and her head barely came up to his shoulder, Mutt and Jeff. She didn't know I'd looked in her wallet, of course, so I hadn't been able to ask her who that was.

"Now, Bette. He was a skunk, that's what he was. Someone nice is going to come along for you. It's in the cards. Wait a minute, let me just see if that child is out of earshot."

I flew. Ollie raced after me, barking joyfully.

Chapter 16

In which my investigation of an old
love affair heats up, and a sleepover
in the barn turns scary.

T he following week, Sarge and I got the barn door open a wedge so
that I could get in there with Ollie while Aunt Bette was away. The
only other entrance was the rickety ladder to the loft window, which Sarge had
insisted was not safe to use.

Mother was adamant that Ollie would not be allowed to sleep in my room,
so Sarge nailed together a box bed that looked like a large bureau drawer for
Ollie. He used odd pieces of lumber from the pile of discards stacked against the
barn on the far side where it wouldn't irritate Mother when she looked out her
dining room windows. Forsythia, lilac, and rhododendron bushes were planted
on the house side, so that she could enjoy them in season, but every blossom
was faded now that the buzzing heat of July had begun. By comparison, the barn
seemed marvelously cool and dark. I layered a folded horse blanket with sprigs
of pennyroyal in Ollie's new bed, smoothing a favorite blanket from Snow's on
top so he'd know that all this effort was for his comfort, that this was his place.
He sprawled on the wood floor with only his nose on the blanket, which I took

to mean that, although not ungrateful, he wasn't to be so easily mollified for being banished to the barn.

Carefully, I set Romeo's cage on the high workbench out of harm's way. He was getting to look like a real grown-up rabbit. Soon I'd be able to let him loose in the woods. Maybe he would find some cousins to show him around. My dad had always let his patients go as soon as they seemed able to fend for themselves. "Freedom is dangerous," he told me, "but better a short life running wild with your own kind than a long life in a solitary cell."

I left Ollie in semi-contented exile with a bucket of cool water nearby and took off for the library. My books weren't due yet, but I was nagged with curiosity about Margaret Carver and decided to find out what I could about her from Miss Pratt.

It was a longer than usual walk in the sweltering late morning. My thoughts kept returning uncomfortably to Mr. Carver as I trudged along. How he must have hated Winston Snow for discarding the beautiful Margaret, his mother, just as Lancelot had abandoned Elaine. Yet it was before Mr. Carver read the love letter that he'd introduced himself to Snow and had been offered the job of cataloging that strange collection of books. Now why would Mr. Snow do that? According to Aunt Bette, that first night they talked, Mr. Carver told Mr. Snow about his mother being the town librarian. Did Mr. Snow connect the young man with his youthful passion for Pan? And after reading the letter, why did Mr. Carver continue to ingratiate himself with someone who had jilted his mother? I remembered how he had cried on the night of Mr. Snow's accident.

By the time I'd walked halfway down Fisher Street toward the Circle, I was beginning to feel dizzy from the heat, so I sat for a while by the side of the road under a giant copper beech tree, its dark red leaves offering a haven of dense shade. The events of last winter continued to prickle like an itch in my mind. Winston Snow under the ice, his nails clawing at his frozen tomb. Winston Snow dragged up in spring, swollen with bloat and eels. I shivered as a light finger of breeze touched my sweat-drenched back.

Mr. Snow had been old, but his arms were muscular and his step firm. He must have fought desperately to keep his head above water. When Mr. Carver saw what had happened, why hadn't he been able to save the struggling man? Couldn't he have grabbed a plank or a fishing rod from one of those shacks on the ice and snaked it out there for Mr. Snow to grab? Or had Alex Carver just stood there smiling with satisfaction as he watched his mother's lover lose his breath in the clutch of freezing water, witnessed him sink under the ice for the last time. Worse, had Mr. Carver lured the old man out onto that thin ice *on purpose*. Had Mr. Carver believed this was what Winston Snow deserved, that justice was being served and his mother's honor avenged? I shook my head, as if that would shake off these distressing visions, jumped to my feet, and continued my walk.

At the library, Miss Pratt took pity on me as I collapsed cross-legged on the floor between two cool stacks of bookshelves.

"LORD, AMELIA," she said in her usual loud voice, the better to hear herself, "you sure look heat-struck. You stay put right there. I'm going to get you a drink." She inched to the back room with the help of her cane and came back with a bottle of Moxie from the Sewing Circle's old refrigerator. "Here, drink this, child. It's good for what ails you."

The dark liquid had a bitter taste, but it was wet and cold. I drank it down eagerly and burped. Not an auspicious beginning to my cross-examination of Miss Pratt, so I decided to spend some time with the town reports first.

The letter had been dated January 15, 1910, so I began by looking for the 1911 and 1912 reports. Unfortunately, all the town reports seemed to be shelved in a long, gray, dusty row on the floor behind Miss Pratt's desk.

"If you don't beat all, Amelia," she said as she swung around in her well-padded oak swivel chair and watched me crawl about on my hand and knees. "Now what are you after? Have you taken a fancy to town finance?"

"I might do a history paper on Whitford for school," I said. "How come these only go back to the thirties."

"OF COURSE THEY ARE DIRTY. Dust-catchers, that's what books are. And those who pull a bunch of books off the shelves, causing other people to hack and cough, are the DUST DISTURBERS."

"NOT DIRTY, MISS PRATT. THIRTY. HOW COME THESE ONLY GO BACK TO 1930, THAT'S WHAT I'M ASKING."

"BECAUSE THAT'S AS FAR BACK AS ANY SENSIBLE PERSON WOULD TAKE AN INTEREST, that's why," she hollered back. "The rest of them are in the back room somewhere. Look up over the refrigerator. There's some more town stuff up there, as far as I remember."

I found the rest of the town reports under some empty flowerpots near the ancient set tub. After I dusted off the cobwebs with my shirttail and got them in order, I took an armful of 1900s to the ramshackle reading table near the window.

The geraniums' red blossoms in the windowbox outside were like a row of Raggedy Ann heads on a shelf. The window was propped open with a stick and the sheer white curtain pulled back. I could have loved sitting there if I weren't being impaled by Miss Pratt's suspicious gaze. I wondered if it would be possible to live in a library when I grew up.

After reading through Marriages in 1911, 1912, and 1913, I finally glanced through 1910, and there it was: February 1, 1910, Margaret A. Carver to Jeremiah Carver. *Wow*, I thought, *that was some fast rebound romance!*

The Eliot twins had schooled me in how to read the town reports the way their grandma and her cronies did. They poured through the pages avidly as soon as a copy arrived in the mail each year. First they checked the dates under Marriages, and they flipped over to the dates under Births. "Ah ha!" Daisy would say. "Another premature birth, Mellie!"

So I skipped ahead. Births. September 7, 1910, Alexander Percival Carver to Margaret B. and Jeremiah Carver. I counted the months on my fingers, seven months from February, nine from December, 1909. The twins would have been proud of me—I'd unearthed another scandal. It must have been common knowledge at the time. All the ladies relished the Census in the town report, and it probably wasn't any different in Margaret's day. Seven months though. Jay would shrug and give eight months the benefit of the doubt. It depended on who the mother was. One time it was a second cousin of their father's, and Daisy said the young woman had been out hanging sheets and that'd brought on an early labor. You weren't supposed to lift your arms over your head after the seventh month, she explained. So eight months could squeak by okay. Seven, not likely.

Yes, but what had Mr. Carver thought? There had been a date on the letter. Maybe he'd seen Winston Snow as a double deserter, who'd not only discarded the fragile Margaret in order to marry Frances with her trusts and her social contacts, but who also may have left a child to be brought up by the rough, quiet undertaker who had taken a fancy to gentle Margaret.

Brooding on this romantic tragedy, however, didn't prevent me from feeling rather hungry, as it was now well past my usual lunchtime. Thoughts of a toasted cheese sandwich or even peanut butter and jelly loomed large in my imagination.

Miss Pratt took a brown paper bag out of the drawer in her desk. It rattled intriguingly. "Cucumber on whole wheat. Gingersnaps," she said. "Always pack for two, just in case. Got enough for you, if you like. AREN'T YOU HUNGRY?"

"YES, THANK YOU," I shouted, not wanting there to be any mistake in my meaning. I got two more Moxies from the back room, and we picnicked together. The second Moxie tasted better. I sat in the banister-back oak chair beside the desk and looked through the recruitment brochures the post mistress had left there, choosing "Dogs for Defense" as my lunchtime reading. *Thousands of dogs are needed. New recruits are being inducted daily at the War Dog Training Center, rushed into training courses which skill them as sentries, message carriers, airplane spotters, pack-carriers...* Airplane spotters? What did they do—bark once for Allied planes and twice for Japs? In one fleeting moment, I imagined Ollie dashing through enemy lines to carry a vital message to Allied headquarters.

"For goodness' sake, take the darn thing," said Miss Pratt. "Maude's just cluttering up my desk every week with more of that government stuff."

"I could lay them out there," I suggested, waving at the other side of the room with the whole wheat crust of my sandwich.

"Good idea. Throw them all out. There's a barrel out back for trash."

"I SAID, I COULD LAY THEM OUT IN THE READING ROOM."

"All right. All right. I suppose Maude will be poking around here to see where they're at. That's a good girl, Amelia."

"MARGARET CARVER," I said, making a neat row of stacked pamphlets on the reading table. "DIDN'T SHE USED TO BE THE LIBRARIAN HERE?"

"Good Heavens, you *are* a one for ancient history, aren't you? That goes back…let me see…about seventeen, eighteen years since she died. That's when I took over, on a temporary basis only."

"DID YOU KNOW MARGARET CARVER, MISS PRATT?"

"CERTAINLY I KNEW HER, just the same as I know everyone else. Well, I used to, anyway. So many new faces now. Youngsters running in and out. Margaret was a fool, if you want to know. Lived in a fairy tale world, full of *la-de-da* notions she got in books…not unlike present company."

"Was it consumption?"

"NO GUMPTION? That describes her, all right. All that mooning around will sap a body, as you'll soon find out if you keep reading yourself sick."

"I SAID, 'WAS IT CONSUMPTION?' "

"Oh, consumption. Yes indeed. She'd had it for ages and wouldn't get any medical attention for it after she got mixed up with that religion, what's it called? Jesus Science? It's hard to have sympathy for someone who doesn't even take care of herself. Just after Christmas 1925. Nice present it was for the boy. He found her downstairs on the couch. Now any sensible person knows that the library doesn't have to be open in bad weather like that. You wouldn't catch me coming in here when there's so much as a flake of snow in the air. It's not worth catching my death just so someone else can curl up by the fire and read a novel."

I knew that. I'd walked up to the library in winter weather I thought passable only to find the door locked and a sign on it: "Library Closed Today Due to Ill Health."

"THAT WAS A VERY GOOD CUCUMBER SANDWICH."

"Have some gingersnaps. Now that boy took on about his mother like you wouldn't believe. Never got on well with his father. Jeremiah was a real Yankee—careful, you know. Some would say frugal. That boy had some idea his mother wouldn't go to the doctor because Jeremiah begrudged the money. All the ladies from the Sewing Circle were in here to take care of things, with the tragic loss, and we heard from the boy how the Carvers scrimped and saved at home. To hear him tell it, his mother wasn't even getting the nourishing food she needed. Not that I believed it. Jeremiah was not a stingy man. He just wouldn't allow waste and foolishness in his house, that was all."

"HOW OLD WAS ALEX CARVER THEN?"

"Yes, Alex. That was his name. A fifteen-year-old boy doesn't know what's what, no matter how smart he thinks he is. Same for girls."

"DIDN'T HIS FATHER, JEREMIAH CARVER, DIE SHORTLY AFTER HIS WIFE?"

"They kept fighting about money. Some expensive college Alex had his heart set on. The boy always had big ideas, thanks to his mama. Brought him up on King Arthur and other nonsense. Well, it took Jeremiah's broken neck to lay the argument to rest finally."

Just at that interesting juncture, Waldo Whitcomb banged in the door, looking red and beefy.

"Ma says it's too hot for you to be baking in here, so I'm to take you home," he said, pulling a chair over to the history shelves and allowing his bulk to fall onto it. "Says she's invited the two new teachers over for lemonade and cookies. Says she's going to use your sugar so you might as well be there to share it." He took a piece of paper out of his pocket and handed it to Miss Pratt. "Here are a few books I think you should buy for this section, in case you're interested. There's a couple of great books about the Civil War on the list. I just thought you might not have had a chance to read about their publication."

Miss Pratt held the list away from her as if she were examining a strange bug. "You know, Junior, I've been holding down expenses this year, and everyone is mighty pleased about it. Now, if you'll give me your arm, and Amelia will shut that window and lock the back door, we can talk about your list on the way. TWO NEW TEACHERS, YOU SAY?"

"Two new ones, and one old one to convey them around town. Alex Carver is chauffeuring, so they'll see the lay of the land, so to speak, before Labor Day."

"Speak of the devil, WHERE'S HE GOING TO GET THE GAS FOR SIGHTSEEING?" hollered Miss Pratt as we stepped into the summer furnace. "When a good citizen like Maude puts her car up on blocks for the Duration! Those young teachers should walk around on their own two feet if they really want to see Whitford. Whizzing through by car at twenty, twenty-five miles an hour you don't see half as much." Waldo locked the front door, and Miss Pratt hung the "Ill Health" sign on it.

Actually, Maude Whitcomb had quit driving, to the great relief of her neighbors, after a series of small collisions had culminated in her plowing into a school bus one icy morning. None of the schoolchildren were hurt, but the bus driver broke his toe kicking Maude's Caddy.

Miss Pratt boarded with Mrs. Whitcomb, who was widowed and "liked to hear another body breathing in the house," as she often said. Waldo ran the funeral home and lived in the big yellow house adjacent to it with his house-keeper, Mary Kelly. Mrs. Whitcomb and Miss Pratt were on the other side of the Whitcomb Funeral Parlor, in a white saltbox on Frietchie Circle, so they didn't have very far to walk in the blaze of the afternoon.

But I did, and by the time I got home myself it was five o'clock. Mother had already gone up to the telephone office, leaving me a cold plate in the refrigerator with a note that read: "Your share of ham is on plate in icebox. No extras! If you're still hungry, have more tomatoes. Cake in breadbox—one piece only! Wash your dishes. Sarge is down the Poor Farm to fix tractor. Dish of scraps is for dog. Keep him out of house, or else! Love, Mother."

After I took out my dinner and Ollie's, I stood there holding the two plates, deciding what to do. It seemed a shame to eat alone. For all she couldn't stand animals, Mother had patiently picked over the bones of Sunday's roast chicken and stirred in some vegetables and this morning's leftover Ralston for Ollie. I put the dishes on the table and went to fetch him. He was sitting on the floor by the workbench watching Romeo, his whole expression one of such attention, eagerness, and intelligence as wins the hearts of dog show judges. The rabbit was frozen in the farthest corner of his cage, his eyes like glass.

"Come on, Ollie," I said. "You're going to give Romeo a heart attack. Let's go have dinner."

It was a word he understood well. Immediately abandoning his rapt pose, he bounded toward me. We slipped through the small space where the great unhinged door was leaning. Ollie dashed back and forth, covering the distance to the kitchen three times to my once.

I checked his paws. They looked dirt-free to me. "We can't leave any evidence, Ollie," I explained. He did his best to clean his plate and the surrounding floor so that not one scrap remained to incriminate us. After I finished the dishes, I packed up a few supplies: my radio, my flashlight (although the batteries were weak from being used to read in bed), my pillow and a sheet from the linen closet, some *Punch* magazines from Mr. Snow's attic, cookies, matches, and a couple of Parliaments I'd hooked out of my aunt's open pack. Leaving a note on the kitchen table—"Sleeping in the barn, okay?"—Ollie and I headed out there and dropped our gear. Then we went out to the backyard and untied Aunt Bette's old hammock from where it swung between two pines. Ollie liked this game, which he took to be tug-of-war.

Just as I'd imagined, it was possible to hang that hammock between the posts in a former horse stall in the barn. A single bulb with a second plug, hanging from the ceiling under the loft, served to hook up the radio. Clearing the worktable of everything except Romeo's cage, I plugged in the radio and turned up the volume rather loud to dispel the eerie shadows in the corners of the barn. The dance band seemed to enliven Romeo, who thumped around in his cage at odd intervals. I looked forward to letting him go free where I'd found him. Perhaps I would put Merlin back in the pond, too, before the cold weather came. I didn't want to have to hide the turtle under my bed to keep him from freezing in winter.

I smoked a Parliament, using an old cold cream jar as an ashtray, and admired the Gibson girls in *Punch*, wondering how they managed to swim in those bathing outfits. That reminded me to check on Merlin. I found him sitting on top of his rock, motionless, possibly thinking to sun himself in the feeble light of the single bulb. I pulled his dishpan under my hammock, out of the light.

This has the makings of a fine clubhouse, I thought, but I couldn't imagine who'd want to join my club. Certainly not the fastidious twins. Minna, maybe—although hanging around a barn would hardly seem like a treat to her. After a while, Ollie curled up in his new bed, I stretched out in the hammock, and we both fell soundly asleep, the music still blaring.

The next thing I remember, there was a great thud. Ollie sprang from his bed, barking crazily. I peeked out of the hammock and saw the dog throwing himself at the barn door in a frenzy.

"Oh, come back to sleep, Ollie," I said lazily, turning over in the hammock, which no longer seemed ideally comfortable. "There's probably a skunk out there you wouldn't want to meet."

Ollie refused to stop barking and jumping, so there was no point trying to get back to sleep. I rolled out of the hammock and stood up, thinking I'd take the dog for a little walk, on leash so that he wouldn't chase after whatever he was hearing out there. Slipping on my loafers, I paused to turn off the radio, which now seemed terribly loud. I could guess my mother wasn't home yet or she would be yelling at me about the noise disturbing the neighbors.

The door was in deep shadow. Clipping the leash to Ollie's collar, I didn't even notice that the thick, heavy plank door somehow had shifted, had shut tight, and now filled the entire door frame, not hung on its original hinges but just with its own weight holding it in place, immovable. When I tried to slip out the way we'd come in, I found our sliver of entrance had been sealed as if by a new wall.

This was strange, this was impossible. Sarge and I had sweated and tugged to open that door a slice just that morning. Now, mysteriously, it had fallen back into place with a thump that must have scared Ollie. I pushed and banged and got splinters in my hands, but the big old thing just wouldn't budge an inch.

As I was looking around for something to use as a lever or battering ram, something even worse happened. The light went out. *I don't believe this,* I thought. Ollie hadn't stopped barking for a moment, which made it more difficult to think what I should do. I felt my way to the stall and found my flashlight. I had no idea what time it was, but I felt it was late enough for Sarge to have come home.

Just as I began to holler for Sarge, something terrifying happened. *I smelled smoke.*

Chapter 17

In which I'm trapped in my worst nightmare
with three little creatures in need of rescue.

At first it was just a whiff—*maybe from the cigarette I smoked*, I thought irrationally. Immediately, I realized that had been hours ago, and I'd put the lid on the jar to hide the butt. The smell of smoke oozed in stronger and thicker, and with that horrid, choking odor came a crackling sound that was even more frightening. It was unmistakable. The barn was on fire!

I shone the weak beam of the flashlight to the far wall where the snapping sound was coming from. Thick gray smoke was pouring in from cracks between the boards. Panic rose in my throat like stomach acid. But even while I felt nauseous, trapped in the dark with smoke fouling the air, my mind cleared for an instant. Wide awake now, I was thinking madly.

My exact thoughts were: *I have to get out of here! And I have to take Ollie, Romeo, and Merlin with me.* There wasn't much time. Already I was coughing.

With the dim help of the flashlight, I found Merlin and stuck him way down in the pocket of my shorts. Then I grabbed Romeo's cage. Up the ladder to the loft, wire fencing digging into my hands. Ollie was at the foot of the ladder, barking and scratching to follow me.

I heaved the cage onto the loft. Scurried back down for Ollie. Up the ladder again with the dog under one arm, squirming and twisting and pawing the air. All of us in the loft, but the smoke seemed even denser up there. Crawling on the floor, I flung open the hinged board that covered the loft window, grateful for the rush of sweet night air.

The ladder was gone!

I aimed the weakened flashlight at the ground below. There it was, lying on its side. No good to me at all.

"Sarge! Sarge!" I hollered. There was only one little light shining in the kitchen. But I'd forgotten to leave on a light. That meant Sarge *had* come home. I aimed my flashlight, spearing it at the side window of the front bedroom. The beam didn't quite reach, faint as it was. Maybe he wouldn't wake up at all.

Now I could see the source of the crackle and smoke. The odd-lots pile of lumber was ablaze. The side of the barn had caught in it. Surely someone must see it! Fingers of flame were curling around the corner of the building, reaching for me. I was trapped in my worst nightmare.

The brightness of the fire lit up the woods behind the barn. Was that someone moving in there? "Help me, help me!" I shouted to the shadow. As I watched, the indistinct figure seemed to drift away. It disappeared among dark trees.

I hung onto Romeo's cage and Ollie's leash with a death grip. If someone didn't come to rescue us in a minute, we would have to jump.

I looked down at the ground. Never had it seemed so far away! I'd throw the cage down first. If I had a rope, I could lower it. I looked around with the flashlight. Nothing but cobwebs. The loft was completely empty. No way to improvise. Unless I used Ollie's leash. But if I did that, I might lose him. He might dash off the ledge of the loft. Romeo would have to take his chances.

Lying on my stomach, I lowered the cage as far as my arm would stretch. Ollie tugged madly at my other arm. He wanted to be gone, poor pup. Anywhere but here. "It's okay," I said to him and myself. "We're going out next."

Just as I let go of the cage, I looked up and saw Sarge. He was running from the house. He ran like a football player trying to intercept the ball. Not quite catching the cage, he broke its fall nonetheless, fell himself on the grass and was up again in an instant.

It seemed like forever, but it must have been just a few moments before he had the ladder up, swinging it toward the windows. I jumped back as it hit the barn with a reassuring thwack.

"Come down," he shouted. "I'll get Ollie after."

"No, I can't let him go," I sobbed. "He wants to run back. He'll get caught in the fire. The big door is shut tight."

Sarge was up the creaky ladder in three jumps. "Give him to me," he said urgently. I pushed the struggling Ollie into his arms. "There, there, Mellie, climb down right after me. Be quick, quick!"

Jumping down the last half of the ladder, Sarge rolled on the ground with Ollie, holding fast to the leash all the time. I started down as soon as the ladder was clear. Halfway, a rung broke. My leg plunged to the next rung, scraping against the broken wood painfully. But I hung on and didn't fall. Then I was on the ground and Sarge was holding me. Grabbing Romeo's cage, hanging on to each other and to Ollie, we raced toward the house.

"We have to call the Fire Department," said Sarge, pounding over the lawn. "I looked out, saw the flames and you in the loft window. I didn't stop to call." Suddenly, however, we could hear them. The fire whistle. The blowing horns. The firefighters were on their way. Someone else must have seen the flames and given the alarm.

"Maybe Beryl," said Sarge, running for the hose. "Civil Defense and all. Keeps her alert."

"It won't reach, Sarge." I ran after him, looking back at the fire. The blaze in the pile of lumber was shooting up the barn to the corner of the roof.

"I know. But I'm going to wet down this side of the house, in case. Run inside and close the windows. Then you'd better call your mother."

"Oh, she's going to be awfully mad!"

"And she's going to be awfully *glad*—that you're all right. Now get going. And take this dog. Keep him in the house, so the trucks won't run over him." Sarge had the hose unrolled and turned on, wetting the lawn and the foundation, waiting for me to slam the windows down. So I rushed inside, pulling a panting Ollie after me. I could see Beryl and Nate on their back lawn. It looked as if Beryl were jumping up and down in one place, like a jack in the box. Even in the midst of disaster, they wouldn't run over to help because Sarge was here.

On the first floor, every window was open, it had been so hot that day. I started on the barn side, then closed all the remaining first floor windows. It took me a few minutes. With dread in my soul, I rang the operator. Surely I would be blamed for this disaster. I didn't know why, it wasn't my fault, but I knew that somehow it would be labeled my fault. Because that's the way life was. Any little thing you did unsuspectingly, or maybe even with good intentions, could turn out to be a sin or a crime or at the very least, terribly stupid and any fool would have known better. I rang again and again. No answer. But there was always an answer at the phone office.

I went out and told Sarge. "She's on her way, then," he said. "She knows already. You'd better check on Romeo. He took quite a fall back there."

Feeling something in my pocket squirm, I reached in and pulled out the turtle. "Look," I said. "Merlin's okay!"

Romeo had survived our escape, too. Just a little scratch on his back thumper. I left the cage on the back porch, on the side away from the barn, and dropped Merlin in the milk box beside the kitchen door. Inside, I could hear Ollie whining and jumping at the door. "You have to stay out of harm's way," I soothed him through the door. "Good boy! Brave boy!"

Back in the yard, I looked up and saw that the roof would be catching soon. Sparks were flying into the pines. I ran down the porch steps and waited with Sarge for the firemen and all the cars to stream into the driveway. And Mother.

In that long few moments—for they were on Pond Street already, honking and blaring, my mother with Dom Ferro in the police car, the telephone office abandoned—with the fire eating away at our barn, I tried to visualize that shadowy figure. Who had I seen fading into the trees?

Someone who wouldn't answer my call for help.

Chapter 18

In which Mother takes charge, I am interviewed by the chiefs, and Aunt Bette comes to a reluctant decision.

It wasn't until my mother jumped out of Whitford's only police car, closely followed by Chief Ferro, that I began to cry, half in terror at the danger I had passed and half in defense against being found guilty of—*what?* Especially since she rushed at me, arms flung wide, screaming in a voice that went straight through me like a spear of ice, "I knew it! I knew it!"

With a quick, fierce hug, she checked me over as if looking for missing parts. Immediately after, she went to the more pressing business of directing the fumbling efforts of the volunteer firemen to control the blaze. Watching how she took command, I realized two things: that she was indeed marshalling everyone into more effective action and that Fire Chief Gil Ott's face was red to the point of apoplexy, and not with exertion.

"What a general she would have made," Sarge said as we passed each other in the acrid, firelit night, carrying out our orders, he to hose down the house again and I to make the inevitable huge pot of coffee. Coming from anyone else, that would have been a sarcastic remark, but Sarge's tone was admiring.

Nevertheless, Mother lost the battle for the grand old barn, defeated by a sudden stirring from the west, the breeze we had longed for in the stifling afternoon. The smoking, steaming hulk that remained by night's end was beyond repair. But the house was safe—sooty and sour, but safe.

Because the fire had occurred past midnight, the usual overflowing crowd of enraptured onlookers in cars and trucks was absent. Just the volunteer firefighters, the police chief, and our immediate neighbors on Silver Sand Pond, in ill-sorted, hastily donned outfits, were in attendance. Among them, I saw Alex Carver, in a seersucker robe, being especially solicitous of Mother, who being busy directing operations, brushed him aside for once. Beryl and Nate Whitcomb still hung back in the shadows of their house, watching the action. And Gordon Fisher was among the sooty volunteers.

Jason Fisher, often the chief suspect when a fire of unknown origin erupted, was "home, tucked up in bed" his brother Gordon said when Gill Ott asked the question. He swung around the heavy fire hose so furiously that the fire chief had to jump back to avoid being struck. It seemed that no one was more enraged at the destruction than Gordon, not even we Byrds, helplessly watching our own barn being consumed.

I was sleeping with my head on the kitchen table and one hand on Ollie's collar in the early morning hours when Dom Ferro and Gil Ott, looking like a disheveled Mutt and Jeff, finally tramped in to question me. I let go of the dog, who limped away tiredly and disappeared into the hallway. I hoped he would find his way upstairs to my room before my mother spied his departure. If there was one thing to be Pollyanna-glad over in this whole mess, it was that Ollie could no longer be exiled to the barn when Aunt Bette wasn't around to protect him. But what about Romeo and Merlin?

The roly-poly police chief's permanent "five o'clock shadow" was now the start of a full beard. His chins shook and his voice was gruff, but his button eyes were kind, as they always were when he questioned youngsters. "Now, Amelia," he said, patting my hand. "I want you to tell me exactly what happened right from the beginning, starting with why you were sleeping in the barn."

So I told them about Mother being at the telephone office and Sarge at the Poor Farm and Aunt Bette in Boston and Ollie relegated to the barn all alone.

Chief Ferro said something about the sad plight of latch-key children. Mother shot him a look that would have felled a horse, but it seemed just to bounce off his round bulk. I went on to explain about the thump that had roused Ollie and how the door had been inexplicably wedged back into the frame.

"Impossible," Sarge said emphatically. "I had to work hard as the devil just to stand it aslant for passage in and out. I was going to ask you men at the firehouse to give me a hand getting it onto the new hinges. There's no way that door could have shut by itself. It must have been pushed into place, and by someone with plenty of muscle. Mellie couldn't have budged it. She had to run up to the loft to escape. Mellie's no fool, you know." He gave my shoulder a reassuring squeeze.

"That raises several disturbing questions," Chief Ferro said solemnly, tapping a chewed pencil on the wrinkled brown notebook he laid on the kitchen table.

"Indeed it does," Sarge agreed. "But let's allow Amelia to finish her story first."

Gill Ott was leaning his tall, thin frame against the wall by the back door. With his stooped shoulders and concave chest, his whole body looked like a question mark. When he spoke, his words hissed out between teeth clamped on a pipe. "You must tell us the absolute truth here, Amelia. It's very important. Did you light a match in the barn for any reason, like, say, to sneak a little cigarette while the coast was clear?"

I looked him straight in the eye, unblinking. "No, Sir, Chief Ott," I said. "I promised my mother that I would never smoke." Besides, I was absolutely certain I'd put the cover on that cold cream jar. What if they poked around in the rubble and found it? I'd have to find it first.

"Look here," Mother interrupted, pounding a fist on the kitchen drainboard. "Are you out of your mind, Gil? No daughter of mine skulks around lighting fires. As you well know, you've had a fire bug running loose in Whitford for months. Furthermore, you think you know who he is. I'm not so sure you're right. I rather think there's more than one person involved. Be that as it may, isn't it about time you take *some* action before the whole town is burned down around our ears? Instead of wasting your time questioning innocent little girls!"

It wasn't often Mother defended me. It gave me a warm, safe feeling. Her eyes blazing straight at him, the fire chief decided not to pursue that line of questioning any further.

"The suspect was home in bed, and Gordon says his parents will back him up. Now you go on, Amelia," Dom Ferro said.

I told them about the lights going out, about finding the weak flashlight in the dark and taking Romeo and Ollie up to the loft. "But when I looked out the loft window, the ladder was on the ground."

"That ladder *was* standing up when I got home, so someone must have taken it down later," Sarge said. "I looked over first thing, because I could hear the radio playing. I just figured Amelia was having a slumber party or something. I wish now I'd checked. She's such a sensible young lady, I believed everything was all right."

"She shouldn't have been out there at that hour for any reason, and why you didn't make her come in, I'll never know, " Mother said, looking like a furious queen. *Uh oh,* I thought. *Sarge and I are both going to get it. Off with our heads!*

"If it weren't for Sarge," I said quickly, "I'd have had to jump. Probably would have broken my ankle. Or my leg. Or both."

"Let's go back to the window for a minute," Dom Ferro said. "Did you see anything else when you looked out and discovered the ladder was on the ground?"

"Well, there was a kind of shadow in the trees. It moved, so I thought it was some neighbor, and I yelled for help."

"Ah ha!" Gill Ott exclaimed. "Now we're getting somewhere. Did you see who it was? Are you sure it wasn't Jason?"

"I didn't see much, but it wasn't Jason."

"If you couldn't make him out, how can you say that?" Gill Ott banged his pipe in the kitchen wastebasket.

"Mind you don't start a fire in my kitchen," Mother said to him sharply.

"Because the way the shadow moved was too slender and graceful to be Jason."

"Tall?" asked Dom Ferro, writing something in his notebook.

"No, not tall, but not heavy and clumsy like Jason either. I know it wasn't Jason. I'm pretty sure it wasn't, anyway." Now that I was thoroughly awake and the center of attention, I was almost beginning to enjoy myself. "Of course," I added, "just because I saw a shadow that might have been a person doesn't mean that person lit the fire. I mean, it doesn't necessarily follow."

Sarge chuckled, and Gill Ott hissed through a freshly filled pipe, "If you called for help, and the person in the woods didn't answer, dollars to doughnuts it was the local firebug."

"Maybe whoever it was didn't hear me," I said.

Then Mother said something that chilled me and instantly took all the pleasure out of being in the limelight. "Why would anyone push that door shut, cut the lights, and torch the barn, knowing my daughter was in there? If Sarge could hear the radio, it must have been playing full blast. What kind of degenerate would do such a thing? I just can't believe this of anyone we know, someone here in town. It simply doesn't seem possible."

"He may even have deliberately kicked that ladder away from the window," Sarge added. "Now Jason would never have done that kind of thing, But I'd like to get my hands on the bastard who did."

"Something about this doesn't make sense, that's for sure," said the police chief, studying his notes as if they were a column of figures that refused to add up. "This fire seems different than all the rest. The others were summer cottages or sheds. No one was threatened. Even Sarge's place was empty when it got torched, but he got home in the nick of time, gave the alarm, so we were able to save a few things for him. And you're right about the lights. Gil and I checked the electrical connection first off, thinking a worn-out wire might have sparked the blaze, but we found it had been cleanly severed." He swung his round figure around on the chair toward Gil Ott. "What are you seeing in all this?"

"I'm seeing just what I've been seeing all along. A pyromaniac you're letting run loose."

Dom Ferro sighed in a perplexed fashion. Everyone fell silent, and the interview petered out to general exhaustion.

"I'd say all he had to do was use an ordinary match. Didn't take much with that stack of brush and lumber next to the barn. Everything's dry as a bone,"

Gill Ott said, lighting his pipe again. "A miracle that the woods didn't go up with the barn, I'd say. Lucky that breeze came from the west, blew the sparks right over the pond."

"I lost my radio," I said. "My dad's woodworking tools are all burned up. Ollie's new bed. I don't think that's so lucky." Even Pollyanna had her off days.

"There's no need to be a smart alec," Mother said and went to the sink where she stood with her back to us, facing the window, her shoulders slumped with fatigue. Sarge went over and took the cups out of her hands.

"Amelia and I will do these, Catherine," he said, giving me an imperative wave to the sink behind her back. "Sure that's an ugly mess you're looking at, but it can be cleaned up, just like we cleaned up Beryl's yard. You'd never even know there was a cottage there once, now would you?"

"It's the stinking waste of it," my mother whispered in a bitter tone. "Do you know how long it takes to grow a rhododendron that size? And what was he after? Kicks?"

What was he after? That's what I wondered about, too, in the silence of my own room as I stretched out on the sheets. Ollie was curled up on the cushioned bedroom chair between two stuffed animals that Skip had won at the Brockton Fair, a giraffe and a bear. The cool morning air drifted over us from the open window, bringing with it the sharp odor of the night's disaster. When I woke just before noon, a weird idea surfaced, full of menace, a dream monster.

What if the mystery went back a long way, to Mr. Snow's accident that January night? What if Alex Carver hadn't come along afterward but was out on the ice with him? What if Miss Pratt had remarked to Mr. Carver and the new teachers, over lemonade and cookies, that Amelia Byrd was in the library asking fool questions about Alex's mother?

Maybe Alex Carver thought, meddlesome Amelia is the only other person who's knows about the letter, and now she's found out who wrote it. Amelia, the snoop, the only one who might raise questions about the accident.

Maybe Mr. Carver, walking home to his rented cottage past our place last night, had known somehow that I was in the barn. Heard the radio? Or had he dropped into our kitchen and seen the note I left on the kitchen table?

I got up and looked around for Ollie, but he was gone. Dogs don't loll about till noon, no matter what went on the night before. Pulling on blue shorts and an old Camp Pocahontas shirt with a tiny campfire embroidered on the pocket, I tried to wash away all these disturbing notions by splashing my face with cold water until my skin burned.

Outside, it was a beautiful summer day, full of sun sparkle and the glad cries of swimmers. Maybe I *did* read too many mystery stories. Surely no one could smile at me as warmly as Mr. Carver did and still have malice in his soul, like a worm at the core of a ripe, red apple. Surely wicked thoughts should show in his eyes. I'd seen them shining malevolently in so many movie villains. I wished I were like The Shadow and could see the evil that "lurks in the hearts of men" more clearly. I ran downstairs to get Ollie, finding him where I feared I would.

"Get this dog out from under my feet," said Mother crossly, by way of greeting. "I just don't know why Bette keeps him. Take him outside, for heaven's sake. Minna's waiting for you on the porch. But don't you forget that you're going to be needed to help today. Here, take these sandwiches with you. There's a pitcher of iced tea on the porch table."

Minna was full of sympathy, smiles, hugs, and gossip. The Fishers swore that Jason had been home all evening. Gordon had been threatening to punch Dom Ferro in the mouth as his last civilian act. People had thought Mr. Carver would take Gordy's place as town moderator, but now Mr. Carver had been called up, too. One of the new teachers, just out of school herself, would have to take over his classes. Lively Ames had called on the Cronins wearing his church clothes, and had taken Bunny Cronin to the movies. Dr. Tyrell was moving to Falmouth and no one knew what we'd do for a doctor in Whitford. There'd been some sort of ugly scene, and Inez was staying in Whitford.

These great gossipy news items washed over me in a blur, except for one— *Mr. Carver had been called up.* What a relief!

Perhaps now I'd be able to forget about that old letter and everything that happened afterwards, or that I imagined had happened. We devoured the sandwiches, which were ham salad with pickle. Ollie tasted his and looked at me with reproach.

"If you don't like the pickle, don't eat it," I said to him.

"I've got my suit on underneath," Minna said. "Will your mother let us go for a swim?"

I asked her. She was on the phone, so she covered the mouthpiece before hissing, "Wait half an hour before you dare to go in the water. Take the darned dog with you, and be back here by two or I'll kill you." Then she continued in a chatty tone to the operator. "Emily! I want you to get me the Statler Hotel in Boston, Miss Bette Cabot's room. Yes, of course, I'm calling to tell her what happened. Well, that's very nice of Beryl and Nate. Tell them I'll call if there's anything. Now would you please make that connection for me?"

Aunt Bette returned on Friday in a new pink linen outfit and a nervous frame of mind. We were all milling about in the yard, trying to cope with the devastation, when she sprang lightly out of the Olds.

"My God, what a mess you're in here," she said and spun around in a circle. "Bonwit Teller. What do you think? Mr. Fenner took me to lunch at the Ritz. I thought I looked as good as anyone. Oh, what a terrible, terrible week I've had!" All the time, Ollie was greeting her with effusive running and barking, and my aunt was hugging and kissing us all. She smelled of lily-of-the-valley cologne. "Mind the stockings, Ollie. I see they've been fattening you up. Now, Catherine, tell me everything! Have they arrested that creep Jason yet? I knew immediately that it was he. Amelia, are you going to adore what I bought you! Now who saved whom? Ollie saved you or you Ollie? Your mother told me the whole story on the phone. I nearly screamed when I heard, and then what would the bellboy have thought? I'm going right home and put on my slacks so that I can give you a hand cleaning up. But first, after I hear all about this"—she gestured with pink-polished fingertips toward the black skeleton of the barn—"I have to tell you my own news. And that wretched, greedy bishop calls himself a Christian!"

It was obvious that we weren't going to get any more accomplished in the yard right then, so Mother trudged indoors in her rubber boots to make us lunch. She'd been up before any of us that morning, and there were two irresistible blueberry pies, oozing purple juice and a delectable aroma, on the countertop.

"Take your dirty finger out of the pie, Amelia!" Mother ordered briskly. "Now go wash all that soot off your hands so you can set the table. Well, Bette, this isn't the Ritz, but I bet you'll eat better here. All doilies and parsley sprigs, wasn't it?"

"I'm really not very hungry, it's so hot today." Aunt Bette paused to light a Parliament with a slim silver lighter I'd never seen before. She held out her hands to me. "Precious Pink. Sort of discreet and sophisticated, isn't it?"

After I'd admired the new nail polish, I washed my hands at the kitchen sink so I wouldn't miss anything, and set the dishes around the table, putting a giant clam shell ashtray at my aunt's place.

"I've had such a hard time getting cigarettes, I can't tell you what I've been through, you wouldn't believe it. Do you know, I went to every cigarette stand and drug store in the heart of Boston, and the most I could get was a pack here and a pack there. Oh, Catherine, I think I'm going to have to agree to a settlement, you know. Otherwise, the whole thing could drag on for years, Mr. Fenner says, with lawyers' fees just eating away at that fortune. That so-called man of God is going to bring suit against the estate claiming undue influence or some such nonsense. As if anyone could have influenced Win out of his money. Heaven knows Eunice tried for years. So depressing! I don't want to wait forever. Mr. Fenner's advice is to settle promptly and move the estate through probate as swiftly as possible."

"Even though he won't make as much out of it that way? Generous of him. Are you sure there isn't a little collusion going on there?" Mother chopped viciously at onion and bell pepper and threw the mince into sizzling bacon fat in her largest black iron skillet. She began to beat the dickens out of a dozen eggs with a fork.

"Win always relied on him. Wouldn't have anyone but a Harvard man, he said. I have to trust someone, you know."

"Do you think a little glass of sherry would pick up your appetite? Amelia, go tell Sarge this omelet I'm making won't keep, he should get himself in here now. He's just wearing himself out trying to get all that cleared up in a day. And while you're at it, run out into the garden and get me some parsley."

"It's too hot for sherry. Now, about that jewelry, Catherine." My aunt dropped her voice to a whisper. I lingered, one foot out the screen door. "That's something else again. It's worth every penny I hoped for, *and more*. And you know what? I bought these. They're only twenty-twos, but they'd stop an intruder, for sure." She took a small package out of her handbag. "Since those dear little revolvers are real, I'll feel more protected over there at Snow's all alone. I'm going to learn how to load and shoot them, too. I bet Dom will give me lessons."

"Amelia, if you let one dirty fly into my kitchen..."

I let the door slam and ran.

Chapter 19

In which Miss Cronin gets engaged, Aunt Bette receives an upsetting letter, and Mr. Carter is given a farewell party.

After lunch, I rode back with Aunt Bette and Ollie to Snow's to help her unpack her bundles and see what she'd bought me at Bonwit Teller that might dazzle Daisy Eliot. It was a pale green cashmere sweater that she assured me would bring out the color of my eyes, and a darker green plaid skirt. They were awfully plain, but I supposed they were classy.

"These weren't cheap, so don't slop anything on them," she said, holding the sweater under my chin and studying the effect. "If you'd give up coke and chocolate, your complexion would be a lot better, you know."

I peered into her vanity mirror. What I saw was rather hopeless, I had to admit. But I didn't think my skin was all that bad compared to some of my classmates.

"Try that lipstick, the Coral Pink one that's about half gone, not the new tube," said my aunt. "There, that's an improvement. You can have that, if you like, but don't tell your mother. Now, how about helping me with a quick dusting around the downstairs—that is, if you think you can do it without breaking anything. That baby-faced Carver is liable to show up here later, and I do want things to look nice."

The shock to my system was like a bucket of ice cubes. "What's *he* coming here for?"

"Because in a weak moment, I said he could call on me when I got home, if it's any of business of yours. Don't you approve of your old maid aunt entertaining gentlemen callers?"

"Oh, Aunt Bette, you're not an old maid. You're young and beautiful. It's just that you always said how boring and self-centered Mr. Carver is and everything. I bet there are a lot of handsome and interesting men who would like to marry you, if they could only meet you."

She didn't seem displeased "Tell your mother I'm not an old maid. *She* thinks I should grab the first thing in trousers that walks in my door. But don't worry, Amelia. I wouldn't marry unctuous Alex if he were the last man on earth."

"You won't change your mind, will you? I mean, like Elizabeth in *Pride and Prejudice* kept saying how much she disliked Darcy, and then in the end she got engaged to him."

"I'm happy to hear that you've been reading something worthwhile this summer." She gazed out the open bedroom window, looking a million miles away while taking a shred of tobacco off her tongue with her pointed pink fingernails. Ollie, who was snoozing on her bed, turned over rapturously and almost rolled on the floor. He clawed his way back over the bedspread, pulling out threads, but my aunt didn't even seem to notice.

"But you won't, will you?" I persisted.

"Won't what?" she asked vaguely.

"Won't change your mind about Mr. Carver."

"Well...not if you're perfectly sure there's a tall, dark, handsome stranger right around the corner." She grinned impishly and hugged Ollie. "Now are you going to get busy and give me a hand, Miss Worrywart?"

She started downstairs, trailing her hand lovingly on the shining mahogany banister, with Ollie bounding beside her, but I stepped back into her room for a minute to check out the drawer in her bedside table, where sometimes she kept an open pack of cigarettes. I meant to tuck a couple in my pocket for wages. But there weren't any Parliaments there. What I found instead was the miniature mother-of-pearl revolver with the gold handle. Beside it was a small cardboard box of bullets. Quickly I shut the drawer. The last thing I wanted to discover was any more dangerous secrets. Still, as I ran downstairs, I couldn't help wondering what had happened to the other ladylike revolver, the one with a silver handle, so small it could easily be concealed in a beaded evening handbag.

When I wanted to be, and my spooks weren't deviling me, I was an expert duster, lifting objects carefully, rather than swiping around them and leaving a ring of dust. And I had the knack of putting things back exactly as they had been placed. That afternoon was one of my good days, unlike the infamous day when I'd stared absently at the niche in the stairwell and the blue and white vase that stood there had rocked back and forth before my mother's horrified gaze. My diminutive aunt had flown up the stairs as if shot from a cannon, thrown her arms around the Canton export china, and ordered me out of the house. But on this day I was praised and called "Honey" and given two quarters, *a fortune,* enough for bus fare to Kates Hill and the movies. I tucked them into my shirt pocket and enjoyed their happy jingle all the way home.

During the last week of summer vacation, I studied a book on firearms while I sat between the stacks at the library, because I didn't dare ask Miss Pratt to sign it out for me. I was just rather curious to know how a person went about putting the bullets into a revolver. Sighting and firing were easy enough, I supposed, since I'd finally become a pretty good shot with Skip's BB gun in the good old days of shooting cans off a stump.

I'd just had a letter from Skip, whom I hadn't heard from in several weeks, although I'd written him faithfully every Sunday. This letter, dated July 25, was different from the other three I'd received. He'd been wounded, he wrote, but nothing to worry about, just his left leg. It was healing okay, but he "might never play the piano again, ha ha!" They'd been putting down pontoons when the LST he was on got hit below the tank deck, exploding the ammunition stored there. He'd been lucky when another LST, with a section of pontoon still attached, had been able to swing around against the stern of the burning ship and save him and the other men trapped on the fantail. They'd taken him to Africa, to a real hospital where a pair of pretty nurses waited on him hand and foot. He expected to be "back in action" in a couple of weeks. For the first time, he added a line to say that he was glad to be getting my letters, and he liked hearing the home news from me because I "told it straight, without the dirt." Sometimes he got letters in a bunch, he wrote, but he always read them in order of postmark date.

I tried to remember what I'd been doing when Skip got hit. So many unreal things had happened this year, and here was another. It was real enough to Skip, though. I wondered if it hurt much, and I hoped they gave him really strong drugs for the pain, the kind that Dr. Tyrell would never prescribe as he seemed to have some kind of prejudice against medicines. And I wondered if Skip wanted his mother to know. To tell my mother would be the same as telling his, I thought, and that was the best way to pass on the news without getting into trouble with Skip. Maybe Cora would write to Skip, and Skip would forgive her for her fling with Dr. Tyrell and write back.

After Dr. Tyrell moved to the Cape, somehow Whitford had been fortunate enough to get Dr. Douglas Woodward. I loved Woody from the first. Although he treated some people like animals (so they complained), he treated animals like people and willingly provided free medical consultation for the wounded waifs I sometimes rescued. Fortunately, he was quite gentle with Aunt Bette, too, and seemed to understand her need for pills and potions.

"With doctors as scarce as hen's teeth, too," said Aunt Bette, visibly relieved to have medical attention again—little white pills for her nerves, a nasty viscous stuff for her insomnia, and some huge brown iron pills for her anemia. "Horse pills" she called the latter, "filled with iron filings, no doubt. I suppose we should be thankful that Doug's practically blind and 4-F. Those glasses he wears look like coke-bottle bottoms. I just hope he never has to sew any of us up. Someone would have to thread the needle for him and point him in the right direction. You just keep that in mind, little one, and don't go jumping out of any more barn windows." She loved to call me "little one" now that I was inches taller than she and felt like a clumsy giant beside her.

There was no more barn to jump out of, not even the black skeleton of it, with Sarge out here every day clearing up the debris. Mother joined him whenever she wasn't on duty at the telephone office. She wore her rubber boots, an old blue work shirt and overalls that had belonged to my dad, and a scarf around her head like Mrs. Korhonen. When she did have to take her shift at the telephone board, she left a clear set of instructions on just how Sarge was to proceed, but once the coast was clear, he pretty much did things his own way.

Wonder of wonders, Sarge talked Mother into letting him build a new shed "to store the tools and the gardening things and, who knows, maybe a car some-day." At first she said no, with the high cost of lumber, and it wasn't really a necessity. There was always the cellar for storage. She didn't know how much longer she'd be getting a pay envelope from the telephone company. Rosemary was back in town and nearly recovered, working a few hours during the day, and as soon as she was ready, the night operator's job would, of course, go back to her.

But Sarge said Nate owed him something for the land where the cottage had stood. It was Sarge's land, and he was willing to just let it go back to Beryl if they could make some reasonable trade. He knew there was no way to broach it to Beryl without her getting hysterical, but he'd just have a private talk with Nate over at the lumber yard.

"Well, maybe so," said Mother doubtfully.

"You could draw up plans showing just the way you'd like it to be built," Sarge said.

"As a matter of fact, I do know just how a proper shed ought to be laid out," Mother agreed. "There should be shelves for pots and garden tools all along one side, a recess for the mower, hooks for rakes and shovels on the other wall, and a good sturdy workbench in back."

"Why don't we get some paper and make a sketch of your ideas," Sarge said. I was pleased to watch Mother become enthusiastic about this project. I'd finally released Romeo into the woods, with many a warning to find himself some proper friends, but once winter set in, I would be glad to have a warm roof over the heads of any needy animals I might adopt.

"Do you think that Mr. Carver likes Aunt Bette?" I finally ventured to ask my mother. "I mean, likes her for a girlfriend even though she's much older than he is?"

I was standing on a chair while my mother pinned up the hem of the blue wool jumper she'd made me for school. It was the kind of outfit Mother described as "smart" that I thought made me look like a sixth grader just when I was entering the rarefied ranks of the high schoolers. Her dressmaking, stitched up on our own pedal Singer sewing machine, always looked oddly bunchy around the zippers and pleats. The buttons she sewed on by hand were meant to last for all eternity; I can't remember one of them ever falling off, or a seam she had triple-stitched ever loosening its death grip. Although not on very intimate terms with God, I thanked Him silently that I had the green cashmere sweater and matching plaid skirt Aunt Bette had given me to wear on the first day. And the gold (so I thought) locket she'd given me out of her safe deposit box loot.

"I can't see that it's any of your business," Mother said through a mouthful of straight pins.

"You don't think they'd get married or anything?" I persisted, although I knew I was treading dangerously.

"Nothing would make me happier than to see your aunt settled at last," she muttered, sticking in what I imagined must be the thousandth pin. "There, I think that does it. Get down now and take off that jumper. I can't think of a finer man. But I must say I don't believe it's in the cards. So you'd better not count on having Alex as an uncle. Too bad! And don't you go saying a word to either of them. Who knows what miracle might happen if nobody makes them skittish."

I'd as soon have Jack the Ripper for an uncle, I thought, and wisely did not say so as I gingerly removed the jumper, which by now was as prickly as a porcupine pelt.

"Minna told me Mr. Carver has been called up. One of the new teachers is going to take his classes. So he'll be leaving soon, won't he?"

She folded the jumper, smoothing it carefully, and sighed. "I'm afraid so. What a shame! Every damn farmer gets deferred now because of so-called essential employment. Even tobacco farmers, for God's sake! You'd think they'd have sense enough to value teachers over farmers, now wouldn't you!"

"Miss Cronin told me that nothing except munitions is more important than our food crop. *The Army travels on its stomach*, she said. *America is the breadbasket of the world*."

"Miss Cronin is delighted that Lively Ames has been deferred on account of that miserable truck farm of his. Well, I can't blame her, Poor thing can't have had too many chances. This jumper came out rather well, if I do say so myself. I think I'll finish the hem tonight so that you can wear it this week. Wait until you see how smart you're going to look in it!"

At Whitford High that first week, I saw more of Daisy and Jay Eliot than I'd seen all through August while they'd been hobnobbing with friends in Plymouth. Being trapped in school made us buddies again, as close as captives in the clutches of the enemy. Despite my being a lowly freshman, Daisy even sat with me in the cafeteria. Maybe Jay would have liked to join us if having lunch with girls wouldn't have made him the butt of stupid jokes. I couldn't understand why clever, amusing, talented Jay always looked like a pale hanger-on at the end of a boys' table, his chair pushed back as if he were getting ready to run if a fight broke out.

After school, too, the three of us hung around together, smirking over local scandals, like the rumor that Rosemary's soldier husband, home on furlough, had walked out on her after a big noisy fight. We were confidantes who shared everything we managed to find out simply by being invisible listeners among the adults, never drawing attention to ourselves when an interesting tidbit was being passed around. And the Eliots, of course, could always listen at that informative heating grate.

One afternoon, when local gossip paled, after making them swear an oath to eternal secrecy, I foolishly confided in them my suspicions about Mr. Carver. The fears I'd held inside so long were beginning to hurt my head and stomach. I needed comfort, sympathy, and someone to believe I wasn't crazy. So while we sat on the cement steps of the school waiting for the bus (ours was the second trip on the big old yellow clunker that broke down continually in the absence of new parts for proper repair) I related the whole story to Daisy and Jay as I imagined it to have happened.

"Mellie, are you making up another fairy story?" demanded Jay. "Do you really believe all that stuff about Mr. Carver? I mean, do you honestly think he goes around bashing old men and burning barns?"

Daisy unwrapped a Hershey bar, divided it into thirds, and handed it around. "That's interesting about his mother," she said dreamily, nibbling her chocolate in tiny bites. "Are you sure it was she who wrote that drippy love letter? But it can't really matter now. After all, that was ages and ages ago. And everyone knows it's Jason Fisher who's been setting those fires. That's what Grandma says."

"If anyone has a reason to do away with old man Snow, it was your Aunt Bette," Jay suggested. "The heiress."

"But Aunt Bette wasn't out on the ice that night. Mr. Carver was right there with Mr. Snow when he drowned. Oh, Mr. Carver *said* he just happened to be walking along the shore and saw Mr. Snow struggling in the water. But what if he'd purposely gone along with Mr. Snow to check those ice traps, and then misled his victim into walking back across the thin ice?"

"Well, if we're playing 'what if,' your aunt could have slipped old Snow a Mickey Finn cocoa or something like that before he went out," Jay said. He picked up his assignment notebook, flipped to a blank page, and began to draw a deadly looking bottle with skull and crossbones on the label. "Not that I think she did or anything, Amelia, so there's no need to get all red in the face. But if you're intending to go around telling stories about Mr. Carver..."

"I am not either! You're the only ones I've told. How come you believed those ugly stories about Rosemary and her husband, and you don't believe me?"

Would other people get the same dumb ideas that Jay and Daisy did? Could they take away Aunt Bette's inheritance?

"People say your Aunt Bette was Mr. Snow's mistress. I bet you know all about it, too," Daisy said with a sly dig in my ribs. "That's why she got all his money and that grand house."

I could feel my flushed cheeks getting even hotter. "Don't be a jerk, Daisy. Mr. Snow was twice as old as my aunt, sort of like an adopted father." But even while I thought the idea incredible, there was a small click in my brain as if the last piece of a puzzle were being snapped into place. Suddenly I hated these two, their knowing smirks and clever ideas, doubly despised. I stalked off to where other students were waiting, clustered around the oak tree at the edge of the driveway. When I glanced back, Daisy and Jay were whispering to each other in a huddle of two—laughing at me, I thought.

For a few days after that conversation, I avoided the Eliot twins' company, but they hardly seemed to care. Their own companionship was intense and satisfying, and they always had a best friend in one another. But not wanting to provoke them into any more weird notions about my family, I waved in my usual fashion if we passed in the halls while changing classes. Meanwhile, I hung around with Minna. Since it was still warm enough that September, I persuaded her that it would be fun to eat lunch outdoors, sidestepping having to choose a table in the cafeteria.

With after-school time on my hands, I wrote more often to Skip, who reported that my letters were arriving, although not as regularly as I mailed them. He asked me how Rosemary was doing, and added that she hadn't answered his letter, but he had received some goofy letters from Daisy with sketches by Jay. "I can hop around pretty good now," he told me, "and I'll be glad as hell to get back in action now that things are heating up. Getting dull here. No all-night poker games. I even wrote to Ma."

"I'm glad Skip wrote to his mother." I said to Minna, who was always a sympathetic listener. "I can't imagine not writing home if I was away, no matter what anyone in my family did that wasn't proper. Isn't it lucky that Skip was still in the hospital and not in a landing craft when the invasion of Italy began!"

"I could never go against my family either," Minna said. "I get so mad at my father sometimes, though. He thinks we all should behave as if we were still back in the old country. I don't know what he'd do if I went with a boy that wasn't Finnish. Lock me in my room, maybe. I wish I could write to the servicemen like other girls, but I'd be in big trouble if my father found out."

"You could give my address," I offered.

She wrinkled her brow and gazed off into the woods behind the school. When Minna thought things over, you could almost see the machinery working. "I guess not," she said finally. "If my father went up to the post office, Mrs. Gilbert would probably say something about it, and my lies would make him even madder at me."

"It wouldn't be *real* lying. It's just not telling the whole truth. He wouldn't beat you, would he?"

"No, but he would come close, shouting in my face. The last time it was because I put on eye shadow and perfume. 'Tabu' it's called, and I think it's heavenly. But he threw it all out, all my cosmetics it took me ages to save up for." She sighed, but her expression was as placid as ever. I must have looked horrified because she added, "It was only a push up the stairs. Does your mother beat you when you make her real angry?"

"Slaps me, unless I duck in time. I don't stay around for more. I run off till she cools down. But my dad never hit me or raised his voice, not once."

"That must have been so nice." Minna sighed again. I thought of Mr. Korhonen yelling as he grabbed up all Minna's make-up. And I thought of my father, with his clever hands creating such wonderful animals out of shapeless wood, his gentle hands dissolving into bone under the earth. I wished he were here now. He'd have believed my suspicions about Mr. Carver. And he'd have known what to do.

I wanted to tell Minna about Mr. Carver, but after the way the twins had turned the story around to accuse Aunt Bette of horrid things, I didn't dare. Now I thought that any question about Mr. Snow's accident might only raise ugly ideas in people's minds about Aunt Bette rather than pointing a finger at Mr. Carver. All I'd had for proof was the letter, and that was out of my hands, probably torn into a million pieces or burned. No one would believe me, not even Minna. Everyone thought Mr. Carver was the greatest thing since sliced bread.

Of course, if he killed me to shut me up, and they caught him red-handed, holding the knife over my poor bloody body, they'd believe me then. Everyone would come to my funeral and cry. Reverend Pinch would tell everyone what a good, honest girl I'd been, that folks should have listened to me when I told them about Mr. Carver. Mother and Aunt Bette, draped in mourning and black veils, would sit in the front pew and sob. Ollie would wear a black bow. Daisy and Jay Eliot would weep buckets.

"Oh goodness, Amelia, did I make you cry?" asked Minna. "You shouldn't feel so bad for me. Here, do you want to use this napkin?"

"I am not crying," I said, grabbing the napkin and wiping my eyes. "It's only the ragweed. It always makes my eyes water."

That fall Miss Cronin got engaged to Lively Ames. Her students, who always seized on any opportunity to be unruly, saw in this romance a perfect opportunity for some merciless fun. I was part of her freshman biology, first class on Tuesdays and Thursdays, which routinely began with her erasing whatever caricatures had been drawn on the blackboard by an enterprising cartoonist. I remember one particularly crude drawing in which she was pulling a plow while Lively cracked the whip. Miss Cronin was unfailingly good humored about these barbs, although they often made her blush. She even laughed about some of them while we were taking the school bus together, since she was saving her gas allotment for weekend trips to Kates Hill.

On one of our rides home, I heard the welcome news that the teaching staff was having a party for Mr. Carver on that Friday, the last in September, because he was leaving the following day for Fort Devens. From Minna I heard that Gordon Fisher was also headed for Fort Devens but traveling separately. Our ex-town moderator was still angry about the way the engagement with his sister Penny had been broken off when, as he put it, Alex Carver had seen "a mile-high pie in the sky." I guessed that meant an alliance with my Aunt Bette. What a hateful thought!

When Aunt Bette was at our house (a frequent occurrence at suppertime), there would be more smart remarks about Miss Cronin and Lively and their future at the Poor Farm. Although she was soon to be rich, my volatile aunt was often in bad spirits over little things. When she no longer had a hoard of Parliaments and was reduced to smoking despised brands like Fleetwoods or Orbits, she was especially sarcastic about love and marriage. This was a good sign, I thought. Mr. Carver had taken to calling on my aunt regularly, much to my mother's delight, so I relished every nasty thing Aunt Bette said about wedded bliss.

"I certainly envy you," she said to Miss Cronin over a Friday supper of pan-fried perch and corn on the cob. Actually, Aunt Bette was having corn *off* the cob. Just for her my mother cut off the kernels and served them in a little sauce dish with a pat of butter because that's the only way she would eat corn. "You'll be like a queen among those poor demented creatures at the Farm."

"More coleslaw, Bunny?" asked Sarge, trying as usual to deflect Aunt Bette's barbs.

Miss Cronin shook her head and smiled cheerfully, putting a modest dab of apple butter on a split baking powder biscuit. "It's true that I've been thinking of ways to brighten up the place. I don't mean that there's anything wrong with the Farm. Lively and Merry are doing an admirable job of taking care of their little brood. And it's a fine structure, a real New England farmhouse. Maybe if I brought in a piano…"

"Merry's been boss of that place for a long time, Bunny," Aunt Bette said with a tiny, superior smile. "If you start trying to organize the crazies into a happy band, you'll probably have to march them over her dead body."

"I think my future sister-in-law is a delightful person, the last one in the world to be opposed to new ideas."

"That's because you're not living there yet" Aunt Bette said. "As soon as you move in, it's going to be a pitched battle for possession of Lively and the old homestead. That's the way it always is with in-laws, so don't kid yourself. I don't know which is the worse part of marriage, putting up with in-laws or catering to a man's whims."

"Oh, it's having to cater to a husband," I piped up at great risk. Mr. Carver didn't have any relatives left alive to become burdensome in-laws.

My mother spooned coleslaw onto Aunt Bette's plate. "You need to eat more vegetables," she said, then added: "When you two girls get married yourselves, you'll be able to speak with more authority on the joys and tribulations of matrimony. I'd say Bunny has the right attitude. What that depressing Farm needs is a good, strong woman to make it into a real home. Merry just doesn't have the knack. I tasted her pea soup once. Ugh! Nothing but split peas and water."

"Catherine makes the best pea soup I've ever tasted," said Sarge, who had been silently eating his supper during this exchange of views.

"Well, you have to put in a decent ham bone, some onions, celery, carrots, and lots of fresh herbs," my mother explained. "Any fool should be able to make a good soup." She looked pleased but didn't exactly smile in recognition of Sarge's compliment.

"You certainly have a way with fish, too," Sarge said. "These perch didn't die in vain." He'd been fishing early that morning and brought back a basketful of fat, pink fish. Now they were crisp golden-brown. My mother slid the platter nearer to Sarge's plate.

"Nice and fresh they are, too," she said.

Sarge eased another crusty perch onto his plate, humming softly to himself. Had that been I, my mother would have reminded me sharply that she did not allow singing at the table, but by now we all knew that when Sarge was quietly working out a problem, an undercurrent of song accompanied his thoughts. Sometimes I could guess which project he was reflecting upon from the tune he was humming. This time it was "Rock of Ages." He was probably figuring out how to repair the damage at the Friendship Unitarian Church where the cross, struck by lightning and broken off during a recent thunder storm, had impaled itself in the roof of the adjacent parish house.

I could have spared myself all the worry about Sarge's disinterest in gainful employment. He might have been indifferent to wages, but he was always fascinated by challenges of repair—the more devilishly difficult, the better. Never in memory had things at our house run so perfectly. Not only was our ancient washing machine chugging away dependably, but the roof didn't leak over the front dormer any more, the kitchen drawers no longer jolted down several inches when pulled out, all the windows could be opened—top and bottom—with one finger, so smoothly did they glide, and the radiators no longer knocked, gurgled, and spat upon the floors. All the demons had been exorcised from attic to cellar.

More than ever, Sarge was Whitford's unofficial Mr. Fix-it. Although this was not exactly a salaried position, folks paid him for his work, in cash or in goods, and he passed these bonuses on directly to Mother. Thus we had two bushels of apples from Lively's orchard, a bolt of maroon velvet left over from the church drapes, an old bicycle from Fisher's garage (now oiled, painted, and fitted out with a makeshift half-black headlight, so that Mother could ride it to her night job at the telephone office), and twenty-five pounds of King Arthur flour from the general store. He also received a few wrinkled dollar bills and fifty cent pieces from fixing the sagging floor at the library, the shorted plugs at the school office, the sink hole at the cemetery, the fire station's sump pump, and whatever else broke down or wore out in the town buildings. He even found a way to rid the town hall attic of flying squirrels. It was almost as good as if he held a regular job, I told myself. He was on call twenty-four hours a day, just like Dr. Woodward. Between delicate repairs around town, he cleared away the debris of the barn and began the construction of our new shed.

"Sarge knows how to get things done right," I heard Mother say to Merle Gilbert, paying him one of her highest compliments. Merle was at her wit's end over the post office boiler, which was grumbling and smoking its way toward extinction. "You mark my words, let me send Sarge over here tomorrow to have a look at that old dragon, and he'll soon have it purring again. There's money in your budget for maintenance, isn't there? Just pay him for his time, like you would anyone else."

"Well, it's worth a try," Merle said, stamping my parcel. Without even turning around, she pitched it into the large canvas bin that stood directly behind her, then picked up her knitting. "Must be a Christmas box you're sending to Skip, isn't it?" she asked me. "I just sent one from Cora, too. He finally wrote to her, you know. Be a wonder if either package gets there, I'd say, but at least you're giving it plenty of time to catch up with him. I told Cora you'd been hearing from her son pretty regular. That's the way it is with young folks these days. Plenty of time for their pals but none for their parents." She sighed and clicked into another row, her fingers moving so fast they didn't seem to be related to her heavy body. She sat in a high padded chair at a counter where everything was arranged to be within her reach. Once a day, with a great groan, she heaved herself up and sorted the incoming mail into the postal boxes or arranged it for rural delivery, which was shuttled around town by her big, handsome son Glenn, who hadn't yet been called up. Glenn never had much to say, but he was always smiling and he could drive their wheezing Dodge from either side of the front seat with equal dexterity.

"I hear Rosemary's going to be taking her old job back soon. Amazing she recovered at all," the post mistress remarked to Mother "Guess you'll miss the paycheck, won't you?"

"Oh, we'll get along just fine without it," Mother replied airily. "I'm getting a mite tired of working nights anyway."

" 'Course, with Bette coming into all that money, things should be looking up for you folks. I hear Alex Carver has been a steady visitor over there at Snow's where your sister is setting herself up. She plan to stay there, does she? Isn't going to sell the place and move to Philadelphia?"

"Now why on earth would she do that?" Mother looked genuinely mystified.

"Well, seems like I sorted a letter for her today from Philadelphia. And guess who it was from!"

"I'm sure it's none of our business," Mother said, grabbing my sleeve and moving toward the door.

"Letter from Jack Wallace down in Philadelphia," said Merle Gilbert, turning the olive drab scarf for another row. "Now what do you suppose he wants? Wouldn't you think he'd caused enough grief already?" Merle remembered every word she read on an envelope or post card, and she must have read them all as she sorted. I often wondered if she coded the names and dates into her knitting, like Madame Defarge, so that the gist of the town's correspondence was always at her fingertips.

My mother, who'd paused for just a moment in the doorway as if tempted in spite of herself to hear the news, said "Good afternoon, Merle!" in an icicle voice, pushed me out ahead of her, and slammed the post office door. I glanced back as we flew out. Merle, still placidly knitting, never even looked up from her work.

"That damned old busybody," Mother said, stalking off down the road while I raced to keep up with her.

"Who's Jack Wallace?" I asked.

"Now don't you start," she said. "Curiosity killed the cat."

Silently I repeated the rest to myself. *And satisfaction brought her back.*

"Don't you be a smart alec, either." She gave my arm a good pinch. I never could figure how she knew what I was thinking.

With admirable restraint, Mother did not call Aunt Bette, but the juicy details came to us fast enough anyway. Aunt Bette went into a screaming fit over the contents of that letter. She had just about enough breath to call Mother for help. It wasn't even a real letter, only a clipping about Wallace's engagement to some society girl from Philadelphia.. I had a look at it while my mother was sponging Aunt Bette's forehead and wrists, waiting for Dr. Woodward to arrive with a shot. The newspaper item showed a picture of the happy couple. The bride-to-be looked like Carol Lombard, only snootier. Apparently Jack Wallace was some big wheel in real estate, a partner in his fiancée's father's firm. *Another ill-fated love affair,* I thought, folding the clipping and putting it back in the envelope. *I think I'll stay out of this one.* I just hoped unrequited passion wouldn't cause my aunt to do anything foolish, like get engaged on the rebound.

The Friday night of Mr. Carver's farewell party, I began to worry again. "I think I'll walk over to Aunt Bette's," I said after supper, "and see if she has any heavy work she needs help with. She's been looking a little tired, don't you think, Ma?"

"How thoughtful of you, Amelia." Mother, who was playing gin rummy with Sarge, looked up at me shrewdly from her hand. "But Bette's been invited to the party, and the last time I talked to her, she planned to go. She may want to invite Alex back to her place afterwards, and I don't want you hanging around there, making your aunt nervous."

"So Alex is finally on his way. Perhaps it's just as well," Sarge said. I couldn't have agreed more.

"I don't think anyone understands that boy except me," my mother said. "He's really very thoughtful and sentimental. You know, once he told me that he's never felt so close to anyone since his mother passed away. The night Mr. Snow went under the ice, when Alex went to pieces and I took care of him, he actually said that I'd been like a mother to him. I was quite touched."

She was "touched" all right. What had happened to my usually shrewd mother? It was enough to make a sensible person throw up.

She picked up a card and deftly arranged the others in her hand. "Gin!" she exclaimed, laying her cards down on the table with a flourish of satisfaction. "That's five, twenty, thirty-five, fifty, sixty points, counting what you have left in your hand. How much do you owe me now?"

Sarge sighed and wrote down the new score. "Comes to over eighty dollars now," he said. " Don't know how I'll ever pay you all I owe."

"Not bad!" she said with a smile of triumph. Then she turned back to me, and being in rare good humor, offered an alternate plan. "Why don't you take the bike and ride over to Minna's? I think it will be safe enough if you keep the darklight lit. Just stay on the main roads and be home by nine-thirty."

I grabbed my lumber jacket off the hook by the kitchen door and hurried out before she could change her mind. "Okay. So long," I yelled back once I was safely beyond the screen door.

"Aren't you going to phone her first?" Mother called after me. I pretended I hadn't heard her.

By bicycle it only took me ten minutes to get to Snow's. I would have a long chilly wait before my aunt got home. But Ollie heard me out in the rose garden and began barking and scratching at the door. So I reasoned it would be better to climb in the pantry window and let the dog out to relieve himself. Probably it was what Aunt Bette would want me to do.

After we had our walkabout through the back yard trees, I brought Ollie in and made another little tour of the upstairs, looking for open packs of cigarettes. The doll's gun was still in her bedside table drawer. Sure enough, it was loaded, too. I put it back very carefully, just as I'd found it. My aunt had a sharp eye for detail.

I wondered where she'd put the other gun, and having time on my hands, I poked around looking for it. Now where would I hide an extra weapon if I were Aunt Bette? With an entire houseful of cabinets, cubbyholes, and curios, this was a real puzzle. I went through the shelves in the library, the canisters in the pantry, and the shelves in the spooky old cellar before I figured out the answer. I remembered how she'd brought the jewelry to our house in a large second handbag.

I raced up to the attic, followed by a scampering Ollie who thought this was a marvelous game, to the built-in cedar closet where my aunt stored out-of-season clothes. Not the jewelry that glittered with gold and precious gems, but some of the chunkier, tarnished pieces were in the very same handbag from which they'd been spilled to my astonished gaze. And the other dainty little gun with the silver handle was there, too. It fit into the palm of my hand just right. She didn't keep this one loaded, I found. I wondered if I'd learned enough from the text I'd read in the library to load a gun myself. Taking the tiny thing down to my aunt's bedroom, I fitted it with two of the bullets from the little cardboard box in her drawer. It seemed to me I'd done it right, but there was no means of testing my handiwork right then.

Before I went downstairs at nine, I put everything back exactly as I'd found it. I hugged Ollie and went back out through the pantry window. The glider in the rose garden hadn't been put away for the winter yet, so I sat in that and rocked back and forth for a while, trying to name the constellations I'd studied in a little book on astronomy from Mr. Snow's library. *How much more difficult the stars were to recognize when you were looking at a real sky, not a picture,* I thought. It was pretty near time for me to scoot home when I heard Snow's Olds rolling into the garage.

As I peeked around the side of the house, I hoped my aunt wouldn't catch sight of the bicycle leaning against one of the two beech trees in her front yard. No, she was busy talking and laughing with Alex Carver. They were carrying some kind of party banner with foot-high letters on it. *Now that Alex is in it...We're sure to win it!* My aunt and Alex were doing a tap dance down the flagstone walk with the red, white, and blue banner stretched between them. What a shock! She really seemed pleased by his attention after all, no matter how much fun she'd made of him in the past.

At the front step, she handed over the key so that he could unlock the front door. I thought I saw him take her elbow as they went inside. *Yeech.* Things were getting worse and worse.

The parlor drapes were closed, so I couldn't see what else was going on until Aunt Bette went into the kitchen, where there was a slit between the curtains, and began to make coffee. Mr. Carver followed and stood too close to her wherever she went as she moved from getting cups, cream, sugar, and a plate of cookies. Finally I saw him take the tray from her hands and carry it into the parlor. How revolting! My clever, canny aunt had been completely deceived.

I came up closer to the kitchen window, hoping to see farther into the house. I guess my face was practically pressed against the glass, but I couldn't make out anything beyond the dining room table. I heard the radio turned on in the parlor, some dance band playing "I'll Be Seeing You." Good Lord, I prayed that man wouldn't dance with my aunt. Anything could happen when two people were dancing. I must have shut my eyes for a moment, because when I opened them, I was nearly nose to nose to Mr. Carver, who was holding the coffee pot and looking out at me where the curtains didn't quite meet. His face was more than expressionless. It was like the cold scowling stone face on one of Mr. Snow's glazed pottery figures, the one that my aunt called "The Implacable Warrior." With one terrified look at my enemy's eyes spearing into mine, I bolted.

Since I was already terribly late, I pedaled home as furiously as one can when fueled by a raging imagination and fear run wild. My only comfort was that Mr. Carver would be leaving in the morning. If "thoughts are things," as my mother always said, the man whose murderous expression filled me with abject dread would never return to Whitford, so strong was my wish never to look in those hateful eyes again.

Chapter 20

In which Ollie and I have a narrow
escape in the woods, and we pay the
Korhonens a surprising visit.

F eeling carefree, almost giddy, knowing that Mr. Carver had left town
yesterday, *at last, at last*, I walked over to the Eliots' place on Sunday to
listen to their new records. We had to sneak Ollie up the back stairs. Mrs. Eliot
didn't allow animals in the house, not even for a visit. It had been a fine warm
day, and I was dog-sitting while Mother gave Aunt Bette a hand at Snow's, the
combination of sunshine and brisk fall breeze being perfect for washing windows. I was glad to escape from this bustle of activity.

After we'd listened to Glenn Miller and the Andrew Sisters a few times, the
usual Sunday boredom set in, and Daisy and Jay fell to making jokes about Miss
Cronin's engagement. Jay winked and held up a new sketch, a caricature of the
bride and groom. Daisy clapped her hands and laughed, which sent Ollie into a
frenzy of dashing around the bed while we tried to quiet him down.

Mrs. Eliot knocked on the door. "Jay? Daisy? What's that strange scratching
and clicking noise?"

"Jay's teaching us some new jitterbug steps," Daisy assured her grandmother. Ollie barked! I threw my jacket over his head.

Mrs. Eliot knocked again, crisply.

"Poor Amelia has a terrible, terrible cough," Daisy added.

The sun was a red ball just touching the trees behind the Eliots' house when Ollie and I started home after Mrs. Eliot practically threw us out, although her frozen, ladylike smile never wavered. "Give my very best to your mother," she said, scrubbing her hand with a lace-edged handkerchief where Ollie had licked it on his way past. Daisy and Jay waved and made faces from his bedroom window.

In the still bright sky, a pale crescent moon was rising, the kind that gives little light even when the sky darkens later. As I crossed School Street, I noticed a big yellow school bus turning from West Street. Must have been returning from some football game, I thought. I ducked off the street into the woods road, knowing it would be fully dark beneath its overgrown arch of trees. I wasn't supposed to walk in there after sunset, but I could say truthfully that the sun hadn't gone down yet. If I took the long way home through Frietchie Circle, I would surely get in trouble coming late to supper. And besides, I knew the woods way too well to get lost. I'd never seen anyone else in there. There was really nothing at all to be afraid of. Besides, I had Ollie to keep me company. He pranced at my side, wiggling with delight at the prospect of a long walk. The sound of his breathing and his trot beside me broke the quietness of being alone in the woods. I hooked the leather leash onto his collar, just to be certain I wouldn't lose him to a squirrel chase, and we started out.

I'd just gone past the first bend of the old road, where School Street is lost from sight in a maze of overreaching leaves, when I heard it—a great roaring motor revving up. I thought a truck must be lumbering by on School Street, since no one ever drove into these woods anymore. But the sound of the motor was strangely louder and nearer. Ollie began to tug to the right. I heard an awful cracking of branches as if tires were crashing over dead wood on the road behind me. Twisting to look back, I hurried forward around the second bend.

Wild blackberry bushes were waist high on both sides there. Beyond that, the woods were filled with scraggly new oaks growing so thick you could hardly squeeze between them. Still there were no lights, just that enormous noise in the dark. I wished I had brought a flashlight. Ollie began to pull harder and bark nervously.

Then, suddenly, there was a light! More blinding than the blackness of the woods. I couldn't see anything but the light. Jumping to the right, with Ollie right ahead of me, I dodged the truck bearing down crazily toward us. We scrambled over the road's right shoulder, falling into one tangled bush after another. *Just in time!*

But instead of moving straight ahead and lumbering on past, the heavy vehicle swerved after us with a screech of monstrous wheels. It was as if the truck itself had gone mad. Or the driver was stricken with some kind of fit, slumped over the wheel unconscious while the truck ran amok. I jumped up from my knees and threw myself sideways through the thick fence of new trees. Ollie yelped like a puppy when I jerked his collar to pull him through.

The truck rammed into the first line of saplings, pushing them over so that they tilted toward us. It stopped with a splintering crash. Some of those new oaks had two-inch trunks of tough green wood. One headlight went out. Then the truck backed up onto the road with an ugly squeal. That's when I knew the driver couldn't have been the victim of a heart attack. Now I was sure that someone behind the wheel was after *me.*

I screamed and threw myself farther through the crowd of trees. No one to hear me except my pursuer! I pulled Ollie after me so hard that I could hear him gasp as the collar choked off his breath. My wrists ached from catching my fall in the blackberries. My palms were stuck with pebbles. My arms and legs burned from scratches. But I just kept pushing my way deeper into the resistant scrub.

The tearing, grinding noise sounded as if the truck had backed up into the underbrush on the road's other side. I could smell foul motor oil. The truck hurled itself forward again but stopped just short of the oak wall, its one bright eye shining like some mythic ogre through the scrawny trunks.

By this time I was sobbing and could see even less. But I knew where I was, almost. That is, I knew I was somewhere near my secret hideout at the edge of First Bog, where I had buried my treasure chest. I could hole up there, in the ground hollow I called a cave, hidden by sweeping low branches of pine. If I didn't move or breathe, and if I could keep Ollie quiet, no one would be able to find me. How to find the place in the pitch-dark? *Go back to the road's edge and turn in at the huge fallen pine trunk*, I told myself. Because everything looks the same at night. More so right then, with the truck light still imprinted in my eyes. I needed some sure landmark, and the downed tree would do it.

Waiting until the truck heaved itself onto the road for another thrust, I struggled back to the road's edge. Pushing through brambles that grew there, I used them as a guide to the turns of the trail and stayed out of the road itself. Crouching, I stumbled down out of the light, hauling Ollie behind me. Finally my knees smashed against the pine trunk, so hard I almost somersaulted over it. My mouth was full of dirt where it had hit the great root ball. A front tooth ached.

Turning abruptly, I dashed into the woods, tumbling Ollie right off his paws, and aimed for my secret place. There was a small clearing, then the stand of pines. No underbrush grew in the thick needle carpet. Footsteps made barely a sound. I raced over the open ground. In a minute, the two of us had rolled into the hollow I called my cave. Ollie fell on top. He squealed and panted and scratched his way off me. We lay there gasping together, our chins in the rug of pine needles, with the comforting smell of pine pitch in our noses. The heavy branches covered us completely. I figured Ollie knew not to bark. My heart was pounding in my ears as well as my chest. I thought about praying but there wasn't time before I heard the truck lurching into the woods again.

It had raced past the fallen pine, then swerved to the right through the clearing. The Cyclops had seen my flight and was following. But we were well camouflaged under the sweep of low pine branches. It roared right past our hiding place and didn't stop until it nearly rolled into First Bog. Stuck on the brink, it rocked noisily back and forth, screaming, a huge wounded monster struggling in a trap.

The crescent moon over First Bog gave a sliver of light reflected on patches of water in the ditches. I could see a little now. Not a truck. The school bus! And I could see a dim silhouette of the driver, jerking back and forth as the bus tried to yank itself free. The shadow of a hat. A profile. A shoulder.

It looked like the broad-rimmed hat Ed Lyons, the school bus driver, wore. But something was mismatched about the picture I was seeing at the wheel of the bus. I knew that profile from somewhere else. The tip-tilted nose, the smallish chin. *It was Alex Carver!* I was practically positive, except for the hat.

I didn't even wonder why he was trying to run over me. It was to stop my mouth. Mr. Carver hadn't tried to save Mr. Snow from drowning. He'd pushed the old man to his death. No one except the Eliot twins knew that I'd given the letter to Mr. Carver, and Daisy and Jay didn't believe me. And no one else realized—except me, too late—what that letter must have meant to him. Then there was that other accident—or was it?—his father's falling down the cellar stairs. So Alex Carver could sell the house and go to college. Then the burning of our barn—with me in it! And courting Aunt Bette, knowing I was watching, knowing what I knew. Hoping to marry Mr. Snow's fortune, and only I stood in his way.

A girl hit by a bus at night could be an accident, too. Mr. Carver specialized in accidents.

Finally, with an immense grinding and tearing, the bus backed out of the ditch and stopped dead. The Cyclops headlight went out. A terrifying quiet descended on the woodland clearing. I held my breath twice, once for myself and once for Ollie, as if I could wish him into perfect silence.

Suddenly, a piercing new light. A different eye, brighter and sharper than the last, shone over First Bog. It was the bus's spotlight making a slow, careful circle around the edges of the bog. With little stops and starts, it overlapped itself, patiently ferreting through each stand of surrounding trees. It snaked yard by yard toward our lair in the pines. Moving forward, moving back, moving on again.

Ollie gave a very low whine and wiggled, as if to get going. I scratched the base of his tail, and he settle down to enjoy it. He was still panting from our run. There was time now, and I prayed: *Dear Lord, please keep Ollie from barking. Dear Lord, please get us out of this before I die of fright.* And all the while, I inched out of my lumber jacket, making a tent of it over my head and over the white blaze between Ollie's eyes and on his chest. I held the bulk of it up so that Ollie wouldn't get scared and bolt. *Please Lord, let this green and black plaid look like a mossy boulder!*

The terrifying eye-beam reached into the pines now. I pulled one side of the jacket over my face, holding the other half high with my left arm, out straight above Ollie's head. After a minute, some of the light shone through on Ollie's side, moving back and forth. I knew the beam was right above us, searching.

But my cave was a sheltered cavity scooped out of earth, and the pine branches hung thickly there. The light moved on. I lifted a corner of the jacket-tent. The eye found itself back at the road and slowly came full circle to the bog's edge.

The spotlight went out. Silence returned, an endless time. Then the motor turned over with a reverberating roar. The one headlight came on. Slowly the bus began backing up toward the road. It turned in the clearing and headed out the way it had come. I breathed a full breath.

Suddenly Ollie came up from our hiding place with a jerk, all stiff-legged, barking loudly. He shot forward with a quick leap. The leash, which had looped itself on the ground under me, took half the buttons off my shirt as he went. The handle burned my fingers flying out of my grasp.

Like an arrow loosed from the bow, the dog was off into the clearing after the bus. Jumping and barking at the back of the bus, dancing back and forth, nearly under the wheel, a frenzy of fearlessness. The bus slowed sharply, as if surprised at this tiny buzz of attack. But Ollie speeded up, so that he was snapping at the front wheel, leaping ahead of the bus. Did he mean to meet it head to head?

The bus swerved to catch him, tire against flesh. Ollie catapulted clear. Bounding like a tennis ball, he went back to his attack.

There was no thought in my head as I ran out of the pine shelter after the dog. I just did it.

I didn't think again until I had grabbed the thrashing leash and jerked Ollie away from the bus. Still barking and hurling himself forward, his legs went right out from under him. He rolled over several times before he got his paws under him again, while I just kept racing out of danger.

The question knifed through me, *where could I run? Where would I be safe in this dark, lonely stretch of woods?* The answer flashed up faster than thought. I'd have to escape across the bog. If I ran straight across First Bog I'd come to

Korhonen's farm. I could see their lights faintly glittering on the other side. Old Mr. Korhonen kept a gun. We would be safe there. I could call my mother. I felt hot tears in my eyes at last.

I'd have to jump the irrigation ditches. I'd done it many times for fun and knew I could clear them. But Ollie's legs were much shorter. I thought of Eliza in *Uncle Tom's Cabin*, jumping the ice floes in the river at night to escape the evil slave trader. Carrying her baby. Well, I would carry Ollie if I had to. Already on the move, I would see what he could do for himself first.

I cleared the ditch and Ollie almost did, scratching at the second bank, held up by the leash. I gave it a mighty pull and up he came. Right then was the only time I looked back. The bus's interior light went on for a moment, then out again, as the driver came down the step and shut the door behind him. But in that instant of dim yellow light, I saw the face for sure. Hat or no hat, it was Alex Carver all right.

Now the night was completely dark except for that sliver of moon. I thought I heard footsteps thudding toward First Bog. When we reached the second ditch, Ollie balked, leaning back against my pull on his leash, digging his paws into the spongy ground. I didn't wait. I scooped him up in my arms, backing up for a running start, and jumped, clearing the ditch by so little that I almost fell backward into it.

Ollie scratched and twisted to free himself from my grasp, so I let him go, hanging onto the leash for dear life.

It probably took us several minutes to cross the bog that way. It seemed an eternity of pounding through squishy cranberry vines, hearing the old berries pop under my feet. I ran so hard I thought I would die. At each ditch, I had to pick up Ollie, who squirmed in protest. Finally, at the last ditch, I couldn't quite make it with Ollie wriggling in my arms, and we slid into the water up to my knees. I let the dog go and scrambled up, pulling him after me.

Looking back then, I could see no one behind us, nor could I see the bus. At first I thought, *Thank God he's gone.* But then I figured, maybe he'd driven back to School Street and was circling around. At that moment I remembered the little gun in my aunt's cedar closet. So clear was the image, I almost felt my hand close around it. Then, just as suddenly, the idea slipped away like a live fish from my hand and dove back from whence it came.

When at last I reached the farm house, I wasn't really running. It was more like staggering, with Ollie limping and whimpering. The light from the windows shone in the yard, and I could see Mr. Korhonen and his son, Will. They were scampering from their steam hut toward the house. Will was wearing a towel around his middle, but the old man was naked and frisking around in the cold air as if he were a kid.

When they saw us, they froze for a minute, like a game of Statues. The sight of the two grown men playing around like boys seemed to revive Ollie, who trotted over to join them, making a grab for Will's towel But then the father gave a mighty bull-roar and pushed through into the house, his wrinkled little thing wagging in front, his rear end shiny and white. He slammed the back door.

Will with the towel stayed. He had a small funny smile, but his eyes looked concerned. I noticed how deep set they were, with dark shadows. Afterwards, I realized it was because I'd never seen him without his glasses before. Or without his clothes, for that matter. There are times when embarrassment is worse than fear. I felt myself blush to the roots of my muddy, wild hair.

"My goodness, Amelia," Will said. "What the devil happened to you?"

I wanted to say everything at once, and that was the trouble. I was crying and words just came out that couldn't make any sense to him. It was something like, "bus coming after us, ran and ran, Ollie couldn't jump them, he wanted it to be an accident, my mother will kill me, is Minna home?"

The last part gave him something to hang on to. "Minna's gone to a Grange dance. I'll call your mother," he said. "Do you want to come in?"

I was afraid his father was angry at my materializing out of the night at that embarrassing moment. So I said I'd just sit on the side porch. I lifted Ollie up beside me on the glider and rocked us gently back and forth, hugging him, rubbing my chin on his short bristly fur. He smelled doggy from being wet. After a while, Will came out, bringing a glass of cold lemonade for me and a bowl of water for Ollie. Now dressed in neatly creased workpants and a plaid shirt, he sat with us on the porch until Mother and Aunt Bette drove up to the house in Snow's black Oldsmobile.

"Amelia, this is too much!" Mother jumped out already scolding me. "Look at you! Your shirt is a wreck. Your legs are all scratched. And your shoes! Where is your jacket? Is that tooth bleeding?" Putting her strong hand around my wrist like a handcuff, she rushed me into the car with accusations and questions, while Aunt Bette apologized to Will for his trouble. She took Ollie's leash and brought him into the car.

I crouched down while we drove home, but Ollie looked out the window, wagging his rear end.

"Young lady, you have a lot of explaining to do. You are a perfect fright." Mother was right. I was a real mess, and not just on my soiled, torn, scratched surface—my thoughts were equally muddy. On the way home, I tried to explain what had happened. First I started at Korhonen's and worked backwards.

"Amelia, what in the world are you saying? You're not making any sense. Bette, do you think a blow on the head...?"

By then we had reached home, and I felt safe. I collected my wits and told the story from the beginning when I had left the Eliots', while Mother was making me a cup of cocoa and Aunt Bette was dabbing at my cuts with warm water.

I said, "I'm sure it was Alex Carver. I saw him when the bus's light went on." Although I feared my mother wouldn't believe me, I thought Aunt Bette, who never used to like him, might.

But it was Aunt Bette who said it first. "Honey, that's just not true. You must have imagined that. Alex Carver has already left for Fort Devens. He took the bus to Ayer yesterday. Some of the teachers and I saw him off ourselves."

"That Ed Lyons is a disgrace," Mother said angrily. "I'm going to speak to Guy Fisher about him tomorrow. No way should he be driving the school bus."

"Must have been drunk to take that old road. Didn't see her. Unless he thought he'd corner her in the woods, the old pervert," Aunt Bette added.

"I'm going to put some iodine on that nasty cut over her eye." Mother got out the little brown bottle with the skull and crossbones on it.

"It wasn't Ed. Mr. Carver isn't gone," I wailed, as Mother swiped at me with the stinging stuff. "Call the camp at Ayer and find out! Probably he saw me and Ollie on our way to visit the Eliots. He still has the key to Fisher's garage from when he was working at the store. I bet he stole the bus and waited for me to leave for home. Probably thought I was going to walk down School Street."

"I kept some macaroni and cheese for you," Mother said. "Your favorite." She put her hand on my shoulder for a minute and looked at me sadly. I thought she was missing Daddy at that moment.

"Where's Sarge?" I asked.

"Gone to Kates Hill with Bunny Cronin to fix the Cronins' furnace. He sure is popular these days." Mother's melancholy expression turned into a satisfied smile.

I sipped my cocoa gloomily, trying to avoid the little beads of undiluted bitter stuff at the bottom of the cup. Aunt Bette finished cleaning up Ollie with a soft brush, and he walked over stiff-legged and dropped down on my feet. I leaned over and scratched behind his ears. What a funny baby he was to carry through the night. No matter what anyone else believed, I knew I had saved us, at least for now.

Maybe I could have cleared up the confusion if I'd told them of my suspicions concerning the ice fishing accident. But then I would have to confess about the letter.

The whole thing had started with that letter. So in a way, it was all my fault. With everything I had on my conscience, at least I could be glad that Aunt Bette got rich out of it. I guessed they'd never want to know how it all really happened. So I'd just stay safe in the house until Mr. Carver went away again. He'd been drafted, and he'd have to go. And when he came home on furlough, I'd be ready.

The big pain in my chest slowly became a small pang in my stomach. "Could I have that macaroni and cheese now?" I asked

Chapter 21

In which Aunt Bette has good cause
for hysteria, Mr. Carver courts a
fortune, and I confide in Sarge.

N o matter how much I whined and insisted, that was the end of it as far
as Mother and Aunt Bette were concerned. They even managed to convince Sarge that their version of the evening's events was the only sensible explanation. Never had I felt so deserted! Why didn't my mother's usual lightning intuition hit on a truth so close to home? Even when Sarge found out later that Ed Lyons had been square dancing that night, my mother and aunt simply transferred their wrath to some unknown teen-age bully. Mother gave Dom Ferro " a piece of her mind" for being too soft on "juvenile delinquents," a new phrase being hurled at us from magazines and pulpits.

My family's fierce capacity for indignation soon found a new target, however, when Aunt Bette became embroiled in the final settlement of her estate— the detestable greedy Snow family. Finally, it all came down to Aunt Bette's agreeing to give up one third of the estate's value, calculated down to the last piece of carved jade dragon and Canton export platter, in an out-of-court settlement with the Bishop. Aunt Bette was forced to sell several stocks that had been carefully selected by Mr. Snow for long-term growth.

This major setback drove my aunt, whose disposition was hardly tranquil at the best of times, to the brink of a hysterical breakdown. The new doctor, Dr. Woodward, made frequent house calls. The pills and potions on my aunt's night table grew in number and variety. I made frequent house calls myself, with a hamper full of home-cooked remedies that my mother hoped would keep up Aunt Bette's strength. Aunt Bette never finished any of these savory dishes. Leftovers frequently went to Ollie, who did seem to grow quite cheerful and roly-poly on his share of the chicken soup and egg custard.

When the time came for her final signing of papers and the Bishop's release of all claims against the estate, Aunt Bette left me in charge of Ollie while she took care of her affairs with Attorney Fenner in Boston. Before bringing my little friend away from the empty Snow house, I browsed through the rooms, looking for Ollie's longest leash and something out of Snow's library that I shouldn't read to sneak home with me.

What I found was a stack of letters from Mr. Carver lying right out in plain sight on the Governor Winthrop desk in that forbidden room.

Had I learned my lesson about letters—or would I read them?

Well, I reasoned, *for my aunt's safety, as well as my own, I'd better at least peek at one or two pages and check out his plans.* After the first cold-water shock of finding that these were not the usual serviceman's newsy notes but actually a bundle of love letters, I sat right down and read the whole lot. Ollie sighed and stretched out under the library table. I thought I would be sick to my stomach, but I persisted through the smooth compliments—"your beautiful mouth...your musical laughter...your sweet dainty hands" and the passionate declarations..."a life together after the war... give me something to hope for." Heaven help us, that devil Mr. Carver was trying to get Aunt Bette to marry him. Or rather, he was trying to get his hands on her money. And then what? Another accident? My pretty little aunt turned into a twisted heap of blood and bone? *Never!* I vowed. I would find a way to stop that monster in lover's clothing.

Sarge was still the most reasonable adult I knew, the only one who really listened. Deciding to have one more go at convincing someone of our danger, I offered to help him work on the new shed. With the aid of Will Korhonen, Sarge had erected the frame where the old barn used to be. The walls had been enclosed, and the roof shingled. Now Sarge was building the potting shelves Mother had designed, and he agreed that he could use a hand putting them together. Ordinarily he enjoyed working alone, but he seemed to know I needed to have a heart-to-heart talk.

"Hold this board in place while I nail it," he said when we were alone in the new building with its clean, sharp smell of fresh pine wood. "While it's thoughtful of you to offer to help with the finishing, Amelia, it's also surprising—when you could be up in your room reading some contraband book and munching apples. Is something troubling you? You look as if you were carrying the weight of the world. Let's see if I can lift some of those worries off your shoulders."

"No one believes me about Mr. Carver. I thought at least I could depend on you, Sarge."

"The culprit must have means, motive, and opportunity, Amelia. Alex Carver was long gone when you had that adventure in the woods, so he didn't have *opportunity*. With no further access to Fisher's Garage, especially since he jilted Penny, so that eliminates *means*. And I can't imagine what motive he might have to chase down a student with a school bus. Surely your book reports weren't *that* bad. But I'm willing to listen with an open mind. Lay out your evidence."

"It all began with a really old love letter, but you must promise that you'll never, never tell this part to my mother or Aunt Bette."

"I'll give you a qualified promise."

"What does that mean?" I whined.

"Unless someone's life depends upon the information, or you're planning some criminal activity, I will take your secrets to the grave with me."

"I wish you wouldn't put it that way."

"This is starting to sound rather serious." Sarge stopped adjusting the shelves, and sat down on an upturned wooden crate. He motioned me to do the same. "Tell me about the letter, then."

So I did. I started at the beginning, quoting as much of the letter as I could remember. I explained to Sarge that, since Mr. Carver was cataloging Mr. Snow's books, I'd asked him to return the letter to the green book on Greek gods that later, Mr. Carver had behaved strangely when I questioned him about the letter. I reminded Sarge that Mr. Carver admitted to having been out on the ice the night of Winston Snow's accident, but we had only his word for it that he tried to rescue and not drown the old man. I told Sarge how I'd discovered the identity of Pan in the school yearbook, and then everything had fallen apart ... or together, depending on which way you looked at it. I added that, on the day I was researching Margaret at the library, Miss Pratt had been on her way to tea with the new teachers and Mr. Carver, that she may have mentioned my interest in old yearbooks and town reports.

Sarge whistled with surprise. He put down the small hand drill he'd been holding and wiped his hands on his overalls. There was still sawdust, however, on his drooping mustache. "Winston Snow and Margaret Ann Burns! I'll be damned. So you gave the letter to Alex, and he must have been devastated to think of his mom being jilted by that old devil. Alex worshipped his mother to an unhealthy degree, if you ask me."

"And right where we're standing now, Sarge, we used to have a barn. Remember how the lights were cut, the heavy door pushed into place, and the barn set afire with me in it?"

"As if I could forget! What you're saying is, Carver figured you knew he had a revenge motive for pushing old Winston under the ice. Ice and fire, fire and ice. How did he know you were in there?"

"I left a note on the kitchen table. And I was playing the radio in the barn. There's more..."

"I can hardly wait." Sarge mopped his brow with a large red handkerchief. His round brown eyes looked at me thoughtfully. It isn't often that an adult actually gives his full attention to a kid. I felt as if I were in the spotlight on stage, with someone at last really listening.

"I found the Town Report for the year Margaret Ann Burns married Jeremiah Carver." My face was beginning to feel hot, so I knew I was blushing. I looked down at the pennies in my scuffed loafers. "And Alex was born too soon after the wedding. So when Mr. Snow learned that Mr. Carver's mother used to be the librarian in Whitford, maybe Mr. Snow realized she was his former girl-friend, and he got to wondering about Mr. Carver's birth date. Aunt Bette said it was strange the way the old codger took an immediate interest in Mr. Carver and offered him the job of cataloging the library."

"The plot thickens... and sickens..."commented Sarge. "What do you suppose Alex thought about that?"

"Well, nothing at all. Mr. Carver always thought everyone adored him, even Aunt Bette who despised him. She used to, anyway. Not any more, I'm afraid. But when Mr. Carver read that love letter...he can count as well as any of the ladies at the Old Home Day sewing circle. Did he think to himself, this rich man should have married my mother and raised me in luxury, instead of letting her die of consumption and her son struggle to go to college?"

"Yes...I guess he might have followed that line of thought. What a plotter he must be! You wouldn't think anyone we knew...but stranger things have happened. I guess you haven't been reading Sherlock Holmes to no purpose. I feel as if I'm a regular Dr. Watson here. And you, my dear girl, you're the one Alex Carver must fear the most. But how could he be sure you haven't already told half the town?"

"Because I told him how afraid I was that my mother would find out I'd taken a letter of Mr. Snow's. But he wouldn't know how long he could count on my feeling guilty. And now he's writing lovey-dovey letters to Aunt Bette. I think he means to marry her and get old Snow's money after all. I don't know what to do to prevent it, since no one believes me." I could feel my eyes fill with tears, so I squeezed a few out to trickle down my cheeks.

"Now, now, Amelia. You've told me, and you've made a good case against the man. It may be hard to believe, but it's plausible. The important thing is to protect you and your family, and I'll do everything I can in that regard. And I think we have some time on our side. Alex may have managed to leave a day later than we thought he did, but the army is very strict about the whereabouts of its new recruits. The man has been in basic training for three weeks, so we have at least three more weeks of grace before he finishes boot camp and gets himself assigned somewhere. Alex will be due a weekend pass right about then." Sarge got up and picked up the drill in a businesslike fashion, as if to finish the shed before the day of confrontation was at hand. "The wisest course would be for both of us to have a talk with your mother."

"No, no, *no*! What if she thinks you're crazy and asks you to move out?"

"That's a possibility," he replied mildly. "Nevertheless, she has a right to be informed of any threat to her daughter and her sister, has she not?"

"Sarge, you promised, you promised," I cried out, although I knew in my heart that promises made to kids didn't count for much.

"Yes, but I believe I qualified my promise. I said I would keep silent unless someone's life depended on it. You've done your best to convince me that your life does, and you know you're very dear and important to me." He smiled, turned, and started to drill, discouraging any reply. At first my heart felt warm and good that he cared about me. But my second thought was that this ought to teach me never to trust a grown-up again as long as I lived. Which might not be all that long if Mr. Carver got me somewhere alone.

I shot my last arrow. Over the whine of the drill, I said: "Sarge, they don't want to know how come Aunt Bette is now a rich heiress. It will spoil everything if they have to think about the letter I gave Alex Carver and how it drove him to push Mr. Snow under the ice. Aunt Bette will feel guilty, and she'll hate me for it. You know how she is."

He stopped the drill for a moment. "I'll reflect on all this, and I'll let you know what I decide is the right action. Will that do?"

"Before you squeal?"

"Yes, before."

I felt cheered. I had a stay of execution. And three weeks to plan my strategy.

Chapter 22

In which Aunt Bette gains a new admirer, and I get myself ready for trouble.

Mother was still pinch-hitting for absentee telephone operators, day or night, but she quit altogether when Aunt Bette got sick. The flu had begun early that year, storming through Whitford in October like the Allies mopping up Nazis in Italy. In the case of Aunt Bette, who wasn't as strong as ordinary people, the flu naturally turned into pneumonia. After what had happened to my dad, when Dr. Woodward pronounced this dread diagnosis and called for an ambulance, my mother screamed and collapsed. She began sobbing from somewhere deep inside her chest. This was scary, because normally my mother never cried no matter what. But when she did cry, it seemed she couldn't stop.

Dr. Woodward put an arm around her shoulders. "Now, now, we have some new wonder drugs to fight pneumococci. I'm sure that Bette will respond very well to the treatment I've prescribed. But until her lungs are clear, I'd like her to be in Jordan Hospital."

Dr. Woodward must not have been all that sure of the new drug's healing power, because he spent a lot of his own time at my aunt's bedside. He even brought her flowers from Rosie's Posies in Plymouth, which seemed to cheer Mother as well as Aunt Bette.

Visiting my aunt wasn't easy. We couldn't ask anyone to waste precious gas carting us to Plymouth. Even the Olds was worthless to us, since Aunt Bette had used up all her gas stamps in trips to Boston. So Mother would hitch a ride with Dr. Woodward when he did his morning hospital rounds. Doctors got all the gas they needed. Patients were not supposed to have visitors in the mornings (that was when doctors performed examinations and various nasty tests) but Dr. Woodward fixed it so that Mother was treated like a private nurse.

Once I went along at Aunt Bette's request. I was pleased that she called me specially from the hospital, even when she whispered, "For heaven's sake, Amelia, bring me some cigarettes. You know very well where I keep them. And don't let your mother discover what you're doing, or she'll take them away. She and Doug are in league against me, but I know I can count on you to be on my side. That's a good girl. You're a real pal."

Whenever Aunt Bette and I shared a secret, it almost seemed as if she were my sister rather than my aunt. I thought about how much I'd wanted a sister, or a brother, or something, at least a dog—although I almost had Ollie—while I worked on a hiding place for the cigarettes. It took me hours to cut away the inside of one of the books Miss Pratt had discarded as unworthy of Whitford's library. First, of course, I had to read it. *Bad Girl* was the story of a foolish teenager who let a young man kiss her on a bed, and in the next chapter she was pregnant. While the kissing scene was passionate and exciting, the rest of the story was disappointingly unromantic. When it came to disreputable young men, I far preferred Sydney Carton in *A Tale of Two Cities*.

Unfortunately, I wasn't allowed to bring Ollie to the hospital. Another of the world's stupid rules, I thought, since a visit from one's own dog, providing the animal had a minimum of good manners, might be quite as healing as a dose of medicine.

Aunt Bette was propped up on several fluffy pillows, her face pale, her expression brave, and a faint glow of Fatal Apple on her lips. She really did have a beautiful mouth.

Her dark hair was a bit lank from not being washed, but it was tied back with a fresh blue ribbon that almost matched her eyes.

"Hi, honey! How about a big hug for your old aunt."

I hugged her gingerly, feeling how slight her bones were, like a bird's. "Did you bring my pajamas, Catherine?"

From the cloth shopping bag she was carrying, Mother unearthed Aunt Bette's satin pajamas with the Chinese jacket. "Really, Bette. How inappropriate do you plan to be? Besides, this red and black stuff is going to make you look even more washed out than you are already."

"Thanks for the compliment, dear. I need something pretty to lift my spirits. I'm feeling rather down in the dumps today."

"I brought you a present," I volunteered, hoping it would prove to be a spirit-lifter, also. I fished it out of my pocket—a bottle of Tabu I'd bought at the Whitford drugstore. I'd liked the advertisement that showed a Victorian woman at the piano being swept into the arms of her handsome male accompanist, who seemed suddenly overcome with passion. It had taken most of my savings to buy even a very small amount.

She thanked me with a funny smile that made me wonder if there was something amusing about my gift, but she put a drop of the heavy sweet scent on each of her narrow wrists. "Just the right thing to go with my satin outfit," she declared. "Doctors will be swooning right and left." She eyed the other package in my hand with eager interest. My mother began to dust the windowsills and rearrange the pink roses.

"And I brought you a book to read, too," I said, handing her the copy of *Bad Girl,* which I had wrapped in red tissue paper out of the Christmas decorations box. The book's heart contained a treasury of Parliaments, nearly two boxes of them emptied into the carved-out interior. The few cigarettes that wouldn't fit I hid in a leather pouch I'd made at a Camp Fire Girl meeting, stashed behind the row of Bobbsey Twins in my book case.

"Thank you, honey. I'll open this later when things get dull around here. Which is all the time."

"Speaking of swooning doctors..." said my mother, looking at her sister inquiringly.

"As you see." Aunt Bette gestured toward the cascade of pink roses in a vase on her windowsill. I wandered over to see what could be seen from the window. It was a pretty decent view, a rolling lawn that was still green and some woods beyond in the last of the autumn colors. Some other rooms only looked out on the parking lot.

Aunt Bette sighed and said, cryptically, "But it will never be the way it was with Jack."

"And a good thing, too. Now tell me, Bette, what did they give you for breakfast?"

"Oh, I couldn't eat a thing. Some kind of hot white cereal, and a cheese thing. I had a half a slice of toast and a swallow of orange juice."

"Just as I thought. They have no idea how to feed sick people in any hospital. I know what you need to build you up," Mother said, bringing out a little brown pot of custard and a baked apple in a glass dish from her shopping bag. "You eat these now. I made them specially for you, and they'll do you a world of good." I guessed Aunt Bette should be grateful that milk toast wasn't portable.

"Well, well, how's my loveliest patient today? Having a bit of homemade nourishment, I see," Dr. Woodward said in a hearty doctor tone as he joined us at Aunt Bette's bedside. Most people called him Woody, so I did, too, but Aunt Bette and Mother always referred to him as 'Doug' or 'Dr. Doug.' He was a tall, fair-haired, pleasant-faced man who walked a little stooped over as if the better to see whatever he was peering at through the thick lenses of his tortoise-shell glasses. It was not surprising to learn that the army had turned him down. "I'd like to put you in charge of our convalescent diets, Catherine. I'm sure you could show those dietitians some wholesome restorative dishes to bring back a patient's strength."

Woody knew how to win over my mother with no shots fired, I noticed. She blushed with pleasure. Aunt Bette winked at me over her shoulder. Dr. Woodward took hold of my aunt's thin wrist and seemed to lose his train of thought, for it took him several minutes to check her pulse. Then he put his stethoscope against her chest rather low down between the lacy inserts of her nightgown. "Hmmmm," he mumbled, flushing slightly. "A little clearer to-day—that's good news. You'll be going home soon. I don't know if I'm glad or sorry about that. You really brighten up this old place, you know."

I didn't get a chance to observe any more of his examination before my mother grabbed my hand and pulled me out the door into the corridor.

"We'll go down to the cafeteria for some of that dishwater they call coffee now. You may have a half cup, if you like. With lots of milk," Mother said. I wasn't thrilled. I thought about the rich coffee that Mrs. Korhonen brewed in her blue enamel pot, then laced with thick cream and sugar. When I grew up, I would learn how to make Mrs. K's coffee and have endless cups of it morning, noon, and night.

While we were sipping the tepid tan stuff in the cafeteria, I asked Mother, "Is Dr. Woodward sweet on Aunt Bette? He called her lovely, and he treats her more like a princess than a patient."

"Your aunt could do worse. A nice professional man with a satisfactory practice and a decent income. Clean cut, no objectionable personal habits." It sounded as if Mother were filling out a report card on Dr. Woodward, at the bottom, in the space provided for *Remarks*. Personally, I knew Aunt Bette could do worse. A lot worse, like the village murderer.

"Do you think he'll ask her to marry him soon? Like maybe during the next week or two?" I asked.

"That will be none of your business, I'm sure, young lady," Mother said. "But if he should ask her, and she accepts him, that would be all right with me. I would have preferred Alex Carver, but *a bird in the hand*, I say. Alex is gone and the Lord only knows when he'll be back." And that was as close to having a gossip with my mother as I was ever going to get.

When Aunt Bette got out of the hospital a few days later, she insisted on going home to Snow's, even though my mother pleaded with her to recuperate at our house. "No, no," said my aunt, "I've been enough trouble all ready. Just send Amelia to me after school to do my errands and take Ollie for a walk. She'll be well-paid, of course. I don't expect her to dance attendance for nothing. Doug will be stopping by when he makes his evening house calls. He's going to save me for last. 'Dessert,' he calls it." She smirked, and my mother chuckled.

How I looked forward to making some money! And Aunt Bette paid me fifty cents a day, top wages for an hour's work. But my aunt didn't make life any easier for us by convalescing at her own place. Now Mother felt she had two houses to clean instead of one. Every Friday she gave Snow's house a thorough mopping, scoured the kitchen, and changed Aunt Bette's bed. I was expected to help after school on that day, unpaid. We took the laundry home to be washed and ironed by Mother.

Aunt Bette, who still wore her red and black satin pajamas a great deal, would wander around us with a small feather duster, exclaiming over the beauty and value of certain pieces, or telling us more about their history. She would dust and rearrange the mantle while Mother Hoovered the Oriental rugs.

Mother often stocked Aunt Bette's pantry with freshly made muffins and cookies to feed Dr. Doug Woodward through the week. Sugar was no problem for us now, because Mr. Snow had hoarded ten-pound bags of it in his cellar. The only problem was that the sugar had hardened to rock and had to be pounded and sifted back to its former granulated state. My job, naturally—in complete secrecy, lest the neighbors get riled. That meant hammering away in the cellar's cold room, making all the mason jars tremble on their shelves.

Sarge said he was reminded of Edgar Allen Poe's "The Tell-Tale Heart," which made me curious enough to read it. It was about a murdered man's heart thumping under the floorboards louder and louder until the murderer confessed. A good tale to read aloud on Halloween. I would try it out on Daisy and Jay.

Along with the extra cleaning, there were pots of soup, custard, and cooked fruits to transport to the invalid. Prunes especially, since Aunt Bette was always constipated. I wondered if discussing these practical matters put a crimp on Woody's courtship style.

Meanwhile, time was ticking away like an unexploded bomb. Sarge and I had several talks about the possible return of Alex Carver when he finished basic training. "If Carver comes back to cause us any trouble, I'll be on his backside like a coat of paint," Sarge declared. "But I'll hold off on explaining matters to your mother until we see what happens. I agree it would be too bad to throw a bucket of cold water on your aunt's inheritance if it doesn't turn out to be necessary. Maybe Carver will have the good sense to stay clear of Whitford in case you've had a word with Chief Ferro about that accident. Nothing we can prove though, and well Carver knows it. We don't even have Margaret's letter to establish motive. The uncorroborated word of a young lady like yourself would not be enough to bring a serious charge like murder. I guess you realize that."

I wished life were more like novels, and that some ghostly manifestation of Mr. Snow would entrap Mr. Carver into a guilty outburst. I thought about arranging something, but it seemed to me that Mr. Carver was too cool a character to be driven by Halloween tricks into a hysterical confession. Instead I had better arm myself with something solid, like one of Aunt Bette's little handguns. Since I was at Snow's every afternoon anyway, there was no difficulty in running upstairs for an armful of magazines stored up there—*Punch* with the drawings of Gibson girls and *Esquire* with the naughty cartoons. I helped myself to the silver-handled handgun and the extra box of bullets hidden in the cedar closet.

But I needed to know if I was able to load the weapon and shoot it. I decided to practice somewhere deep in the woods road where no one would hear me. After returning Ollie to my Aunt's care one afternoon around four o'clock, I trotted about a quarter mile into the woods road, shivering as the October evening turned freezing. My teeth chattered and my hands shook as I loaded one bullet into the chamber. Holding it straight out, I sighted down the miniscule barrel, but that seemed too cowboyish for such a ladylike weapon. Perhaps one should just bring it up casually about waist-high and squeeze the trigger gently in the general direction of the target. After all, a man was a pretty fair-sized target. Looking around for something of a similar size, I spotted a bushel basket stuck between three birch trees. Perhaps I would prop that up shoulder high into the one of the trees and see if I could hit it while aiming from the waist. Laying the silver and pearl handgun down on the ground, I set about rearranging the basket.

The basket mewed! For a moment I was frightened, thinking of some nasty wild animal like a rabid fox, but then I steeled myself to look inside. It was only four kittens curled up together, all the colors of fallen leaves in a heap. Three of them were moving, but the last seemed too still. Someone must have dumped them here to die. Surely they could never survive on their own. An unexpected litter of kittens was not a highly valued item in Whitford. Tenderly, I patted each little head in turn and debated our best option—bringing them home to Mother's screams or to Aunt Bette's house to be terrorized by Ollie. Since I was nearer to Aunt Bette's, I'd try tugging at her heartstrings first, a tactic that would never work with my mother. I almost went off without the gun but at the last moment I remembered and stuck it into the pocket of my lumber jacket.

Lucky for those kittens, Woody was making a house call on Aunt Bette earlier than usual that day. Although she loved animals, my aunt may not have made such a fuss over the little dears had Woody not been there to admire her womanly concern. He inspected them carefully, listening to their chests with his stethoscope. As I had thought, we'd lost one, but the healthy kittens were old enough to be weaned and could be saved if carefully nursed and fed several times a day, Woody said. I offered to bury the kitten who had died.

"Oh, don't look at me all teary," Aunt Bette said. "I'll take the day shift, and you can tend them after school. Let's keep them in the pantry for the time being, with a good big box of sand. Maybe they'll turn out to be good mousers. But you'll have to find homes for them, you know. This is only a temporary arrangement." With that, she went into the kitchen to check the percolator. It smelled to me as if it had boiled over already. Leaning over to say good-bye and admire their sweet doll faces, I forgot about the gun and it fell out of my pocket right at Woody's feet.

"Water pistol," I said, scooping it up and shoving it back into my pocket before he got a good look.

"Fancy little thing," he commented, but his attention was swept away by Aunt Bette appearing with a tray. "Here, let me help you with that! I'm supposed to be looking after you, Bette, not the other way around. Mmmm … those muffins do look grand." Gallantly, he lifted the tray out of her hands and set it on the coffee table while my aunt smiled modestly.

Ollie ran downstairs, fresh from a nap on Aunt Bette's bed, to see what sort of party was brewing. I took the opportunity to remove the kittens to the pantry, where I gave them a pie tin of milk they could all fit around. Their tiny pink tongues seemed to get the idea right away. I fixed a flat sand box and shoved it under the counter below the pantry window. The basket I tipped over on its side, stuffing it with some old toweling used for dusters, so the kittens could crawl back into it when they got sleepy. I could hear Ollie sniffing all along the edge of the closed door, so I left by way of the pantry window.

As soon as I got the chance, a few days later, I tried out the handgun, far into the woods road. It went off okay, making a big sound for such a little thing, and a fearful smell of burning powder. My target this time was a disappointing history test I didn't want to bring home. I stuck the stapled papers on a pointed tree branch and winged it right through the C minus. *Not bad,* I thought. *So much for the Industrial Revolution and Its Effects, about as dull a subject as even a history teacher could drone about while the real-life invasion of Fascist Italy was happening right now.*

I had a calendar in my room where I'd been marking off the days from the time Mr. Carver left for Fort Devens and was sent for basic training. Six weeks came and went uneventfully. Maybe Sarge was right, and Mr. Carver would go off to win the war without killing anyone else on the home front. At the end of the sixth week, I went into the Friendship Unitarian Church after school to say a prayer of gratitude at the altar. No one was there. The place was as cool and quiet as a tomb, with a sweet odor of decay wafting from flowers leftover from the last service. I only wished that Unitarians had a bank of money candles. I would have liked to pay my nickel and light a candle to go with my prayer. Perhaps I should become a Catholic. Maybe even a nun.

Someday when Mr. Carver lay dying and I was the nun tending his last agonies, he would be wracked with guilt and confess his crimes to me. Or would I have to be a priest for that?

Chapter 23

In which Aunt Bette plans everything, my mother is thrilled, and I can't stop worrying.

It's a sad business to bury a small dead thing. My little cemetery was in back of our house, among oak, birch, and pine trees, beside a natural path that generations had marked as the easiest footing for traveling from one side of the woods to the other. Once we'd used it as our short cut to the lumber yard when my father owned it. I wrapped the kitten in a scrap of soft wool and laid him to rest in the ground near Geraint, the baby squirrel I hadn't been able to save. Stone markers were more lasting than wooden crosses, which tended to fall into disrepair over the winter months. Scratching a name or at least an initial into its surface was a way to honor the lost life, only this little fellow didn't have a name. So I called him Baby K. Perhaps his spirit would keep some child's spirit company in the afterlife—if there was an afterlife.

I wondered if Mr. Snow's ghost was still hovering around the scenes of his former life, like Hamlet's father, waiting for someone to punish his killer. A scary idea. Shivering, I hurried home to find a hiding place for Aunt Bette's handgun, which I fervently hoped she would not remember and go looking for. Otherwise, I might become an untimely ghost myself.

My scheme to smuggle cigarettes into the hospital had been such a success, I decided to sacrifice another book rescued from Miss Pratt's wastebasket. I took *Coney Island Casanova* out to the new shed where the sturdy workbench made cutting away the interior of the book easier and safer than working with the volume in my lap. I'd read most of the book anyway, celebrating some guy's under-the-pier affairs, a grimy story that probably deserved its fate. The silver and pearl gun and the box of bullets fit into its interior nicely, and the book was shelved inconspicuously in my bedroom between *Ivanhoe* and *Robin Hood*. As soon we knew Alex Carver was safely overseas, I'd unload the ladylike gun and return it to the handbag in the attic cedar closet. And no one would be the wiser.

Meanwhile, the only way I could keep track of my nemesis was to read the letters he sent regularly to Aunt Bette, which she continued to stash in a pigeonhole of the Governor Winthrop desk. I was relieved not to find them tied up with a pink ribbon, not only because that might indicate she was taking his sweet talk seriously, but also because I might not be able to retie the bow as elegantly as she did. Aunt Bette had an eye for detail.

One more good thing about animal friends—they never squeal. Ollie lay with his nose between his paws, looking up at me with ears perked, watching me intently every time I read a new letter. If anyone came in the door, front or back, he was off like a furry flash to greet Aunt Bette or Woody or Mother or whomever, which made him an ideal lookout.

The three kittens (temporarily named Winkin, Blinkin, and Nod until we found them new homes) had the run of the kitchen now, with their sand box still under the pantry shelf, but they were not allowed to roam through the rest of the house. It was one of my jobs to clean out the sand box every day after school. Twice a week I changed to fresh sand and stirred in some baking soda. Aunt Bette said if her pantry began to smell badly because I neglected to keep the box clean, I could count on her dumping the kittens back in the woods. I didn't think she'd really be that mean, but I wasn't taking any chances.

Whenever I went through to the other rooms, I had to be careful to close the kitchen door before the kittens scooted out into forbidden territory. Fortunately, Ollie had made friends with the new residents after all—and more than friends, because he behaved rather like a parent, alternately cuddling and correcting the little creatures. Sometimes when the door was shut between them, he sighed with relief, and other times he got nervous and whined at the crack under the door, seeming to wonder if Winkin, Blinkin, and Nod were getting along all right without him.

Late one afternoon, while Aunt Bette was driving around with Woody on house calls, I took the opportunity to read the latest letter. It included a snapshot of Mr. Carver in uniform, casually posed against a cannon. Every photo of a serviceman sent home to his family seemed to stress an easy familiarity with something he was leaning on—an airplane, a jeep, a buddy. I bet all those guys were scared to death, just as I would be if I were in their boots. Mr. Carver was smiling his engaging Ronald Colman smile. I had to admit he looked pretty handsome, but I counted it a good sign that the picture was still tucked in the letter and not on display.

The letter itself was a humdinger. Mr. Carver pleaded with my aunt to send him a hopeful word to sustain him while he went off for his next assignment. He wrote that her friendship was the most beautiful part of his life, that he thought of her every day, and dreamed of her every night. (*Oh, puke!*) He wrote that he'd been tapped for Army intelligence and so transferred to a civilian post with the OSS. because of his proficiency with languages, especially Finnish which he spoke fluently, having perfected his abilities with the Finnish community in Whitford. He was being sent somewhere in the south to train, and they wouldn't even let him have a weekend pass. (*What luck!*) Still, after all the work I'd put into cutting up *Casanova*, I thought I wouldn't return the weapon and bullets just yet.

Something about the photo nagged at me to take it out and study it again. Did Mr. Carver's features look just a bit like those of Mr. Snow when he was a young man? Especially as he appeared in the yellowing photo that Mrs. Snow had kept on her bureau. Had Aunt Bette noticed the similarity? I ran upstairs with the photo to compare Mr. Carver with Mrs. Snow's picture in its ornate frame, silver with tendrils and fronds.

Big mistake! Because I missed the warning my four-footed lookout gave when he scampered to the door to greet his mistress. I only realized my danger when I heard Woody's warm, low laughter and the sound of my aunt rattling the percolator in the kitchen. The letter was only partly pulled out of its pigeonhole in the library. I had almost put it back before I decided to have another look at Mr. Carver beside Mr. Snow—a look that confirmed my suspicions. Wouldn't Aunt Bette's sharp eyes notice the out-of-line letter? But how was I to get the snapshot back and get myself out of the house undetected? Aunt Bette thought I had left the house when she did, but I'd returned through the pantry window.

I crouched at the top of the stairs, listening intently. There were more sounds of coffee being prepared and served, laughter, and low murmurs. They took their coffee into the living room at last. I would have to sneak down the stairs into the library, put the snapshot back in the letter, and then get out through the kitchen. I sure hoped Aunt Bette and Woody were concentrating on each other as I tiptoed down the carpeted stairs. Ollie came bounding out of the living room and stood at the bottom of the stairs wagging his rear end, eager to join in whatever game I was playing. I ducked around the corner into the library with the dog right on my heels, slipped the photo into the letter and the letter in line with the others.

So far, so good.

Suddenly I heard my aunt's laughter and light footsteps as she left the living room and started upstairs. Flattening myself against a bookshelf inside the library door, I heard her murmur, "That's odd...I don't remember leaving on any lights upstairs."

"What's the matter, Bette?" asked Woody, coming out of the living room into the hallway.

"It wasn't dark yet when we started your calls. So I didn't turn on those lights upstairs. You don't think there's anyone up there, do you? No, there can't be. Ollie would be barking like crazy. Ollie? Where are you, honey?" Ollie bounded out of the library. "See, here he is, my good little watchdog, keeping an eye on everything for his mommy."

"I'd better go up and check around anyway," said Woody. "You stay right here near the phone." After a few minutes of opening and closing doors, he called down, "Everything's okay up here."

I stopped breathing as he came back downstairs. He and my aunt were standing in the hall right outside the library door. Then I heard another sound—a soft, rustling, whimpering sound. *They were kissing!*

"A beautiful woman like you shouldn't be living alone," Dr. Doug murmured.

"What do you suggest I do?" asked my aunt coquettishly

"Bette, you know what I'd like, but I'm not in a position...It wouldn't be fair to you. I'm just starting out here in Whitford. I don't even have a real house, just my office and the two rooms in back that I use for living quarters. But I love you, and I worry about you. You're a woman who needs care, real care."

"I have enough house for us both," Aunt Bette assured him. Her voice was clear and crisp for someone who was just coming out of a major clinch. "Why don't we get married, and then we can live here together. Surely this would be an ideal doctor's residence. In fact, it's right next door to where Dr. Tyrell used to live before he split up with Inez."

Woody murmured something I couldn't hear.

My aunt laughed, a tinkling affectionate laugh. "Of course, darling. I wouldn't expect you to move your office in here, with a steady stream of patients traipsing in and out. Your medical practice can stay right where it is. And we'll have a fine life together. You know, I have a marvelous diamond I want to use as an engagement ring...nearly four carats!"

I still couldn't hear what he replied, but it didn't matter. When Aunt Bette laid out her plans, hardly anyone dared to drag his heels. She might be small in stature but her spirit was mighty forceful.

Whatever Woody mumbled into her hair, she continued, "Just a small wedding, I think. We'll have a quiet civil ceremony in Boston, and a wedding lunch at the Ritz. We'll go on our wedding trip by train, and Sarge can drive Catherine and Amelia home in your car so that gas won't be a problem."

It did seem as if Aunt Bette had figured out everything in advance in case the subject of marriage happened to arise. Finally she stopped talking for a few minutes while they were kissing again, and after a while they went upstairs together. I wondered if they were going to kiss on the bed, like in *Bad Girl*. Somehow, I couldn't imagine it and shook away the image of my petite aunt pressed onto the chenille bedspread by the doctor's angular frame.

What a narrow escape I'd had! I patted Ollie good-bye and slipped out the kitchen door, which wasn't all that easy with three kittens underfoot.

Thrilled as I was at the thought of Aunt Bette marrying anyone besides Alex Carver, and especially someone as gentle and good-hearted as Woody, I knew if she ever found out I'd heard *her* proposing marriage *to him*, I would be in big trouble. That wasn't the accepted way. The suitor was supposed to be on his knees and the gal flustered at the suddenness of his proposal. But maybe Aunt Bette's method made more sense, since weddings always ended up being planned by women anyway.

My mother cried when she heard the good news from Aunt Bette, and I acted surprised, perhaps too surprised. Aunt Bette looked at me sharply. I studied the library book in my lap, *The Fifth Column.*

"Oh, I won't have to worry about you anymore!" Mother declared. "You'll be settled at last. Not only a professional man, but a *physician* to look after your health. What could be better than that!" She took my aunt's hand and studied the ring on her left hand. The diamond looked enormous on Aunt Bette, whose hands were slim and dainty, The stone kept rolling around on her finger, too heavy to stay in one place. Her nails were faultlessly manicured in Debutante Blush. Her dark hair was a perfect page boy, and she wore gray flannel slacks and a rose-colored twin set, set off by a small string of pearls I knew were real.

"Well, that rock should knock everyone's eyes out," said Mother dubiously. "But you'd better get a ring guard on it before it ends up in some sink trap."

"Now here's what I want to do," said Aunt Bette, studying her sister. Mother looked tired after an afternoon spent baking tarts for Inez Tyrell's bridge party, and her flowered blue housedress was spotted with raspberry jam and dusted with flour. "I want us to have a real day off together on Friday...go up to Boston on the train and choose our wedding outfits. Ollie can stay with Sarge. I'm going to buy something simply lovely for you and for Amelia, you'll see. And here's the other thing, Catherine. You've been perfectly wonderful helping me with the housework after I got out of the hospital, but enough is enough. As a married woman, I should be able to manage on my own, with maybe a little weekly help from one of the girls who works at the Whitford Inn. They're often looking for an extra dollar or two from some daytime work."

"Well, if you want to tolerate slipshod help," my mother said, getting up heavily to put on the kettle for tea. "Dirt under the rugs and no respect for fine china."

"No one will ever be as careful and capable as you, Catherine. I know that. So I'll have to watch them closely and train them properly, without any doubt. But you need to take things a bit easier now. Let Inez bake her own raspberry pastries. My sister shouldn't have to do that sort of thing, for the pittance Inez pays."

"Oh, yes? Well, I've never been ashamed of doing an honest day's work, and I never will be. It won't be that easy to make ends meet with all my boarders gone. Now Bunny Cronin is getting married next month and moving over to the Poor Farm." Mother must have been distracted, because she set out three cups, which must include me. Could it be that tea was no longer stunting my growth?

"Don't worry about a thing," said Aunt Bette. "There are always interns and even some nurses at Jordan hospital looking for a pleasant place to stay with some decent food. I've told Doug to send two or three of them here to you. Medical personnel have C stickers and can drive all over the county if need be. So what do you say to that!"

Where would poor Sarge end up when Aunt Bette got our bedrooms filled with young doctors? I worried this problem over in my mind while nibbling on an oatmeal cookie from the plate Mother set before us. We always had cookies now that I was pounding out Mr. Snow's rock sugar in the cellar.

"You've got to get Sarge out to make more room," my traitorous aunt said, as if reading my mind. "No wonder you're going broke with him eating you out of house and home."

"Listen, Bette," Mother said, getting up to quiet the whistling kettle. "Sarge has put everything in this house from cellar to attic into perfect running order. He's cleared away that mess of a burned barn, and now he's almost completed the most beautifully designed shed and workroom a person could ask for. Why, as far as I'm concerned, the man is worth his weight in gold."

A heaviness lifted off my heart. We were going to keep Sarge after all!

Aunt Bette poured from the tea pot my mother had filled. It was a special blend of S. S. Pierce tea that she'd given us, fragrantly smoky. "Well, at least move him from that big front bedroom into my old room. It's perfectly nice and snug."

"I'll think about it," said Mother. And she did move Sarge during the weeks that followed. But not upstairs. Instead, they cleared out the old sewing and storage room, which was on the first floor next to her bedroom. It was a tiny place, but big enough for a single bed and bureau, once the sewing machine had been packed away in the attic. I only hoped this meant Mother wouldn't be making me any more of those strangely puckered jumpers for school.

During the confusion of clearing-the-storage-room day, I seized the opportunity to get rid of that bolt of rick-rack remnants, a trim Mother applied with abandon when the sewing mood was upon her. At first it refused to sink, and I had to weight it down with stones. What a good feeling it was to see that mint green, pink, and baby blue zig-zag stuff gradually disappearing into the greenish depths of Silver Sand Pond.

Now there were four empty rooms upstairs available for boarders, plus my room in back, which I still thought the nicest since it was the only one with a view of the pond. One by one during that October, as promised, my aunt got them filled with boarders. First there was a big nurse named Rita. Then a Southern woman and her pregnant daughter. The girl spent a lot of time in the bathroom, and the mother frequently had to pound on the door. "Beatrice, get out of that bathroom," a refrain that made all of us giggle ever afterward. And finally, an intern, Dr. Fred, who looked more like an exhausted patient than a doctor, took the big front room.

Mother suggested that Sarge build some bookcases on each side of the fireplace in the living room. Probably she was tired of looking at the orange crates he'd been using to store books rescued from the fire at his cottage, plus others that he seemed to attract out of thin air, the way a blossom attracts bugs. Everything was beginning to look snug and safe at last. The boarders brought in enough money for us to get by, not to mention a stack of ration books with blue and red stamps, and Mother made sure that Sarge charged cash money for repairing people's irreplaceable appliances. The best part was Mother and Sarge really seeming to like each other. That gave me a safe comfortable feeling inside my chest.

Aunt Bette postponed the date for her wedding to Dr. Doug until the tenth of November. For some odd reason, even though she wasn't getting married in Whitford, she resented the idea of getting married the same month as Miss Cronin. My aunt didn't even want to be a wedding guest because the ceremony was taking place at the Poor Farm. Reluctantly she agreed to attend the reception, after absolutely forbidding us to wear the new dresses she'd bought us for *her* wedding. I tied a pink satin bow on Ollie's collar anyway. It turned out to be a great and memorable party.

The Cronins—father, mother, brother, and sister of my science teacher—provided the music with a sort of family band they had formed, since the elder Cronins taught musical instruments in Kates Hill. They played some Gay Nineties hits like "By the sea, by the sea…" and "If you were the only girl in the world…"and a medley of show tunes from *The Merry Widow,* which seemed like a odd choice to me.

My mother had outdone herself with a three-tiered wedding cake and a fancy buffet of little sandwiches and preserves, her gift to the bride. The inmates of the Poor Farm had slicked up their appearance for the big event and were obviously quite excited at the thought of having Miss Cronin (now Mrs. Ames) to brighten up their drab lives. Her frequent visits to the Poor Farm had often been enlivened by lectures on cultural subjects, arts and crafts, and concerts. Sarge said people might start paying to stay at the Poor Farm after Bunny Cronin moved in, like for a visit to some kind of educational camp.

In her princess-style cream-colored dress with long sleeves and a sweetheart neckline thinly edged in lace, Miss Cronin looked radiantly happy but not exactly what I would call a beautiful bride. I guessed she was pretty to her new husband Lively Ames, though. With his shock of red hair and permanently sunburned complexion, he beamed at her like a small earthbound sun.

Lively's sister Merry had made two bowls of strange punch with Kool-Aid. My mother, who was flushed from serving food, had several glasses of the orange stuff that was half-gin, so Aunt Bette said. I supposed that's why Mother and Sarge did a rather wild dance together, loudly singing "I go back to Maxim's where fun and frolic beams" as they whirled around the Poor Farm's big empty living room. A mother who is having too good a time can be an embarrassment, but Aunt Bette pinched the back of my arm and told me to stop scowling, it was doing my mother good to let her hair down. And down it came, her usually neat gold-gray braids unraveling wildly as they waltzed.

The new bride and groom planned to take the bus to Bangor, Maine, for their wedding trip, which made Aunt Bette laugh all the way home. *Her* wedding trip would be spent in New York seeing Broadway shows and touring museums.

"We can't all be heiresses, Bette," my mother said. The gin had worn off and she was her gloomy old self again—what a relief! But my aunt just zoomed along the road (thirty-five miles an hour!) smiling with satisfaction, the huge diamond glittering as she turned the steering wheel.

While we were on the subject of weddings, I took the chance of asking, "You haven't written to Mr. Carver about your wedding, Aunt Bette, have you?"

"Well, well—why do you ask? As a matter of fact, I've been meaning to do just that."

"Good heavens," said my mother. "Don't you think you owe it to him? Here he is thinking that you two... You know what I mean. He has some hopes, and you ought to let him down as quickly and kindly as possible."

Aunt Bette sighed. "I guess you're right. I suppose he'll be devastated."

"He'll get over it," my mother said. "You're not the only pebble on the beach, Bette."

I wondered if Mr. Carver *would* get over it all that easily. How might he really feel about losing Aunt Bette and all of Mr. Snow's estate with her? My stomach began to ache just thinking about that. I exchanged glances with Sarge who was beside me in the back seat of the Olds, and he looked rather grim.

"Maybe you should wait until after the war, then," I suggested, "when Mr. Carver won't have so much on his mind, like fighting the Nazis."

"Oh, will you all leave me alone about it. Do you mind if I keep a little of my personal life to myself?" Clearly, Aunt Bette was getting irritated, so we were all quiet for the rest of ride home.

Chapter 24

In which my birthday is celebrated, sort of, and Aunt Bette's wedding plans are jeopardized by Woody's weird accident.

W hen Daisy and Jay's parents finally got divorced, I shared their feelings of despair and helplessness at the unpredictability of grown-ups. Would the twins be sentenced to a boring life with their conservative dad in Boston, or endure a rootless existence with their mother and the trombone player in New Jersey? Or even worse, would they be split up in some crazy division of property? But finally, the reprieve! It was decided that, since school had already begun, they would stay with their grandmother at least for the rest of their sophomore year.

Which is how Jay and Daisy talked me out of having a party for my fourteenth birthday. Given the okay by Mrs. Eliot to stage a *Hooray-We're-Staying* party on Halloween, the twins explained, two parties so close together would be an unpatriotic waste of sweet treats and decorations. But if my mother would bake a birthday cake big enough to feed twenty or so kids at the Eliot party, we could combine our two events. It seemed to make sense, and yet I felt let down. A person is supposed to be the star on her own birthday. This was carrying wartime sacrifice too far.

Mother agreed to make the cake with surprising readiness, declaring that it would probably be the best thing ever served at the Eliot house. We still had plenty of Mr. Snow's rock sugar and eggs from the Poor Farm chickens. Perhaps Mother was secretly relieved not to have my friends leaving black shoe marks all over her carefully waxed hardwood floors, as they had on other occasions.

On my real birthday, October 29 (Black Tuesday!), Mother gave me a flannel nightgown she'd made. It was decorated with pink ribbons, since her bolts of rick-rack had curiously disappeared on the day she'd moved the sewing machine up to the attic. Sarge's gift was a record player he'd rescued from the town dump—revamped, refinished, and in prime working order, plus an actual new recording of *White Christmas*. I guessed the record had been part of his payment for fixing the Cronins' furnace. And Aunt Bette thrilled me with an aqua sweater and a gold locket set with three seed pearls. Inside were two tiny glassed frames on hinges, with clipped photographs of people we didn't know. Someday I'd replace them when I decided who I wanted to keep on my heart.

Minna and I hitched a ride with Woody to Plymouth. We hung around Plymouth Rock, eyeing the sailors who never even noticed us, then had a big lunch of fried clam rolls and milk shakes, topped off with a matinee at the Plymouth Theater—*Shadow of a Doubt.* Joseph Cotton as the murderous uncle reminded me eerily of how dangerous my life might have been if Aunt Bette had married Mr. Carver.

On Halloween, Aunt Bette drove the Olds to our house so that Sarge could transport Mother's birthday cake, as big as a sofa cushion, to the Eliot's house. Even though I had to wear a navy blue skirt my mother had made, the bunchy zipper was hidden by my new aqua twin set, and I'd scuffed my saddle shoes through the dirt around the shed so they wouldn't look too new. Just before it was time to leave, Aunt Bette grabbed me in her surprisingly steely grip to curl the hair around my face with Mother's curling iron, which was a scarier experience than going to the dentist. That sizzling odor! I expected to go up in flames at any moment, like Joan of Arc.

"Do you have to wear those terrible bobby things?" she asked. "They hide your slender ankles, which you get from me." She held out one slim leg so that we could admire its silk-clad shape. Then she arranged my gold locket precisely in the center and patted my cheek. "You're getting on all right."

"And she's got your chest as well," my mother commented, giving me the same sharp once-over that she might have used to assess a prospective roasting chicken, gauging its skimpiness. The satisfaction of wearing one of my two new bras under my sweater was instantly deflated.

Still, I thought Sarge and I made a grand entrance, like the Queen of Sheba with her native bearer carrying treasure to King Solomon. And I felt really glad that the twins weren't moving away after all. I'd have missed their company, which was like belonging to an exclusive club of secrets, gossip, and laughter. Minna was generally too kind-hearted to repeat the really juicy stuff.

On the other hand, Jay and Daisy always turned up one rock too many, such as when they insisted that Skip was the reason for Rosemary's "women's trouble," that the lonely wife had seduced her young handyman, according to the sordid tale Daisy had pried out of Tristan Fisher. Skip had been barely sixteen at the time! I couldn't believe that, and I wouldn't.

Unfortunately, I hadn't been able to stay mad at the twins for long. After all, I hadn't wanted to miss my own party. Also I'd needed them to practice the jitterbug, which I'd only danced once at the Freshman Sock Hop.

Since it was Halloween, we'd festooned the living and dining rooms with orange and black crepe paper streamers. There was a cider punch, apples for bobbing, marshmallows to toast, and doughnuts that Mrs. Eliot had made herself that were as heavy as horseshoes. Later in the evening, some of the boys did use them to play a kind of hockey game out in the backyard, where there was a fire in the stone fireplace and a grinning candle-lit jack-o-lantern on the picnic table.

Although they were the hosts, Daisy and Jay had to share the limelight with me as the birthday girl—and also with Tristan Fisher and Glenn Gilbert, looking grown-up and handsome in Army uniforms, on a weekend pass from Fort Devens. Skip, Tris, and Glenn had always gone everywhere together, but Skip had signed up earlier by lying about his age, and had chosen the Navy, like his Dad. How I wished he were here, too, looking dashing in his uniform. But would he have danced with me? *Fat chance* with Daisy around.

When Glenn asked me to dance, an easy slow number, I took the opportunity to press him for information about Mr. Carver. "We didn't hang around together much, him being a teacher and all," Glenn said. "But we had a few brews the night he took off for OSS training, he couldn't say where. I heard they have a camp in Maryland. Once he gets in with that outfit, technically he'll be a civilian again."

"Did he say anything about Whitford?" I asked.

Glenn said that Carver had urged Tris and him to keep in touch, to let Carver know how they were getting on, what was happening at home, and all that. Maybe they would if they had time. "Any news from Skip? We heard he was in a North African hospital with a leg wound."

"The Last Time I Saw Paris" ended, and "Deep in the Heart of Texas" began, so with all the stamping and clapping, we could hardly hear each other. Glenn got two Cokes out of the cooler, and we joined Tris in the backyard. Tris poured a little of Glenn's coke into his own glass and spiked it with rum from a flask in his hip pocket. From the look of his eyes, he'd had a few already. Glenn and I declined his half-hearted offer to share. It smelled like the ruin of a good Coke to me.

"Skip's leg healed up okay," I told his friends. "He's back on his ship now. I think they're probably patrolling the Mediterranean, now that Italy has declared war on the Germans. Why don't you write to him? I bet he'd love to hear from you guys. He's still the same old Skip, playing poker and making jokes. Seems to be in high spirits now that he's back in action." I asked about Tris's older brother.

"Gordon's training with a demolition unit." Tris said. It seemed an odd assignment for our former town moderator. "The house is damned near empty now. Pa wanted to rent out a couple of the rooms, but Ma doesn't want to pack up all our clothes and gear. Bad omen, she says, as if we were dead or something, another of her loony ideas." Even their sister Penny had joined the WACs. Only Jason, was still at home.

The day after the party, while we were taking down the crepe paper streamers and eating soggy chips, Jay remarked that we weren't having any more of those unexplained fires in Whitford now that the Fisher family was scattering.

We thought that was strange, considering the fact that the chief suspect Jason no longer had his brothers around to watch over his activities.

I thought about that as I pedaled home on Sarge's reconditioned bike through the gray, chill November afternoon. Skip, Glenn, Tris, and most of the Fishers were gone from Whitford now. The Eliots might get snatched away by their mother or their father in the spring. Dr. Tyrell and even Mr. Carver had vanished from the scene (no loss there!). People were disappearing from Whitford one by one like the last brown leaves on the trees. Maybe that old Holmes poem was more true than tiresome after all.

> "And if I should live to be
> The last leaf on the tree ..."

At least I'd always have good-hearted Minna to talk to. Who else would have taken in two of the kittens I'd found in the woods? Now they would live the useful life of barn cats on her farm. And I had Sarge as a friend, even though he was quite old.

"It's like the curious incident of the dog in the night-time," I said to Sarge when we talked about the Fishers the next evening. We'd just switched off *The Green Hornet* and were drinking mugs of steaming cocoa at the kitchen table.

"But the dog did nothing in the night-time, Holmes," replied Sarge, his eyes twinkling. He stroked his drooping mustache while putting on a bemused expression in his best Dr. Watson manner.

"Well...don't you think that's curious? Jason at home with no big brothers to keep an eye on him, and not one mysterious fire among the summer cottages? What do you make of that, Watson?"

"I'm glad that Chief Ferro never got tough on Jason just to please everyone who was suspicious of him. It looks mighty like the culprit has left town, maybe for the service. Now what does that bring to mind, Holmes?"

"The thing about Jason is he'd always be lurking around at every fire scene with his mouth hanging open and that stupid pleased look in his eyes," I said. "But the other person who was always with Jason, watching that he didn't get too close or that no one teased him, was Gordon Fisher. Remember how concerned Gordon was about Simpson's barn, dashing in to help bring out the horses and all? He and Jason were there before the fire trucks even. That one looked particularly bad for Jason."

"You know, I managed to put up with the thought that Jason might have torched my cottage and burned up all my books and wrecked my best tools. I told myself he couldn't help it. He's slow compared to the rest of the family, but he's smart enough to know he's dumb, and that must be continually frustrating. But if all the time that miserable firebug was someone like *Gordon*—well, I'd be happy to wring his neck. Gordon's got no good excuse for pyromania or any mania. He's good-looking, well-liked, and an important fellow in town politics."

I loved it when Sarge talked things over with me. It made me feel grown-up, a pleasant change from having my every opinion being the cause of scorn or laughter. "Well, if it *was* Gordon, that makes the whole family a bit strange. Besides Jason being retarded and Gordon maybe a firebug, Tris has been drinking heavily since he was my age, and Penny used to sleepwalk right out of the house and down the street, but maybe she outgrew it."

"Many other families in town would seem strange, or eccentric, if you really looked into their behavior and history," Sarge suggested.

"Aunt Bette always said that Fisher blood was weak from way back."

"Not so far back," Sarge said, but he got up then and went to the sink to wash our cups. I thought there must be more to the story about the Fishers than Aunt Bette had revealed, but Sarge wasn't about to fill in the rest. Maybe Aunt Bette would, if I got her in a good mood.

My aunt was in a cheerful frame of mind more often these days, now that she was engaged, with a diamond so big she had to hold her hand out in front of her for balance. She agonized, of course, over all the details of her wedding, now set for the second week in November, and the elegant lunch at the Ritz she was planning for afterwards. She'd bought a satin suit in a shade of pink so pale it looked like eggshell when you glanced at it sideways, a dainty "doll hat" with blushing flowers and a wisp of veil, and matching satin high heels in her amazing size three, the same as shoe stores displayed in their windows and later sold at marvelous discounts. And she'd insisted that Woody buy a grand new suit at Lebow's in Boston, charcoal gray that made him look like a Harvard professor, with those Coke-bottle-bottom glasses he wore.

Besides ourselves and Sarge, Inez Tyrell had been invited, along with Woody's sister, Laura, a genuine war widow whose husband had been a naval officer killed at Pearl Harbor, and their son Stan who was supposed to be some sort of genius and I would love him. It made me gag just to think of having to sit near him and be polite. I'd bet a quarter that he'd turn out to have zits from ear to ear. Beryl and Nate were invited also, which must have caused Beryl to have a terrible struggle with herself, on the one hand wanting to attend the social event of the season, and on the other hand maintaining her refusal ever to speak one word to her ex-husband, Sarge. Then Nate broke his leg while plane-spotting when he backed up off the high school roof, and Woody had cemented him into a cast from his toes to his groin. So Beryl had to stay home to take care of him, or as she put it, "to cater to his every whim while he plays the invalid." Ollie, who was not invited, would also get to spend Aunt Bette's wedding day with Beryl. A sad fate, I didn't doubt.

Aunt Bette still had little Nod left from the litter, and I figured she'd adopted the kitten as her own. After all, she'd renamed him Bing, after Bing Crosby and because the kitten had learned to ring the bronze frog bell on the library desk by hitting it with his paw. No longer confined to the kitchen, Bing and Ollie had become so close that they slept together on Aunt Bette's bed. They strolled through the backyard together, too, so that the indoor sandbox was largely unused. But I didn't mind going over to Aunt Bette's to check it out most days, anyway. In her present humor, she was affectionate more often than caustic, always calling me "honey," and it made me feel good just being with her.

I told her of our suspicions about Gordon Fisher. True to form, Aunt Bette said, "Weak blood in that family, and from way back, too." It was five days before her wedding date. We were in her bedroom, where she was polishing her nails with a new color, Victory Vermilion, while one of the girls who worked at the Whitford Inn at night was cleaning downstairs and began making a mighty racket with the Hoover. Although totally occupied with her nails, Aunt Bette was wearing her housework outfit of navy blue slacks and an old pink sweater. She despised housedresses.

"How does that weak blood thing happen?" I ventured to question. Ollie came dashing up the stairs and jumped onto the bed as if fleeing some great danger. Bing followed at a more leisurely pace.

"Do you know what Lillian Fisher's maiden name was?" she asked.

"Nope."

"Fisher. Doesn't that tell you something?"

"Sure. But what?"

"Second cousins. And they're not the only close Fisher relatives. Well, no need to go into all the details, but Guy's grandmother..." Suddenly she looked at me suspiciously, and demanded, "Why are you so interested, young lady? It's just one of those weird family trees that happens sometimes. But let sleeping dogs lie. And take care never to marry one of your cousins."

"I don't have any cousins," I pointed out. *Not yet, anyway.* Aunt Bette had finished her artwork and was blowing on her nails.

I brushed some Victory Vermilion onto my little fingernail, but my aunt instantly swiped it off with a Kleenex. "That's too mature for you, honey. Your mother would kill me. Try this one instead," she offered, handing me a bottle of insipid pink called Ingenue. "And clean your nails first, Miss."

Downstairs, the Hoover switched off for a moment, and a voice called up the stairs, "Miz Cabot, there's a call for you from the hospital."

My aunt sighed and got up from the vanity, holding her hands in front of her as if she were a zombie. "That must be Doug. I simply have to get an extension installed in this bedroom, if only I can get my hands on one. Everything's so difficult to find these days."

The phone was in the hall downstairs at a little telephone desk, as it was in most homes. The only person in Whitford with a bedroom extension was Inez Tyrell, because Dr. Tyrell used to live there. Clearly, Aunt Bette would have to have the same for Dr. Doug after they got married. I followed my aunt downstairs. Ollie and Bing peeked out from the bedroom hopefully—maybe the thunderous noise would not resume—and padded after me. The girl from Whitford Inn began polishing the living room furniture.

"No! No! No!," my aunt screamed, bringing all of us to a startled halt.

"What happened?" I gasped.

Aunt Bette stopped screaming and began to listen to whomever was on the line. After a while she looked a little relieved. "Oh, thank God. Tell Doug I'm on my way."

Grabbing her car keys off the hall table, she ran out the front door, completely forgetting her coat. I paused for a moment in front of the coat rack, decided on her navy wool, and ran after her carrying it, just as my mother would have done. I knew it would take her several tries to start the Olds.

"What happened?" I asked again. She was already pressing on the starter for the second time. The garage was filled with the smell of gasoline.

"Oh, get in, if you want. Here, give me that." She stepped out of the car for a moment to shrug her way into the coat. Then we both got in, the odor somewhat dissipated, and fortunately, it started at once this time. "Some fool hunter, it must have been, shot at Doug. The bullet went right through his arm and came out the other side. The person who called said it was only a minor wound. But he can't drive his car, of course, and he'll need a ride home."

I think I stopped breathing for a moment. When I could speak, I said, "Where did it happen?" I could be wrong, after all. Hunters were crazy enough in November.

By now we were zooming in the big black Olds along the familiar back roads to Plymouth. "Oh, how in heaven's name will he be able to wear his new suit!" my aunt wailed. "He was in the hospital lot, for God's sake. Just finished his rounds and was going to make some house calls before dinner. He must have parked on the side near the woods where some bastard was chasing a deer, that's all I can think."

But that wasn't the only explanation that leaped into my mind.

Chapter 25

In which Sarge consults Chief Ferro, and my secret fears cannot be kept secret any longer.

By the time we arrived at the hospital after a hair-raising, twenty-minute ride swerving through the curvy back roads to Plymouth, Woody was sitting up in the emergency room, smiling, his arm freshly bandaged. "Now, now," he said, trying to dam the flood of my aunt's hysterics, a losing battle. "The bullet went right through my arm and did hardly any damage at all. I'm all sewed up, medicated, and ready to be devotedly nursed at home. Your home, I hope."

"Oh, Doug, we'll have to postpone the wedding," my aunt wailed, once she had been assured that Woody wasn't seriously maimed.

"I doubt that, I doubt that very much, Bette. If I can get my good arm into that fancy suit jacket, and you don't mind half a hug, our plans don't have to be changed one whit by this mishap. People may think ours was a shotgun wedding, but what do we care?"

My aunt was in no humor for humor. "Where's Chief Ferro?" she demanded. "I want that hunter arrested and charged immediately. Shooting to endanger. Or whatever. We ought to put him in jail and throw away the key. He's a menace to society."

"There, there…" Woody was fond of repeating words twice, part of his reassuring doctorly manner. "I've spoken with Chief Ferro, and he's helping the Plymouth police to look for the culprit right now. The matter is in official hands, and I think I'm going to fall off this chair from that whopping big sedative my vindictive nurse gave me if you don't take me home immediately."

"Oh, that Ferro is good for nothing," Aunt Bette declared shrilly. "He'll never find the son of a bitch. I ask you now, when has Dom Ferro ever made an arrest?"

"He arrested that senior from Kates Hill last month for beating up one of the Poor Farm people," I reminded her, although I knew it was always a mistake to talk sensibly when Aunt Bette was revving herself into a nervous state.

"Oh yes, sure," she said sarcastically. "He saved the boy's life, you mean. After Bunny had nearly killed him with a jujitsu throw and a couple of quick jabs. Dom's wife told me the boy was begging for mercy. Amazing to think Bunny Cronin knows that Jap thing, isn't it? I wonder if I could get her to teach me how to toss someone around the way she did. Being small makes no difference, she says."

What a good idea, I thought to myself, vowing to visit my old science teacher, now mistress of the Poor Farm, and get her to show me the moves.

"Ferro will find the shooter all right, all right," Woody said, standing up and weaving toward the hospital entrance so that we jumped to help him. A nurse rushed over with a wheelchair, but he waved her off in an imperious medical manner.

After we'd driven back to Aunt Bette's—at a stately pace—I ran home in a sweat with the disturbing news and spilled it to Mother the moment I slammed the door. Before I could get all the words out, she had taken the big pot down from the shelf to make "a nice, nourishing soup" for Woody.

"Scotch broth," she murmured. "I'll make it with the pork rib bones. I don't know why anyone would go hunting in back of the hospital," she continued musing to herself rather than to me, gazing out the window over the big porcelain sink. "I feel there's more to it than that."

For one hot moment, I had the urge to tell Mother all that I knew or surmised, but I caught myself with the thought that I would have to begin with Mr.

Snow's death, and worse, the letter. And then I would have to implicate her darling Alex in murder. *Forget that,* I told myself. As soon as Mother became absorbed in chopping onions and carrots, I slipped out the kitchen door to talk over my suspicions with Sarge.

I found him in the new shed, tinkering with our vacuum cleaner, a big old monster that belched more dust than it snuffled up.

"Alex shot Woody!" With Sarge, I could start out at the heart of the matter.

"What! What! Where is he? You can't mean it," Sarge stammered and grew silent, for once at a loss for words.

Jumping to a conclusion, even when you know it's true, never works too well with grown-ups. I began at the beginning, with the phone call from the hospital, concluding with, "Chief Ferro is helping the Plymouth police comb the woods, but he won't find anyone, I bet. I've read about that OSS training. They're taught to be stealthy and deadly, leave no tracks, and take no prisoners."

"Stow the drama, Amelia," Sarge said. "It might really have been a hunter. It's the season to shoot a nice plump doe, you know. Solves the problem of meat rationing. Or it may have been some idiot teaching his neighbor how to shoot a .22 rifle, as the National Rifle Association has urged us all to do for the war effort. But there's a slim chance, and a frightening one, that you're right, so we have some serious thinking to do. The time has come to call for reinforcements. This matter has become very grave, very threatening, and we need help. Suppose I have a quiet word with Dom Ferro, and see what strings he can pull to find out Alex Carver's whereabouts. I would think the first step was to make sure that Carver actually had the opportunity. Remember, Holmes—motive, means, and *opportunity.*"

"You don't think Chief Ferro will tell my mother?"

"If it comes to that, *I* will tell your mother. She would never, never forgive us if she had to hear what's been going on in her own family from an outsider, now would she?"

"Never," I agreed. I could just imagine. I'd be restricted for life. Still, I *had* tried to explain matters to Mother and Aunt Bette after Alex Carver attacked me in the woods, and I hadn't been believed. "The Chief's in Plymouth, and we don't have a car," I pointed out.

"What's your mother making for the invalid?" Sarge asked.

"Scotch broth. She thinks Woody is a descendent of Robert the Bruce because his mother's maiden name was Bruce."

"Good. It will be ready in an hour or so, and we'll volunteer to deliver it to Bette's. Then we'll see if Bette will let me borrow the Olds."

"Not a bad idea, Watson," I said, admiring his inventiveness.

Later that day, we carried the big pot of soup to Aunt Bette's. She lifted the lid and sniffed. The savory aroma made my mouth water. "I suppose your mother doesn't think I can make a decent soup," my aunt said by way of thanks, clapping the pot shut.

"Oh, no, Aunt Bette," I hastened to mollify her. "She thinks you make lovely soups, but you might be too busy tonight watching over Woody to be fussing in the kitchen."

She smiled and pinched my cheek. "Right you are, honey. We're getting married in a few days, and I'm keeping a close eye on the groom."

Sarge asked if she'd loan him the Olds so that he could check on the progress of the investigation with Chief Ferro, and she readily handed him the keys.

"Aunt Bette, I was just wondering if you ever wrote to Alex Carver and told him about your engagement," I ventured to ask after Sarge had departed.

"It's none of your business, my dear, but as it happens, I did, and Alex was pretty broken up about it, I can tell you. He begged me to reconsider and wait for him to return from the war. He said he knew in his heart that we were meant for each other." She giggled. "Who would have thought I'd become a femme fatale at my age!"

"You're only thirty-six."

She shot me one of her freezing glances. "It's twenty-nine now," she hissed. "And keep your voice down. You'll be waking Doug if you're not careful."

I walked home with a heavy heart. Mother was looking tired and flushed at the stove, so I said, "Aunt Bette thanks you from the bottom of her heart for the soup and says you're an angel."

"That doesn't sound like Bette. Maybe love is mellowing her," Mother said. She asked me where Sarge had gone. I said he was off to do an errand in the

Olds. Although I didn't exactly say so, I know she got the impression that the errand was for Aunt Bette.

At any rate, he was home again by suppertime. "Mmmmm," he said, "do I smell fish chowder with salt pork?"

I tugged his arm to step out of the kitchen. "Never mind that, Sarge, what did you tell the Chief? What did he say? Is he checking up on Mr. Carver?"

"At first, he seemed flabbergasted at the story I told him and looked at me as if I'd taken leave of my senses. But then he did say he'd always thought it was strange that Alex couldn't save the old man out on the ice that night. And what was Snow doing out there in the first place? Everyone in town knew the ice wasn't safe near the ice house. The whole area is posted. Ferro admitted there were some pretty big questions in his mind about that accident, but there didn't seem to be any reason to suspect a fine upstanding citizen like Alex Carver of foul play, so he'd just accepted Carver's version of events. And as for finding out whether Carver could be traveling on a pass from his training unit, Ferro doesn't hold out much hope. Any information about the OSS is kept strictly secret, even from law enforcement officials. But he will pursue the matter and see what he can find out. 'And again, it goes to the question of motive,' Ferro said. 'Why would Alex want to shoot Dr. Woodward?' "

"Because he wants to marry Aunt Bette and get all of Snow's money, which he thinks is rightfully his, that's why," I said hotly.

"A twisted mind, that," Sarge said solemnly.

Then we had to stop talking when Mother called us back into the kitchen and started dishing up the chowder. There were hot rolls, and a big three-bean salad from the green beans and wax beans and shell beans we'd put up from our Victory garden. And baked apples for dessert from the bushel I'd lugged home myself. Foods tastes even better when you've slaved over it. I remembering the hot sun on my back as I hoed those rows of beans.

"We've got to tell Mother," I said finally, as I was drying the last of the pots and pans Sarge had washed. It was a decision that filled me with dread, but the alternative was worse. Alex Carver, out there somewhere, plotting to kill dear Woody and become my murderous uncle, might not fail the next time.

"It's the right thing to do, Amelia," Sarge said. "I'm proud of you."

Why is doing the right thing always as heavy as a sack of potatoes lying on your chest?

Chapter 26

In which Mother tells Aunt Bette how she got rich, and I prepare for the war at home.

There *is* no perfect time to tell your mother that her favorite former boarder is a murderer who has set himself upon a course of doing away with everyone who might keep him from marrying her sister for the money she has recently inherited due to his villainy. So I didn't wait for a moment when Mother would be resting in a rocking chair with a restorative cup of tea in her hands. Sarge and I found her in the kitchen ironing the boarders' sheets and pillowcases, the hot smell of sunshine and bluing rising from the sea of white percale as she smote the folds. *This was it!*

Sarge and I sat in two of the kitchen chairs, as solemn and respectful as two mourners at a wake. "I have something important to tell you, Mother," I began tentatively.

"Haven't you two got anything useful to do? Sarge, do you have that vacuum cleaner working yet? All right, all right, tell away. And while you're at it, Amelia, hand me that stack of pillowcases you're leaning on. I don't need any extra wrinkles."

"Alex Carver is probably lurking around somewhere trying to kill Doug Woodward," I started out. Then I realized I'd done it again, started at the end of the story.

Mother laughed her deep hearty laugh that usually made me feel good, but not now. "This would be funny...if it didn't make me worry...about your sanity," she gasped.

"Better start at the beginning," Sarge suggested. "The letter."

So I did. It didn't take as long as I thought it might, a whole year's worth of chilling events boiled down into a half hour's telling. As I kept talking, Mother's merriment dwindled down to silence except for the thump and slide of the heavy iron. Gradually this rhythmic sound, too, went slower and slower until finally Mother was leaning on a motionless iron. She screamed. *"Now look what you made me do!* There's a scorch mark here right in the middle of this pillowcase." She rushed the injured fabric to the sink, trying to wash out the mark with a vigorous scrub.

We waited quietly until she spread the pillowcase on the sink's rim and returned to face us, dropping heavily into a chair. "Alex...Alex...it's so incredible," she whispered, as if talking only to herself. "Can it be? Are you sure?"

"Mother, I did see his face clearly when he drove the bus at me in the old bog woods. Don't you remember that I tried to tell you it was Mr. Carver?"

"Alex had no reason to go after you, to try to injure you...or... Oh, God! So I thought at the time. It didn't make sense. If you had told me about his mother's letter back then, I might have understood. Margaret Burns and Winston Snow, who ever would have imagined it? That old goat. And the fire in the barn, too? The fire?"

"Yes, the fire. It all fits together," Sarge said. "Alex thought he'd take advantage of the town arsonist's evil doings to get rid of Amelia, the one person who knew he had a motive to arrange Snow's accident."

"I'll kill that bastard," Mother said softly, reaching out as if to gather me into her arms. I felt tears filling my eyes. But in the next moment she sprang to her feet, electrified by resolution. "Good God, if Alex is back in town, hiding somewhere, I have to warn Bette and Doug. We need to talk to Dom Ferro."

"I've already talked to the Chief," Sarge said quietly, standing now and putting his hand on Mother's arm. He patted her affectionately, and I noticed that she didn't shake him off. "Dom is trying to find out if Alex is on leave, as we suspect. But it's unlikely Ferro will be able to get anywhere with his inquiry, since it's OSS, and that's not even Army. The one thing we do know is that Alex can't have more than a day or two at most away from his unit. If the OSS has given him a pass, they're probably planning to send him somewhere real soon."

Mother moved away from Sarge briskly and put on her old wool jacket hanging by the back door. She took her shiny, square pocketbook from its regular hiding place hanging on the doorknob behind the open kitchen door. "Finish the pillowcases, Amelia, and put the iron and board away. Sarge, you watch out for her while I go over to Bette's."

"Shouldn't we come with you?" I asked.

She smiled grimly. "I don't think you want to be there, Amelia. When Bette realizes how she came by her inheritance, she's going to be pretty upset. She's going to blame you for finding that letter, for giving it to Alex instead of to her, and probably for being born. If I were you, I'd stay out of the way until she calms down. I know how to handle her hysterics. When she's reasonable, she'll want to talk to you, ask a lot of questions, and that will be okay. I'll phone. *Stay put.*"

The pillowcases didn't look all that wrinkled. I smoothed them out and folded them carefully, stacking them under the ones Mother had already ironed. Quickly I stashed the linens in the linen closet, and got rid of the iron and board. Meanwhile, in his usual unhurried, unworried fashion, Sarge went around locking up windows and doors, and then began to make tea for the two of us. While his attention was elsewhere, I took the opportunity to run upstairs to my room to get the little silver-handled gun out of *Coney Island Casanova,* the fake book shelved between *Ivanhoe* and *Robin Hood.* Carefully, I loaded the gun with one of the small bullets, and stuck it into the pocket of my corduroy slacks. For good measure, I put a few more bullets in the other pocket. Then I went downstairs and had tea with Sarge. We were mostly silent, as if waiting for a sword to fall.

It was more than an hour later when Mother finally called. "You can come along now," she said. "Your aunt wants to have a few words with you. Let me speak to Sarge."

Sarge said, "No, we haven't seen anyone. Yes, I'll be with her every step of the way. No, I don't think it's necessary to carry the fireplace poker. We'll be just fine, Catherine. Now don't you worry. How's Doug doing? Still resting? Good...good."

I already had my green lumber jacket on and was standing at the door by the time Sarge hung up. We set out in the lengthening shadows of the bone-chilling November afternoon, the sun a fiery ball just edging below the horizon. Dark came on fast as we headed for the family fireworks.

When we reached Frietchie Circle, Ollie came running to greet us, a black and white blur of barking. I leaned over to hug him, and he licked my face. "They must have forgotten this poor little fellow," I said. "Aunt Bette doesn't usually let him run off leash after dark. I'd better walk him around back to do his business and get him into the house." Slipping off the belt to my slacks, I looped it around his collar for a leash. Sarge went in the front door, and Ollie and I strolled around to the bare-branch rose garden.

Ollie was in one of his fussy moods, sniffing here and there without settling on any suitable spot. Having found no likely place in the rose garden, we ambled around the side of the house where there were a few bushy pine trees between Aunt Bette's house and the Tyrell place. I studied the sliver of crescent moon that was rising over the church, then glanced into my aunt's living room windows. The blackout curtains had not been drawn, and the scene inside was lit up like a stage play.

Aunt Bette was lying on the living room sofa with a cloth on her forehead. My mother sat beside her holding her hand, with Sarge standing behind her nervously stroking his drooping mustache. I guessed I was in for it all right. Ollie finally took care of business, and we headed for the back door. The kitchen windows were dark; the gleam of something metallic inside the house caught my attention. Then I saw a shadowy form moving toward the hall stairs. I couldn't see his face, but I knew who it was all right. Alex Carver!

How I wanted to scream out to Sarge, but I stopped myself instantly. My heart was beating so loudly I could hear it in my ears. What would Mr. Carver do if he knew he'd been discovered? Shoot whoever got in his way, no doubt, and that would be Mother or Sarge. As a kaleidoscope of schemes tumbled hotly through my brain and were discarded one by one, I watched my nemesis creeping nearer the stairs. He must have been watching the house and had figured out that Woody was up there alone.

I couldn't take a chance on Ollie. I left the dog on the back step, looking puzzled and whimpering for the biscuit he felt he'd earned, while I eased my way into the pantry window. I nearly stepped on Bing's tail. The ungrateful kitten spat at me, shot into the kitchen, and jumped onto the refrigerator, a favorite refuge. I tiptoed through the pantry door into the kitchen, leaving the door open a crack in case I had to make a quick getaway. Mr. Carver had started up the stairs, and the metallic gleam I'd spotted was the pistol he was holding down by his side. Dressed in black from head to foot, he crept along the wall invisibly.

There was no time to think out a proper plan or even to cry out. I simply took the gun out of my pocket, aimed it at the man from where I stood just inside the unlit kitchen, and pulled the trigger.

Mr. Carver cried out, "Shit! Shit! What was that?"

Immediately crouching down, I duck-walked into the hall and hid behind the Dutch marquetry chest that stood against the wall. Now I peeked around the edge of the chest cautiously. Mr. Carver had fallen forward on the stairs and seemed to be groaning and wringing his hands. Was he dying? Had I killed him?

Mother rushed into the hall, followed by Sarge, who snapped on the light. "Oh my God!" she exclaimed, clutching her chest. Alex Carver turned in a flash, aiming the pistol he was holding directly at them. At that moment Aunt Bette came running into the hall after the others, her face as white as flour paste. Woody appeared at the top of the stairs, looking incredulous. "Stop! Don't" he shouted.

Laughing at Woody's expression, Alex Carver looked down at the blood running from his left hand. "Now we've both been winged. Don't any of you move. Whoever has the pop gun better drop it right now. Ah, Bette, my sweet, was it you who shot me? What trouble you could have saved us all if you'd fallen for *me* instead of this four-eyes 4-F lover here. Let your weapon drop to the floor, Bette, or I'll kill him right now."

"No. No. You can't hurt him. I don't *have* a gun to drop," Aunt Bette cried out, leaning against the living room door frame as if her knees wouldn't hold her up. "Amelia must have it."

"Amelia," he snarled. "And where is that stupid brat?"

My mother stepped in front of Aunt Bette. "Amelia's not here. She's at home," Mother said firmly, not a tremor of fear in her voice. "Bette is having one of her spells, and she doesn't know what she's saying."

Alex Carver couldn't see me behind the chest, but from where they stood, Mother and Woody could. I wasn't so sure about Aunt Bette and Sarge. Yet somehow Mr. Carver knew Aunt Bette spoke the truth, because he said, "She's here somewhere, the little bitch, and I'll be taking care of her in a minute. But first you come down here, Woodward. Join the party. I want all of you in the library right now."

I peeked out again. Mr. Carver stood up, the blood falling on the blue stair carpet in dark drops, and let Woody slowly pass by him to the library door. Mr. Carver motioned with his pistol for the others to follow. Mother marched in after Woody, and then Aunt Bette followed, moaning and leaning heavily on Sarge.

While Mr. Carver was herding my family into the library, I loaded another bullet into the gun, which was surprisingly warm. An ugly heavy smell of burned gunpowder hovered around me. I was glad that Mr. Carver hadn't simply let his nose find my hiding place. Fortunately, that was the darker end of the hall, where the light from the living room didn't reach, and I was behind a massive piece of furniture.

I heard Alex Carver's steps come down the stairs and follow his prisoners into the library. When I thought he'd reached the doorway, I took the chance of standing up, looking over the chest this time. He must have heard me, because he swung around quickly and fired several shots in my direction, shattering the Chinese vases that stood on the chest but missing me. *Oh well*, I thought, *I'll never have to dust those again.*

My mother screamed a piercing scream I hadn't heard since a cake of soap I was holding slipped into a pot of peach preserves bubbling on the stove. She tried to push her way back into the hall, but someone—Sarge or Woody—held her back.

Creeping into the kitchen, I eased the door closed. Then I waited behind the refrigerator for Mr. Carver to follow me, holding the gun ready to shoot him as soon as he came through the door. *But he didn't.* I could hear nothing at all except the hum of the refrigerator and the small sounds the kitten was making as he cowered on top of it.

Okay…back out the pantry window, I decided. Maybe I could fire at Mr. Carver through the library window. But before I could dodge into the pantry, a scuffle began in the hall. Mr. Carver's pistol fired, and Sarge swore.

I stopped in my tracks as if flash-frozen to the floor. As I listened, I heard my mother shout and my aunt scream. Then Woody yelled something. That must mean they were all right, so far. I could have thrown up with relief, but I didn't have time. I crept back to the closed door, opened it a crack, and listened with all my might.

The door was flung back against me as Mr. Carver hurtled through. I sank to the floor, the little gun spinning out of my hand. As he thundered toward the back door, a shot rang out toward his retreating back and struck the door chime above the frame. *Where did that come from?*

Startled out of his wary crouch, Bing leaped off the refrigerator onto Mr. Carver's head, digging in with his claws. Outside, Ollie began to bark and snarl. Cursing, Mr. Carver pulled the kitten free and threw him against the wall. Yanking open the door, he kicked Ollie out of the way, then sprinted into the night's shadows. Soon his black-clothed figure blended with the dark trees on the other side of Frietchie Circle. Ollie ran after him, barking, but he turned back uncertainly at curb's edge, no more able than I was to follow the disappearing form.

He's gone. We're safe now, I thought, and turned on a small light over the kitchen table, taking some satisfaction in the blood drops on the kitchen floor where Mr. Carver had run past me. I picked up Bing in my arms and rushed back into the hall. Woody was on the phone dialing Chief Ferro with his good hand, Aunt Bette collapsed against his bandaged side. My mother was wrapping a bureau scarf around Sarge's leg. "Tighter than that," ordered Woody, wincing as Aunt Bette shifted her weight.

"Oh, Sarge, you've been wounded," I cried. At the same time, I could feel Bing stirring in my arms and mewing, which was a good sign. Looking down, I saw the kitten had a lump growing on his head. His head was tiny, no bigger than an orange, which made the lump look even bigger, poor baby. Then my attention went back to Sarge who was making a noise as if trying not to moan as my mother tightened the tourniquet with cruel strength. I took his hand and squeezed it, still holding Bing in my other arm.

"Where has that bastard gone to now?" my mother demanded.

"Ran off across the circle. And it didn't look as if he planned to come back," I said.

"You should have seen your mother," Sarge told me between clenched teeth. "She turned into a she-devil. While Carver was holding us all at pistol-point in the library, he made the mistake of turning his head toward Woody for a moment. Catherine seized that half-second to punch Carver right in the jaw. The man staggered back—I bet you're familiar with the wallop your mother can deliver. His pistol went off and you see what happened here. I got shot. Your mother jumped Carver, wrestled for the gun, and got hold of it. That's when Alex ran for his life out the back."

"I'd have got him, too, if I'd had a clear shot," Mother said grimly, "but I wasn't sure where Amelia was hiding. Speaking of weapons, was that Bette's little pearl handgun that you shot off in the hall, young lady?"

"I saw Mr. Carver through the window. It looked like he was headed upstairs to get Woody. I thought he really meant to kill him this time."

"Thank God he didn't hurt my Doug again!" my aunt wept. "That madman! Oh, I hope he hangs for this! And those lovely Chinese porcelains were worth a small fortune. You might know that Amelia would be involved!"

"You can stop thanking God and thank Amelia for sounding the alarm and plugging the son of a bitch," my mother said sharply.

That reminded me that I ought to retrieve my aunt's handgun, hoping my mother and aunt would forget about it later, what with all the mess we had to sort out. "I'll go check on Ollie," I said.

The silver handle was gleaming on the braided rug under the kitchen table. I put the handgun back in my pocket.

Ollie limped in as if he'd been chasing Mr. Carver for miles instead of merely watching him take off. Padding tiredly through the open back door, he sniffed the air of the room for a moment, then heaved himself into his kitchen basket-bed and curled into a black-and-white furry ball. "What a good watch dog you are!" I praised and patted him. He sighed and shut his eyes contentedly. Once an emergency has passed, dogs really know how to let go of trouble.

Chapter 27

In which we attend a fabulous wedding luncheon at the Ritz, Mother cries all the way home, and two strangers call at our house with questions.

We couldn't believe it! Alex Carver had got clean away from his attack on us. Chief Ferro could neither locate the culprit nor get anyone else interested in bringing him to justice. The Army had released Mr. Carver to the OSS, and the OSS wouldn't communicate with the Chief. At least, not by telephone. But soon afterwards, two officials from the OSS arrived at the police station one afternoon to inform the Chief that Mr. Carver had departed for an extremely sensitive mission in Eastern Europe. They warned Chief Ferro that this was a top secret matter and reminded him that he could be prosecuted for talking about it.

Officer Wayne Bugbee, who'd been taking a nap in the Police Department's one tiny holding cell, draped in an old horse blanket, overheard the whole conversation between his boss and the two strangers who were trying to intimidate him. Within hours, everyone in town knew the story.

"Must be Finland," I said to Sarge. "He speaks Finnish real well. He bragged to Aunt Bette that's why the OSS was able to pluck him out of the service."

"How do you know that?" Sarge asked.

I may have blushed a little. "I glanced through the letters he sent to her. But only to keep a check on what he was up to. Ordinarily, I never read other people's mail."

"Indeed! And if that were true, none of this would have happened, my dear," Sarge said. "Perhaps you may consider this a lesson in life. A really big one. Never, *never* read letters not meant for your eyes. Well, Alex won't have an easy time of it in Helsinki these days. The Finns are in bed with the Nazis, you know."

"Maybe he'll volunteer for a dangerous mission and everyone will call him a hero," I said. "Wouldn't it be horrid if they want to name a street after him! Alex Carver Boulevard."

"Ironic, yes. But Dom Ferro and I won't allow him to be honored among the real heroes," Sarge assured me. "The trouble is, as long as Alex is sheltered by that crazy OSS that suits him so well, we'll never know exactly where he is. Unlike those neat little mysteries of yours, Mr. Holmes, in real life we encounter situations that never get resolved."

I sighed. I would be relieved not to have to deal with any more drama for the Duration. "I don't think Mr. Carver will have the nerve to come back, do you?"

"Not really. Almost any peril would be preferable to facing your mother again."

After the Carver episode, things changed around our house. Mother began to lock up every door and window at night, something we'd never thought about before Mr. Carver's rampage. Beside her bed, she kept a walking stick that my father had carved from teakwood, a wolf's head with wickedly pointed ears and a snout capable of doing a great deal of damage if used as a weapon.

It was the same story at the Snow place. Not only did Aunt Bette keep her small loaded gold handgun in the night table, but she also had Mr. Snow's rifle cleaned and made ready as well. No longer were we the innocent trusting family we once had been. The National Rifle Association would have been proud of our preparedness, just what they recommended for every American family. We were ready for Mr. Carver or the German invasion, whichever came first.

Fortunately, neither one materialized.

⟶

Our wedding party looked like the Spirit of '76. Woody hadn't been able to dispense with the sling and wore his suit jacket draped over his wounded arm. Sarge was on crutches. And I had a livid bruise on my forehead where Mr. Carver had slammed the kitchen door against me. All we needed was a drum, a flute, and a flag. Except, instead of being dressed in rags, we were all gussied up for the Ritz, the wedding luncheon that Aunt Bette had planned down to the last *petit four*.

Mother wore a crepe dress in a shade of blue the dressmaker had described as "heavenly," and so it was. Her hat was a circlet of blue and gold flowers set like a tiara on her regal crown of braids. I thought she looked like a Norse queen straight out of my favorite fairy tale book, *East of the Sun, West of the Moon*. Sarge cleaned up better than any of us had expected, and looked quite dashing in a sincere navy blue suit he'd borrowed from the funeral director, Junior Whitcomb, who shared the same short rotund frame.

The bride's palest pink satin suit, with its darling little peplum and matching satin shoes, was set off nicely by the really real pearls she got out of the Snow loot. Eunice Snow might have got the best ones, but I thought Aunt Bette's petite strand looked especially elegant. And of course that enormous diamond engagement ring was practically hanging off her finger. With a "doll hat," decorated in tiny roses and a dotted veil, set forward on her head at a fetching angle, she looked adorable. Her dark blue eyes were glowing with triumph as she stood in front of the Justice of the Peace with her doctor, the bemused and devoted Douglas Woodward, wearing the expensively tailored gray suit she had chosen for him.

I got a green wool beret, not a regular hat. My dress was a princess-style green velvet. I thought it was nice enough but a one-shot deal. I would never be able to wear this outfit to a dance because its lace collar would have made me a laughing stock of the school.

Since it was nearly Thanksgiving, all of us had to have natty coats, too. Mine was camel's hair. Aunt Bette was draped in a fur stole that fastened with tiny fox faces whose glittering vengeful eyes were lifelike enough to scare a little kid if you waved it and hissed. As a matter of fact, Ollie had growled and backed up when he first saw those malevolent faces, then tried to act nonchalant when he realized the poor dead things posed no threat. Dogs have their embarrassing moments, too.

The Ritz was hushed and plush, the curving stairs to the second floor dining room so wide and inviting even Sarge on crutches waved away the notion of taking the elevator.

Woody's sister Laura Grimes and her son Stan met us at our reserved table. They were as tall and fair as he, and judging by their thick eyeglasses, shared the same vision problems. I had expected Mrs. Grimes to be draped in black and heavily veiled due to her bereavement. My mother had worn black whenever she went out for a whole year after my father died, but Mrs. Grimes had graduated to pearl gray. Her son wore a mustard-colored corduroy jacket, a bit too short in the sleeves. He wasn't as homely as I had thought he would be—not a zit in sight.

Inez Tyrell, the only other guest, was calculated to be the witness who would gab to everyone in Whitford about the splendors of Aunt Bette's wedding party, the next best thing to inviting the whole town. She wore a flowered crepe dress that made her look like an advancing lilac bush, a fluffy fur jacket, and a purple hat with a cascade of more purple flowers.

And Mrs. Tyrell didn't miss a trick. "Oh, what a divine table," she cooed when the suave waiters, dressed like escapees from *Penguin Island,* had seated us overlooking the Public Garden. All of us admired the table linens of pale yellow and the fall flower arrangement muted into barely recognizable shades of orange, blue, and gold. Silver glowed and crystal gleamed. It seemed almost too much to expect to be fed as well as dazzled.

But fed we were, while Inez Tyrell *ooohed* and *ahhhed* her way through every rich course. Wartime austerity seemed far away, somewhere among the colorful peasants sporting in the leafless park that was spread below our lofty windows. I'd never had caviar canapés or squab duchess before. There was cake for dessert that Aunt Bette had specially ordered, with a tiny ceramic bride and groom on top, but the couple at the next table ordered something the waiter had to light on fire before serving, which I thought was a lot more fun. Since my aunt smoked between every course, our waiter was constantly springing forward to empty her ashtray, a silver scallop shell.

My mother muttered to Sarge that this stuff was "bridge club food," her criticism of any dish that was fussy, dainty, wobbly, or decorated with paper ruffles.

He stroked his drooping gray mustache, patted her hand, and reminded her in a low tone, "It's your sister's day. Let's enjoy every bite of it in her honor. When we get home, we can reheat that lamb stew you made for us yesterday. You make a better stew than anyone else on earth."

My mother smiled and ate the rest of her endive with chiffonade dressing in pleased silence. Although she had been a little teary during the brief wedding ceremony, she seemed to be her old self now, looking around her at the crystal chandeliers and blue brocade drapes as if checking for cobwebs.

"I bet those heavy drapes hold a lot of dust," Mother said with satisfaction, pushing away her empty plate. The vigilant waiter refilled everyone's glasses from a fresh bottle of champagne. That is, everyone's except mine and Stan's. Stan ordered a Moxie. I'd been served a ginger ale with sliced fruit and cherries in it. For some reason I thought of Skip, how he would have made fun of any drink described as a "Shirley Temple." I hoped he was getting plenty of brews out on the Mediterranean and staying out of trouble. When no one was looking directly at me, I took a sip of Sarge's champagne and made a little silent toast to Skip's good health.

"How do you like it?" Sarge asked.

"Sour," I said, "but good. May I have another taste?"

"You'll get us all arrested. Do you want to spend tonight locked up in a cell with your aunt? Suppose she ran out of cigarettes?" In one corner of the long dining room, a woman in a flowing gauzy dress began to play an anguished harp. "La belle dame sans merci," Sarge murmured to me.

"...our party hath in thrall," I parodied the next line, noticing how Sarge seemed to be able to speak everyone's language except that of his ex-wife Beryl. Maybe because she mostly screamed, and that does tend to shatter communication in the home.

Stan, the reported genius, looked at us all in a confused way. But when Sarge got Woody's nephew on the subject of buzz bombs and rockets, the boy seemed to come to life. Soon the two of them were drawing rocket designs on the back of the dessert menus. Aunt Bette frowned menacingly, but Mrs. Tyrell drew her attention away from their doodling to the subject of sterling silver, on which my aunt felt herself to be quite an expert. There were many silver service items in the hotel's dining room, gleaming expensively.

Mrs. Grimes smiled in a doting manner at her son. "Stan's building his own working rocket as a science project," she confided to Mother. "He's trying to give it an aerial guidance system. Works on it in our garage every day after school."

"You'll be lucky if he doesn't blow up the place," Mother said. "Can't you get him to build something a little less incendiary?"

"A budding genius should never have his wings clipped," Woody's sister said piously.

"You'll give that boy a swelled head if you don't watch out. No child of mine would ever be called a genius, even if she were one," Mother summed up a favorite child-rearing theory.

After the feast, we put Mrs. Grimes and Stan on a bus. "Oh, I do hope Stan and Amelia can get together again some day soon," Woody's sister cried out warmly, turning in the midst of boarding the bus for one more shot at Mother. "They have so much in common." Stan looked incredulous, which was pretty much how I felt.

"Don't fret," Sarge muttered in my ear. "You'll probably won't see Stan Grimes again until the next family wedding, which may be his."

"Or funeral," Mother added. "Rockets! What can that woman be using for brains?" Fortunately, I don't think Woody heard her, since he was following the bus and waving.

Then we saw Aunt Bette and Woody off on a late-afternoon train to New York Many of the cars seems to be simply bulging with servicemen, but my aunt had made a special reservation in the first class club car. Since Sarge and Woody were in no shape to haul luggage, I was thankful for the red-capped porter who relieved my mother and me of the many blue suitcases that Aunt Bette had packed for her honeymoon. The bags smelled expensively of brand new leather, and the monogram was also new—E.C.W. Aunt Bette was carrying two sets of calling cards, too. The first read: *Dr. and Mrs. Douglas Woodward, The Frietchie-Snow House, Frietchie Circle, Whitford, Massachusetts,* and a second was embossed with *Elizabeth Cabot Woodward*, ditto. She would have preferred The Frietchie-Snow Mansion, but was talked out of the phrase by her fiancé, who managed in his soft-spoken way to convince my aunt that "mansion," like "saint," was a title properly conferred by others, and besides, it sounded as if they were advertising to host tour groups.

We kissed and hugged, and off they went, with one last wave of Aunt Bette's lace handkerchief from behind a sooty window. "Whew!" said Sarge. "I feel as deflated as yesterday's parade balloon. How about you ladies?"

"Champagne always leaves me with a headache," Mother said wearily, as if she'd had a lifetime of experience quaffing the bubbly stuff as a lunchtime beverage. "Let's get out of here before someone steals Bette's Olds out of the lot. I don't trust this dirty city."

We had planned for Sarge to drive the car back to Whitford, but his leg wound made that impossible, so we were left to the uncertain driving skills of my mother, made even more hazardous by her weeping all the way home. Once she even turned on the windshield wipers, as if that might help to clear her vision. Begging her to stop where there was a pull-over on the shoulder of the road, Mrs. Tyrell offered to take over the wheel, at least until Mother could quit crying. But Mother refused with an angry shake of her head, and drove doggedly forward, mile after sodden mile, until with many sighs of relief, we made it to Whitford. We unloaded Mrs. Tyrell in Frietchie Circle and took ourselves home.

When I ran next door to retrieve Ollie from Beryl, our neighbor was already on the phone with Inez Tyrell. "Champagne at lunch!" Beryl was exclaiming. "I'll bet that cost a pretty penny." She waved absently when I ran out the door with Ollie.

At home, I fed Ollie the liver pate and squab I'd saved, wrapped in a Ritz linen napkin. I wished I had been able to tuck away one of those little silver shell ashtrays, as well, but I guessed that might be considered stealing rather than souvenir gathering. Ollie crunched the squab appreciatively, keeping a weather eye on Mother. Dogs learn fast who the pack leaders are. Sarge clumped around on his crutches, putting on the kettle while mother went to bathe her eyes with cold water in the new downstairs bathroom Sarge had installed where there used to be a closet under the stairs.

I laid out the tea things. "How come she didn't cry through lunch," I wondered aloud.

"She had other things to think about at lunch. The fancy food and decor took her mind off losing her baby sister."

"But Aunt Bette isn't a baby, and she isn't lost. She'll be back in a week, living less than a half mile away. Mother's dearest wish always was for Aunt Bette to get married and be taken care of for the rest of her life, if she only could find a husband at her age. She's thirty-six, you know. And thank heavens, she found the doctor, so she can be sick every day if she wants and always get free medicine and the best treatment, even though there's a war on. So what's to cry about?"

Sarge hotted the pot, as he'd been taught. "Beware of your heart's desire, Amelia. You never know what may happen if you get it."

Coming back into the kitchen, my mother looked refreshed as she took out her bottle of ginger brandy. "I should save this for emergencies," she said, setting it on the table near her teacup. "God knows when I'll be able to buy more now that Schenley has switched to making alcohol for the war effort. Amelia, go change out of your new dress before that dog gets it all greasy. What in the world did you give him to eat?"

"Just a biscuit," I said. I headed for the bathroom, but looking out the front window, I saw a strange black car in our driveway. Two men in city clothes got out of it and headed for our front door. Before they could ring the bell, which actually worked now, thanks to Sarge, I had hotfooted it to the kitchen with news of the strangers' approach. Mother put the brandy back in the cupboard, smoothed her hair, and went to the door, murmuring, "Well, I don't know who that could be, I'm sure." Ollie ran beside her barking protectively. "Amelia, get this dog on leash at once," she added, her hand on the doorknob.

"FBI, Ma'am," said the younger man, who was sandy-haired and pink-cheeked. The second man was older, shorter, and balding. Both were dressed in blue suits, white shirts, and funeral ties. They removed identical felt hats and held up identification cards without smiling. "Are you Mrs. Catherine Byrd? We'd like to ask you a few questions about Alex Carver, Mrs. Byrd. May we step in for a few moments?"

Ollie tugged on the leash and growled, pulling me into the hall. I could tell that Mother was flustered although she assumed a very dignified air in ushering the two strangers into our living room. To my surprise, she said, "Amelia, I think you had better stay. And Sarge, too. But first, put that animal outside at once."

After shoving Ollie out the back door with a consolation biscuit, I perched on the windowseat and folded my hands in my lap, glad that I was still wearing my new Ritz dress for this exciting interview. The two agents sat on the sofa, with Sarge in a chair opposite them, his crutches leaning against the arm of it. But Mother still stood by the door. To my embarrassment, she insisted that the G-men share our tea. The heavily laden tray she brought in a few minutes later included a plate of hermits she'd baked last night.

"It's come to the attention of the Bureau that you've made a serious complaint to the Whitford Chief of Police about a member of the OSS. Alex Carver, a former English teacher," said the older man, who looked considerably less intimidating with a cup of tea on his knee and a cookie in his hand. "According to our informant, the matter has not been properly followed up by the OSS, and Alex Carver is now unavailable to answer questions due to his involvement in a matter of national security. It may be that due process of law is being subverted in this case. If so, the Bureau takes an interest. Therefore, what we'd like to do today is to take a statement from you with full particulars of the case. This information will then be placed in our files until such time as Alex Carver returns to this country."

"Good enough," Mother said. "I should think *someone* would take an interest in that murdering villain." And she began to tell the two FBI investigators the whole story, only backwards. She started with Mr. Carver herding Aunt Bette, Woody, Sarge, and her into the library at gun point, and how he had wounded Woody in the hospital parking lot a couple of days earlier, that he wanted the doctor out of the way so he could marry her sister Bette. Then Mother related the tale of her sister's inheritance from "her friend and patron" Winston Snow. Finally she thought to explain that Alex Carver may have believed himself to be the son of Winston Snow and somehow entitled to lay hands on the Snow fortune.

The sandy-haired agent, Bill Cassidy, who had been making notes as Mother talked, stopped writing and looked at his partner, Russ Berman, with a puzzled frown. The older man raised a questioning eyebrow. This led Mother further back in time to accuse Mr. Carver of the strange fire in our barn, of trying to run me down with the old school bus, and of the drowning of Mr. Snow. The sandy-haired agent began to write furiously again. Finally Mother explained about the discovery of the letter, and how it led back to the affair between Mr. Carver's mother and Mr. Snow in the early 1900s.

"It was my daughter who found the letter, and in all innocence, gave it to Alex to return to the Snow library, since he was employed there by Winston Snow as a cataloger. Apparently Alex convinced the old man that he'd accumulated a valuable collection of books. It's certainly an unusual assortment, I'll give you that. More tea, anyone? It won't take a minute to make a fresh pot."

"Let's see if we have this right," said Agent Berman. "You're accusing this man Carver of the murder of Winston Snow, and the attempted murder of your daughter and of Dr. Douglas Woodward. You believe that revenge and the desire for gain were his motives. The evidence, the letter, has disappeared, but you have witnesses to verify your story. You've made a complaint through proper channels. The Whitford Chief of Police has contacted the OSS, but that office has refused to cooperate and produce the suspect."

I was amazed that this FBI man had followed the thread of Mother's discourse back to the beginning and sorted out the relevant facts, something like reducing *War and Peace* to a twenty-five-word synopsis. By now, the November sun had set and, despite having lunched at the Ritz, I was beginning to think about supper. On the other hand, I prayed that Mother would not insist on the two agents staying for reheated lamb stew. I think she might have if they hadn't risen to their feet just then, Agent Cassidy pocketing his notes with care. Before they departed into the night, Agent Berman gave Mother a card with a telephone number she was to call if there was any sign or word of Alex Carver.

"No love lost between those two," Sarge commented later that evening, as he tinkered with Mother's irascible toaster in the new shed. I sat on the potting bench, swinging my legs, feeling free and comfortable in my old corduroy slacks.

"The two agents?" I asked, bewildered.

"No, my dear. Between the Bureau and the OSS. Plain ordinary small town murderers do not normally fall under the jurisdiction of the FBI. Hoover is probably compiling every scrap of information that might embarrass the OSS later on, when those glory boys have tarnished somewhat."

"How do you figure that, Sarge? Aren't we all on the same side, after all?"

"I read and I think, Amelia. For myself, that is, not just what the *Whitford Enterprise* and *Life* magazine tell me to think." Then he chuckled. "So if you want to be a success like me in later life, you'll do the same." Sarge plugged in the toaster, which immediately sparked with a weird blue light. There was a strong smell of burning coils. Mother would not be pleased if the toaster died. And I'd have to go back to toasting bread on a long fork over the burner, a boring job that gave the toast a scorched flavor.

"Don't worry. I can probably rewire this baby so she'll quit shorting out," Sarge assured me. "So maybe if Carver makes it back to the U.S. in one piece, the Bureau will pursue him to confound the OSS. I believe we can all breathe easier if J. Edgar Hoover gets on the case. His G-men are smart, thorough, and relentless. Nice to have them on our side."

But as it turned out, it would be many months before we had news of Mr. Carver.

Chapter 28

In which my sleuthing turns up a few troubling truths, and Aunt Bette gives me a little grown-up advice.

"Sarge suspects Gordon Fisher of being the Whitford firebug," I confided to Minna when I was spending another weekend at the Korhonen farm early in December. I thought she would be appalled, but her placid face betrayed no surprise.

"Mr. Curry spoke to Will about the matter, and Will talked to Chief Ott," she said, ladling another birch dipper of water over the hot rocks. The steam was so thick in the little sauna hut, it seemed as if I were breathing water, but it was good to feel thoroughly warm right down to my bare toes. Everyone's house was kept very chilly that winter, conserving the limited fuel supply. When I went to bed at home, I even wore socks with my flannel pajamas, but refused my mother's suggestion of a kerchief nightcap. We burned logs from the old apple tree and Sarge's other prunings in our fireplace almost every night. Our boarders brought their journals and notes to the living room after supper to enjoy the warmth of that cheery blaze. At Korhonen's, however, the gathering place was the kitchen where the big black stove kept us all toasty. After our steam bath, there would only be the manic dash from the sauna to the house to endure.

"There hasn't been one fire since Gordon went into the service, although Jason is still around town." I adjusted my towel to resemble a Dorothy Lamour sarong. "He can't drive and deliver groceries the way Gordon did, but they keep him busy at the store anyway, stocking shelves and helping customers with their bundles. Even so, some people still suspect Jason, because of the way he looks, sort of slow and vacant-eyed. My aunt and Beryl Whitcomb believe it was Jason all along. They insist the only reason we haven't had a fire recently is because Jason's parents are keeping a closer watch on him, that's all."

"Gil Ott told Will he doesn't want to get into that can of worms. As town moderator, Gordon could make things pretty hot for the fire chief," Minna said, unaware of the pun. "But it's true that Gordon as well as Jason hung around every time an empty summer cottage got torched. Maybe Gordon will get his fill of fires while he's fighting over there in Europe. He was in Italy for a while, but now no one knows where. Penny's with the American forces in Britain. Are we cleansed enough, do you think? Want to run outside for a while?"

"Only as far as the kitchen. Don't you know how cold it is outside? We'll freeze in a minute, Minna. If it was Gordon, why do you suppose he burned out poor Sarge? All his wonderful books, too."

"Oh, come now, put on your boots and bathrobe, Mellie. You'll see how grand you'll feel. Didn't you know that some folks got tired of Gordon throwing his weight around and wanted someone else to run for town moderator? And Sarge was a favorite candidate with Chief Ott, Dom Ferro, Lively Ames, and some of the other guys. Not the Whitcombs, of course, or the other town bigwigs." As soon as we got our clothes on, Minna opened the door to an Arctic blast and pushed me out ahead of her.

"Eeeeeee! Isn't this great," I screamed, dancing around in my flapping galoshes, my skin tingling, a flush of pure joy invigorating my whole body.

"So…what did I tell you?" The cold was silent and intense, the night sky cloudless, every star brilliantly clear. Minna grabbed my hands and we foxtrotted twice around the well before scampering toward the house, where the windows glowed with cozy warmth and a plume of fragrant wood smoke wafted from the chimney. "Apple pie and cocoa," she encouraged me along.

We banged in the kitchen door, wild and exuberant, and rushed upstairs to put on our flannel pajamas before settling down in the kitchen for the promised snack. Mrs. Korhonen's apple pie was different from my mother's, flavored with spices I couldn't name and studded with walnuts and raisins. The cocoa was richer, too, no bitter lumps and laced with cream.

"I can't imagine Sarge wanting to hold public office," I said as we dug in. "Still, I suppose it may have seemed a threat. What will Chief Ott do when Gordon comes marching home?"

"They will watch. They have ways," Minna said enigmatically.

"Maybe Gordon will have had enough kicks. He's in demolition, after all."

Later, when we were tucked into Minna's snug, slanted room under the eaves, looking out at the cold stars, Minna said, "What about Mr. Carver? Will said he's not even in the service anymore. He's working for some spy outfit instead."

"I hope he never comes back," I said with passion.

"Oh, Mellie, what a thing to say! How can you?"

"Remember that night last year when Ollie and I ran into your yard from the bogs? You were out, but Will must have told you about how bedraggled we looked."

"Hunted, Will said."

"Mr. Carver had just tried to run me over with the school bus."

"No!"

"Yes," I assured her, and proceeded to relate the whole story. Minna never once questioned the truth of what I told her, but only listened quietly, sometimes drawing in her breath sharply with surprise. But toward the end of my tale, she fell asleep, wheezing lightly, and I thought, *oh well, I suppose she won't remember any of this in the morning.. Or she'll just think she had a crazy dream.*

But that wasn't the case. In the morning, when we brought the dishpans of warm, smelly mash out to the chicken house, Minna said, "Will was called in, you know, when Mr. Carver's father fell down the cellar stairs and broke his neck. My brother always said there was something funny going on with his friend Alex. And afterwards, the money from selling the Carver place sent Mr.

Carver to college just when everyone else had to drop out because of the depression. But perhaps it was only coincidence."

We hurried back to the house, shivering despite our knitted hats and mittens, hers bright blue and mine dark green. Her cheeks looked as if they had been brushed with crimson paint. The tip of my nose felt frozen in the breathlessly cold morning air. But Minna seemed cheered by the hardships of winter, and wanting to comfort me.. "If Mr. Carver comes back to this town, at least the police chief can arrest him for threatening your family with a pistol. So don't you be afraid. What a terrible man he turned out to be, and he used to read those Shakespeare plays to us so thrillingly—do you remember?"

"If he comes back, I'll turn him in to the FBI," I muttered between teeth aching with cold. It was a relief to step into the fragrant kitchen and warm our bones. Minna cut thick slices of bread and heaped two plates with eggs and potatoes staying warm on the back of the stove. She poured us big cups of coffee from the blue enamel pot. We stirred in sugar and plenty of cream.

"The FBI!" Minna said admiringly. "How exciting to have been visited by real G-men! Your life and your family's are just like a movie. And your aunt getting rich and marrying the nice new doctor in town, sort of like Kitty Foyle."

Looking back at the past year through Minna's eyes, I saw that she was right, it was a story, only it didn't have a neat ending—at least, not yet.

Minna and her family were having Sunday dinner with Will's fiancée at Kates Hill, so I left the Korhonen's early and found our house surprisingly empty, even of boarding nurses and doctors, and rather chilly as well. Since the roads were clear and the sun shining brightly, if coldly, I decided I'd bicycle up to Fisher's General Store, buy a Coke, and see if any of my school mates were also hanging around on this dull Sunday afternoon. I went into my mother's room looking for spare change.

The book lying open, face down, on her night table was *Science of Fishing, the Most Practical Book on Fishing Ever Published* by Lake Brooks. This didn't seem like my mother's sort of book. She was more the Marie Corelli *Romance of Two Worlds* type. Also, the fragrance of Sarge's pipe tobacco was stronger in Mother's bed-room than in the converted sewing room, a tiny adjoining space which he had gallantly agreed to occupy in order to rent all the big upstairs bedrooms to pay-ing boarders.

Suddenly it seemed clear to me, like a blindfold pulled off at the end of a game. Sarge had spent the night in Mother's room while I was visiting Minna. That's why Mother had allowed Sarge to install himself so conveniently in the old sewing room.

Peeking under the bed, I found a cracked saucer which, although empty, looked as if it had been used as an ashtray. No wonder I'd had such an easy time getting permission to sleep over at Minna's!

I shivered with a new chill, not sure of how I really felt about this. Sure, I loved Sarge, but I definitely didn't want to think about my mother and Sarge in bed together. Maybe they were only trying to keep warm, I hoped, not actually "doing it." I shook away the embarrassing images running through my brain like one of those penny arcade movies where you peered into a box and saw people cavorting around in crazy ways.

Mother kept a fat change purse full of coins on her bureau. I helped myself to thirty cents. Then I cycled up to Fisher's on the bike Sarge had reconstructed for Mother, with much to think about over the mile and a half route.

The best thing would be if Mother married Sarge. But my independent mother might rather settle for an "arrangement" like Waldo Whitcomb, Jr., with his housekeeper Mary Gloria Kelly, as if the whole town didn't know. Then I would have to suffer the winks and smart remarks at school, the same as I had with Aunt Bette and Mr. Snow, or Skip had with his mother and Dr. Tyrell. And I couldn't even run away to the Navy. After I had worried so about Sarge's precarious position in our household, he'd betrayed my friendship. It just showed that no grown-up could be trusted, no matter how many books he had read and how many fascinating facts he knew and how comforting it was to confide in him. I vowed never to let down my guard again.

After pedaling all the way to the General Store and getting my nose and cheeks frozen, I was disappointed that none of my friends from school were anywhere to be seen in the street front with the old hitching posts or on the wide porch that ran the length of the red-shingled building. I bought a Coke from Jason, then sat on one of the wooden chairs that circled the woodstove. Jason returned to his task, lugging in big cartons of cereal and crackers to stock on the high shelves that could only be reached by ladder or with a long metal grabber. Some kids from school had been hanging around the store earlier, he said, but then they'd gone to the cranberry bog woods to play Scatter. That was a rigorous kind of hide-and-go-seek that I'd never enjoyed. After a while, Jason took a root beer out of the cooler and sat with me, his round face wreathed in smiles that I had not immediately bolted to join my friends.

"My brothers and sister are all gone," he said, pointing proudly to the 3-star flag prominently displayed in the store window.

It occurred to me that I needn't waste my bicycle ride after all. I could do some sleuthing while I was here. "You must miss them," I said. "Especially Gordon. I bet you and he used to have a lot of fun together going to fires."

Jason' smile faded and he looked toward the back room in a worried way. "We didn't do nothing," he said over his shoulder. The Fishers had never allowed Chief Ferro to question Jason alone, and here I was with an opportunity too perfect to let pass.

"It wasn't you, Jason. I know that. But Gordon liked fires, didn't he? Were you with him when he set Sarge's cottage on fire?"

"That Sarge Curry is a bum. Gordon said so." Jason grabbed a sour pickle from the barrel and took a big bite.

At that most inopportune moment, Lillian Fisher, Jason' mother, came in from the back room with several new bolts of cloth for the yard goods table. "None of that lazing around to gab, Brother," she demanded. "You go out back now and bring in the Wheaties. Stack them up there next to the corn flakes." Jason dropped the rest of his pickle back into the barrel and lumbered away carrying the empty bottle of root beer.

"I was just asking after your boys and Penny, Mrs. Fisher," I explained.

"We had a letter from Penny just yesterday," Mrs. Fisher said, lining up bolts of cloth. "She's in London, you know, secretary to General Cooper. Very popular with the British officers, too—gets escorted to all the best places. She was having a drink at the Connaught Hotel, she wrote me, and *you'll never guess who she saw there!* Alex Carver, who used to be her fiancé. What a small world! Isn't it funny how Alex went in and out of the Army like that, and now he winds up in London, big as life. Well, I can't say as I wish him very much luck, after the shitty way he treated Penny. But I bet he's sorry now, seeing her so cute in her uniform, being treated like a queen by those Brits."

An icy spider of fear crawled over my scalp and down my neck. "I've heard he's in the secret service, Mrs. Fisher," I said.

"Oh, well, that explains it, then." Lillian Fisher stepped back and surveyed the table with satisfaction, a rainbow of florals, ginghams, and heavy solid colors in cotton broadcloth, plus huge spools of ribbon and that rick-rack my mother liked so much. Then she looked over at me in a perplexed fashion. "What secret service?"

"It's called the OSS. No one knows very much about them, but I guess they spy on the Nazis and collect information to send to Washington."

"Hmmmm. Sounds dangerous. Good enough for him. All the time I thought maybe Alex had become a foreign correspondent. Penny said he was there with a journalist from *Colliers* who was on her way to Finland."

Jason had brought in the Wheaties and was standing listening, a vacant look in his eyes. Then, like a lightning strike out of the blue, he said, "Amelia asked me about Gordon setting fires."

There was a lurch in my stomach as Mrs. Fisher dropped a spool of lace trim she was rewinding and glared at me menacingly. "Why you miserable little busybody…" she hissed, picking up a yardstick from the counter. I scrambled to my feet and backed out the door. Jumping on Mother's bike, I pedaled madly away down the road not looking back when Mrs. Fisher came out on the porch and shouted at me.

At home I told the news of Mr. Carver and what Jason had said—how could I resist? But I didn't smile back at Sarge when he said, "Great work, Holmes. You almost got Jason to admit that Gordon torched my little house."

My mother was wearing a pretty yellow dress. I remembered it was the same stuff that had been tacked onto the dress dummy in the old sewing room with common pins for ages. "You'd better stay out of Fisher's for a while, Amelia," she said, basting the chicken she was roasting for our dinner. We always had our dinner at night, even on Sundays, although many people in Whitford consumed a big meal right after church. But then, we didn't go to church, either. We were different from regular people in so many ways, I reflected, and now there was this embarrassing romance going on—how long would it be before Beryl got suspicious and told everyone in town?

⸻

"What's going on with Sarge and my mother?" I asked Aunt Bette. I'd dropped in for a visit after school on Monday to see if she wanted me to take Ollie for a run. My mother had already called and related all that I'd learned at Fishers, so I didn't have to get into that. I could go straight to the heart of what was really bothering me.

Aunt Bette was opening several cans of S.S. Pierce vegetables and stirring them all together in a pot with some chopped meat. "There," she said. "I guess stew isn't all that hard to make." She clapped a lid on the pot and turned to look at me, her eyes narrowed, her smile impish. "I told your mother you'd catch on."

"I think you'd better turn down that gas a little," I said. She'd left it on full blast under the pot.

"Oh, yes—well, maybe you're right. I just want to get the damned thing cooked before Doug gets back from the hospital, not that I ever know when that will be. So...want a cup of cocoa and a chat?"

"Yes, thank you, Aunt Bette."

"Good. You make the cocoa while I go doll up a little. Then we'll have a good heart-to-heart. Besides, I don't think Ollie really wants to run, do you?"

Having greeted me loyally, Ollie had soon returned to snoozing on his cushion by the radiator. Bing came along and fitted himself like a shawl alongside the dog, who sighed with contentment. Aunt Bette's house was always comfortable, warm, and well-stocked. I felt like sighing with relief myself as I checked out the pantry for cocoa and noted all the wonderful cans of fruit, vegetables, and Vienna sausages that were lined up there. Mr. Snow's legacy lived on!

A quarter of an hour later, Aunt Bette, all primped and prettied, and I in my old corduroy slacks and shrunken wool sweater sat in her living room with china cups of steaming cocoa and some stale raisin biscuits I'd found in the pantry. My aunt stirred her cup daintily and said, "Your mother and father were something special, Amelia. They loved each other deeply and truly, the kind of love that is rarely found a second time. It may be that your mother will never bring herself to marry again. Or maybe she will. Who knows what that girl will get up to? Anyway, everyone needs some affection in life, and you mustn't blame your mother—or Sarge who's always been your good buddy, hasn't he?—for seeking a little human warmth with one another. You'll just have to be grown-up about this, that's all there is to it. Besides, you'll soon notice, if you haven't already, that your mother is much better humored than she had been for years. And you know what a grouch she can be!"

It was always warming to be treated like a grown-up with Aunt Bette. But I said, "Can't they be affectionate without sleeping together?"

"No," she said in the firm manner that suggested there was no debating that point.

Nevertheless, I retorted, "What about Heloise and Abelard?"

"Abelard was missing some necessary equipment. Otherwise he would have behaved like any other man. In fact, he did. That's what got him caponed. You know, Amelia, I'm not one of those who claims you read too much, but sometimes I wish you'd stick with the Bobbsey Twins."

"I've read them all already—twice. What if everyone finds out and talks about Mother?"

"Who cares what little minds find to natter about? I dare say they've done plenty of talking about me, but you don't see me pining and fretting, do you?"

She looked wonderful, her dark blue eyes sparkling and her slim little hand glittering with its huge diamond flanked by the brand new gold wedding band as it rested on the arm of her chair. There was an elegant emerald ring I thought I remembered on the other hand that held a flowered cup to her lips.

"*Sticks and stones will break our bones, but names will never hurt us,*" I recited.

"That's my little honey!" She always liked to call me "little" since I towered over her. "Now don't you say a word to your mother. Simply pretend that you haven't noticed anything, and go on about living your own life. Speaking of which..." she reached into the pocket of her pink cardigan and handed me a tube of lipstick. "This color is a bit light for me. You can have the rest of it, if you like. It's called Cotton Candy."

There was at least a quarter of an inch left in the gold tube! Delighted with the gift, I hugged my aunt, noticing how frail she felt in my arms and how big and clumsy I felt next to her.

"Now tell me again everything you learned from Mrs. Fisher," said Aunt Bette, and I repeated all that Penny's mother had quoted from her daughter's letter.

"Well, we can all hope that bastard will drown in one of the fjords, or whatever they have up there in Finland," she declared, narrowing her eyes and waving her hands as if they held a magic wand, glittering rings and all. Perhaps she put a spell on Alex Carver with those words.

Chapter 29

In which Skipper Davies comes home
in a very bad mood, and I regale Daisy
with the story of a shooting.

In March, Skipper Davies came home in a wheelchair. His right leg, wounded in the fighting off North Africa, had been struck again and nearly shattered when the Germans bombed his ship in the Mediterranean. In time, the Navy doctors had promised, he should be walking again, although he might have a permanent limp. I heard all this from Woody, who made house calls twice a week to check on Skip's progress. From Woody I also learned that Skip was refusing to see any of his friends, so it would be better if I waited for an invitation before calling on him. Not knowing what I could possibly say to cheer Skip, I was cowardly enough to feel relieved.

When they met at Fisher's General Store one afternoon just before Easter, Cora Davies told my mother that Skip was surly and critical, fuming at having to sleep in the living room like a visitor because he couldn't get upstairs, wrecking the house with his wheelchair, and finding fault with everything. Her son had refused to discuss any of his experiences in the war but was angry to be out of it before the finish, so he said, envious of his father Frank who had shipped to the Pacific to fight the Japs. My mother replied that if Cora would only build him up with good nourishing food, his spirits might improve. She volunteered to send me over to the Davies' house with a pot of chicken soup, the ultimate embarrassment.

A soup pot not being something I could transport on the family bicycle, I had to lug the stuff sloshing in its container the quarter mile between our houses. Ollie, who was visiting our house while Aunt Bette attended to some business with her broker in Boston, trotted along with me faithfully. He acted as if it were his dinner dish I was carrying, hopping up from time to time to get a better whiff of the fragrant soup.

Skip in his wheelchair was parked in the front yard under the apple tree, smoking and drinking beer. When Ollie ran up and greeted him effusively, Skip bent over to pat him, a lock of straight brown hair falling over his face to hide his expression. "Hi, Byrdie," he said without looking at me. "How're you doing?"

"Fine. It's good to see you, Skip," I said, feeling stupid. "My mother sent this pot of soup to your mother. I'll just leave it on the stove. Want anything from the house?"

"Yeah. Bring me another brew, will you?"

When I came back with the beer, he offered me a swig. I didn't like the taste much—it was even worse than Moxie—and he laughed at my expression. For a moment it seemed just like old times between us. I relaxed, sitting cross-legged on the grass with Ollie by my side, and asked Skip what he'd heard from Tristan and Glenn. As it happened, Skip had recently received a letter from Glenn, who was with the 82nd Airborne Division, paratroopers, in Britain. Soon Skip and I were chatting about his "Troops" while he smoked incessantly and wouldn't offer me even one. Now that he really was eighteen, he looked older, his face leaner and tighter around the jaw than I remembered. Wearing a t-shirt with rolled up sleeves, his packet of Camels twisted into one cuff, his arms were tanned and muscular. An anchor tattooed on one bicep made him look like Popeye, there was a new crescent scar on his forehead, and his right leg, stuck out in front of the chair, was encased in a metal brace.

I wondered how long he'd been out under the apple tree—alone, since his mother had gone to work at Whitford Inn. So I said a dumb thing. I asked Skip if he wanted to go for a walk. Of course, I meant with me pushing his chair. Immediately his face closed down with a mean, hard look. "Fat chance of that," he said and began to roll himself back into the house. I could see it took great effort to move himself over the knobby brown grass. So I ignored the glare he threw at me over his shoulder when I grabbed the handles of his chair, pushing him out onto driveway and nearly toppling the chair in the process.

"Well, what will it be? The stuffy old house or a ride down to Silver Sand?" I asked. "Ollie votes for the pond. Of course, you'll be taking a chance, going with me. I haven't forgotten how when we played cowboys and Indians, you once left me tied to a tree and went home for lunch."

He laughed then and leaned over to drop his beer bottle on the ground, where several more dotted the yard. I pushed his chair down the dirt road to a lookout spot that was midway between our two houses. The sun was shining on the barely budding trees and tiny blue waves were lapping the narrow beaches. Someone was painting an upside-down sailboat on the other side of the cove. Someone else was out on the water, paddling a red canoe. Rubbing my arms, I said, "Wow. That's like real work. I'll probably build up some muscle, going out walking with you."

"You always did like to play nursie, so don't start complaining now," Skip said. "If you can get me into a rowboat to go fishing one of these days, I'll do the rowing, how's that?"

"Nice change from the old days," I commented.

"You'll still have to bait the hooks," he said.

After that, we went for walks almost every good day. Some of his other friends called to see how he was doing, but Skip was pretty nasty to anyone who seemed to pity him the least bit for being stuck in that chair, so only a few came back more than once. I was very careful not to sympathize with Skip as he struggled to get around on his own, so we talked about everything else, especially the progress of the war. We still had our two matching atlases to follow the headlines of the day. I helped him catch up on all the town gossip. He seemed especially interested in news of Rosemary, who never came to see him, even though her husband had left her after being discharged with a punctured eardrum.

Eventually, one afternoon, the conversation got around to Alex Carver, and I told Skip the whole story while we sat under the tree in his front yard. Boy, did I ever have his rapt attention, for once. I felt like Scheherazade.

"Didn't I always tell you those English teachers were no damned good," he teased. "But I admire your old lady. She's got real guts, tackling an armed guy who's been trained by the OSS."

I thought that was true, my mother was practically fearless.

Skip said that by summer he hoped to be up on crutches. And if he could get by with a cane next year, he'd take me to the Junior Prom. "But don't expect me to do no jitterbugging."

I couldn't believe it! That would make me the first girl in my class to have a date for next year's Junior Prom, when I wouldn't even be a Junior yet. Maybe I could even get Skip to wear his uniform. Would my mother think he was too old to take me out? I resolved to bring Skip over to our house really often to let Mother feed him all those thick soups and baked apples she swore were the proper foods for an invalid. By next year she would be convinced he was one of the family.

⁓

"What's this I hear about your being thrown out of the general store?" Daisy's gaze was on the sky-blue honor bead she was threading onto a leather thong, an impish smile twinkling at the corners of her mouth. "Mrs. Fisher told Grandma that you've been up there pestering Jason and if she catches you in her place again, she's going to give you a good hiding."

We were hanging around in my bedroom, listening to Frankie on the record player Sarge had restored, and decorating our ceremonial Camp Fire Girl gowns. Since Mrs. Lively Ames, the former Miss Cronin, never questioned our somewhat creative list of craft honors, we'd accumulated so many beads and badges, we were running out of places to show them off. How different she was from Aunt Bette, who never believed a word I said without proof positive. Like if I told Aunt Bette I'd observed and recorded the activities of a family of birds for one whole season, she'd demand to see the nest and the notes before she handed over a nature bead.

"Oh, Mrs. Fisher's all over being mad at me," I said airily. "Aunt Bette drove me up there with one of her shopping lists as long as my arm, and Lillian Fisher might have glared at me, but she never took that yardstick off its hook while she was waltzing around filling the order and writing down the prices."

"Yeah, well I wouldn't go up there alone for a while." Daisy took up a green health bead and added it to her headband. "So…tell me! What did you find out? You know, you've been holding out on me and Jay. Grandma heard from Mrs. Tyrell about that ruckus at your aunt's place a few days before the wedding. Shots fired back and forth, that's what she claimed. Gave Mrs. T such palpitations, she had to take an extra shot of her calmative tonic. Jay said, maybe you were fixing to have a shotgun wedding?"

"Ha, ha. Your Grandma sure is a gold mine of information. Well, isn't it remarkable that Mrs. Tyrell's nerves didn't prevent her from attending Aunt Bette's champagne luncheon at the Ritz. And just where is that smart-mouthed Jay?"

"Gone down Silver Sand to sketch boats. He goes off like that sometimes, when he's worried about stuff."

"Let's walk down there later and find him. Maybe you two could stay for supper."

"Oh, goodie. Something sure smells good downstairs."

"Oh, it's nothing special. Some stew. They killed another pig at the Poor Farm, so it's probably pork. New peas—you can help me with the shelling. Cornbread. Strawberry and rhubarb pies made this morning." I thought I heard Daisy's stomach rumble. She sure loved my mother's cooking. "What's Jay worried about now?"

"We both are. Our mom's getting tough about our spending the summer in New Jersey with her. But we absolutely *have to* stay at Grandma's. I mean, all our friends are here…and we have plans for the summer. You know that. Just suppose Mom gets the notion that we ought to change schools next year?" Daisy looked down at her lapful of beads and sighed. "And besides, her boyfriend is always hanging around playing that blasted trombone. Jay sure hates him." She tried to blink back the tears, but one escaped and ran down her cheek. Frankie was crooning, "I'll Be Seeing You," which was enough to make anyone sob, even if they weren't saying good-bye yet. "Grandma can be cranky and all, and everything she cooks is sort of boiled and tasteless, but we can count on her not to wreck her life and then try to drag us into her messes."

This wasn't like Daisy, who was usually so cheerful and even-tempered, always ready for gossip, mischief, and adventure. So to make her feel better, I not only told her about Gordon torching Sarge's place, I also told her about Mr. Carver's last visit, how he'd wanted to marry Aunt Bette so he tried to kill Woody. It worked like a charm—she was soon giggling. I swore her to secrecy, of course, and I didn't bring up Mr. Carver's murdering Mr. Snow. Maybe she'd forget about that old love letter. I didn't mind everyone knowing that Mr. Carver was a villain. I just didn't want any more gossip about Aunt Bette's inheritance.

Daisy's grin sparkled, sun after rain. "With a gun? You shot him with a real gun? Where in the world did you get it?"

"Oh, just something we happened to have around the house in case the Germans invade the East Coast. You know, like the NRA advised we all practice for?"

"And your mother punched Mr. Carver in the jaw? Oh, Jay is going to be so sorry he missed this! You're going to have to tell the whole story again."

"You two won't tell anyone, will you? Like your Grandma, and everyone else on the Old Home Day committee?"

"*Cross my heart and hope to die an old maid.* Now did this business with Mr. Carver have anything to do with that old love letter you found last year?"

Uh oh. Daisy's cleverness and curiosity just naturally steered her into the heart of every secret. Maybe that's why she was fun to be with. I sure hoped her mother wouldn't steal her and Jay away from Whitford. It was terribly unfair how parents could ruin your life and think they were doing you a favor. Like that puke-yellow corduroy jumper my mother had just made for me, with the puckered pockets and the zipper left over from an old sofa pillow.

Chapter 30

In which we learn the story of a top secret mission, Mother and Aunt Bette drink a toast, and June brings a day of glory.

A few weeks after my first visit with Skip, in the middle of April, Mother had another surprising visitor. A dark car drove up to our front door, and the driver jumped out smartly to open the back door for his passenger. Looking as if she had just stepped out of *Vogue*, the lady who emerged was wearing a tiny fur hat tilted over one eye and a fur trimmed cape with a matching rose wool dress.

"Mrs. Byrd? Catherine Byrd? I'm Natalie Laine from *Colliers* magazine," she introduced herself when Mother opened the door. "I've been wanting to visit you in person to talk to you about a friend of yours and a colleague of mine, Alex Carver."

Standing in back of my mother, I felt her start as to ward off a blow, and my own heart knocked fearfully. But Mother spoke calmly: "Yes, I'm Catherine Byrd. Won't you come in, then, Miss Laine," showing the attractive blonde woman into our living room. We sat down, the three of us more or less on the edges of our respective chairs. For once in her life, mother seemed to forget to offer refreshments.

Natalie Laine explained that she was here to offer her condolences. Her large blue eyes filled with tears as she spoke, leaning forward to pat Mother's hand in a consoling manner. Mother sat as stiffly as if she were one of my father's carved figures. Then Natalie took out a tiny lace-edged handkerchief and dabbed at her eyes as she continued, seeming to be oblivious to the stunned silence around her.

"Alex was on an important mission to Finland when it happened. For the OSS. I'm really not supposed to talk about his activities, but under the circumstance, I think you of all people, Mrs. Byrd, have a right to know," she said, dropping her voice to a stage whisper. "They asked me to use my role as a journalist to provide Alex's cover and access to certain government friends I have in Helsinki. Alex posed as my assistant. We both tried unsuccessfully to turn these officials against cooperating with the Nazis. I can't tell you more, but something went wrong and Alex disappeared. I was forced to flee for my life." She paused to wipe away the tears that welled up in her eyes. "I'm so sorry to be the bearer of this sad news. Just recently I learned that Alex was not as fortunate as I. The Finns' Nazi advisors got hold of Alex. My friends in Helsinki say he was found on the shore near Lovisa, on the Gulf of Finland. It appeared to be an accidental drowning."

"Thank God," said my mother.

"Yes," said Natalie Laine. "We were all so relieved that he wasn't a victim of torture. But I was assured that his body was relatively unmarked. Sympathizers to our cause buried him in a little cemetery in Lovisa. Perhaps after the war we can return him to Whitford. I'm sure that would mean so much to folks around here."

"Knowing Alex Carver's fate means a lot to me," said Mother. "But still, it's hard for me to understand why you've taken the trouble to come here and tell me what happened. The man was merely my boarder. If he had a next of kin, I don't know who that would be."

"That's just it," said the journalist. "There is no next of kin. So, as you may be surprised to learn, Alex Carver named you as his beneficiary of his National Service Insurance just after he was called up. Yes, I see from your expression that this comes as something of a shock. But you should be notified by the administrators any day now."

Mother was clutching the arms of her chair for dear life. I was feeling dazed myself. *Alex Carver's beneficiary? How could this be?*

Natalie Laine tried to explain. "And I think I understand why. Once, after we'd both consumed rather a lot of vodka with our Finnish contacts, Alex got quite weepy and told me that you had been as good and kind to him as his own mother who died when he was fifteen, and that he regretted bitterly that you two had parted with some kind of misunderstanding between you. If anything happened to him, he begged me to ask you to forgive him. Now that his fate is known, his death benefits and insurance will be paid to you, my dear. It's such a beautiful story, isn't it? Too bad the details must be kept secret, for now. How I would love to have written a piece for Colliers about Alex and you and your sweet daughter and this lovely old farmhouse, such an example of Americana at its finest in time of war. What a photo spread that could have been!" Natalie sighed and put away her hankie in a business-like leather handbag of generous proportions. "Well, who knows? Perhaps after all this need for secrecy is over, I may write a book about my wartime experiences."

As Miss Laine rattled on, my mother, the fearless, went all ashen and queer looking, and nearly passed out. I rushed into the kitchen to put on the kettle for some strong, sweet tea to revive her.

I thought maybe I was getting too old to be sitting on the stair landing eavesdropping on the conversation in the kitchen, but the sound of my mother and aunt laughing fit to kill was too much of a temptation. The bottle of port must be out on the table. They were alone, of course. They never laughed in quite that same wholehearted, wicked way when anyone else was present. Mother must be telling Aunt Bette about Natalie Laine's visit, Alex Carver's insurance bequest, and the wonderful photo-illustrated story that would never appear in *Colliers*.

"I hope to God she never writes that book she was talking about," Mother declared vehemently.

"Did you believe her? I mean, here she just shows up on our doorstep with all this hush-hush business about Alex." My aunt took a long drag of her Parliament and gazed into air as if looking for a revelation of truth to appear in the smoke.

"Yes, I did. I can't say why. Just a feeling I got that Miss Laine came here to make amends for something that had happened in Helsinki. Maybe she feels a little responsible for Alex's fate, who knows?"

"*If she knew Alex like we knew Alex*...she wouldn't be wasting her tears. Oh well—speak no ill of the dead!" my aunt declared.

"The less said, the better," my mother agreed. "Under the circumstances."

"Agreed! *Loose lips*, and all that. But now, I propose that we drink a toast." From my perch on the shadowed stairs, I pictured my aunt raising her glass of port with a dainty gesture. "Here's to Alex Carver, the man who made us both wealthy!"

"Bette! You should be ashamed of yourself," Mother scolded before she collapsed into more deep hearty laughter.

"Oh, come on down here, Amelia," called my aunt. She leaned over the stairs and peered up at me, crouched against the wall on the landing. "It's high time you joined us."

In the kitchen, the heavy blackout curtains were drawn and the single lamp above the enamel kitchen table threw long shadows of us three against the wall. The smoke from my aunt's cigarette curled upward around the lamp like a wreath. Just looking at each other, the two sisters would begin to chuckle again. I imagined—and hoped—their merry mood had been inspired by relief. *Surely my mother would never accept the benefits of Alex Carver's death*. I drank the shot glass of port I was given by Aunt Bette, feeling grateful to be included in their indomitable circle.

"Now Catherine," said Aunt Bette. "As soon as we can arrange a day off together, I want you to have a talk with my broker about investments."

By June, Skip and I could manage, with Sarge's help, to take the rowboat out on Silver Sand to fish for bass, just as we used to before the war. With his leg out of the brace, Skip got around on crutches as nimbly as a monkey. We'd catch a few bass or pickerel. I still baited the hooks with worms we had dug out of Mother's lawn. I called him "Captain;" he called me "Matey"—even though I did the preparation and planning.

One morning, we brought a picnic over to the tiny no-name island in the center of Silver Sand Pond. From its minuscule beach, I could look straight over to the town boat landing and the old ice house, which was falling into disrepair as if slowly merging with the stand of trees beside it. I remembered the night Winston Snow had drowned there, how Alex Carver had cried and been comforted by my mother. I could see the rocks where Snow's body had been pulled out the following spring. I thought about Alex Carver drowning somewhere halfway around the globe, strong hands holding him under the water while he struggled, his mouth and lungs filling with icy water.

"It all seems so far away now," I said to Skip, who was lying on the grass, crutches discarded beside him, his face upturned to bask in the day's warmth.

" ...So far away," Skip agreed, but it was his own bad memories that were dissolving like shadows in sunshine. With his eyes still shut, he reached out to take my hand, as if to make sure I hadn't disappeared, too. "Where'd you put the bass we caught, Matey?"

"Don't worry, Captain. The bucket's in the water keeping cool. Mother will make us a fish feast tonight—but you'll have to clean them first."

"Why me?"

"Because I'm a girl. Girls don't clean fish. And from now on, you can bait your own hooks, too."

"What is this—some kind of mutiny?"

I just smiled. Skip was still holding my hand.

Then we saw the tiny figure of Sarge down on our dock waving excitedly for us to return right away. I might have been fearful that there'd been some terrible accident, but there was something about Sarge's antics, even from a distance, that was more a dance of joy.

When we'd packed up and rowed back, the reports of D-Day were blasting out on radios everywhere. People were running out of their houses to make sure everyone else had heard the glorious news. That night, it was like a blind carnival with everyone out on their docks sharing the hope and triumph, but mindful of covering flashlights and keeping their heavy curtains drawn. Mother, of course, kept busy making giant pots of coffee and trays of sandwiches because "people always need to eat," which was like her religion. And Aunt Bette drove over in the Olds with Woody to carry a basket of goodies to the party.

Then Nathan Whitcomb, our block warden, entirely broke the blackout rules by rowing out to the center of the pond to set off a few hoarded fireworks. Amid cheers from shore, the rockets rose splendidly for a few magic moments and then dove down into the darkness. But far above all that, the summer stars continued on in their brilliant, eternal way.